THE SNARE

J.H. HARRISON

To Eme Harrison,
with love and gratitude.

PROLOGUE

Silence.

That's all I hear. I don't know what the time is, but the silence tells me it's too early to be awake. No birds tweeting, no trains chugging along, just sweet stillness.

What is it about quietness that upsets people? I don't know why people go to such great lengths to fill their lives with noise. Guilty conscience? Self-hatred? Fear that they may have to think about anything other than pointless activity? Dreading the realisation that they spend most of their days trying to bleed meaning out of what is essentially meaningless?

The silence pleases me. It helps me think, and plan, and reflect. I do not fear introspection. I came to terms with myself a long time ago and though the thoughts of my past actions are amplified at times like this, I know that all the things I did were for the greater good. I know that they were right. I did them for love; I did them because someone had to. I know who I am. I welcome the silence. It probes me and I stand unmoved and unashamed by it.

I roll over to my side, try to shake the nasty feeling my latest nightmare gave me. I may find silence therapeutic, but even it is no cure-all. I may consider my conscience clear, but the memories of things I've done linger still.

I reach for my clock, peer at it closely. 2:17am.

Like I thought, it's too early to do anything useful. If insomnia is to be my constant companion, at least I have silence to comfort me. Until sleep sees it fit to return, I'll lie here planning for the day ahead. There's nothing else to do.

PART I

I

NOVEMBER 21ST, 2019

DONNA

Three thousand, six hundred and fifty-three days ago, my life changed forever. William's sudden death meant that freedom was handed to me, as though on a platter of fine gold. That freedom has come with unforeseen challenges. It's ok, I've been through worse. Right now, I am enduring an unpleasant experience, but nothing akin to the violence that occupies my memories.

Daryl Blake has been talking, uninterrupted, for four minutes straight. This might be tolerable if he had anything interesting to say, but he doesn't, because he is uninteresting. His green eyes sparkle like tiny emeralds as he proposes one bad idea after another.

I can hardly believe I hurried in to work for this. I got to my desk 5 minutes before this meeting because I overslept. Had I woken up in time, I would have had enough time to mentally prepare for this horror show. To my despair, rather than switching my alarm to snooze, I turned it off. This means that I not only had to skip breakfast, but I had to take the tube – instead of the bus – to work. Of course, today some poor commuter decided to bid this world adieu, lengthening my journey time. I sacrificed a relatively pain-free trip to work for an extra 30 minutes of sleep.

Days like this get me down, but I cannot escape them. I am an adult with responsibilities, and this is the price I have to pay. I've been in this meeting for what feels like an eternity but is only 79 minutes. As I expected, it's overrunning. We were supposed to leave within an hour, but Daryl loves the sound of his voice more than flies love faeces. He would never pass up an opportunity to try to bore a captive audience to death.

I watch as he paces in front of the white board, the light bouncing off his light hair, his mouth moving non-stop. He is about 5ft 11, but his posture is good enough that he could be mistaken for a taller man. I suppose that has worked to his advantage. He is a proud man who holds his head high despite having nothing to be proud of. I do my best to avoid speaking to him on matters unrelated to work.

I've learned that he was raised by his father, Spencer, after his mother, Nancy, left them and his two older brothers for a married man who had once been her teacher. (Why break up one family when you can break up two?) That sounds wild but Katrina Murray assures me that it's true. She would know. You'd think knowing about his background would make me feel sorry for him. It doesn't.

Kat, also present at this life-threatening meeting, is the resident investigator at Sanders Staunton & Co, the legal firm that I've worked at for a little over three years. She and I get along well, despite the fact that she excels at making morally dubious choices. She's good at her job, therefore I respect her. She's also good-enough company in small doses. Her success in her role is no doubt related, at least in part, to her appearance.

Kat always looks attractive – her hairstyle frames her face nicely, drawing attention to her big hazel eyes and her full lips. She wears minimal makeup that enhances her features, and casual, well-fitting clothes. It doesn't hurt that she's got a tiny waist that makes her look like a 1950s pin up model. People – especially men – seem more willing to talk to a good-looking woman, to tell her all their secrets. I've seen her pout and bat her eyelids in order to get information. It's somewhat depressing that that's all it takes.

Though I've worked here for a while and I'm a year post-training contract, I don't feel like a real lawyer yet. That might be connected to the fact that I was denied the opportunity to lead this team. You see, a little while ago, Daryl and I were both trainees. My work was outstanding, his mediocre. That may sound cruel, but it's a fact. So clear was this fact that at some inane work party, the senior partner, William Sanders, took me aside and told me that my 'remarkable intelligence and fierce determination' would have me leading my own team 'in no time.' I believed him.

Alas, it was not meant to be. At the time Old Bill dispensed that little piece of encouragement, he didn't know that the incompetent yet ambitious wasteman known as Daryl was sleeping with his beloved daughter, Veronica. He found out when she was 6 months pregnant, much to his distress. I hear that he's the sort of man who would rather kill a baby than release a portion of his fortune to someone like Daryl. The baby was lucky it was out of his hands. I don't know how his fortune is holding up.

After the shotgun wedding (a lavish affair that must have cost the entire GDP of a small country), the job I'd set my sights on and worked hard for went to none other than Sanders' new son-in-law. Upsetting though that was, it gave me clarity. I now see that Old Bill is a rat. I've hung around since then for one reason alone – I need more experience. Within the next two years, I will have worked on enough cases to get a more lucrative job in a better firm. Better in terms of reputation, for I'm old enough to know that behind closed doors, they're all the same.

My attention returns to the meeting room, which itself inspires misery and hostility. The windows don't open, the air conditioner is on too high (despite my protests), the walls are an ugly shade of grey and the air is stale and dry. Unlike some of the other meeting rooms with glass walls, the room's walls are solid. I can't even distract myself by looking at the passers-by. To make matters worse, the chairs are uncomfortable. My back hurts, and my bum feels flat as a board. I want to choke on my own saliva just to get out of here.

"Donna, what do you think?"

I don't know. I wasn't listening.

Daryl… he has no interesting thoughts or original ideas and wouldn't recognise a good strategy if it spat in his face. He did very well for himself by knocking up the boss's daughter. Come to think of it, maybe he does know a thing or two about good strategies.

I look at Kat, and then at Shane Smythe, the other member of the team and Daryl's rival for the title of Least Worthy of a Job at This Firm. He smiles, clearly amused by my lack of focus.

"I'm sorry, Daryl. What do I think about…?" The words come out of my mouth sounding like a yawn.

"Am I keeping you up… or did someone do that already?" He has the nerve to wink at me.

I wish I could cut his tongue out and pin it to the wall. You'd think that being married to the boss's daughter would curb his inappropriate behaviour but he can't help himself. To be more accurate, he refuses to. It's disappointing when a man has all the traits of a dog except the positive ones.

Despite oversleeping, I'm still quite tired. It's hindering my ability to concentrate. It's not entirely my fault that I slept for too long. Last night, I was struck with a bout of insomnia. It always happens around this time of year. I was awake for over three hours, from around 2am. I dreamt that I killed someone. Like the sleeplessness, that dream isn't new.

I was 17 again, working at the newsagent near the house I grew up in. I hated that house and all that happened in it; my job was an escape. It was the evening shift and my friend and I were hanging out, just fooling around. No customers, no problems. She was in a bad mood and I was trying to cheer her up. Then someone walked in, brandishing a gun. He had no face and he robbed the till. He went to attack my friend, but I shot him. I stood over his dead body with his blood all over me.

When I woke up, I could still hear the gunshot ringing in my ears. And for a moment it felt like I had sticky, drying blood on my hands. This month, every year, such dreams plague me, robbing me of sleep and peace of mind. I've learned to cope with them, but they're still an unwelcome intrusion.

"What was the question, Daryl?"

"Should we advise Mr. Matheson to settle out of court?"

Ah yes, Connor Matheson – our current no-good client. Mr. Matheson is the latest in a string of obviously guilty people that we will be helping evade justice. The man shot his wife's lover, although he denies attempted murder. I can't say I blame him for his efforts, but he wasn't smart about it and for that I disdain him.

According to him, he arrived home a day early from a business trip to Singapore and, upon entering the house, was confronted by a man he presumed to be a robber. Said man – given name, Pierre Benoit – was eating breakfast in Matheson's kitchen. A cinnamon bagel was the man's meal of choice. Good choice, in my opinion – tasty and light, yet filling enough to fuel you for the morning.

Shocked, Matheson ran to his study and retrieved his gun, and then proceeded to shoot the 'robber' in the back as he fled the house shirtless and barefooted. Both items of clothing have yet to be recovered, by the way. Matheson's wife, Sarah, denies knowing the man and claims that she had no knowledge of his presence in the house. Can you believe that garbage?

In all the time I've worked here, I've never come across a robber who would flee the home he was robbing barefooted or shirtless. I've never even heard of one pausing to eat before, during or after a robbery. People are getting dumber and dumber as each generation gives way to the next, but no one I know is dim enough to believe this tale. Mr. Matheson is a liar, and a terrible one at that.

In my teens, I was more cunning than half the criminals I've encountered during my short legal career. I didn't let my feelings cloud my judgment. No, each time, I put them – the anger, the hatred, the fear – aside and focussed on the task at hand. If you fail to prepare, prepare to fail. I prepared for weeks before I made my move. The nightmares I have are my payment for a well-planned and executed murder. Although what others call murder, I think of as justice. The law and I differ on that point but it's all semantics. When the police arrived at the scene, all they saw was a potential rape victim and the friend who killed a criminal in order to stop him. No one suspected the truth, not even to this day.

But let's get back to Mr. Matheson. It's obvious that Sarah (who is 37 years younger than he) married him for his money (his art collection alone is rumoured to be worth millions), but needs a little side action because, well... her husband is old and he looks it. I don't understand how every rich man with one foot in the grave thinks that a woman young enough to be his daughter is marrying him for the love of him, not the love of his money. It's true what they say – there is no bigger fool than an old fool. I suppose she's not ready to go back to being poor, so she's siding with her husband on this one. I wonder how their relationship will fare... I wonder where the missing clothes are.

Speaking of old fools; Old Bill took this case because he and Matheson are friends. In his words, "What sort of friend would I be if I didn't lend a hand?" He's charging Matheson twice the going rate for the privilege of having the least competent defence team on his case, so I guess he's not the best friend. I hear that Veronica and Sarah are friends, too... I wonder if Veronica knew Sarah was cheating.

"Well," I say, "that sounds like the best course of action to me. Mr. Benoit doesn't seem keen on having his dirty laundry aired in public. I reckon he'd be happy to receive a cheque and be done with it."

"But the client wants to go to court," Daryl says.

"And I want to win the lottery. Wanting doesn't always lead to getting, Daryl."

"I think we should respect our client's wishes."

"That is absurd!" I say.

"Why do you say that, Miss Palmer?"

I look across the table to Rebecca Staunton, the firm's other partner. She's one of those people who rarely ever raises her voice. Sometimes, she speaks at such a low volume that I have to sit still, or move closer to her, in order to hear what she's saying. It's like her subtle way of controlling people. I at once admire and resent that.

For some reason, she invited herself to this meeting. Too much time on her hands, perhaps. Or maybe she likes being punished. She's worked in various in-carnations of this firm for around 30 years, which is longer than I've been alive, and has been a partner for more than fifteen of those years. In that time, the firm has thrived. I respect her work ethic and hope to one day achieve at least as much as she has.

Today, her salt-and-pepper hair is in a bun, which gives her appearance a slightly stern edge. Her shrivelling neck is decorated with a string of pearls, and her long-sleeved black dress hugs every bone on her petite frame, while making her look like a widow who took out a hit on her husband. Her blue eyes are steely, almost certainly matching her will.

I compose myself. Then I let loose.

"The only hard evidence we have of Matheson's encounter with Benoit is the CCTV footage from Matheson's driveway, which we know shows Benoit getting shot in the back as he hurries out of the house. Even as he tries to crawl away, all bloody and wounded, Matheson goes after him. If the police hadn't got there so fast, Benoit would be dead for sure. Matheson doesn't look like a man who was defending his home. He looks like a man hell-bent on murder. He wasn't trying to scare the 'robber'," I say, using air quotes, "he was trying to kill his wife's lover. You know the prosecution will want to play that video in court, which is why he should settle instead."

"You think the video evidence points to his guilt?" Staunton asks.

I nod. "The only person in that video who looks scared is not the one we're defending."

"Well, that's just your opinion—"

"Which was requested," I say to Daryl.

"That is the one piece of visual evidence we have of any interaction between the plaintiff and defendant. Matheson may look dangerous to you, but he might not look that way to a juror. And there's no guarantee that the video will play in court," Daryl says.

"I don't know," Kat says, "everything Donna said makes sense. There's no way they won't play that video, especially since it paints Matheson as someone out hunting rabbits or some other helpless creature."

"Are rabbits helpless?" Shane asks. For once, he's not jumping down Daryl's throat, trying to choke him with disapproval. Maybe he's coming down with an illness.

"I'm not sure, but my point—"

"We should vote," Daryl says, cutting Kat off.

There's a brief, awkward silence before Staunton nods in agreement.

"All in favour of advising Matheson to settle…?" she says. She, Kat and I raise our hands. To my surprise, Shane doesn't. He really must be feeling unwell.

Staunton continues, "And against?"

Shane and Daryl raise their hands. Even Daryl looks surprised to have Shane on his side. He shakes his head a little, disappointed to have been overruled.

"Well that settles it," Staunton says. Pun intended?

I'm pleased that logic has prevailed. And yet, my heart sinks. I became a lawyer because I wanted to deliver justice to those who've been victimised. I wanted to help people, somehow make the world a better, fairer place. Yet here I am, helping the guilty go free. Sometimes I tell myself that this is only a phase and that one day, I'll be able to switch sides. I don't know how true that is.

At least the meeting is over. When we leave the room, I catch up with Shane as he walks back to his desk.

"Hey, Shane, are you feeling ok?" I ask, with a half-smile. My curiosity has got the better of me.

"What do you mean?"

Shane is another person I try to avoid speaking to. He insists on talking even when he has nothing to say, and he steals ideas. All the time. His main aim when conversing with anyone is to pick their brains, then pretend that their ideas or work originated with him. He's a snake. In meetings, he devotes an inordinate amount of time to arguing with Daryl over something, nothing or anything. Their competitiveness is both distracting and embarrassing to witness.

Shane's sole redeeming feature is his face – though it will never win him a modelling contract, on the whole, it's not distressing to look at. Yes, his chin is weak and destined to double in size unless he stays vigilant, but he has pretty, light-brown eyes with long lashes, and his skin looks healthy. He has a beard, but it isn't one of those atrocious heavy metal-style ones. It's more… responsible

– short and neat. Despite the darkness of his hair, he's afflicted with ginger-beard syndrome. There are worse things. In addition to all that, he spends a lot of time at the gym (I know because he won't shut up about kettlebells and the cross-trainer) and has a body that reflects that. It's a shame that he isn't interesting or pleasant.

"You didn't really think that Daryl's proposal was good, did you?" I say, narrowing my eyes.

He smiles and shakes his head. He looks over his shoulder, as if checking that no one is within earshot. Then he looks at me, beaming.

"I woke up this morning and realised that I've been going about this the wrong way," he says, his eyes widening.

I shake my head. "Going about what the wrong way?"

"We all know Blake doesn't have a clue, yet he's still running this silo. Maybe if we let him… expose himself, the partners will see that they made a mistake. They'll do the right thing and get someone more competent to lead the team."

I take a moment to think about how to respond.

"When you say expose himself, you don't mean—?"

"Of course not! Although… that might speed up the process."

He grins.

"Oh ok. And by someone more competent, you mean… you?"

He shrugs as we get to his desk, which (unlike mine) is brimming with mountains of useless paper.

Part of me can't believe Shane is this deluded. It's a reasonable plan but unless Shane also plans to impregnate Veronica Sanders (improbable, though not impossible), I think it'll fail.

That won't stop me from having fun watching this slow-motion car crash.

***

I generally go to lunch at midday. I say I go to lunch but in truth, I take a walk in the surrounding area. It's always nice to get some fresh air. And by 'fresh', I mean 'less stale' for there's no such thing as fresh air in the centre of London. The pollution is so severe that I don't remember the last time I didn't have smog-infused mucus. I am lucky enough to know a few green spots in the vicinity, so I often wind up walking to one of them.

As I prepare to leave my desk, Kat comes over to me with a sober look on her face. She gently brushes my forearm.

"You want some company, flower?" she asks.

I never want company. And I hate it when she calls me 'flower.' Of course, she doesn't know this.

Like everyone else I encounter, she knows little about me. She knows where I was educated, knows I'm 27, that I have a sister – Ivy – who is two years younger. She knows that we live with our mother, Selene, and she's even dropped me at our apartment building on more than one occasion. She knows nothing of William. She's never asked. I assume that she thinks I never met my father or have no memory of him. I'm content to let her do so.

I consider telling her that I'd rather spend the time by myself, but it seems like she's being considerate. I'm sure it's ultimately to her benefit. That said, she's a well-spring of useful information – acquired by means both fair and foul – so there's unlikely to be any harm in letting her tag along.

Before I can respond, my phone starts ringing. I reach into my pocket, holding my breath. I look at the screen, and exhale when I see that it's Ivy. I smile at Kat. "Excuse me."

She nods and steps away. I slip past her and leave the office, walking into the corridor. I find a spot in the stairwell and answer the phone.

"Hey Ivy, how goes?"

"I'm alright. Sorry I missed you this morning. How's work?"

"Same as ever. How's your church thing?"

"Yeah, it's ok. Um, I wanted to ask a favour, if that's ok…"

"It depends on the favour." I know at once that it has something to do with William. I brace myself.

"Mum's decided to make a meal for us, you know, to mark the day," she says, putting it delicately. "I know you might have to work late or do exercise or something, but I was hoping you could… maybe be home earlier than usual so we can all have dinner together. Would you try? Please."

I blow air into my cheeks before letting a slow stream of it filter through my nostrils. I had no intention of working late tonight, but I hardly ever do. I had hoped to go to the gym and I don't want to have a family dinner. Definitely not tonight. I suppose I shouldn't be surprised that mum made no mention of this to me... I should have expected her to use Ivy as a go-between.

This morning, for the first time this month, I was able to leave the house without seeing either of them. It was unusual, more so because I was later than I should have been, but I was relieved all the same. I imagine mum stayed in bed wallowing in some form of self-pity, crying over her 'bereavement.'

As for Ivy, she was almost certainly alternating between thanking God that William is dead, and asking God to forgive her for thanking Him that William is dead. Her relief and guilt are most evident this day each year.

My memory of that day remains fresh. He was already dead when mum found him. She was almost inconsolable. Ivy, though shaken, tried to calm her down. When she did eventually cry, I wondered if Ivy's tears were real or if, like me, she was putting on a show. Having to pretend irked me but it was good practice for the future.

And by the future, I mean the present I currently occupy. I'd rather dance on his grave than have a meal in his honour. But... his death is an event worth celebrating and I respect Ivy's efforts to keep the peace. I'll say yes.

"I'll see what I can do, Ivy. You know they just spring these things on me sometimes."

That, in my mind, is a yes.

"OK, cool. I'll keep a plate warm for you." She sounds uncertain.

"Thanks. See you later."

I end the call and lean against the wall, tilting my head towards the ceiling.

I cannot wait for this day to end.

The door to the stairway swings open, startling me. I look over and see Kat beckoning to me.

"What? What is it?"

"Old Bill just called. Emergency meeting in his office, ASAP!"

"But it's lunch t—"

"Ha, funny. Come on, no room for stragglers."

She retreats and leaves me staring at the door.

***

Daryl, Kat, Shane and I troop into the lift and go all the way to the twelfth floor. I make a point of standing in between Daryl and Kat. The last thing I need is for her to find reasons to whine. Shane, still in a good mood, yammers on about all the possible reasons why we've been summoned to The Top, as he calls it.

"Maybe we're the best team and we're all getting a raise."

"Or maybe we're the worst and we're all getting the sack," I counter. Daryl lets out a laugh, one that says, 'I have a job for life.' For some reason, I have a strange knot in my stomach and a growing sense of unease.

When we get to The Top, Sanders' assistant, Charlene, greets us. She and Maria, Staunton's assistant, are the only other people on this floor. They know all the gossip and are always happy to share it with Kat. Before he had a chance to tell the team, Charlene let Kat know about Daryl's engagement and pending promotion, and the reason for both. When she found out, Kat came running to me. I can always rely on her to spill other people's secrets.

Charlene leads us into Sanders' office, where Staunton is already sitting, cross-legged, waiting. Charlene leaves, shutting the door behind her. There's nothing unusual about the noise but in my head, it sounds like the slamming of a prison cell door. All of a sudden, everything feels so ominous.

William Sanders has a commanding, somewhat intimidating presence, all 6 feet and 4 inches of him. He's no spring chicken (65, last I checked), but he still stands upright, and despite his age, he's one of those in-the-gym-at-6am sort of people. Unlike Mr. Matheson, who at 63 is aging like poorly preserved milk in a heat wave, Sanders could pass for a man in his late forties. It helps that his hair isn't all grey. Maybe it's the exercise, or maybe he's well-acquainted with moisturiser and sunscreen, or maybe he's had some work done. Whatever the case may be, it looks as though he pays attention to his appearance and that is to his benefit.

I tend to feel uneasy around him. I don't know if it's his stature, or his beady-eyed stare that makes me feel like he's x-raying my innards, or the fact that he bears the same name as my deceased father, but being around him puts me on edge. I wouldn't want to run into him in a dark alley. I try to hide my discomfort and always make a point of keeping my distance physically.

We stand around like naughty children in the principal's office who are waiting to be chastised. Sanders smiles at us, though the smile doesn't reach his eyes. "Please, sit."

We do as we're told. He sits down as well, and then clears his throat. "We're taking you off the Matheson case effective immediately. Davis and his team can finish that off."

Shane starts to say something, but Sanders cuts him off.

"Jeremy Haywood was arrested earlier today on suspicion of sexual assault," he says. "Your team will oversee his defence. He's the most important client we have, and we went to great lengths to get him." He pauses for a second, then, "I expect you all to bring your A-game."

The room gets quiet enough for one to hear a strand of hair fall to the ground. This news has left even Daryl speechless.

Jeremy Haywood is one of the richest men living in the country. Legend has it that he made his money from night clubs and casinos, so I know he's guilty the second I hear he's been accused of a sexual offence. I don't have to hear any details – my mind is made up. Casinos, nightclubs and rape go together like Huey, Dewey and Louie.

"He's at the police station waiting for his lawyers," Staunton says. There's more silence.

Finally, Daryl says, "Well, we'd better get over there."

"You can sit out the disclosure and initial interview, Mr. Blake. I'd like you—" she says, pointing to me, "—and you—" she points to Kat, "—to take this one."

I'm too taken aback to respond. I sit in stunned silence. Daryl stutters something unintelligible, but Staunton raises her voice over his. The day is full of surprises.

"That won't be a problem for you ladies, will it?" she asks.

"No Ma'am, it won't," I say, finding my words. I get a glimpse of Kat shaking her head. My heart is beating so fast that I can hear it in my ears. My stomach churns and knots up. I think about the dream that interrupted my sleeping pattern.

"I'm fine with that Ma'am," Kat says.

"Good. The sooner you leave, the sooner we can get him out of there," she says. "You're dismissed."

We get up to leave the room, then she speaks again, "Miss Palmer, please join me in my office."

"Yes Ma'am."

That was an order, not a request. My stomach might have made a noise this time.

"I'll be in the garage," Kat says. I nod and all of us leave Sanders' office together. The others go to the lift, while I follow Staunton to her room.

She walks ahead of me. When I get in, she ushers me through first and shuts the door behind us. I turn and look at her, holding my notebook against my chest. It's been years since I felt this vulnerable.

"You look nervous," she says in a calming tone. Her voice is smooth as a dolphin's skin. "Aren't you going to ask why you?"

I don't know what she's getting at. I look away from her, noting the minimalistic, yet stylish décor of her office. This is the first time I've been in here. I'd imagined that her office would be empty, so I'm not too surprised to find that it's so sparse. The only furniture in here is her desk and chair, and two chairs for guests. There's a table with a fruit bowl and some drinks on it. This is not a place she or anyone else uses for relaxation.

"Why me what?"

"Why you for the interview," she says.

"Why would I ask that?"

She smirks and walks towards me. She stops in front of me and folds her hands. Tilting her head one way and then the next, she examines my face. I feel my facial muscles twitch, though not enough for her to notice. She walks past me

18

and pours herself a glass of… something.

"Scotch?" she offers.

Of course it's scotch. That's all rich people drink, isn't it? Well, scotch in the day and champagne at night. Not that I would know.

"No thanks, Ma'am, I'm on duty."

She shrugs and takes a swig. "I've seen how you work, Donna – how dedicated and tenacious you are. You're smart and resilient and ambitious. You have the makings of a great lawyer. But you're a woman and you're black, so people tend to overlook you. You should be leading that team, but Daryl… Daryl has a benefactor. Maybe you need one too."

"I'm not sure I understand you, Ma'am."

"It is very important to Mr. Sanders that we make Jeremy Haywood's problem go away, and quickly. It's equally important to me that talent rises to the top. That's why I want you to lead the team on this case."

"Oh…"

"I know you have certain issues regarding crimes with a sexual dimension, but opportunities like this don't come about often," she says.

"I see."

"Will the case be a problem for you, Donna?"

Yes, it will be a problem for me. A huge one.

I knew on some level that one day I'd have to work on something like this, but I always told myself that I'd cross that bridge when I got there. Oh joy, here I am.

"Not at all, Ma'am. I— I don't know why you'd think it would," I say with a straight face.

She smiles and walks closer to me. "You're not going to lose control and harm the client, are you? You know, the way you've done in the past?"

My heart misses a beat.

I look her in the eyes, without blinking. "That was self-defence, like the police report says. The boy tried to rob my place of work. And then he…" I look away and take a deep breath. I pick up again, "Things just unfolded that way."

19

I inhale again and swallow hard. She looks like she might believe me, not that it matters.

"I wasn't accusing you of anything, Donna."

I nod. "I will defend Mr. Haywood to the best of my ability, Ma'am."

She looks me up and down, as if trying to detect any ticks that might reveal the contents of my mind. "Katrina is waiting for you. You should go."

I nod again and go to the door. As I open it, I turn to her. "Thank you, Ma'am, for your consideration."

"Make me proud."

I leave the room, making no promises, and walk to the lift. I push the button and wait for the lift to arrive. The discomfort in my stomach persists, until I would like nothing more than to throw up, despite having eaten nothing all day. I take a few deep breaths, lifting my head and focussing my gaze on the lift's progress. I see Alan's face. I blink the mental image away.

The empty lift arrives and I board it, taking sharp, deep breaths until I feel normal again. I look at my reflection in the lift's mirror, carefully inspecting it. I re-tuck my white shirt into my grey trousers and smooth the lapels of my matching jacket. I loosen my bun and redo it, making sure there are no hairs out of place. For a moment, I pause and stare into my eyes. They are the deepest shade of brown, round and full of secrets. I smile at my reflection, though I have no reason to.

The lift stops on the sixth floor, and I turn to face the door. A few people I don't recognise get into it and I smile politely at them. The doors close and the lift's descent continues. I have a feeling today will only get worse.

***

When I get to the garage, Kat is smoking whilst leaning against the driver's side of her VW golf. It's some generic shade of grey which she loves because (according to her) it makes following people easier. Her back is to me. I tap at the window of the passenger's seat. She spins around.

"At last," she says, her eyes bouncing from me to her watch. She stubs the cigarette out and enters the car. She releases the remote lock and leans over to move an outdated mp3 player from the passenger's seat. I don't know why she's holding on to that thing. I get in and buckle up my seat belt, placing my briefcase on my lap.

I point at the music player. "You couldn't do that before… instead of trying to smoke yourself to death?"

She groans and starts the engine. We pull out of the garage and for a full minute, sit in blissful silence. I know it won't last too long, because Kat doesn't like silence any more than she likes happiness. In a flash, she switches the music player on. And then she starts talking.

"Did you hear the way he spoke to me today?"

Ah, I'd hoped it wouldn't be this.

"I'm sure it's nothing personal," I say, keeping my eyes forward.

"I thought things would be easier after we broke up, but now… he treats me like I'm inept."

"He's projecting. Everyone knows he's the one with few to no skills."

She taps the steering wheel. I wind the window down a little, hoping for relief from the lingering smell of tobacco.

"The saddest thing is that I miss him so much. And when he talks to me like that, I feel like such an idiot."

My eyes dart to her, and I notice her blink back tears. The unpleasant reality of this situation is that she is an idiot. Only an idiot would embark on a sexual relationship with a married co-worker, and one as abhorrent as Daryl Blake. In her defence, their relationship started before his marriage (while he was secretly sleeping with Veronica, too) but anyone with a modicum of self-respect would have ruined his life once he announced his engagement. Instead the affair carried on, even throughout his wife's pregnancy. The guy is dirt. Why can't she see this for herself?

"It's been what, a month?" I say, hoping I sound concerned.

"6 weeks."

Whatever.

"These things take time. In another month, you won't even remember today."

She sniffs. I hope she isn't going to cry. I don't want to die in a VW.

"Yesterday, he told me that he still loved me. Said he's going to leave Veronica for real," she offers.

I turn to face her. "He really said that?"

She nods. Surely even she is not dense enough to believe him. Surely, he has not completely lost the will to live.

I shuffle in the seat. "Come on, Kat, you know he's lying. If he really wanted to, he would have left Veronica ages ago. Heck he would never have started sleeping with her in the first place, so why now? Why now that you've moved on?"

"Maybe he—"

"No, he didn't. Whatever you're going to say is a lie. He's trying to control you and you know it. And even if he wasn't, it's pretty despicable to leave your family for anything other than a nap with the fishes."

I know – I interrupted her. Rude though that was, nothing she was about to say would have been worth hearing. I trust that I've spared myself some drivel.

"You're right, you're right," she says, wiping tears away. "Besides," she continues, "he always made it sound like if he left her, Old Bill wouldn't take it well."

At one of their clandestine meetings, Daryl told Kat that Mr. Sanders' nickname at home is 'Old Bill.' And now we call him that behind everyone's backs.

"Exactly! There's no telling what he'd do. At the very least, your career would suffer. Let it go, Kat."

For a moment we stop talking, waiting at a zebra crossing. A pigeon totters across the street and I wonder why she doesn't run it over. She takes the opportunity to dry her tears. When she's done, she accelerates.

Eventually, I speak up. "Maybe you should take some time off. A mental health break, you can call it."

"Since when do you give unsolicited advice?"

Since it was in my interest.

"Since now. It'd be good for you to be away from work and its complications. Stress is like anything else – you can starve it to death."

I'm sick of hearing about this failed affair.

"I don't think that'll happen anytime soon, what with this new case and all."

I sigh and fondle the buckle on my seat belt.

The car goes quiet, except for the music, and my mind wanders to Jeremy Haywood. I'm pleased that Rebecca Staunton has noticed me and my work. This could be a turning point in my career. I hope she isn't a liar like Old Bill.

"Speaking of the case, what did Boss Lady want to talk about?"

Why does she talk so much?

"Nothing interesting."

"Well, what did she say?"

Her grip on the steering wheel tightens.

"Nothing worth repeating."

From the corner of my eye I see her glance at me, clenching her jaw. I look at her as she turns to face the road.

The song that's playing is by one of those rappers with minimal talent, who seems to delight in bragging about how often he trades petty cash for blow jobs. I've not heard this particular song before, and I hope never to hear it again. In fact, I can't stand to hear much more of it.

"Is there anything else you could play?" I ask, hoping to distract her and save myself from this aural assault.

"Don't try to change the subject."

I shift in the seat, feeling uneasy. I look out the window at the grotty streets. The car halts at a red light. It's the beginning of the evening rush, and there are more cars on the road than I'm comfortable with.

This is why I don't drive to work.

In an hour or so, this place will mirror the seventh circle of hell. The pavements are starting to fill up with foot commuters, hurrying to bus stops and train stations, I presume. And here we are, going to a police station to meet a rapist. Once again, I have pulled the short straw in life.

"So, what happened?" she presses.

"What difference does it make?"

"I'm an investigator. It's my job to gather information." She glances at me again and says, "You know you can trust me."

She sounds like she believes what she's saying. I stifle incredulous laughter. This woman who thinks that it's fine to sleep with a married man – a dreadful one that she has to see almost every day – also thinks she's trustworthy. Even if I didn't know about her and Daryl, I would never trust her with anything. Yes, we're on good terms but we're not friends. We're… acquaintances, if you will.

"She told me to pull my finger out, pull my socks up, pull myself up by my bootstraps. That sort of thing. She also said we need to win this case," I say.

"Here I thought we needed to win all the cases."

"Yes, well, this guy's got big money, so it's a big must."

I doubt that answer satisfied her curiosity, but she stops talking at this point. The car approaches another red light.

"While I was waiting for you, I called a friend at the police station. He told me that the accuser is Jeremy Junior's classmate, Aisha Thompson."

"What happened?" I ask

The light goes green and we move off.

"Accuser says she went to a party, and then left with the boy. They went to his house, drank a little, and his dad tried to rape her," she says. Her tone is so monotonous that I wonder if she recognises the gravity of the accusation.

"Right. Where was Junior when the attack took place?" I ask.

"He was passed out drunk in the home cinema room when the alleged attack took place," she says, throwing me a disapproving look.

'Alleged.' Of course, I forgot that special little modifier that we use when we pretend our client is innocent. I nod and look out the window again.

"You think he did it?" she asks.

I stare out the window and, with horror, it dawns on me that we might have another hour of scintillating discourse ahead of us. I hate being trapped in cars with people.

"I'm willing to keep an open mind."

***

Traffic was an ordeal, not helped by Kat's terrible choice of soundtrack and her insistence on talking about Daryl. I shouldn't complain too much. There were no protests on our route. It could have been far worse. Upon arrival at the police station, we were greeted by the most disgruntled receptionist you could ever hope to meet. He was so rude and seemed so angry that I thought, for a moment, that I was at my GP's surgery.

After a short wait, the case officer called Sergeant Philips comes to meet us. Disclosure is brief and he refrains from giving me specific details of the allegations, only revealing that our client "is believed to have tried to rape a young woman at his house last night."

"What are the charges, specifically?"

He shrugs. "There's enough here to charge your client with actual bodily harm, sexual assault and attempted rape. I wouldn't make him any promises if I were you."

Sergeant Philips leads us to the interrogation room where our esteemed client is waiting.

In terms of his physical appearance, Haywood reminds me a little of Sanders – tall, well-built, posture that reveals arrogance. Unlike Sanders, he's not calm. His voice is loud and booming and he paces about and gesticulates a lot, throwing his hands around wildly. He has a long stitch on the left side of his face, starting from his forehead and going down to his cheekbone. It looks like a fresh cut. I notice that there's a small bandage on his left ear as well.

As soon as we enter the room, he yells, "What took you so damn long? Do you know how long I've been waiting? You were supposed to be here hours ago! What the f—?"

I raise my hand, stopping him before he can finish cursing. William swore at us a lot when I was growing up. On one occasion when I was 12, he ordered me to get him more drink from the pantry. I was feeling defiant that day (some might say 'self-destructive') and said something along the lines of, "You know that stuff will kill you eventually, right?" It's one of my favourite things to tell addicts.

As he rained punches down on my head, he went through the A-Z of curse words. I've never heard so much filth in one evening before. The beatings were nothing new and I knew that the bruises would heal. Being subjected to that level of verbal vitriol was uncharted territory for me. First time for everything, right?

I shake myself out of the memory. To this day, profanity makes me shudder and I try my best to filter it out of my consciousness. It appears that Mr. Haywood is also in possession of a potty mouth. This case is going to be challenging in several ways.

"Mr. Haywood, I'm Donna Palmer, one of your solicitors, and this is Katrina Murray, our investigator," I say, "and I would appreciate it if you kept your language clean. We work for you but that doesn't give you the right to speak to us disrespectfully."

His eyes narrow and he steps back. He beckons to me with his hand. I stand stock still.

"Is there a problem, Mr. Haywood?" I ask.

"Have you got a cigarette? I need to smoke," he says, the volume of his voice dipping.

"There's no smoking in here," Kat answers. "That's the law."

He runs his fingers through his dark, thinning hair, still pacing.

"Perhaps you should sit down," I say.

He obliges. The room is as you'd expect – a table, with a couple of chairs on each side. No windows, a mirror, dark paint. I motion to Kat to pick a chair, but she declines, opting instead to lean against the wall next to me. I sit down and take out a notebook and a pen.

I look across the table at him. He taps his foot and keeps making a fist and then releasing it.

"When can I get out of here?"

"We're not sure yet," Kat says. "Can you tell us what happened last night?"

He purses his lips and his eyes dart from her face to mine. He lets out a loud, dramatic exhale. His fingers tap the table rapidly, and then he suddenly stands up again.

"That girl, Jerry's friend, she's lying," he says, his hands flailing.

"We want to hear what happened from your perspective," I say.

"I came home from work, and some girl was leaving the house, looking drunk and dishevelled and… kind of ragged."

"Had you ever seen her before?" Kat asks.

He shakes his head. "I tried to talk to her, find out what was wrong but she just ran off, so I went inside the house."

His hands come to his sides and he carries on pacing. He's doing his best impression of a falsely accused man, but he's not fooling me. I can see right through him. Guilty as sin is what he is. I jot down the nonsense he's said.

"When you say ragged, what do you mean?" I ask.

"Her clothes were ripped and tattered."

"What, like someone had attacked her?" Kat says.

"I suppose," he says. His voice is flat and even.

He sits down and continues, "I don't know what happened to her, but I didn't lay a finger on that girl."

Kat and I exchange a look.

"You didn't think to call the police?" I say.

He shakes his head. "Whose side are you on?"

"We need as much information as possible," I say.

"No, I didn't think anything of it. I thought she'd had a little too much to drink, and maybe had a roll in the hay with some boy—"

"Your son, perhaps?"

"No, not my son. That didn't cross my mind. It wasn't until the police came to arrest me, saying I tried to rape her, that I realised I should have called them. I didn't do anything to that girl—"

"Aisha," I say, correcting him. "She has a name."

"Yes, her. I didn't touch her, but still they dragged me here, and treated me like a criminal. I'm not a criminal."

Even without the clichéd denial, his guilt is clear from his body language. He refuses to make eye contact with either of us, and his eyes bounce from the walls to the table to the floor, never lingering long enough on one surface.

"Why didn't you think she'd been with Jerry?"

His expression contorts into a menacing scowl, with his face turning redder than beet juice. The stitch looks like it's about to burst open. He stands up and looks in my eyes, speaking in a loud, threatening tone.

He wags his finger at me. "When I got home, he was asleep and fully-clothed. Whoever that girl was with, it wasn't him! Understood?"

I nod. "Understood."

He's scum, but not enough to implicate his son. There may yet be hope for him.

"Well," he says, "do you believe me?"

"We're not here to believe you; we're here to defend you. We can only do that effectively if we know the whole truth," I say.

"I just told you the truth," he says, raising his voice some more.

No, you didn't.

"What happened to your face?"

"What?"

"She asked what happened to your face," Kat says, still leaning against the wall. She's barely moved a muscle since we got in.

He touches the stitch. He hesitates. "I had an accident."

"What kind of accident?" Kat asks.

"The kind that happens when you're not paying attention." He stares hard at her.

Kat and I exchange another look. Her brow furrows. Yes, I too am concerned. My gut tells me that this 'accident' is related to the case. I push for more answers.

"When did it happen?"

He sighs loudly, pacing back and forth again, scratching his head. When he's bored or tired of that, he returns to the table and sits down.

"This has nothing to do with that girl, and it can never leave this room." We nod in agreement.

He continues, "When I got home last night, my wife was already asleep. There was a bottle of wine on the bedside table and as I went to pull the covers over her, she woke up. I must have startled her – she grabbed the bottle and hit me over the head."

I look at him as he clasps his hands together.

"I take it your wife is an alcoholic." The words tumble out of my mouth before I can screen them.

"That's none of your business. And it has nothing to do with this— this liar."

"And your ear? What about that?"

He says nothing.

"Your wife again?" I ask, smirking.

No response, only the clenching of his jaw.

"Any other questions, Kat?"

She shakes her head. "I think you've covered it."

"Mr. Haywood, the police will most likely charge you with actual bodily harm, sexual assault—"

"Oh come on!" he says, throwing his hands up.

"—and attempted rape. They might let you go home tonight after questioning, but I can't guarantee that."

I put my things neatly to one side. I stand up and walk to the door.

"Why am I paying your firm so much money if I'm being charged anyway?"

"If you're charged, it'll be because the police believe they have enough evidence to do so. We'll defend you as best we can, but there's nothing else to do right now."

He gets up in a huff and resumes his pacing again. "This is outra—"

I raise my voice above his. "Here's my advice – during the interview, a simple 'No Comment' will suffice. Do you understand?"

"But I didn't do anything wrong!"

"As your lawyer, I'm advising you to say nothing at all. Do you understand?"

He sits down again. "You're useless!"

Ignoring his petulant behaviour, I knock on the door. An officer opens it.

"We're ready."

He nods, closes the door. I go back and sit next to Haywood, taking care to keep some distance between us.

"I'll wait for you at reception, however long it takes," Kat says, heading for the door.

I nod at her.

"Is there someone who can take you home, Mr. Haywood?" she asks. How thoughtful of her. It hadn't even occurred to me that he might need a lift.

"My chauffeur is waiting for me outside."

Kat leaves the room, leaving us alone. If the police are thorough, we probably won't get out of here for at least another hour.

At this rate, I may yet miss dinner.

MINA

Iset the alarm for 7am but wake up fifteen minutes earlier. I want to spend the day job-hunting, and they say that the early bird catches the worm. There's no mention of whether that bird would be more productive if got more sleep. It catches the worm, therefore nothing else matters.

I've been at this shelter for the three weeks since I was released on probation. I was sent to prison for a range of crimes, from possession and sales of class-A drugs, to breaking and entering, and theft. Though I'm still under 30, my record of criminal activity is impressive, if crime impresses you. I should still be in jail, but they let me out on good behaviour... and because the place was overcrowded. Salome, my counsellor/sponsor/friend, put in a good word for me, as did some of the prison officers. She works for a charity that visits inmates and treats us like people. They've got some fancy mission statement but that's really what it boils down to.

Salome is unusual. Her husband, Ricardo, has some high-flying job at a film production company and she spends her free time with prisoners when she could be having spa days and travelling to far-off locations in a private jet. Like I said, she's unusual.

The shelter is basic, has everything you need – bed, desk, publicly-accessible computers and internet, shared bathroom. It's not too dissimilar from prison, except I can go outside without expecting to get beaten up. Also, I don't have to be here. Salome offered me a room in her house, but I didn't feel right accepting. She's already done more good for me than I've ever done for myself. She suggested this shelter because some friends of hers run it. It's a nice place, but it's not home. Nowhere has felt like home for a very long time.

I have a nice hot shower and go to the common area. I've got no degree and next to no work experience in any legal trade, so I'm not expecting much. The only things I was ever good at were selling drugs and getting high, and that's not the sort of experience legitimate employers seek. Oh, I shouldn't think about that. I've been clean for about 6 months now, and I need to keep it up if I'm going to have a good life. You would have thought using whilst imprisoned was impossible but believe me, where there's a will, there's a way. If I can get a real job, that would make my life so much better.

It's early enough that the common area is deserted when I get here. I check my emails and find that none of the jobs I applied for last week have been ac-knowledged. I mean, I received those automated acknowledgement emails, but no human has contacted me to say whether I have been successful or even have a chance. It's getting me down. Salome keeps telling me to keep my head up and persevere, but it's so hard when you feel like you're doing your best and it's all for nothing. I've been at this for three weeks. How much longer? If I was selling drugs, I'd be able to rent my own place by now.

The lack of response dampens my already middling mood. Rather than send out more applications that will only be disregarded, I decide to take a walk. Before I log off, I note the date on the computer and remember that it's been 10 years since Donna's dad passed away. I wonder how she and her family are doing. I haven't seen them for almost five years. I hope they're ok.

That really was something, the way Mr. Palmer died. It was like Donna went from having a normal life to living in a TV show overnight. First, there was the incident at the shop, and then her dad got wasted and tumbled to his death. I didn't even know he drank like that. Life is so fragile. One minute, it seems like the world is a great place and you're full of potential, and the next, all your hopes have been dashed to pieces.

I should know. A month after my 17th birthday, I was invited to the 18th birthday party of one of the older girls at my school. Beth Meyer was the coolest, but not in a way that I would recommend now that I know better. Everyone fawned over her and her piercing blue eyes and hip-length blonde hair, and she took full advantage of the attention she got, flirting with and dating any boy she wanted.

She drank hard liquor, swore like a sailor, got high and had sex with loads of boys, yet managed to never get a bad reputation for it. Maybe it's because her father was one of the local councilmen or maybe she was just lucky, if you can call that luck. Starting with her 13th, her parents threw a lavish birthday party for her at their mega-house every year, and for some inexplicable reason, that year she invited me. It was always an open party but knowing that Beth took the time to speak to me made me feel special.

Donna despised her so much that I sometimes thought she wanted her dead. When she did eventually die of a drug overdose, I think it took every ounce of strength for Donna not to break into song. I remember her saying, "Beth represents everything that's wrong with the world." I often wondered how someone who seemed so calm could say such spiteful things.

I invited Donna to the party, as any best friend would. I wasn't surprised that she turned me down. She said that had to study but felt the need to add that she would rather choke on a dead squirrel than set foot in the home of that 'lout.' I asked if the squirrel had to be dead, she said it wasn't a prerequisite. It was a definite no, and maybe the best decision that she ever made.

My parents didn't like the idea of me going to parties but Beth's dad, Dennis, was well-liked in the community, so they didn't protest. I got to the party not too early, but not too late either. There was so much alcohol; I thought someone had robbed a brewery. I'd never seen so much drink before in my life. I told myself that she'd only turn 18 once, so her parents must have gone all out. There were no adults in sight, but the house was sprawling so I thought that maybe there were one or two hiding somewhere on the premises.

Some other friends of mine were at the party – Charlotte Ainsworth, her boyfriend Aaron Dunn, Suzanne Zhou, a few others. I hung out with Charlotte and Aaron, for most of the evening, while Suzanne snooped around the house, trying to work out the cost of every ornament on display. I knew my parents would have a fit if they found out, but I had a couple of drinks with my friends. It was the first time I had vodka and orange – less vodka, more orange. The taste took some getting used to.

My parents expected me home by 11pm and I didn't want to break curfew. I planned to leave around 10 o' clock so that I had plenty of time to get home on the bus. My dad had offered to come and pick me up, but he'd been at work all day (he was a teacher) and I didn't want to trouble him. I turned him down. Suzanne and some of the other kids at the party lived near me, so I thought we'd leave together. I thought wrong.

Beth's boyfriend, Alan Ellis, had been hanging around all night. He tried to talk to Suzanne, but she walked away from him mid-sentence. Unlike Donna who was more covert about her feelings, Suzanne had a habit of openly disliking people. In all fairness, Alan was well-known for his rudeness and bullying, but as far as I know, no one ever called him out on it. Like Beth, his father had clout in the community.

Louis Ellis – or Big Lou, as he was often called in the paper – was a successful investor with connections to the government, and he'd made his money in banking. He and Donna's dad, William, worked in the same bank at some point. He had friends in high places and gave a lot of money to the community. We were told that one of his donations had single-handedly paid for the new gym at our school. That pretty much ensured that, no matter how despicable his behaviour, people turned a blind eye to Alan's antics. It didn't help that he was a very well-built six-footer. People would have been intimidated by his size alone, even if his father was nobody.

Donna hated him too and had even gone so far as to verbally abuse him at school. It was the first time I ever saw her lose her temper. He touched her backside and she shoved him away, and then bit his hand. I thought she'd gone mad! She told him that if he ever touched her again, she'd scratch his eyes out and feed them to the ducks! Like, are ducks even omnivorous? I still don't know… Either way, I believed her and he must have too, because he looked terrified. He didn't report it, though. He just laughed it off, called her the b-word and went to the nurse.

I needed to use the facilities at the party, but a couple of the downstairs toilets were occupied (with vomiting youths in one case and copulating youths in the other). I ran into Beth on my way to find another one, and she told me that I could use the one in her room. 18 years old with an en-suite bathroom – that's the life. I couldn't believe that she was even talking to me. She'd always been so aloof and seemed somewhat unreachable, but suddenly she'd decided I was worth speaking to! I thought she wanted to be my friend. I was such an idiot.

Once in her bathroom, I let my curiosity get the better of me. I snooped around her cabinet and drawers. It was all very pink and disorganized, ignoring the endless supply of toilet paper in the drawer below the sink. The cabinet was full of drugs, the legal kind. There were birth control pills, vitamin B supplements, anti-depressants and diet pills. She even had some herbs in there in a container that was labelled 'detox tea'. I thought it was a weird place to keep tea, so I sniffed it. It wasn't tea – it was cleverly-disguised weed. In a box near the shower, she had a stash of tampons and condoms. I guess all her needs were taken care of.

I started feeling light-headed, but I didn't feel ill or weak. When I finished looking around the bathroom, I opened the door and was startled to find Alan in the room, sitting on the bed. He smiled at me and even though his smile sent chills down my spine, I smiled back. I thought it was strange that he was there, but then again it was his girlfriend's room, so maybe it wasn't strange at all. I went to the door to leave, but he started speaking.

"How's Donna?" he asked.

"She's fine, I think," I said, standing next to the door. There was a brief pause before I added, "Why do you ask?"

"I thought she'd be here, that's all." He stood up.

"She doesn't like parties."

"That's a shame." He started approaching me.

I shrugged. "Not really."

"Are you having a good time?" he said, standing right in front of me. Looking up at him, I felt so small. I shifted until my back was against the door.

"Yeah, it's fun."

"I can think of ways to make it better." He touched my face. It dawned on me that he was coming on to me. I was taken aback, knowing that he had a girlfriend, who was not only downstairs, but whose house and bedroom we were in. I slapped his hand away.

"I'm not interested, and I don't think Beth would be happy to know you're trying it on with other girls." My tone was stern. I turned to open the door, but he slammed it shut.

"Beth won't mind," he whispered, touching me on my backside, "She likes it when I get with other girls."

I didn't know whether he was lying or not, but my heart dropped to my stomach. I tried to open the door again, but once again, he slammed it shut. He grabbed me and threw me on the bed. He climbed on top of me. I told him no. Firmly, repeatedly, loudly. I kicked and screamed, but it made no difference. He was strong, so much stronger than I was.

"Shut up, you filthy whore!" he said, as I yelled for him to get off me.

He hit my face again and again, punching and slapping me, but I kept fighting, scratching his arms and punching his side. Nothing seemed to work. It was like he had eight hands, the way he was able to beat me and still get my clothes off. Then he covered my mouth and did what he wanted. I never stopped fighting; I even bit his hand so hard that he bled, but it didn't matter. I was always going to lose. It was never a fair fight.

When he finished with me, he slapped me some more as if to underscore the fact that he could do whatever he wanted to me, that I didn't matter, that I was worthless. Then he pulled his trousers back up and left the room. He thanked me on his way out. I don't know how long I was there for before Beth came in. She asked if I'd had fun. I looked right through her. She shrugged and left. I couldn't believe what had happened. I couldn't believe what had happened to me. It was the sort of thing I'd read about, never the sort of thing I thought I'd experience.

My face and body were in severe pain, my mind was in agony and all I could think of was how my parents would react if I got home later than curfew. I don't know how long it was before I put my clothes back on as best I could and left the room. Downstairs, I ran into Suzanne and told that I was feeling ill. She said she could tell and that I looked awful. Tact was not one of her gifts.

"What happened to your face?" she asked, squinting and touching my cheek. I flinched.

"What do you mean?" I asked, touching it. I didn't know what I looked like. I hadn't seen my reflection.

"Did someone hit you? It looks like you had a run in with a boxer," she said, supplying an answer to my question whilst still eschewing tact.

I shrugged and told her I wanted to leave, but she wasn't ready yet.

"It's ok," I said, "I'll see you at school."

"Cool. Be safe."

She looked worried, but I suppose she didn't guess what had happened. On my way out of the house, I caught a glimpse of Alan and Beth. She raised a glass to me, and he smiled that creepy smile again. I felt sick to my stomach. I managed to get out of the house before throwing up in a plant pot just outside. Some kids on the front garden looked at me and cheered. I wiped my mouth and walked down the road, finally arriving at the bus stop.

It wasn't even 10 o'clock yet. I felt disgusting, dirty, used. I didn't understand how Alan could do something so vile and not feel bad. And Beth… she sent me up there. She set me up. Why? He smiled at me. Why would he smile? Why would it make him happy to treat me like I was nothing? Why were they happy to see me in pain? I couldn't believe what had happened.

I knew my parents would be waiting for me, and I knew that once they saw me, they'd know something was very wrong. I needed help cleaning myself up and had no other option – I had to see Donna. Instead of taking the bus home, I took the one that stopped near her house. I called her from the bus stop and asked her if there was any way she could get out of the house and meet me.

"No chance. Why? What's wrong?" she said.

"I... I, uh, just really need your help," I said, sobbing. She knew it was serious. She told me she'd come and get me. I asked her to bring a change of clothes, if she could.

I don't know how she got out of the house after being certain that she wouldn't be able to, but within 10 minutes, she was there, with a change of clothes in her little rucksack. She was always so reliable. I burst in to tears once I saw her, unable to hold them in any longer.

"What the hell happened to you?" she asked. She looked me up and down, with her mouth open and her forehead lined. Her face was a picture of concern and confusion. I couldn't help myself, I just blurted out all the details of the rape. She held on to me tightly, said we should go to the police at once, but I couldn't.

I knew my parents would be disappointed in me for allowing it to happen. Maybe they would blame themselves for letting me go to the party. I didn't want them to feel bad. They would never see me the same way again. I'd just be a dirty piece of trash to them. I couldn't risk losing their affection. And there was no way, with his father's hold on the community, that anyone would have believed me instead of Alan. It wasn't rocket science. I had to forget what happened.

She let me go and asked if I'd showered. I said no, how could I when I'd come right here? She offered to take DNA samples from my person. I recoiled in horror. I knew she was good with science, good enough to do that, but it was more than I could handle at the time.

"Have you lost your mind?"

"I get it; you don't want to go to the police. But what if... what if I go instead and say it was me? I could isolate his DNA and mix it with mine," she said.

"You're serious. I can't believe you."

"We can't let him get away with this, Mina. You can't let him get away with this. He raped you and you're just going to let him walk around like he's a normal person? Like he's an honest person? Does that seem right to you?"

I was taken aback by the anger in her voice. I had never seen her express emotion like that before. Her eyes welled up with tears. "Please, Mina, let me do this," she said. She held my hand. "Let me help you."

The thought of having anyone poking around my body given what had just happened, filled me with disgust. She had a firm grip on science, but even she didn't have the ability to perform a rape exam. It didn't even matter to me that she wanted to lie that he'd raped her and not me. I couldn't bear it. Would that even work? Would that be right?

"I can't do it, Donna. Please, just let me get changed and go home, my curfew is almost up."

"And when your parents see your face, what are you going to tell them, huh?"

"I don't know," I said.

I shook my head and cried quietly, putting my face in my hands. She hugged me again, and then we walked to the garage area of her estate. She stood guard while I changed. In hindsight, it was a bad idea to change in the open, but neither of us was thinking straight at the time. When I finished, she took my clothes from me and said she'd wash them. I cried some more, trying not to be too loud. She hugged me and comforted me, telling me that everything would be fine. I knew she was lying. She knew she was lying. But it was a nice thing to hear at the time. It was what I needed to hear.

She walked me to the bus stop and waited till I got on the bus. She waved at me as it pulled away. I managed to get home in one piece, and as I expected, my parents were waiting for me. It was 5 minutes to 11. They were so happy that I was home in time. In their minds, that meant I was safe.

I told them that the party was average. They asked about my face and I told them that I'd tripped and cut my lip and eyebrow, and bruised my cheek, too. My mother was worried and wanted to take me to the hospital to make sure I wasn't infected. I just wanted to shower and sleep. I told her I'd be alright. I said it was my fault because I was careless. I showered as soon as I got upstairs. I spent most of my time in there crying. It was hard not to wail, but I didn't want my parents to hear me. I scrubbed myself so hard that my skin was raw; I scrubbed till all the evidence was gone. The physical evidence at least.

After my long shower, I looked at my reflection in the mirror. The cut on my eyebrow no longer stung, but it was still noticeable, as was the one on my lip. My cheek no longer throbbed, and it didn't look too bad either. As far as the eye could see, I was not in terrible shape. But beneath the exterior, I was broken. As I stared at my face, I saw Alan's. I jumped back from the mirror, before realizing that my mind was playing tricks on me. I broke down crying again, trying to muffle the sound with my towel.

Eventually, the tears dried up and I got dressed for bed. My mother came to my room and insisted on cleaning the wounds. I was too tired to refuse. She started with my brow. As she disinfected it, it hurt. What hurt more was the memory of how I'd been beaten and abused. I started to cry. She didn't understand why. She asked me what was wrong. I said that the wound smarted.

"Oh, sweet Mina," she said, "you're big enough to take a little pain."

She finished cleaning the brow and moved on to the lip. I thought about telling her what had happened. But then I imagined the look on her face. I imagined how painful it would be for my parents to live with me, knowing I'd been tainted. I could see them withdrawing from me, treating me differently, wishing I'd never been born. I already wished I'd never been born; I didn't need them to do so as well. So I decided that they didn't need to know. I wouldn't tell them, because what they didn't know wouldn't hurt them. I was big enough to take a little pain.

She cleaned up my lip and hugged me. She told me to be more careful, and then she kissed me on my forehead and wished me a good night. She left me to myself… to my thoughts and memories. I spent the next few hours crying into my pillow. I must have fallen asleep at some point, because I had nightmares about being raped by Alan. I woke at various points in the night, terrified, but relieved to know they weren't real. Yet every time I fell asleep again, they returned – different scenarios, same ending. I was glad when morning came. Little did I know that the real nightmare was about to begin.

My mind snaps back to the present. I hate it when I do this to myself. Salome says that I need to stop over-thinking things, but not a day goes by that I don't go over the details in my mind, wondering how I could have stopped it or what I could have done to change things. I wish I could drown out the memories. I know I can't undo what happened, but I wish I could forget. My palms start to sweat as I think about how good it would feel to get high and leave the memories behind.

I have to stop this.

I should go for a walk.

IVY

I sometimes wonder if my mother named me after the poisonous variety of the Ivy plant. I wonder if she hoped I'd be lethal and ferocious – all the things she isn't. You know: the kind of person who is not to be messed with – someone more like Belladonna.

Some of the children at school used to call me Poison Ivy because they thought it was cute and funny (it was neither) and they had no imagination, not because I was particularly naughty or anything like that. It turns out I'm neither lethal nor ferocious, and I spent my childhood being bullied at school and at home or being rescued by Donna from bullies.

I woke up at 5:53am today. It was too early for my liking but I couldn't sleep any longer. The anxiety over the impending day wouldn't let me. Without fail, every anniversary of dad's death leads mum down a road of misery, regret and self-loathing. Donna hypothesizes that she's always on that road, but for most of the year, parks on its side. She might be right, but mother wallows excessively today. And why not? She lost the love of her life, who also happened to be the cause of most of her pain. If he hadn't died that day, I reckon he would have killed her in due time. It's a miracle that he hadn't done so already.

I tried to get back to sleep but after half an hour, realised it was not meant to be. I swung my legs over the side of my bed, got on my knees and prayed instead. Today, I prayed for longer than usual. I asked God for several things but most of all for help and strength, because I know for a fact that these two women I live with will act all kinds of crazy today.

Mum will pretend that dad was a saint, struck down too soon in the midst of making the world a better place; Donna will rightly try to get her to see reason, but in the wrongest way possible. And there I'll be, stuck in the middle, trying to mediate between them. Though the day had barely begun, I was already looking forward to its end. I knew that if it didn't end in tears, it would be by the grace of God.

Whilst praying, I heard Donna leave the flat. She was later than usual. I surmised that she overslept and was kicking herself for it. She always beats herself up for making mistakes. At this time of day, she's better off taking the tube, which she hates doing. Even though we have a car, she prefers the bus. She never drives to work because she hates waiting in traffic and hates looking for parking spaces. I don't know why she puts such limitations on herself.

After I prayed, I left my room and went to the kitchen to make breakfast. I then stopped by mum's room to make sure she hadn't drowned herself in a pool of tears. She was fine, thank God. Or shall I say fine as can be, given the circumstances?

I'd assumed we'd be going to visit dad's grave. Instead, she told me that she'd like to make a special dinner tonight for his anniversary. I shrugged and told her I was cool with whatever she had in mind. She asked me to let Donna know. I promised I would. I kissed her on the forehead and told her I loved her. I do love her, but sometimes I resent her. It's not an abiding resentment, just comes and goes like the waves of the sea. Today, it has chosen to come, which is kind of sad.

I work at the local church for 4 days each week. On foot, it's 15 minutes away from our flat. This has never stopped me from being late before. In fact, I have a theory that the closer one lives to their destination, the later they'll get there. In general, Donna and I get along well, provided I never mention or allude to our father, but my consistent struggle with punctuality is something that she cannot stand. It's not ideal, and I don't go out of my way to get to places late, but I'm just really… disorganized (and possibly irresponsible). I always tell myself 'better late than never', but I know I'm lying to myself. I need to do better in life.

I didn't have to go to work today, as it's one of my days off. However, knowing the day's significance, I made plans to help Lottie with some of her administrative duties. Anything to take my mind off reality. I invited mum to join me, but she said she wanted to be alone. I was initially hesitant to leave her on her own, but I thought about it and decided that she'd be alright.

I got to the church at the time I'd promised. Maybe it's because I didn't want to hang around the house, or because I didn't have to be there, so there was no pressure, but I made it in time and that made me feel good. The morning was uneventful, spent proofreading and sending emails for Seth Tanner, the lead pastor, and then setting up the church hall for the parenting course they'll be running tonight. When that was done, I dug my heels in and called Donna to tell her of mum's proposed dinner plan. She didn't sound thrilled to hear it, but she didn't sound angry either. I suspect she wasn't alone and couldn't react honestly. Lucky me.

Now that I've finished here, I'll go into town and do some window shopping. It beats going back to the flat. Before leaving, I head to the main hall to let Lottie know to lock the door behind me. She's a short, slender woman with thick glasses, pale skin and very curly, brown shoulder-length hair. Though she's very organised, she is often quite… dishevelled.

When I get to the hall's entrance, she's rearranging some of the chairs, because she likes straight lines. She looks over at me and beams her signature gap-toothed smile.

"I'm leaving now, Lottie. Just wanted to let you know," I say.

"Oh, petal, thanks so much for your help."

I find endearing that she sometimes calls me *petal*.

"No worries. I'll see you tomorrow."

"Wait, Ivy."

She runs to meet me at the entrance. She cocks her head to the side and adjusts her glasses. "Is everything alright?"

The low, slow way she speaks makes her sound concerned, although I can't think why she would be.

"Everything is fine. Why do you ask?"

"You just seem a little down."

I let out a sharp sigh. My body language must have betrayed me. I consider telling her about the significance of today.

"I… I'm ok. Just a little tired, that's all." I hope my smile disguises the truth.

"That's not true. Something's wrong and you're not telling. What is it? Maybe I can help," she presses.

There are only two people in the world that I've told about my background. One was a deaf woman who lived in a retirement home I used to visit, and the other was a boy I dated at university. I gave him a vague synopsis of my childhood (dad got drunk and disorderly sometimes – no specifics) and without all the details, he told me that I had to get over it or I would never be 'good enough to be anyone's wife.' I broke up with that clown on the spot. When I mentioned it to Donna, she offered to find him and *ruin his life*. I asked her not to. They say a burden shared is a burden halved, but I didn't find that to be true in either case. Maybe the third time is a charm.

"My dad died 10 years ago, today." I consider telling her how I feel – relieved, guilty – but I stop short of that. As lovely as Lottie is, she is yet to earn my trust.

She pulls me in for a hug. I fight the urge to cry. Even though I don't desperately miss him, there's a sadness that has lingered in my heart since he passed. It makes no sense at all. I find myself wondering if I could have done something to help him or if he could have changed, given more time. Yes, I know that he'd had a lot of time already, but how much time is enough?

Still hugging me, she says, "Oh Ivy, I had no idea."

I break the embrace and shrug. Of course she didn't. I never told her.

"What happened to him?"

I don't want to talk about it, but she looks so concerned, with her brows all furrowed. I feel like I owe her an explanation for caring.

"He got drunk and fell down the stairs."

She inhales sharply. She's very dramatic sometimes. She shakes her head and opens her mouth to speak but I can't take this anymore. Before she can say anything, I say, "I really do have to go, Lottie. I've got some errands to run."

She puts a hand on her chest, twirling the pendant on her necklace. "Oh, alright. Well, if you ever need to talk to anyone, you have my number."

"Thanks."

She smiles at me and we head for the entrance. I leave and wave at her as she locks the door behind me.

IV

DONNA

After the interview, Kat and I waited for what felt like millennia before Haywood was finally allowed to leave. In that time, we read the victim's statement and discussed defence strategies, as well as any angles we thought were worth investigating. You know the drill – try to make the accuser look like a fast, loose, money-grabbing hussy so that no one feels sorry for her, even if they believe she was attacked. Oldest trick in the book.

All our brainstorming will probably be for nothing, though, because despite being the lead on this case – information I'm yet to share with Kat – we're yet to receive input from the men at work. Daryl and Shane will no doubt have some objections, and instead suggest some ridiculous alternatives. For once, I don't mind so much. Nothing would please me more than to sabotage this case if I can do so undetected.

In the time that Kat and I waited, neither of us verbally expressed doubt of Haywood's innocence. I could tell from her deflated demeanour that, like me, she knows he's guilty. Now that I've read the victim's statement, there is no doubt in my mind that he had tried to rape her. She was just lucky to escape. Very lucky.

I forced myself to get through the statement. It took everything in me not to scream while reading it. I felt sick to my stomach, wondering how anyone could do such awful things. I thought back to my dream this morning and to Mina. I see now that Mrs. Staunton's concern was justified.

The victim is Jerry Haywood's schoolmate, Aisha Thompson. By her own account, the 16-year old left a party with Haywood Jr. and went to his house, where he passed out while they watched a TV show. When she went to get help, she ran into his father. The man – seemingly unconcerned about his son's wellbeing – took her to the wine cellar where he exposed himself to her and then attacked her. He would have raped her had she not been lucky enough to get her hands on a bottle of wine, which she then broke over his head. And he had the nerve to lie that his wife injured him.

Her full statement, in all its gory detail, reads as follows:

"My friend, Niamh, suggested that I go with her to Eddie's 17th birthday party because Jerry would be there. She knows that I have a crush on him, and she thought it would be good for me to be there, that maybe he would notice me, or something. I normally wouldn't get invited to something like that, because I don't know the right people. But Niamh is cool with everyone. The party was so boring. I was going to give up and go home when, out-of-the-blue, Jerry came up to me and said hi. I couldn't believe it! He asked me if I wanted a drink, and even though I don't drink alcohol, I said yes.

We drank a little and talked. Well, I drank a little, but he drank quite a bit more than I did. He didn't try to pressure me to drink more. He was really nice to me, very sweet and polite, and he seemed to like me. He said that he was sorry that he'd never spoken to me before, because I was really cool. I was, like, so happy.

After about 30 minutes, he told me that he lived a few minutes away from Eddie and asked if I wanted to go back to his house and watch an episode of The Big Bang Theory, *which I'd told him was my favourite show. He said that his house had its own cinema room, and that everything looked better on the big screen. I was so amazed and happy. I said yes right away, like I didn't even have to think about it! It was like all my dreams were coming true.*

I told Niamh that we were going back to his house, and she said that she'd wait for me at Eddie's, since we weren't going to take too long. We were only supposed to watch the episode about Schrodinger's Cat, so were going to get back within the hour. This was around 9.15pm. I know because I kept checking the time. Jerry was a little tipsy, but he seemed fine. We walked to his place through a shortcut, not the front gate. When we got there, he said that his mother and brother were probably asleep, and his father works late most nights.

He took me to the cinema room (in the basement of the house) and poured out some champagne that he'd got from the cellar next door. He said that everything is better when you've had champagne. I had a couple of sips, and he downed a whole glass like it was water.

He put the episode on and we started watching. We were sitting so close to each other that I could smell his aftershave. I can't even explain how I felt. I could hardly concentrate on the show. It was really nice being there with him. He laughed a lot. And his laugh is so cute. He also drank a lot, but I didn't think too much of it because he seemed in control. He finished the whole bottle within the first 10 minutes of the show.

After a few minutes, maybe about 15, he looked at me and smiled. He asked if I wanted to make out. I nodded and we started to kiss. I guess he'd had too much to drink, because he kissed me, like, twice before he passed out. I didn't really know what to do. I called Niamh. She said to find someone in the house who could watch him, so I could go back to the party and we could leave.

I left the cinema room to go to the kitchen. Jerry had said that he had a live-in maid called Irene, so I thought that maybe I could find her. I got up the stairs and to the kitchen, which was empty. I went to the reception area and just stopped because I didn't really know what to do or where I was going. The house is massive.

When I turned to go back to the cinema room, there was a man standing in the landing area, between the reception room and the kitchen. He was old and taller than Jerry, but they looked alike, so I figured he was Jerry's dad. He asked me who I was and what I was doing in his house. I told him I was Jerry's friend and that Jerry had fallen asleep downstairs and I was looking for someone to keep an eye on him. He then introduced himself as Jeremy Haywood Senior. He shook my hand.

I said that since he was there, I should just leave, but he asked if I was Jerry's girlfriend. I said no, we were just friends. He asked if I wanted to drink something before going home. I wanted to say no, but I didn't want to be rude to him. I wanted him to like me. I thought if he did, he'd encourage Jerry to date me. He said that the best drink was wine and that we should go downstairs to the cellar. I didn't say anything; I just nodded and followed him.

When we got to the cellar, he shut the door behind me and told me that we should drink the wine in private. I started to get a little scared because I suddenly realised that I was alone with a man I didn't know. I asked him if we should check on Jerry, to make sure he was ok, but he said that Jerry did this all the time, and that he would be fine. He's like his mother, he said, the alcohol doesn't hurt them much.

He started coming really close to me and unzipping his trousers. I was shocked, but I just stood there. I was too afraid to do anything. He exposed himself to me and I stifled a scream. I couldn't move, it was like I was paralyzed. I told him that I didn't feel well. I started backing closer to the door. By then I was terrified, but I told him that I thought all the alcohol I'd drunk was making me sick. He said he didn't mind, and then he grabbed my hair and slammed my back against the cellar door. He slapped my face really hard, twice, with the back of his hand, and then he started tearing my clothes.

I screamed. I told him to stop. I begged him to stop, but he just hit me again, and pulled at my trousers. He started unbuttoning them and touching me really hard. I scratched him and tried to push him away, but he was too strong and it didn't work. He was just groping me, and he put his hand down my underwear and kept pushing. Then he removed his hand and pulled my trousers down some more, pushing his genitals against my thigh.

I bit his ear as hard as I could. He shouted and moved his hand to hit me again, but I reached for a bottle of wine and smashed it on his head. He fell over and I opened the door and ran up the stairs and out of the house. When I got to the garden, I heard someone calling my name. I didn't look back – I just kept running as fast as I could, through the shortcut, until I got close to Eddie's house.

I tried to make myself look normal, but when I realised that my clothes were in too bad a state, I called Niamh. I told her that I couldn't come into the house and that she should come and meet me. She came round with her car and couldn't believe how messed up I looked. She thought that Jerry had attacked me, but I told her who did it. She wanted us to go to the police right away, but I begged her to take me home. I just wanted to go home.

When we got to my house, I told my mother everything. She had only got back from her shift 15 minutes before we got in. She thanked Niamh for bringing me home in one piece. I felt so dirty and disgusting but she wouldn't let me clean myself up. She said we had to go to the police immediately."

The thought of a man using his strength and size to overpower and try to violate anyone – in this case a girl who could be his own child – makes me feel sick. Sick and angry. It's not good for me to get angry; it usually ends badly for others.

At long last, I'm at a point in my life where things are relatively simple. I'm on cruise control. The past is neatly tucked away, done and dusted. I can't afford to mess things up for myself. But the dream, was it an omen, a sign of things to come? Was it a warning or some sort of direction? A cosmic reminder of who I am and what I have to do? I know it's not the first time I've had that dream, but maybe there's a reason for it, a reason other than me being punished.

I'm not opposed to killing Jeremy Haywood, but it won't be easy. Well, none of my prior kills was particularly easy, but they were easier than this would be. I wouldn't necessarily be a prime suspect, however committing the act undetected would prove… trying, if not impossible.

When he was finally released into the reception area, it took all my willpower not to walk up to him and snap his neck. The rage I felt within was difficult to ignore and even harder to contain. But I hid it, like I always do. I remembered that I had what it took to be in the same room as William and not once stab him to death with a carving knife. If I could restrain myself then, I can restrain myself now. Besides, it would be foolish to kill this man in public.

Haywood was fitted with an ankle monitor and will be permitted to leave his house for work alone. We all left the building together and he got into his car, where I presume his driver had been waiting for several hours.

As it drives away, Kat and I get into her car.

"This one's going to be tough, isn't it?" she asks. I'm not sure if it's a real question or if she's just thinking out loud.

"I think you might be right."

She turns on the ignition and drives off.

Let the games begin.

V

IVY

After hours of aimlessly wandering around the shopping centre, I sit down on a bench to rest my feet. When I was with Lottie, I made it sound like I had urgent business to attend to. In truth, all I wanted to do was buy a birthday card for my friends, Freya and Nana. I haven't seen either of the twins for almost a year, but we keep in touch by email. I'll see them next month in our old neighbourhood when I attend their birthday party.

Dad is buried there. Every year, mum and I visit his grave on his anniversary. For reasons I don't know, she didn't want to do that today. Whenever we go, we stop at Mr. and Mrs. Boateng's house. They're always so gracious and generous and kind. Freya and Nana still live with them. I've never met a happier family. I know appearances can be deceiving but having grown up in a house brimming with fear and gloom, I think I can tell when a family is happy. Besides, I don't think those girls would have moved back into the house after university if they weren't happy there.

The Boatengs were the first people mum called when we got home that evening. She had hoped that dad would join us at the food bank's celebration, but he had refused, saying he would rather stay home. We all knew that he was going to spend the afternoon drinking and watching porn. No one said anything, though. We didn't expect more from him. Even Donna managed to keep her thoughts to herself. She was probably just grateful that we got to spend some time away from him. She didn't want to 'invite' a beating, not that any of us had to do much for that to happen.

We got home from the food bank and dad was in the basement, as expected. We came home in time, so we didn't think he'd be stomping around, waiting for us. Had we been even one minute later than mum had promised, there would have been hell to pay. Mum wouldn't have to make dinner, as we'd taken some leftovers back with us. It had happened before that dad had asked her not to make dinner for him, then had come home and given her a furious beating for not making dinner. The man acted like a genuine lunatic. I have no idea how he managed to hide his craziness from his colleagues, or how he held down his job for so many years. I guess it was in his interest to keep up appearances. Not drinking at work must have helped, too.

We weren't expecting him to break away from his virtual girlfriends to see us, but after 15 or 20 minutes of being home, pottering about, warming the food and waiting, mum decided to see if he wanted anything. We avoided going into the basement regardless of whether he was down there, but we especially avoided disturbing him when he was. Yet we weren't sure if we were allowed to eat without him or not. My arm had healed about a week before, and no one was gagging to be next in line for broken bones. Mum knocked on the basement door. There was no response. She knocked again, and still got nothing. A third time yielded the same – silence.

"Maybe he's asleep," Donna said, shrugging.

It was not unheard of. Once when he'd fallen asleep down there (I say fallen asleep, I mean passed out from drunkenness), he almost beat mum up for having the nerve to come in without his express permission. I honestly don't know how she put up with his cruelty for so long.

Only after she explained that she was worried he had choked on his vomit, or something similar, was he pacified. I remember thinking that it would have been a blessing for such a thing to happen to him. So mum was inundated with lousy options – risk a beating for checking on him, risk a beating for not checking on him and eating in his absence, or risk letting him die from alcohol poisoning.

At last, she decided to go in and check on him. She opened the door. The light was on, which was strange. Dad liked the darkness, the reflection of his soul. She hadn't got far before we heard her scream. As we heard her bound down the stairs, Donna and I rushed to the door. When we got there, mum was crouching next to him. He was on the floor, face down. As far as I could tell, he was unconscious. My heart started racing, and my legs felt weak. I found it hard to stand. But I not only stood, I ran down the stairs to meet her. She was crying, calling his name, shaking him, the works.

Donna stood at the top of the stairs for a moment, and called out, "Is he ok? Should I call an ambulance?"

Her voice was calm and measured, as was the way she came down the staircase. She stood, looking down at me and mum.

Again, she asked, "Should I call an ambulance?"

"Yes. He's not breathing," mum responded, through tears. I was scared. That surprised me. In general, I only felt scared because of things dad had done to me, or things I thought he would do to me. But seeing him so helpless, maybe even lifeless, also scared me and I didn't know why.

Donna rushed upstairs and I heard her voice in the distance, telling the person on the phone to hurry because her father wasn't breathing. She didn't sound too agitated, but she didn't sound unconcerned either. In what was obviously a crisis, I couldn't understand how she could be so composed. I've always found Donna difficult to read. Dad had always mistreated us, but I still felt like she should have worried about his safety.

Then again, her behaviour changed after she killed Alan Ellis. She had just started seeing a therapist about that when dad died, and she seemed even more disconnected from everyone than she was before. It was like she was just putting one foot in front of the other, going through the motions. I've heard that taking a life changes your life, that it changes your outlook on life, your view of yourself. I can understand why.

God didn't create us to be killers, but sin has changed the game. Regardless of our initial design, we can – and some of us do – kill. Maybe that's why Donna seemed too calm. Maybe she was still recovering from the last dead body she'd seen, the one she had dropped. Maybe she wasn't calm, maybe she was numb. Whatever the reason, she came back and told us that the ambulance would be with us within half an hour.

Mum was inconsolable by then. She'd turned dad over and was giving him CPR. It looked to me like he was dead, and I didn't know whether or not to hope that he was. I knelt beside him as mum hit his chest and yelled at him to wake up. Then there was Donna, standing there, motionless. I wondered if she understood what was happening. I barely understood it myself.

I watch people go about their business, shopping. Women pushing prams; girls who don't look old enough to be mothers, also pushing prams; a mentally unstable man talking loudly to himself about bees (he's well-known in these parts); a bunch of youths hanging around, doing nothing. I don't like this shopping centre, and I find it extra depressing at this time of year. Even then, there's more cheer here than there will be at home.

Christmas is round the corner and every shop is decorated with lights and baubles, flogging everything from stationery to perfume to (my personal favourite) booze. Dad always topped up his stash at Christmas time. Oh, the memories.

When the ambulance arrived that night, it was crystal clear that he was dead. Mum refused to accept it, though. The paramedics declared him D.O.A. I was shocked and speechless. It was then that Donna broke down and cried a little. I wanted to cry as well, but I felt like I had to be strong for them. Donna wasn't distraught, but her tears hurt my heart. To this day, I don't know if they were tears of joy or sadness or neither or both. I moved to hug her and she just cried on my shoulder. Mum was slumped on the floor being comforted by one of the paramedics.

Once the ambulance took dad's body away, mum called the Boatengs and they came over at once. I was really touched. Freya and Nana were so sweet to me and Donna. I've never forgotten their kindness. Nana asked me if I was ok, and that was when I started crying. To my shame, I wasn't crying because of my 'loss,' as everyone called it from then on, I was crying because of my gain.

For the first time in my life, I felt like I didn't have to be afraid anymore. I felt like I had a chance to have a good life. I cried like a new-born because I felt like one, like I'd just entered the world and the future possibilities were endless. Freedom was within reach.

A few more minutes pass, and I'm still people-watching. I decide that it's time to go home. I'd rather not, but then I think about mum sitting there all alone, mourning the death of a man that she loved more than herself despite all the awful things he did to her. I remember her on the ground, with the paramedic trying to console her. The thought almost brings me to tears, but crying in public isn't something I do.

With this newfound compassion for her, I determine that I will do all I can to make tonight easy on mum. I only pray that Donna can find it in her heart to do the same. There's a part of me that feels that prayer will go unanswered. But I live in hope.

In this spirit, I decide that the shopping trip doesn't have to be a total waste. I'll buy a little gift for mum. She needs some cheering up today, and since I can't go back in time and save her from her tragic marriage, I can at least buy her some chocolate. It won't blot out her mistakes, but it's the next best thing. I'll get the truffles from the supermarket, and then I'll go home.

VI

DONNA

When Kat and I get back to the office, I lie that I have a late doctor's appointment so I can leave. There's no way they'd let me go otherwise. I don't really want to go home, but I'm not in the right frame of mind to work or exercise either.

I manage to get away from the office without running into Mrs. Staunton. Out in the cold, I consider taking the tube, but I know it'll only erode what's left of my mental health. I decide to take the bus instead. At this time of the day, it'll take a while to get home. I don't mind.

I walk to the bus stop three stops away from the one closest to the office, in the hopes of avoiding anyone I know. When I get there, there are several people waiting, all with their faces glued to their phones. As I look from one blue-lit face to another, the remaining desire to go home evaporates. I know what is waiting for me at home – irritation. I decide to go to my favourite spot in a nearby park instead.

The park is emptier than I imagine it was at lunch time. I sit on the bench I usually occupy when I come here. There are some runners and a lot of dog-walkers. I never come here in the evening, especially in the winter. Everyone knows that parks are dangerous. But today, it seems worth the risk. Better this than dealing with mum and her misery.

My memories of William's death are so vivid that it's odd to think that so much time has passed. There's a part of me that feels like nothing has happened in the last decade, though I know that's not true. I completed my education, from secondary all through law school, and now have a good job. That all happened. Yet sometimes, none of it feels like a triumph.

At times I forget that William is dead. Some days I wake up in a cold sweat because I think he's still alive, even though I watched him die, even though I killed him myself. The murder wasn't brutal, despite the fact that that is what he deserved. I didn't even plan to be there when it happened but as fate or luck or God would have it, I got home that day and there he was, on the verge of expiring.

About four months prior to his demise, as was the pattern back then, William had come home late at night from a visit with his mistress, Paula Wilson. To no one's surprise, he was drunk and angry. I saw her the next day on the bus and her face was bruised. William knew how to spread pain. Paula was a strange, tubby little woman. Her skin was blotchy, her long red hair was unkempt, and she always looked like she'd eaten too much. I never understood what it was about her that William liked. Sure, she was pretty enough and her boobs were large, but… she seemed to lack any real personality. Maybe that's the answer to my question.

Anyway, the day had been uneventful. Ivy had spent the late afternoon and early evening practicing her interminably long piano piece (by one of those ancient dead people – I forget which one) for her concert recital; I'd waited for her at school, studying for a physics test. She picked up piano very quickly and used the lessons as escapism.

Music was Ivy's thing, and Science was mine; that's the way it was. Learning how the body and nature and the solar system worked helped me make sense of parts of the world. It didn't quite take my mind off our home life, but it eased the pain. Under normal circumstances, I would stay at school studying while Ivy took her lessons, then we'd go home together. In those days, I wanted to be a doctor. In the end that changed. I guess one way or another, everything changes.

We got home, and had a nice quiet meal, knowing that William was either in or breaking Paula's arms for the evening. How did we know? Relaxing with The Mistress du Jour was his Thursday night activity. The man's temper was unpredictable, but his habits? You could set your watch to them. He was so regimented and made sure we were, too. He always did his best to control everyone around him, yet he never tried to control himself. We had a lovely evening without him. Mum even talked to us like she thought we were interesting, which she never did when he was around.

Under normal circumstances, Ivy and I would have waited up for him. That's what he preferred but her recital was the next day. She was anxious and stressed, despite having devoted the entire month to practicing almost non-stop. She'd spent so little time away from the piano that she'd fallen ill. I guess all the practice in the world can't eradicate nerves. Being ill didn't help either.

Mum let her go to sleep. "Dad will understand," she said. I didn't think he would, but somewhere in my heart, there lay the hope that I was wrong. When he got home, that hope was eviscerated. He'd barely got through the door before he ordered mum to get him another drink. As was her way, she did as she was told. She wasted most of her energy doting on him. After downing the drink like he was trying to win a competition, he realised that Ivy wasn't there to greet him, and was asleep instead. *How dare she!*

In his drunken rage, he went to her room and dragged her out (by her braids, no less) talking about how disrespectful it was of her to go to sleep before he got home. Didn't she know the rules? It didn't matter to him that she was recovering from a cold. It didn't matter to him that her concert was the next day and she needed to rest. No, none of that mattered to him because she didn't matter to him.

He hit her multiple times, ranting on about how he provides food, clothing and shelter for her (as if that wasn't his basic duty) and she needs to be more grateful. Of course, Ivy cried. She begged him to stop hurting her. But as we've already established, he didn't care. I'd had enough. I got in between them, as mum cowered in the corner, leaving us to fend for ourselves. There are animals that do a better job of protecting their young, but I guess free will gives you the option to not do your best.

I stared him down as I often did, and told him to back off. This time, it was different. I'd come to the end of my rope.

"Or what?" he said, lifting his hand. In that moment, I felt something inside me break. It was as if I heard a piece of my soul snap off and crumble. And before he could drop his hand, I pushed him. For the first time in my 17 years of life, I physically retaliated against my father.

A Jack Russell terrier without a leash runs up to the bench and yaps frantically, returning me to the present. My first instinct is to slap it away like a fly, but from the corner of my eye, I see its owner running up behind it. It's a man, likely in his mid-twenties (or as I like to think of it, prime serial killer age), wearing baggy trousers and a vest.

It's a bit cold for a vest.

He smiles and starts talking.

"Hey, sorry, he's friendly," he says, taking sharp breaths.

Is nowhere safe?

"No worries," I say.

He smiles again and carries on running. I'm lucky he's got things to do. The dog stays behind, wagging its tail. The man whistles and the dog runs after him. In no time, it's in front of him again. The two disappear round a bend.

As I was saying, William couldn't believe I'd done that – pushed him, that is. He was too drunk to recognise the significance of the gesture. The sand was shifting beneath his feet but he couldn't feel it; the tide was turning and he couldn't see it. He didn't understand the chain of events that had been set in motion.

He growled at me, "You stupid cow!" and pushed me out of the way, and against the wall. In her attempt to help me, Ivy crossed his path and he grabbed her. He slapped her and pushed her on the ground, then kicked her over and over again. When he got tired, he kicked her down the stairs.

Only when she went tumbling down the steps did William stop raging, and did mum manage to move. She called an ambulance. That was all, but I guess it was something. Poor, delicate Ivy lay crying at the bottom of the stairs. I'll never forget the look on her face. She knew she didn't deserve any of it, but there was no way she could escape. No safe way, at least. I ran to her and comforted her as best I could. I told her that she'd be fine, and that one day she wouldn't have to live like that.

I was tired of waiting for that day. I started crafting an escape plan in my mind. All that changed when we got to the hospital. The doctors told us that Ivy's arm was broken. The fracture was severe and would take a long time to heal – many weeks at least. That meant that she'd miss the concert. She'd worked so hard and had practiced that irritating song for so long, and it was all for nothing. Worse yet, she had to lie that she'd fallen down the stairs because she was careless. It was so hard to look at her – the pain in her eyes didn't just come from the broken hand, but more so from her crushed spirit.

That was the final straw. I knew at that precise moment that I had to kill William. I knew that it was up to me, because mum would rather watch us die than run away, and Ivy simply didn't have that sort of malice within her. But I did. I still do. It had to be me. I was the only one who could save us. I was the only one who had the strength to make the hard choices.

Certain dim-witted students at my school made fun of me for loving science (or as they put it, being a 'science nerd'), but my love and knowledge of science is what secured my freedom. Not the sports or drugs those fools prized. No, a strong will and science gave me what I needed. In this case, it was my beloved chemistry, and to a lesser degree, biology, that got me out of this jam.

The key to safely getting rid of William was to avoid using brute force, no matter how much I wanted to. I didn't just want to be free of him, I wanted to be free. That meant that I couldn't and wouldn't risk going to prison. My first choice would have been to stab him to death with a blunt, rusty weapon. Sadly, that was out of the question.

I needed to kill him in the subtlest way possible. People die every day of natural causes. For the subsequent month, I feverishly studied as many poisons as much as I could, as well as their effects on human physiology.

It was exciting, regardless of how grim it was. For the first time since I was a child, I felt like I had hope. I felt like I was in control. I knew that one day, I'd wake up and he wouldn't be there. I knew that I'd be able to go home and not be afraid. I'd still have a spineless mother, but at least I wouldn't have a weak bully of a father, too. The winds of change were blowing violently, but I was the only one who could feel them. Maybe I was the one who summoned them; maybe they were in my power.

William was so arrogant that every night when he got home, he would make one of us fill his hip flask with vodka. It didn't matter who, he'd pick one at random. He was so confident that we were under his control that it never occurred to him that the quality of his drink might one day be compromised. What a fool. I decided to poison his drinks, knowing that no one else was allowed to (or even wanted to) taste them. I took full advantage of his weakness. Some may think that was unfair, but they'd be wrong. It was warfare and all warfare is based on deception.

I poisoned him slowly. A little each time, not enough to overcome the foul taste of vodka, not enough to kill him on the spot. That carried on for a while, until one day, it took its toll. What a glorious day it was.

It started like any other Saturday. Ivy and I spent the morning at school – she at her piano lessons, I at gymnastics. That day, William chose to forgo his usual Saturday afternoon squash, and stay at home so mum could go to the food bank. It's the one thing he would let her do. She was invited to volunteer at the food bank by a woman at church whose husband William got along with. I don't think he particularly liked the man, Mr. Kwame Boateng, but he was always polite to him. I guess he didn't want to drop the mask.

His wife – Stella – was the kindest lady I've ever met. She was warm and friendly, especially to me and Ivy. Uncle Kwame was always very good to us, treated us like family. At times, I got the impression that they suspected that our home situation was far below ideal, but they never said anything. Well, they never said anything to me.

William would sometimes let us go to their house and play, usually on a Saturday. They didn't live too far away from us, but they lived far enough away that it was a nice break. They had twin daughters, Nana and Freya, who were Ivy's age. It was painful to see how much those girls were loved. I wasn't upset that they were loved; I was upset that we were not. They were nice enough to treat us like we mattered.

The day in question, the food bank was celebrating 5 years of operation. They wanted mum to be there early. In the spirit of acting normal, William agreed for mum to help with the planning and setting up. He even let me and Ivy help her after our activities. I wasn't interested in helping but since it meant leaving the house, I jumped at the chance.

Ivy's arm had healed by then, and with a heavy heart, she'd resumed playing piano. Her lessons ended almost an hour later than my gymnastics session. Waiting around for her to finish seemed like a waste of time. The plan was simple: I'd go home and change, return to the school with her 'special outing' clothes, and she would change before we left for the food bank. That was the plan. That is not exactly what transpired.

I got home around 1 o' clock and went upstairs. I changed into a dark green long-sleeved maxi dress, complete with a yellow scarf. It was a celebration, so I reckoned that some colour was in order. On the rare occasion that we went anywhere as a family, Ivy let me pick clothes for her because, as she put it, I always dressed her up like a doll. I packed an orange dress of hers into my little gym bag, also choosing a scarf that matched mine, and went back downstairs.

On my way out of the house I noticed that something was out of place. I expected William to be in the basement – his den – and he was, but I didn't expect the door to be open. It wasn't open wide, but it was open. He was always so private and cautious (even if we all knew what he was up to), and none of us was allowed in there. I thought it best to leave, but a part of me couldn't resist the urge to find out what he was up to. That's the part of me that always gets the whole of me into trouble.

I pushed the door and peered down the staircase. The den was dimly lit but I could clearly make out the form of someone lying on the ground, a little way from the bottom of the stairs. My heart stopped beating for a second or two, and then it started again, but faster. I switched the light on, and saw that it was William. He made a noise that made me think I'd startled him. He did not get up, though.

I still didn't fully understand what was happening, why he was lying on the ground or why he wouldn't get up.

Then he spoke. "Selene? Selene, is that you? Help me!"

He sounded rattled, frantic even. That's when it dawned on me – the poison had kicked in. At long last. He hardly moved as he continued to call out my mother's name.

"It's me, dad," I said as I descended the staircase. "It's just me."

"Belladonna, help me," he said, in a tone that broadcast his pain.

Belladonna – he's the only one who ever called me that. Little wonder I chose to poison him. I wasn't sure what effect the poison had had, or how mobile he was, though he looked like he'd been paralyzed. For my own safety, I stood a little distance away from him, near his desk, on the off chance that he was playing some sort of deranged game.

"Help you do what, dad?"

My heart was racing. My throat felt parched. For the first time in my life, my father – the man who it seemed had made it his life's mission to stand between me and peace and happiness – was at my mercy. He wanted my help. He needed it. He begged for it. He was afraid and it was up to me to allay his fears, if I so wished. For once, I was the one who was in control. I got to choose whether he lived or died. In that moment of triumph, I should have felt nothing short of pride, as though I myself had called forth the stars at the beginning of time…

Alas, I did not feel pride. I instead felt a strange mixture of sadness, pity and fear. I'd thought for years about ending his life, imagined how good it would feel to watch him bleed to death. But more than that, I'd thought about how it would feel to come home and not have to wonder what innocent action would provoke abuse; to wake up and go to sleep and not be afraid; to have something other than merciless beatings to look forward to; to expect more from life than pain and bruises.

The only way for that to happen would be for him to leave, and I knew he never would. He liked torturing us too much; causing us misery was his primary joy in life. Running away was not a realistic option – I had nowhere to go and I knew what happened to people on the streets… I knew what happened to the girls. I would never volunteer for that kind of life. Besides, I couldn't leave Ivy. I needed her as much as she did me. The police are damn near useless and the justice system is a joke, but even if I turned to them, mum would probably have lied to protect William. His death was the only way out.

I told myself to get a grip. I reminded myself that I'd planned his end. And I'd executed the plan. Still, I had not expected to be around when it happened. I hadn't expected to see him like that – powerless and in pain. Why was it that, of all days, we were both home at that very moment? On any other day, he would have been out at that time. Why were we both home? Was it a test? Was I merely supposed to humble him and not to kill him? Was I supposed to be the bigger man?

"My phone, it's under the desk," he said. His breathing was laboured, his words weighty with urgency, "Call an ambulance."

I looked under the desk and saw the phone. It crossed my mind that I should honour his request but then memories of the events of my eighth birthday party came flooding back. William missed the whole thing, then came home drunk and threw me against a wall. What did I do to deserve that? I asked him why he missed my party. To this day, I don't know what he was doing instead, but from that day, I knew that he was a poor excuse for a father.

I didn't even have to reach that far back to pull out a terrible memory. All I had to do was to think of the events of that night months before, which led me to poison him. I just had to think of any of the multiple incidents before and since then. Maybe I was the immediate cause of his miserable predicament, but I wasn't the ultimate cause. He was. The only surprising thing about all of it was that it took someone – in this case, me – so long to take decisive action. I guess murder is not for the faint of heart. Though it was more like self-defence, no matter how much planning went into it.

"What happened?" I asked him.

"Call the damn ambulance, you stupid cow!"

Despite his pain and discomfort, he spat the words at me as though I were some worthless subordinate. With that statement, any sympathy I may have been entertaining was summarily erased, just like my hope had been countless times before. He hadn't seen the writing on the wall. Even knocking on death's door, William didn't know how to behave.

I shifted a little bit, so that I could see his face better.

"Did you hear me?" he asked.

"I heard you."

His eyes met mine. I remember the piercing look he gave me. I think he saw it; I think that was the point at which he knew. I crouched and stared at his face, searching for any traces of remorse. All I saw was fear and the slow realisation that he wouldn't get out of the basement alive. His breathing got louder; his voice raspier.

"What are you waiting for?"

I let out a soft, mirthless chuckle. "An apology? An explanation? Maybe some sort of admission of wrongdoing."

He blinked rapidly at me.

"Never mind me. Once upon a time I hoped we'd get one of those from you, but that was long ago. I'm older now, wiser. I know how life works. You can't wait for people to do the right thing; you have to make things happen for yourself. So I've finally decided to take matters into my own hands."

"What the hell—"

"You've been poisoned, dad. Or to be more precise, I poisoned you. You're dying."

He started coughing. His breathing got even louder and more uneven. A psychosomatic reaction? Perhaps. He sounded like a steam train moving across the tracks.

I thought I'd be thrilled to see him in so much pain, but by then I was indifferent. Unfortunately for him, apart from refusing to help him, I'd confessed my part in his situation. I'd gone too far to turn back. I knew had to stick around and watch him expire. However, I was conscious of the time.

It would have been alright to hang around for five more minutes, for I would have got back to school without raising any suspicions. But had I left it any longer, there was a chance that Ivy would have been waiting for me. She would've wondered what kept me. I didn't want to take that chance. I suddenly needed a rock-solid alibi.

"Why... why?" he groaned. He really had to ask! I couldn't believe he was that narcissistic.

"Why? You have tormented us for years, made our lives miserable. Ruined my childhood, all for your entertainment. Did you ever feel bad about that? Obviously not, or you would have stopped. You have treated us like rubbish for ages, William. You should have treasured us but you were too weak and evil to do that. And now you will never have a chance to hurt us again."

The words came out in such a venomous tone that I hardly recognised my own voice.

"Please, don't do this," he said.

"How many times did we beg you to stop? And how many times did you listen? Welcome to the reaping. I hope hell really is as bad as they say it is. You deserve no less."

In what sounded more like a rasping noise than a speaking voice, he said, "You— can't do this…"

His voice trailed off, but he wasn't dead. Not yet. I had a choice to make – let nature take its course, or help nature take its course. I looked at the time. There wasn't much left. I took the first option. I watched as he tried his best to drag himself closer to the desk. I knew he wouldn't make it, but still I walked over there and nudged the phone just so that it was further out of his reach. He groaned and yelled profanities at me.

"Reap what you sow, William. You've made your bed. Congratulations – you get to lie in it. Goodbye, dad," I said.

There were so many other things that I would have liked to say to him. So many questions I wanted to ask him. So many things I needed him to explain. I hadn't thought I'd be around in his closing moments, but since the opportunity presented itself, I wished that I'd been able to say more. But I was out of time… we both were. I had to accept that there were some things in life I would simply never know or understand. I had to. He wasn't dead when I climbed the stairs, but he must surely have walked into the darkness soon after.

At the top of the steps I looked back, like Lot's wife. Except I wasn't looking at something I loved more than freedom, I was looking at something that I feared more than death. I had done what for a long time I'd been too scared to even dream of – vanquished my enemy. I felt a weird sense of relief, and yet there was fear and searing anguish. I didn't know how Ivy would react, but I had to put those thoughts out of my head. I'd crossed the bridge and I couldn't go back… I needed to burn it. I heard him groan one more time, and then I crossed the threshold from the basement to the living area, firmly shutting the door behind me. I put on my brave face and left the house.

Another dog comes running past, but this one's owner is on a bicycle next to it. They go by quite quickly. The darkness is falling faster than I'd like. At some point, I'm going to have to go home. Considering that I have an early start tomorrow, sooner would be better than later. Knowing all that awaits me at home, I grudgingly leave the park and find my way to a bus stop.

As I approach the stop, the bus I need arrives and stops right in front of me… like my own personal chariot.

VII

IVY

Walking to the exit of the supermarket, truffles in bag, I spot a familiar face. At first, I'm not sure if it's Mina Kaur. As I watch the hooded figure pick up a basket and retreat into the aisles, I know it's her. She has a backpack and keeps her eyes on the ground the whole time. It looks like she's lost a lot of weight since I last saw her, but she still has the same walk. She didn't have much weight to lose in the first place, so I assume things haven't improved for her.

I follow her into the ready-meal aisle, but not too closely. Even though I'm now certain it is Mina, I'm not sure if I should engage her. The last I heard, she'd been using and selling drugs. They sent her to prison for three years or something. I can't remember the exact sentence, but it was longer than anyone would want to spend in prison. She doesn't look particularly jumpy, actually looks quite normal. I think for a second about what to say. I say a quick prayer, after which I walk up to her.

"Mina?"

She turns around, startled. I smile and for a moment, I'm not sure she recognizes me. Then, without warning, she drops her shopping basket and hugs me.

"Ivy, is that you?"

"Hey Mina, how're you doing?" I ask, disengaging from her.

Her brown eyes are sunken, and her body looks slight and weak. She's wearing a loose, long-sleeved hooded jumper. When she rakes her hand through her black hair, the sleeve rolls down, and I see that her forearm is scarred. The scars don't look too old, maybe they've been there for less than a year. I think it's safe to say she's still cutting herself. She also looks kind of hungry. As my eyes linger on her arm, she hastens to pull her sleeve down and smiles sheepishly.

"I'm ok. I'm... yeah, not bad."

Her hair looks thinner than I remember it, but prison food is not known for being nutritious. Her olive skin looks weathered, perhaps the result of drug-use. Her thin fingers dance on the top of her thighs as I speak.

"Cool. What are you up to these days?"

"Oh, you know – this and that."

Shall I surmise crime? There's a brief, awkward silence, which she breaks.

"How's Donna? And how's Mama Selene?"

"Oh, they're fine. You know, trudging along the treadmill of life as Donna likes to say," I say, miming a power-walk. That was a ridiculous thing to say but still, she smiles. She's one of those people who smiles through the pain. It's both admirable and saddening.

"That's good. Hey, you know what's weird? I thought about you guys today. 10 years, right?"

I'm stunned that she'd remember this detail. Our lives changed the day dad died, but I didn't think it had a profound enough effect on Mina for her to re-member the date. Lost for words, I smile, my eyes losing focus as I look past her. I imagine my expression is pained.

"Oh, I didn't mean to... I'm sorry," she says.

My focus returns. "No, no, I just didn't think you remembered. That's all."

"It was three weeks after Alan died. I remember," she says, her voice getting quieter until she stops talking. How selfish of me to forget that. I look at her as she avoids my gaze. Then it hits me!

"Mum is making a special dinner tonight, you know, in dad's memory. You should come."

Her eyes widen and she shakes her head slightly. "You don't have to do that—"

"I know, but I want to. It's been so long since we've seen you. It'd be great to catch up. I know Donna would be happy to have you over. We all would."

"You really think she'd want to see me?" she asks, probably aware that (among other things) she doesn't look her best.

"Of course she would. You're the only best friend she ever had."

She says nothing. So I continue. Talk until you're told to shut up. That's how I live.

"You can even stay the night if you like."

She looks down and shuffles her feet. I can't tell what she's thinking.

"Um, yeah, you know that would be really nice." She looks up again. Her eyes dance around for a second. "Are you sure that's ok? I don't want to impose."

"It would be no trouble at all. You're always welcome at our place." I hope she can tell that I mean it. Her eyes fill with tears, which she very quickly blinks back.

"Ah, Ivy, you've always been such a saint," she says.

"I should make my own skincare line – St. Ivy's!"

She groans while I laugh at the badness of the joke. We exchange numbers, and I give her our address. I tell her that she's welcome any time after 7pm. I let her get back to her business and I take my leave.

As I exit the shop and step into the frosty evening air, I wrap my scarf around my mouth and nose. And then it occurs to me that I've been careless. Yes, I live in the flat with two other people, neither of whom I consulted before inviting someone to spend the night. Mum probably won't mind too much, but Donna will have my head for this. I was really hoping to avoid any sort of conflict with her today, but if I know her well, Mina's presence will rock the boat.

It's too late for me to rescind the invitation, and I would like to spend some time with Mina. I'll just have to take Donna's wrath on the chin. Besides, it seems like Mina could use some support. I'm not going to let fear stop me from helping someone, especially someone I care about.

Oh Lord, I need Your strength. Tonight is going to be something.

VIII

MINA

Ispent the day walking various roads with no goal in mind, trying to get my thoughts in order. I wound up at a shopping centre a few miles away from the hostel. Even when I'm not actively remembering the rape, it's there in the back of my mind, haunting me, influencing all the decisions I make… maybe even controlling them. I could have taken a shortcut to the shopping centre, but it's through a mini-forest. It occurred to me that someone could be hiding there, waiting to attack and maybe kill and bury some unfortunate woman in said forest. That woman will not be me. I took the long way. Maybe that's smart, maybe that's letting fear control my life. I don't know. All I know is that I've had my fill of pain and I don't want any more if I can help it.

At the shopping centre, I looked at all the things I can't afford and told myself that I didn't need them anyway. I did that for hours, as if trying to challenge my soul to accept the truth of my situation. These things weren't made for me, or for people like me. They were made for those who have their lives in order – the honest, decent folk who went to school and got good jobs and deserve nice things. Or the ones who dropped out and worked hard to start legitimate businesses. These things are for people who've made something of themselves, not parasites like me who peddle death and misery, and steal from those who've done their lives right.

From the way people look at me, I know that they can tell I'm an outlier. Some refuse to make eye contact. And when their children do, they manoeuvre them away, as if I was dangerous. It hurts when people think the worst of you before they ever speak to you. A child in a pram drops her shoe and I stoop to pick it up. When I hand the shoe to her mother, I see the look in her eyes. It's somewhere between fear and repulsion. I don't blame her. Most days I find myself repulsive. She's polite enough to thank me, which is a pleasant surprise. Her child smiles sweetly as children do. It warms my heart, before I remember that I don't deserve such a gift.

It doesn't matter where I go or what I do, I always manage to upset myself and others. Salome says that I can call her anytime of the day or night, but I don't want to be a burden to her, and I don't want her attention to become my next addiction. I'll have to walk off the sadness. Pretty clothes and nice shoes may not be for me, but food is for everyone. I'll use a bit of the little money I have to buy some. I could get some snacks from the sweet shop, but there's a supermarket in here. I'll go there instead. I need to regain some of the weight I've lost over the years so that I don't look so much like... an addict.

In the supermarket, while examining the vegetables, I'm surprised by a vaguely familiar voice calling my name. I turn around and am greeted by Ivy's smiling face. I can hardly believe it! From thinking about her and Donna this morning, to seeing her! It's amazing.

I hug her and then we talk for a little while. She looks really well, with her deep brown skin glowing as though she moisturised it with sunshine. She tells me that Donna and Mama Selene are doing well. I notice that she saw the cuts on my arm, but she didn't say anything about them. Ivy was always so discreet and sensitive. I see that hasn't changed.

Even during our brief encounter, I can't help but bring up Alan's death. When I say his name, regret and maybe disappointment flash across Ivy's face. She doesn't even know the full story. I avoid her gaze, hoping to give her time to compose herself, while feeling bad that I can't stop thinking about him, even after a decade. It's been so long, but it feels like yesterday. He's a part of me, and I don't know how to get rid of him.

She invites me to have dinner at their house tonight. I don't know if she's being sincere, but she insists and says that it would be a pleasure to have me over. She goes as far as inviting me to sleep over. I'm scared to accept, but I reckon even their sofa would be more comfortable than the hostel bed. I accept.

We exchange phone numbers, and she gives me her address. When she leaves, I find myself panicking. I look like a mess and I've done nothing with my life for the past few years. I have nothing to offer these people – why would they be nice to me? I consider calling Ivy right away and making some excuse to cancel, but something inside me feels so… so lonely and I think that this might be a chance for me to make friends. Or re-make friends in this case. If I don't try, I can't succeed. It worries me that Donna doesn't know I'm coming. The last time we saw each other, we didn't part on good terms. No matter, I've got a valid invitation, and I should use it.

I need to go to the hostel and pack up my stuff, and then I'll make my way to the Palmer home. I hope this evening goes well.

***

I leave the hostel and get a bus to the Palmers' flat. I'm nervous. Very nervous. I don't know how Donna will react to seeing me, but I hope we can at least talk. We used to talk so much when we were teenagers. Like the night that Ellis died, we were talking when he came in.

On Wednesday nights, Donna worked late at the newsagent. I say late, I mean her shift ended at around 10 o'clock. It was about 9.30 when it all started. For some reason, there was a lull in custom around that time every night. I don't know why that was, but that was the pattern. She and I were just chilling out. I sat on a stool near the till, and she sat behind it.

She'd asked me to hang out with her, since Mr. Pryce wasn't working that night. She said it would be good for us to spend time together. More than a month had passed since the rape. I'd been coping by avoiding school and people, her included. She said she missed me. It made me feel good to be missed. I missed her too. I agreed to spend time with her.

We were talking, about nothing really, when the shop bell rang. We looked towards the door, and I froze. There was a man pointing a gun at us. He was wearing a balaclava, and he yelled for us to put our hands up. We did as we were told. I was terrified. Sweat dripped down my face of its own accord. I looked at Donna, but she didn't look as scared as I would have expected. She looked like she was trying to maintain control. She asked him what he wanted and he very loudly ordered her to put all the money from the till into a bag that he tossed at her. She did what he said.

When the till was empty, she gave the bag back to him. He walked a bit further away, as if he was going to leave, but instead he locked the shop door. Then he turned back to us. That was when he looked at me. He told me to come to him. I didn't understand. He said it again, "Come here, now!" I started moving towards him, crying. The whole time he had the gun pointed at me. As I got closer to him, he looked me up and down and said, "I'm going to enjoy this."

My heart dropped.

"You have what you want, please just go. Don't hurt my friend," Donna yelled.

"Shut up!" he yelled back.

I got about halfway and couldn't go any further; I stopped dead in my tracks and started crying. And then he smiled. And that was when I knew. I knew it was Alan. Even with the balaclava, it was the same creepy smile as the day he attacked me.

I remembered what it felt like when he hit me. I remembered what it felt like when he did worse things than that. My breathing got shorter and my mind started to shut down. My vision started to blur. All of a sudden, through my tears, I saw him fall to the ground. Something had hit him. The gun fell out of his hand. Donna came bounding towards us and pushed me out of the way as he jumped to his feet saying, "Oh, you want to play, too?"

I stumbled backwards from Donna's push, barely maintaining my balance. The object she'd thrown at him was Mr. Pryce's gun, which I later found out was hidden under the counter at the till. She scrambled to get Alan's gun, but he pushed her to the ground and got on top of her. He started hitting her, and I stood there watching.

When he grabbed her neck, I snapped out of it. I found Mr. Pryce's gun and whacked Alan across the back of the head with it. He fell off her, and she told me to get out and call for help. Before I could move, he grabbed my legs, pulling me down. As I tumbled, I saw him pull Donna to himself again. I hit the ground very hard. I was coughing and felt like I couldn't move. I don't know whether it was physical or mental, but I was rooted to the spot.

Until I heard it. The gun shot. I rolled onto my side and looked up in time to see Alan slide off Donna and onto his back. She'd shot him with his own gun, it seemed. I don't know how that happened, but she'd somehow got the upper hand. I stood to my feet, in pain. Donna was still on her back. I wanted to help her up, but I just stood there, watching Alan writhe. He wasn't dead, not yet. But I figured he would be soon because from what I could see, she'd shot him in the chest.

Donna got up and got in my face. She told me to leave. She said I should go to Mr. Pryce's house and call the police, and that I shouldn't come back if I could help it. She pleaded with me to leave. And when I didn't, she led me to the door and said, "Please Mina, get help."

Mr. Pryce's house was a 5-minute walk away, but it must have taken me more than 10 minutes to get there. I told him what happened. He asked why I didn't call him, why I'd walked all the way to his place. I told him I hadn't thought of it. He was so agitated that he called the police as he left to go to the shop. He left me in the house with his wife, who gave me some tea and made sure I wasn't wounded. I was shell-shocked, couldn't believe that Alan would stoop to petty theft. I don't remember crying. Was it all so he could hurt me again? Was I in the wrong place at the wrong time? Was he stalking me? Was he going to survive a bullet to the chest? Did I want him to survive?

About an hour after I got to his house, Mr. Pryce came back with a police officer. The police had taken Donna home. Despite her attempts to help him, Alan had bled to death by the time the ambulance arrived. The officer said that they were going to investigate, although what had happened was quite obvious. I didn't know what to say. I was numb. She said they'd have to ask me some questions, but they wanted my parents around. She and her partner took me home and asked me and my parents to come to the station the next day. I hardly slept that night.

Donna didn't make it to school the next day. I didn't see her until I went to the police station. School was insane, though. Somehow, everyone knew that Alan had been shot dead, and that Donna did the shooting. Rumour had it that Beth was in a sorry state. She didn't come to school either, apparently because she was in mourning. Her sidekick, Tara, took it upon herself to make the whole incident about her. She was twice removed from the situation, but the way she was carrying on, you'd have thought she'd attempted CPR on Alan, and then wheeled his body to the coroner's office herself.

People kept asking me what happened, how I was, what I saw. Had Alan gone crazy? Did he die instantly? How bloody was the scene? How much money was in the till? How did I feel? It was intense. That last question unnerved me because after the incident and being up most of the night, I felt nothing. And for the first time since he attacked me, I hadn't had flashbacks to that night. It was… bizarre.

Of all the people who spoke to me about the Violence at the Newsagent's, as the local paper called it, Suzanne was the only one who expressed relief over Alan's 'untimely' death.

"It's so sad when people die before their time," Aaron said, to which Suzanne replied, "It's even sadder when they die after their time." Her honesty was always bracing, but Aaron generally welcomed it. Not this time, though.

"How can you say something so cruel and thoughtless?" He was visibly upset by Suzanne's (accurate) observation.

"How can you not? The guy was a bully and a tyrant, and apparently a thief. And if the rumours are true, he was a rapist. The world would have been a better place if he'd never been conceived. But since that mistake was made, this is the closest thing to a course correction we've got. Donna deserves a knighthood," she said without even the slightest of vocal inflections.

"Rapist? What do you mean?" I did my best not to sound too interested.

"Are you kidding me? I heard a rumour last year that he does rape. I don't know how true it is, but no smoke without fire is what I say. Anyway he's dead now, so if it was true… one down."

She shrugged like it was no big deal. Aaron stormed off. I didn't really care that he was annoyed. I was more interested in the rumours Suzanne was talking about. I didn't want to seem too curious, didn't want her to guess my reasons for caring so much. Any normal person would care, but even though he was dead, I didn't want her to know what Alan had done to me. I didn't want anyone to know.

"Where did you hear these rumours?" I asked, doing my best to sound like a gossip, rather than an investigator. She was on her phone, typing a text.

"There's a Facebook group that I stalk sometimes when I'm bored. Someone anonymously posted that Alan had raped her," she said in her usual blasé way.

"Who said that? Did they actually name him?"

"Ok, first of all," she said, looking up from her phone, "*anonymously* means *I don't know who it was*, and secondly, of course they didn't name him. No one's trying to get sued."

"Then how do you—"

She put her phone away. "I put two and two together. Father who worked in a bank donates cash to the school so they can build facilities. Dude is a known bully, currently dating a party girl. It's not neuroscience, it's following the trail. Bada Bing."

I looked at her, dazed. I wanted to know everything. Even though I knew in my gut that the post was about Alan, I still felt like I needed more proof. As if she could read my mind, she carried on talking.

"She said his father was a 'pillar of the community' and that her reputation, future and family would be toast if she accused him in public. Say, didn't Principal Brewster call Louis Ellis a pillar of the community when he was sucking up to him over the gym? I say that's a smoking gun."

She paused for a moment, like she was waiting for me to say something. I didn't.

"Trust me, Alan was trash. It's a good thing he's dead. The world is marginally less unsafe now," she said.

I nodded slowly. She didn't know how right she was. Well, she was always rather self-assured, so she probably knew. As she started to leave, no doubt bored of watching me digest the new information, she turned and said, "I can send you a link to the post if you'd like."

I managed to crack a half-smile. "That would be great, thanks."

She smiled and went on her way. I ran to the bathroom and threw up.

Sadly, the day didn't end there. I still had to go to the police station. I went home in a haze, trying to anticipate all the questions I would be asked by the police. All that thinking stressed me out. The whole situation stressed me out. For the first time since Alan got shot, memories of the rape started coming back to me. I had hoped they were gone for good, but deep down, I knew that was too good to be true.

Throughout our journey to the police station, my mother was eerily quiet. There was a feeling of foreboding in the air. I was so afraid of what would happen with the police, and her silence scared me even more. The numbness had receded. My feelings were all over the place, bouncing from sadness to fear to hope to horror. Alan's death was so much more than the end of his life; in a weird way, it felt like the end of mine, too.

The police station was as dull as ditch water, but I guess it wasn't meant to be a fun place. My mother and I waited outside an interrogation room for 10 minutes before Detective Forsyth invited us in. I don't remember his partner's name, but his hair made him look like a golden retriever, and he never said a word.

Detective Forsyth asked me to describe the events of the prior evening, starting with why I was there in the first place. I told him that sometimes Donna and I liked to hang out at the shop, especially if she was on her own. He seemed to find that odd. I told him that it was fine, as Mr. Pryce didn't mind.

He asked me what Alan had said, how it was that he got shot. I started fidgeting a little, moving uncomfortably in the already uncomfortable chair I was sitting in. I told him everything that had happened, trying not to cry. I managed to hold it together, sobbing quietly instead of bawling my eyes out.

The detective looked at me and my mother. He looked like he wanted to say something but wasn't sure how.

"Can we go now?" my mother asked.

"There are a few things I'd like to know. Mina, had you ever had any run-ins with Alan before?"

I tensed up. I didn't know how to answer him, not with my mother in the room. Even if she hadn't been there, I don't think I would have felt safe telling him the truth.

I couldn't look him in the eye. "He, uh… he was a bully. Everyone in school knows that. I'd like to go home now. Please."

"It's been a harrowing 24 hours, detective. May we go?" my mother said.

He let us leave, but I felt like it wasn't over. How could it be when he asked such a leading question? He knew what had happened. He had to know. Donna must have told him, I thought. I had to find her and find out what she'd said. Luckily for me, she was with her parents, waiting right outside when my mother and I left the interrogation room.

Mama Selene and my mother hugged each other, while Mr. William looked on. Donna stood a few feet behind him. I told my mother that I wanted to use the bathroom and invited Donna to come with me. We were given permission to go.

In the bathroom, I couldn't contain myself. I started crying.

Donna looked puzzled. "What's wrong?"

"This whole thing is insane. I can't believe you killed him," I said between sobs.

"He was going to hurt us. He was going to hurt you. I couldn't let him do that. I had no choice, and that's his fault." Her voice sounded calm and comforting, like she was trying to pacify a sad child.

"Did you have to kill him? Couldn't you have just shot him in the knee?" I asked. I don't know why it bothered me that she'd killed Alan, but it did.

"Yes, Mina, I had to kill him. It was him or us. Would you rather he'd raped you? Again?"

The words felt like a slap in the face. How could she ask me something like that after everything that I'd been through?

"How can you even say that?"

"I don't appreciate you acting like I just fed a saint to a lion. He robbed the shop. He threatened us. He threatened *you*. If we had let him— if *I* had let him, he would probably have raped and killed one or both of us. Is that what you wanted?"

"No, of course not! What the hell, Donna—"

"I did what I thought was best to keep us safe. I'm sorry if that upsets you," she said, cutting me off.

Her words hurt and stunned me. There was not a hint of remorse or regret in them. It was like she didn't even care how I felt. I searched her face for the faintest trace of emotion, but there was none. It seemed as though, overnight, she'd completely come to terms with the fact that she'd taken a life and it didn't bother her one bit. What had happened to my friend?

"Did you tell the police?" I asked.

"Tell them what?"

"Did you tell them… what he did to me?"

"Of course not. I would never. Why would you even ask me that?"

She looked troubled at this point. And then her mother walked in on us. I wiped my eyes and smiled at her. Donna didn't move.

"Are you girls ok?" she asked.

"We're fine, mum," Donna said, dragging her words out.

Mama Selene walked over to us and hugged us both.

"You're very brave. Don't worry, everything will be ok," she said.

When she finally released us, Donna wouldn't make eye contact with her.

"Your father wants to leave now," she said.

Donna nodded, still avoiding looking at her.

She looked at me instead, and smiled. "We'll talk later."

"Your mother is waiting for you," Mama Selene told me.

She smiled again and the two of them left. As I watched them leave, I wondered if I ever knew Donna at all.

Since then, I've seen another side of her — a more aggressive, callous side — that I didn't know existed. I don't know if the act of killing someone unleashed a beast that was locked up inside her, or if it created one. I want to believe that it's the latter, but maybe she'd been hiding that part of herself all along.

I wonder which Donna I'll see tonight. Will she be happy to see me? Will she throw me out like a piece of rubbish? The thought of getting on her bad side makes me reconsider going to her place. I think about getting off the bus, about turning back, when my phone makes the familiar buzzing noise that lets me know I have a text. It's from Ivy: *Dinner is ready. Looking forward to seeing you tonight. X.* The message makes me sigh.

Forward ever, backward never.

IX

DONNA

I t's about 7.45pm when I get home. The flat is warm and smells like a garden. Mum like a floral potpourri mix which includes roses and lavender, though I only ever smell roses. There are small bowls of it in every room. I hang my coat up on the clothes horse in the narrow entrance hall and drop my keys in a basket on the desk near the front door.

Ivy sprints to the hall to meet me. Her cocoa-coloured eyes light up as she smiles.

"Hey there," she says while hugging me. I smile and hug her back, inhaling the citrus scent of her hippie-dippy body spray. Her warm demeanour always brightens my mood, no matter how dark. She steps away from me, takes my hand and leads me further into the flat. Her small frame is hidden by the massive blue hoodie-dress she's wearing. I'll never understand why she bought that thing. As she moves, her braided ponytail sways from side to side.

I walk into the living-dining area and go over to mum, patting her on the shoulder. We exchange polite greetings and I thank her for the effort she's put into making a meal. It crosses my mind to remind her that our lives may have been better if she'd made half the effort to leave her worthless husband, but I pocket that one for now. I've not been home for up to 3 minutes. There's no need to be so hostile so fast.

"Donna, can I talk to you?" Ivy says.

"Let me change first. I'll be back in a minute."

Her eyes widen and she purses her lips, nodding.

I go to my room, take my shoes off and change into a black t-shirt and a pair of baggy grey trousers. These trousers have seen better days, but they still fit, so I still wear them. There's a picture of me and Ivy on my bedside table. It was taken at her graduation ceremony two years ago. It's one of the few times in my life I've felt genuine happiness. My heart was full of warmth. I think that's what genuine happiness feels like. Ivy only ever tries her best for people, for me. All I ever seem to do is cause her stress. I should make an effort to be nice to mum tonight, for Ivy's sake.

But first, I must rest my feet. I plop down on the ground and put my feet in the air, placing them lightly against the door. I'll stay here till they start to go numb, then I'll move. As I look at the ceiling, I think about Connor Matheson and his retirement wife. How will he feel to have his legal team changed so suddenly? I shouldn't worry about that – it's no longer my problem.

I shake my head a little, trying to relieve tension in my neck. When I stop, I think about Jeremy Haywood. I try not to think about work when I'm not there. Most times, I fail. Even after I close my eyes, I can't stop thinking about Haywood… I can't stop thinking about what he did to Aisha. Who in their right mind does something like that?

Obviously, he's not in his right mind. He's delusional, thinking he can do whatever he wants. People like him believe they can behave however they like because of their station in life. And they treat people like things… they treat women like things. I know in my gut that this isn't the first time he's done something like this. Aisha happens to be the only one who's been brave enough to report it. And here I am, taking money to help him escape justice when all I really want to do is skin him and feed him to sharks. I've lived long enough to know that the only way to stop people like him is to kill them. I did the world a favour when I killed Ellis and the others. I have to find a way to end Haywood, too.

I'm still thinking about him when I hear the doorbell ring. I'm usually the last one to get home, and we very rarely entertain visitors this late. In the summers, mum likes to invite women from her church group to the flat (and I like to make myself scarce on those occasions), but that would be in the early evening.

My feet aren't anywhere near numb, but I have to know who is visiting at this late hour. I drop my legs and leave my room. I am in no way prepared for what I see when I get to the living room. Mina Kaur is here, in this flat. She's hugging my mother, who looks happy to see her.

Mina.

I haven't seen her in 5 years. Considering what happened the last time I did, I thought I'd never see her again. Yet here she is… I didn't know she was out of prison. She was supposed to be there for a few more years. I tend to check up on her every three months, just to make sure she's still alive. I have some contacts at the jail she lived in. I've been so busy these past few months, that I haven't got round to doing my duty. When did she get out? Why is she here? I stand still and watch as she and Ivy see me at the same time. I can't help but notice that Ivy looks apprehensive, her smooth forehead suddenly creasing.

"Hey Donna," Mina says, in what may as well be a whisper. She looks away from me, turning her attention to her feet, which slowly but continually shuffle. She looks unhealthy and weary. Her eyes are sallow, and she's thinner than I remember. I can't work out why she's here and I don't really know how to respond. I turn to Ivy. She lowers her gaze and I look back at Mina.

"Hello Mina. When did you get out?"

I don't mean to sound so cold.

"It's almost been a month."

"What are you doing here?"

"Oh, I bumped into Mina today and invited her for dinner. I didn't think you'd mind," Ivy says. Her tone is upbeat but I know she's faking it. It's the same tone she'd use to try to distract or placate William when he was on the brink of flying into a rage.

She lightly shifts her weight from one foot to the other. She knows she's messed up. I guess that's what she wanted to talk to me about when I got in. I wish she hadn't let me relax before telling me this.

"I was going to say something, I just thought I should let you, you know, do your thing," she adds, her eyes pleading with me to apply restraint.

And so I was right. Mina looks uncomfortable and mum has been mum all this while. More than uncomfortable, Ivy looks worried. Her brow creases further. She looks like she can't predict my next move, like she's afraid that I'll do or say something upsetting. It occurs to me that my presence is oppressive, not unlike William's was. With that realisation, I remember my resolve to be nice for Ivy's sake. How quickly that resolve almost dissolved.

"It's good to see you, Mina." I walk over to her and give her a light hug.

It's going to be an interesting night.

DONNA

So here we are, sitting at the dinner table, making nice. Mum has cooked a delicious 3-course meal (well, technically she cooked a 2-course meal, since the dessert is ice-cream from a shop) and we're all sitting around the table in silence, preparing to eat. It's all very civilized. Mina's hands shake a little. I can't determine if she's still doing drugs or if she's just on edge. I want to believe it's the latter, but that might be foolish of me. Then again, it could be both.

Now settled, mum clears her throat. I hold my breath because I fear that I know what's coming.

"As we all know, today is a very special day for our family…"

I look over at Ivy, sitting opposite me, and watch her as mum speaks. Her hands spontaneously ball up into fists. Her eyes dart from mum's face to mine.

"…10 years ago, today, we lost our beloved husband and father, William…"

I feel a knot forming in my stomach, along with a lump growing in my throat. I start breathing again, slowly, trying to calm myself down. I catch Ivy's eye again, see her shoulders rising to her ears. I reckon she's expecting me to kick off and she's bracing herself for it. I hope to disappoint her.

I cannot be sure I will.

"…I thought it would be appropriate for us to mark this occasion with a nice meal. And as God would have it, our dear friend, Mina has joined us. It's so nice that you're here, Mina."

"Thank you for having me over. I really appreciate the kindness," Mina says.

"Would any of you like to say some words about dad, or say grace?" she says, looking around the table for volunteers. My eyes meet hers and I cock my head to the side, narrowing them as I try to restrain myself. I can't believe this woman.

She barely finishes her sentence when Ivy pipes up. "I'll say grace."

Mum looks at her and nods.

Ivy proceeds. "Dear God, thank you for this lovely spread and the ability you've given mum to make it. Thank you that you are a good Father and you were good to us even before we knew you. 10 years have gone by quickly and you've been faithful to us. Thank you for that, Lord. I, um, pray that you bless this meal and our evening, in Jesus' name, amen."

Ivy's prayers are always short and sweet. None of that irritating, self-indulgent huffing and puffing that we were subjected to at the church we used to attend back in the day. And Ivy knows how to get to the point, and to get the point across with little effort. I also couldn't miss that she called God a good father. Relevance? Oh yes, William was not one of those.

We unfold our napkins and mum speaks again!

"I miss him so much."

Is she actively trying to provoke me? Ivy's eyes bounce from her to me.

"Let's just eat, mum," she says.

Once again, I resume my breathing exercises, focusing on the first course – carrot soup. For all her imperfections, mum is a great cook. I sometimes wonder if the only reason William wasn't more deliberate in beating her to death is that he didn't think he'd find anyone who could cook like her. He did love good food.

We eat quietly for a few minutes. It's nice. The only time I ever get quietness in this flat (discounting my nights of insomnia) is when I'm alone here, and that rarely ever happens. Once a month, there's an overnight prayer meeting at the local church we attend. Mum and Ivy go every single month, and every single month, I sit it out. I usually stay here on my own and treat myself to a tub of ice cream (yes, an entire tub). It's refreshing. The pace at which I live is ridiculous. The stress of work and the stress of home and the stress of memories of things past… all of it can feel so overwhelming at times. So that one day a month, I try to reset my mind.

Ideally, I'd forget some of the things I've done, but since I can't, I focus on why I did them. I've never killed anyone for fun, I'm not crazy. Necessity is the mother of invention and – believe me – it was necessary.

Take Ellis for instance. Good old Alan Ellis, the notorious bully and rumoured rapist. I myself had never heard the rumours because I was too busy minding my own business and paying attention to my schoolwork to do so. But other people had heard them. I knew he was a bully and a brute. I knew he'd groped a few girls at school, myself included, but I didn't know rape was one of his infractions.

I didn't murder him for entertainment purposes, but I can't say it wasn't cathartic watching him bleed to death. For the first time in my life, I felt like I was in total control. I planned his execution meticulously and I really felt a surge of pride when it went down more or less smoothly. Sure, there were hiccups on the night, but he's not here and I am, so all's well that ends well. He did his best to cling to life but it was vain, quite like his life itself.

Obviously, the deviant's parents, Louis and Emily, were devastated and the community was somewhat disturbed, but said community, and the country and the world as a whole were all better off for Alan's death. It was a cleansing of sorts… not on a grand scale, but the removal of even one stain makes a surface a little cleaner. That's how I thought of it. I was doing my bit for society. I was protecting people.

The quietness has gone from being comforting to being deafening. We've all moved on to the second course (roasted goat with mashed sweet potatoes and stir-fried vegetables) and all I can hear is the sound of cutlery on plates. Ivy's fork is especially irritating, as she drags it across her plate with speed and deliberation. She tends to take time with her food, but today she's quicker than usual. I imagine the strain of the situation is getting to her. Mum is slower at the moment, and Mina is the slowest of all of them. She seems to be savouring every mouthful, like she hasn't had a well-cooked meal for a long time.

My thoughts drift back to the night Alan attacked her. I was at home that evening, studying for a biology test. I was in my room while Ivy, mum and William were downstairs, watching something or another. William usually demanded that we all watch T.V. together, even though he never allowed us to watch what we liked. He never let us forget that it was his house and we had to live by his rules. He allowed me to study because, despite how he treated us, he was always happy when we did well at school. I suppose he felt that it made him look good.

There I was, studying, when I got a call from Mina asking if I could leave the house. She didn't sound well at all. I knew at once that something was wrong. She said she needed help. She asked me to bring her a change of clothes. I knew William wouldn't let me leave the house so late, not because he cared about my safety, but because he wanted to control my movements as much as he could. And to be honest, I didn't want to leave the house that late either. It was barely 10 o' clock, but danger likes the night.

She told me she was at the bus stop down the road (literally a 2-minute walk from the house) but I still didn't want to risk being out late at night. I never felt safe in the house, and I didn't really feel safe outside it either. Part and parcel of being female, one might say. But Mina sounded so distressed that I knew I had to help her. Something was very wrong, and I wasn't going to let that mad man stop me from doing the right thing. I told her I'd be there.

She ended the call and I hopped off the bed and packed a top and a pair of leggings into my trusty gym bag. I climbed out of my bedroom window and dropped into the garden as quietly as I could. I'd never done that before, though I'd considered it whenever I thought of running away. I ran to the bus stop and found Mina waiting. She was pacing back and forth, looking anxious and somewhat distressed. Her face was bruised and her lower lip had a cut on it. Her brow was cut up, too.

I asked her what had happened and she told me. About how he'd beaten her, about how he'd raped her, about Beth's role as his accomplice. All I could do was hold her. As I did, I felt searing rage rise up within me. I knew Alan and Beth were wretched – both together and separately – but I could never have fathomed just how depraved and dangerous they were.

Mina refused to go to the police. She didn't want her parents to know she'd been *defiled*. I don't remember clearly if she used that word but it was something along those lines. She didn't think the police would believe her. She said Alan's dad had too much sway over the community.

I asked her to let me help her. I offered to take some DNA from her and pretend I was the one he'd attacked. I didn't even know if it was possible to do that, but at that point in time, I was willing to do anything to bring Alan to justice.

After her refusals, she changed and went home, leaving her clothes with me. Her face was a mess and I still don't understand how she explained it to her parents without raising their suspicions. Her parents were nice, but how gullible could they be? Maybe it was because I'd spent so many years on the receiving end of physical violence that I knew that those bruises could only have been caused by fists. Maybe I've always been willing to believe the worst. Maybe, for some reason, her parents weren't so attentive. And don't even ask me how they didn't notice her change of clothes.

As soon as she left, I went back home. On my way, I tried to figure out how to report Alan to the police without getting Mina involved. If he attacked her, there were probably other girls. And I thought that if I could find even one of them and convince her to come forward, then maybe Mina would have been motivated to do the same.

The anger within me did nothing but rise steadily, until I finally realised that any attempts to get justice would fail. Because of his pedigree, because of his gender, because people were afraid of him. But I wasn't afraid of him. I'd spent my life living under the oppressive rule of a tyrant. If I'd managed to survive thus far, Alan would be no match for me.

I couldn't have been gone for more than half an hour, but in that time William had discovered my absence. I climbed back into my room to find him sitting on my bed, waiting for me. My heart sank. It had been almost two weeks since he'd last hit me. I was feeling good, so much so I was considering stopping poisoning his drinks. But there he was to strengthen my hand. He was so angry that he didn't even notice my gym bag. I stealthily slid it off my back and kicked it out of sight.

"Where have you been?" he asked, puffing the words out.

There was almost no point answering. I knew I was in trouble. There was no right answer to that question. Anything I said would be used against me and I would get beaten no matter what.

I shrugged. "I needed some air."

He didn't move. Neither did I.

He raised his voice. "Don't lie to me."

"I needed some air, so I took a walk."

He stood up and looked down at me. And there it was in his eyes – the look he always got before he threw a shoe or a chair or a punch. It really depended on his proximity to the weapon and the target. He liked using his fists most.

"Why didn't you ask permission and take the front door?

I sighed. Sometimes when he got that way, when I knew that violence was inevitable, it was like my emotions turned off. In that moment, I felt nothing. I knew what was coming, so there was no point being afraid or sad, I rationalized. I tucked the fear, the despair, the sadness, the disappointment at my lot in life away in a box somewhere inside myself – somewhere that they wouldn't stop me from functioning.

And I challenged him because I like to earn things, even the punches he was sure to mete out.

"I didn't want to," I said, standing my ground.

His eyes widened as he stared me down.

"Just hit me, dad. It's what you want to do. You don't need an excuse. You never have."

The words hardly left my mouth before he obliged me. Again and again. I fell on the floor and he lifted me up and threw me back down. It was the sort of thing you saw in a wrestling match. There was never any doubt who would win because it was never a fair fight.

When I hit the floor, I felt the air leave my lungs. I coughed, trying to catch my breath. I wish I could say that the pain was unbearable, but in some ways I was used to it. It was still pain, though, and I wanted it to be over.

I wish I could say that I was scared he'd kill me, but we were way past that by then. To die would have been to receive mercy from him, and I knew he didn't understand the concept.

Besides, I'd lost interest in dying long before that night. I wanted to live, to live and see the back of him. I wanted to be there at his funeral pouring dust on his coffin. I wanted to visit his gravesite from time to time and spit on it. And that night, I wanted to be the one to send him to his grave. Not him alone, Alan Ellis too. I was beyond wishing for death, because I had a mission and a purpose, a reason for living. He could kick me and hit me and scream at me all he liked, but I'd get over it. And when I'd healed, I'd finish what I started. I would put a stop to him once and for all. I would be the true victor.

I heard Ivy running up the stairs, asking what was happening. She must have heard me coughing.

"Dad, what are you doing?" she yelled.

I didn't see her face, but her voice told me all I needed to know. She was shocked to find me lying on the floor with a bloody nose, and to see William standing over me. It was sort of cute how his barbaric behaviour seemed to take her by surprise. It was almost as if she'd inherited mum's ability to forget all the awful things he did to us, like with each new day they thought (or maybe just hoped) that he would wake up as a new man.

Ivy ran to me and held me. Only then did he stop. He'd had enough by then. She cried as she rocked me in her arms. Her tears dripped onto my face, and only when I felt a stinging sensation did I realize that he'd split my lip in his fit of fury. Wonderful – Mina and I had matching wounds. It didn't upset me too much. "This too shall pass," I said to myself. I didn't have an exact timeline for William's exit, but I knew it would be sooner rather than later. All I had to do was be consistent and to wait. Patience and determination win the day. Meanwhile, I needed to work out how to kill Alan whilst staying out of jail. That was my next assignment.

Mum came up the stairs when she was sure that William was done. As was her way, she was armed with bandages and disinfectant. She may not have been good for much, but at least she was not good for nothing. William might have said something about how I needed to learn to respect him. I wasn't paying attention. He was a small, pitiful man crumbling under the crushing weight of his own mediocrity, and I'd long given up hope that he could be respectable. I'm a realist – always have been, always will be. All he deserved was a bullet in the head, and I couldn't even give him that for fear of ruining my future. So he'd get less than he deserved, but the end result would be the same.

Here in the present, slowly eating my dinner, I accept that it's good that Mina is spending the evening with us. She's been through a lot, too much to be on her own. Yes, she's made bad choices, done irreversible, stupid things, but after all that happened to her, it's no real surprise. I look at her and smile. She smiles back. However much I want to rekindle our friendship, though, I know that her weaknesses are numerous and that they are strong. I can find out how she's doing after dinner. Right now, I need to finish this meal.

***

In time, all plates are empty. I volunteer to clear the table and wash up, while Ivy offers to get the dessert. She follows me into the kitchen and takes the opportunity to talk.

"How was your day?" She retrieves four bowls from their cupboard.

That is the question.

"Eh, ok I guess," I say, shrugging. I turn the tap on and start washing up.

"Hmm," she says, grabbing the ice cream tub from the freezer.

Hmm? *Hmm?* That's the sound Ivy makes when she's getting ready to deliver bad news.

"What is it?"

She places the ice cream tub next to the bowls.

"How many scoops?" she asks

Deflection – I hate it when she does that.

"Two, please. What do you want to say to me?"

She drops the scoop.

"I'm sorry to spring this on you but is it ok if— if Mina stays over tonight?" she says, her voice getting low. She looks at me, holding onto the back of her neck with both hands.

"Are you serious?" I say, trying to stay cool. Without meaning to, I start scrubbing the plates unnecessarily hard.

"Look at her, she needs help. She needs *our* help. She needs people who've got her back, who can support her."

"Oh, you are serious. After what happened the last time I tried to help her, I can't believe you're even considering this."

She shakes her head and looks up, no doubt praying for strength.

"Do you even know if she's off the drugs?" I ask. I keep my voice low, hoping mum and Mina don't hear us.

She blinks rapidly and then tilts her head to the side, as if it hadn't occurred to her that Mina might still be addicted.

"Please, Donna. I already told her she could stay—"

"Why would you do that?"

She doesn't reply. She steps back and looks away from me, folding her arms.

"The ice cream is getting cold," I say, shaking my head with irritation.

"Do you mean 'melting'?"

I give her a withering look.

"Ok. I'll take it to them. Shall I take yours, too?" she says.

"Please and thank you."

She puts the tub back in the freezer, drops the scoop in the sink, and leaves the kitchen with two bowls. She comes back for the other two. I stay until the sink is empty. I wipe my hands and then bury my face in them, moving them up my face and then sweeping my hair back. I exhale loudly. My hands rest on top of my head and I pause, trying to drown out the sound of voices coming from the dining area.

Eventually, I let my hands drop and I go to the dining area's entrance. I watch for a moment as Mina practically inhales the ice cream. She looks frail but I catch her smiling at mum. Her smile makes her look like a happy child, one who thinks the world is a safe place full of good people. It's a beautiful smile. I beckon to Ivy with my head. She excuses herself and meets me back in the kitchen.

"So?" she asks. Her eyes are wide. I know she's hoping I'll acquiesce. I nod. She flashes a huge smile, and hugs me briefly.

"Thank you so much Donna. This is a good thing we're doing."

"No, this is a good thing you're doing," I retort.

"Either way, thank you," she says, still smiling.

She puts her arm in mine and we walk into the dining area together. I reclaim my seat at the table and start on my melting dessert. With bright eyes, Ivy taps Mina on the shoulder. "When you're ready, I'll get your beddings, ok?"

Mina's smile is so intense that it warms my heart ever so slightly. It's the happiest I've seen her look all evening. I hope this is the right thing to do.

I hope I don't regret this.

XI

MINA

I
t's so awkward being here, in this flat, at the mercy of strangers. Well, they're not really strangers… it just feels like they are. It's been quite some time since we were all together. I can't really think how long, but they're still more or less the same. Mama Selene still has those big, kind eyes, full of warmth, hiding sadness of their own. Ivy is gorgeous enough to sell whatever she wanted on social media, not that she ever would. She's still positive and generous, although slightly on edge in Donna's presence. And Donna… well, she has changed the most.

I recognize her physically – her dark skin and hair, her unreadable deep brown eyes, her slim and strong build – but she's far more reserved and distant than she was. That could be because of all the times I've failed her. If I were in her shoes, I wouldn't want to be near me either. The last time I saw her, she let me stay in her dorm room. I told her I was clean (which was a lie) and that I needed a place to stay for a few nights (which was the truth).

Unfortunately, I made some bad decisions that included robbing her and her housemates. One of them had enough jewellery in her possession to put any member of any royal family to shame. I can't remember her name, but she was foreign. Russian, I think. Or maybe she was Ukrainian. It was some time ago and I think a lot of my brain cells have since expired.

In my mangled state of mind, I took everything that looked like it was worth anything, and I left in the middle of the day. Everyone was out at lectures. It was perfect, like the stars aligned for me. I sold the stash for a healthy amount and proceeded to buy enough drugs to last months. I felt bad but I felt good. It's hard to explain the combination of thrill and misery that I've felt so often over the years. Sadness mingled with excitement. The buzz is always tempered with despair. I get high, then I get low, and the beat goes on. Equal and opposite reaction, I guess. No matter how much I tell myself that I'll do better next time, I know that I won't. Experience has taught me that much.

Even now, in this nice home, having a nice meal with nice people, I know deep down that it's only a matter of time – hours, maybe days – before I wreck this. It scares me to know I'm never too far away from sabotaging good things in my life. Fear has become my constant companion, almost like a shadow. Between it, misery and The High, I'm never alone.

Donna and Ivy go to the kitchen after the meal, ostensibly to wash up and get dessert, but I know they're talking about me. How can they not? Ivy invited me here without telling her sister, and the two haven't had a chance to discuss it. The hostel is always in demand and I know that my place there would have been filled by now. I'm terrified that I'll have to spend the night on the streets. I don't ever want to do that again. I hate being at people's mercy. I hate having so few options. A part of me wants to take control and leave – at least that would be my choice – but it's so nice and warm in here that I have to hope that they'll let me stay, even if it's only for tonight.

Mama Selene tries to distract me with conversation about her church activities. She seems more or less happy. She certainly seems happier than she did when I was younger. There was always a cloud of sadness over her, even though she never stopped smiling. And she was a mess when her husband died. Donna stepped up to the plate and took charge of the household. I can see that she's still in charge. But for sure, her mother seems more alive than she used to, even on a day like today.

She tells me that this flat was bought with some of the money her late husband left them when he died. It seems that all the hard work he did at the investment bank meant that his family inherited a good chunk of change. How nice for them. I'm sure it's no substitute for a loving father and husband, but at least he left them something for their future. I haven't seen my parents since before my most recent stint in prison. They've given up on me, with good reason.

Ivy returns with ice cream for her mother and me.

"Here you go," she says, handing a bowl to me.

She smiles, but avoids looking at me. I know what that means. She goes back to the kitchen and my heart sinks. I try to prepare my mind for a night of rough sleeping. A lump forms in my throat, but I swallow hard. She comes back, still avoiding eye contact, and sits next to Mama Selene. Her shoulders are slumped and she eats slowly. It *must* be bad news for me. Tears come to my eyes, but I don't let them fall. I shut my eyes and will them to dry up.

I should try to be positive. This is the first time in years that I've had a freshly cooked meal. And the meal was stellar. I even get dessert. This is the best evening I've had in a good long while. When I woke up this morning, I didn't think the day would go so well. This is better than I could have imagined. That's something to be grateful for. Yes, I should be grateful. Even if I sleep under the stars tonight, I'll at least do so on a full stomach. With that thought, I dig into the ice cream.

Ivy gets up suddenly, having barely touched her dessert, and I see that she goes over to Donna. The two retreat to the kitchen, disappearing from my view once again. They are there briefly and then they walk over to join us. Ivy looks happier than she did mere moments ago. I want to hope for good news, but I am afraid... too afraid to hope. Donna takes a seat, but Ivy sits next to me. She taps me lightly on the shoulder, like I'm a delicate ornament.

"When you're ready, I'll get your beddings, ok?"

I cannot describe how I feel. It's like my heart is an arid land and someone poured a cup of cold water on it. I want to cry and laugh at the same time. Instead, I smile. I look over at Donna, who is focused on her dessert. I look back at Ivy and mouth, "Thank you." She smiles and nods and pats me on the shoulder.

I can't believe this is happening.

XII

DONNA

I feel quite proud that I was able to contain myself throughout dinner. Despite the lack of confrontation, I'm exhausted. I decide to take my leave and so bid mum goodnight. When I get to my room, I see that I'd left my phone in there. I hate that phone so much that it's no surprise that I hadn't missed it. I grudgingly check the messages and see that Kat has sent two texts – one asking how my (imaginary) doctor's appointment was, and the other talking about how hard she's finding it to get over Daryl. This poor fool. I consider replying the messages but am interrupted by a knock on my bedroom door.

I open the door and find Mina on the other side. She flashes a lopsided smile. Her eyes look less sallow than they did earlier in the evening. She looks stronger; maybe even a little more hopeful. That's nice.

"Hey Donna, can we talk?"

I don't want to talk, especially because I have a sneaking suspicion that I know what the topic of conversation will be. To be fair, I never want to talk. Most times when people ask if 'we' can talk, they plan to do all the talking. It's irritating and misleading. I shouldn't complain too much, since I am an enabler.

Tonight, I'm not opposed to listening. I nod and let her in. I shut the door and the noise makes her jump.

"Sorry."

"That's fine," she says, looking around the room.

"Why so tense?"

I'm not expecting her to admit to still using drugs, but she might.

"Oh, I just… loud noises scare me sometimes."

"Oh."

Neither of us says anything for what feels like a long time. She points at the picture from Ivy's graduation and smiles.

"When was that?"

"Two years ago."

"You look happy."

"I was," I say, smiling.

"That's good. You deserve to be happy."

William and the others would disagree, but no one asked them.

"I have to be up early tomorrow—"

"I wanted to say thank you for letting me stay here. I know I've screwed up a lot, but you've always been there for me. I promise I won't screw up this time. Things will be different," she says.

There are many things I could say, so many doubts I could express, but I conclude that now is not the time to bring up her past misdeeds. I bite my tongue. She ought to have a night of relief. I'm surprised to be feeling charitable tonight. Ivy must be praying fervently.

I smile at Mina, once my best friend, now practically a stranger. "I'm glad we can help you."

"Yeah, me too," she says. After a moment of silence, she adds, "I should let you sleep. Have a good night."

"Thanks, you too," I say, letting her leave.

Once the door shuts behind her, a wave of sadness, regret and disappointment washes over me. It hits me hard enough that I double over and have to hug myself.

I wish I could have been there for her that night at the party. I wish I'd dissuaded her from going. I wish I'd known how dangerous Alan was and reported him to the authorities before he had a chance to hurt her. I wish I'd been able to stop him. How different Mina's life would have been.

I feel my eyes welling up with tears. I squeeze them shut. A few deep breaths later, and I'm fine. I remind myself that I did what I could. I may have been late, but at least he can't hurt anyone else now. That brings me little comfort, but a little comfort is better than none.

My thoughts return to Mr. Haywood, another rotten fruit that needs to be separated from the rest and destroyed. I think that, for the time being, I should apply myself to destroying the case in any way I can. If that fails, I may have to get my hands dirty. That seems like a reasonable plan. Right now, though, I need to catch up on my sleep.

Tomorrow will be a busy day.

XIII

MINA

After dessert, I offer to wash the bowls. Mama Selene tries to stop me, since I'm a guest, but I insist. I clean them like my life depends on it, so much so that they squeak. I don't remember the last time I did something so normal. I can't remember when last I was in such an ordinary setting. I'm more used to park benches and crack dens, and of course, jail cells. It feels good to be here and I want to make it worth my hosts' while.

I put the plates away and return to the living room. Ivy has gone to get beddings for my stay, and Donna has gone to sleep, Mama Selene informs me. Apparently, it's not because I'm here. She's disciplined and doesn't stay up longer than she needs to. Her job is taxing, and she needs all the rest she can get.

I'd like to talk to her, to thank her for being so kind to me, but I'm not sure if I should. I worry that if I thank her for helping me, she'll remember the things I've done to her… as if she could ever forget. Still, I don't want to highlight them. But I do want to thank her. I have to.

"Which room is Donna's?" I ask.

"Well, I'm off to bed myself," she says, "I'll show you."

Mama Selene gets up and takes my hand, leading me down the corridor. She stops in front of a door at the end and gestures towards it. She brings me in for an embrace and then kisses me on both cheeks. She leaves me standing outside Donna's door and goes to her own room.

I stare at the door for a minute, finally mustering up the courage to knock. In no time, Donna opens the door. Her eyes flicker – probably with surprise – when she sees me. I ask her if I we can talk and she agrees, letting me in. She shuts the door with enough force to make me jump.

"Sorry," she says.

It's no problem. It's not her fault I get agitated so easily. She asks why and I tell her loud noises make me jumpy. That's only partially true. I won't bother telling her about the nightmares. It's late and she's tired.

I take in the décor of her room. It's not much different from the one she had when we were teens. It's pretty sparse. There is, however, a picture of her standing next to Ivy, who is wearing a gown. I ask her when that was taken, and she tells me it was two years ago when Ivy graduated. They look happy. In fact, Donna looks so happy that I comment on it. She smiles, tells me she was. That might be the first real smile of hers I've seen all evening.

She starts to say something, but I interrupt her, thanking her for her hospitality. Despite knowing the truth, I feel the need to tell her that I won't screw up this time. Maybe saying the words will keep me on the right path. She looks me dead in the eye and I know she doesn't believe me. I don't believe me; even as I hope what I'm saying is true.

I wish it was possible for me to get my life on track, but this addiction isn't something I can so easily shake off. Screwing up goes hand-in-hand with being an addict. Screwing up is merely one of the by-products of my addiction. She knows that as well as I do. Still, she smiles and says she's happy they can help me. That makes me want to make it worth her while. I really don't want her or Ivy or Mama Selene to regret this. I want to get better, to do better.

We say goodnight and I leave her room. Out in the corridor, I run into Ivy. She tells me that my bed is almost ready. Overwhelmed with emotion, I reach out and hug her. Her skin is soft and warm, like her demeanour. She's an angel. She's my angel. I'm so glad I ran into her today. She might just be the catalyst for my recovery. Because of her, I feel like I might have a chance.

The tears I've held back all night finally fall. When I let her go, I thank her. My words are barely audible, but she says it's nothing. It may be nothing to her, but it's everything to me. I go to the living room and see the bed sheets on the sofa. I sit on the sofa and lift the sheets to my face. They are so soft and they smell like chamomile. I put them down and weep quietly. I don't know if I'm happy or scared, but I know that I'm grateful.

There is a small chance that my life will get better.

XIV

IVY

I walk into my room and head to the drawer underneath my bed to get some spare beddings. I pull out a fresh pillowcase and duvet cover. The sofa bed isn't the most comfortable, but it's all we have. I hope it's comfortable enough for Mina. I'd like to take a moment to pause and collect myself, but I can't. Not yet anyway. For all I know, in the time it takes me to catch my breath, mum or Mina will say something to Donna that will tip her over the edge. I don't want anything to mess up what's left of the evening. I have to get back out there as soon as possible.

It's a miracle that Donna even agreed to have Mina stay. She must be in a generous mood, not that I can tell. She is not unlike a closed book. When we were younger, I would catch occasional glimmers of what she was thinking, insight into how her mind worked, but all that stopped after she killed Alan Ellis. That was when she withdrew. And then dad died and she drifted so far away from me that she feels unreachable.

I'd always thought to myself that if by some miracle he died before he managed to finally beat the life out of us all, his death would bring us closer together. I thought that we'd be free to build a better relationship, like the one we had when we were really small children. That's not how it's happened though. Reality pales in comparison to my expectations. On the upside, we're still alive so there is still time.

I think the spare duvet is in mum's room. I'll get that in a minute. Dinner was delicious. I should let mum know that I enjoyed it and am grateful for her efforts. The evening did not go as badly as I had feared, and for that I thank God. Maybe I spend too much time anticipating the worst. Maybe I need to relax more.

I leave my room and go to the living room, only to find it deserted. Where could Mina be? I place the beddings on the sofa bed and go back towards our bedrooms. I can kill two birds with one stone – find Mina and get the duvet from mum's room. When I reach the corridor, the sound of muffled voices reaches me, and I perceive that Mina is talking to Donna in her room. I freeze, fearing the worst. Donna can be unpredictable and there's no telling what Mina could say to set her off. I hold my breath and stand still, silently praying.

Oh God, please let the night end well.

The door opens and I jump a little. Mina steps out of the room, looking contemplatively at the ground. She's managed to get in and out of Donna's bedroom without all hell breaking loose. A wave of relief washes over me. I do my best to compose myself before she sees me. When she looks up, I smile at her.

"Is everything all right?"

"Yes, everything is fine," she says.

"Cool. Your bed is almost ready… I'll get you a duvet."

I walk past her to get to mum's door, and she grabs my arm. She hugs me as soon as I stop. She grips me tightly. Her hair feels limp and greasy on my face. Her arms feel weak. I pat her back gently and hope for the hug to end. She gets the message and releases me from her clutches. Her eyes are wet. She wipes the tears from them.

"Thank you," she whispers.

"It's nothing."

We part ways, with her going to the living room, and me going to mum's room. I knock on mum's door and wait for an answer, all the while thanking God for a chance to help someone in need. I hope and pray that the rest of Mina's stay is as good as tonight. I hope it's even better.

XV

NOVEMBER 22ND, 2019

DONNA

Today I manage to wake up in time to get the bus. I didn't sleep too well but after how disappointed I felt being underground yesterday, I knew better than to make the same mistake. I even had breakfast. I hope this is a sign of good things to come. Considering that I have to deal with my nincompoop colleagues, I shall manage my expectations.

A smooth journey got me to work at 8.30, which gave me a good amount of time to review Mr. Haywood's case file and read more about him. My research was not exhaustive, but I read enough to know the basics: humble beginnings, self-made millionaire, model-like wife, Audrey, who was a waitress when they met – so far, so generic. She's 12 years younger than he is so like I said: generic. They've been married for 18 years, since she was 24, and have two sons – 16-year old Jeremy Jr. and 12-year old Noah.

The boys attend the same school and are A-students, according to a profile I found on the website of a high society magazine. Audrey now owns a chain of small cafes and spends her free time opening envelopes and cutting ribbons. The boys enjoy school and especially love tennis and hockey. In the summertime, the family sail the high seas on their yacht, The Great Escape.

Started from the bottom, now they're here.

It's the picture-perfect aspirational family, if you believe the article.

I'm not gullible enough to believe the article. I know that people on the outside can never see the full picture. Compared to the photographs from before they were married, his wife has lost a fair amount of weight, which is probably unintentional considering that she wasn't fat. She looks too thin to be happy. And I can see in his eyes that the darkness inside him isn't the sort that can stay caged. He has the look of a man who delights to feed the beast within. I imagine that he's made a habit of giving in to his base desires but this time, for whatever reason, he miscalculated. Now if only I could find a way to prove it.

My train of thought is suddenly hijacked, as I remember how vile Alan was until his dying moments. He had the nerve to swear at me, repeatedly, as if I was the one in the wrong. He did not for even one second express shame at the behaviour that led him to such a violent death. Prideful to the last breath. I needed no more confirmation that my actions were justified.

Though I had wounds of my own that needed healing, my mind was sharp and I spent a few weeks following his attack on Mina plotting how best to make him pay. I'd already decided to kill him (and decided on how I would go about it, too), but then I thought that on the off-chance that he felt something like remorse, I ought to give him the opportunity to confess his crime to the police. It seemed fair.

I approached him at school with that proposition. It was no surprise that he laughed in my face and told me where to go. That pleased me. In between classes, I had told him to meet me at the chemistry lab (my favourite place in the school) during lunch, alone. He did. There were security cameras in the lab but they had no audio, which was perfect for my purposes. I knew he wouldn't try to hurt me in there.

When he got to the lab, he looked excited and strangely expectant. I don't know what he thought would happen, but I don't think he could have ever guessed. I did my best to convince him that I had enough evidence to convict him, and that I wanted him to do the right thing and turn himself in. He said that it didn't matter how much evidence I had – he was untouchable. *Un-touch-a-ble.*

Faced with his brazen disregard for people's safety, common decency and the law, what was I to do? I showed him pictures of the clothes I'd taken from Mina and told him that I had irrefutable DNA evidence of his crime. His demeanour changed very quickly. A picture is worth a thousand words, so I suppose I should have shown them to him to begin with. But I had wanted to give him a chance, and he didn't take it. With the colour drained from his face, he insisted that I was bluffing and that I had nothing on him. He didn't know that I was recording our meeting, as a backup. He wasn't very clever.

"Would you bet your freedom on that?" I asked, smirking.

"If you have all this proof, why haven't you gone to the police already? Why hasn't Mina? Why are you talking to me?"

"Like I said, I want to give you a chance to do the right thing. And Mina... I asked her not to tell anyone until I talked to you," I said.

He paused briefly, jaw tightly clenched, thinking, I presume. And then he said, "There's no way I'll go to the police. And you won't either."

"Then I have a proposition for you."

His eyes narrowed and he moved closer to me. I didn't move a muscle. You can never let anyone think they're intimidating you.

"What do you mean?"

"I can take the evidence to the police, and then watch you get tarred and feathered in court before spending the rest of your youth in prison... or you could do me a small favour," I said.

He looked at me like he needed subtitles, slowly shaking his head. "I don't understand."

No surprises there.

"I have to leave home. To do that, I need money... money I don't have," I said.

"What's that got to do with me?"

"You're going to get me that money."

He turned around and walked towards the wall of the lab, before turning back to me.

"Blackmail? Is that what this is about? Fine, how much will it take to shut you up?" he asked.

"I don't want your money, Alan. I know where to get what I need; I just don't have an easy way to get it."

I shrugged.

"Ok, I'm intrigued."

"The till at the newsagent's where I work is always loaded with cash. You're going to rob the place and give me the cash. I'll run away and your secret will run with me."

"Not if Mina sticks around," he said.

"I can handle Mina. She won't go to the police unless I tell her to."

"Wouldn't it just be easier to take money from me?" he asked, once again moving closer to me.

He was actually thinking. That was a bad sign. I knew I needed to distract him, to draw his focus away from the bigger picture and redirect it as I saw fit.

"Most the money that's in that till, I would have made. I've earned it. I deserve it. I don't care about raiding your little trust fund; I'm not a thief. I just want what's mine."

He looked unconvinced. If he refused to rob the shop, I would have had to kill him less discreetly. I knew that wasn't smart. I was determined to do all I could to make him want to help me. I relaxed my shoulders, softened my tone and, despite how much he disgusted me, mustered a half-smile.

"You come in, point a gun at me, and I hand over the cash. I know you're not very clever, but it's not really that complicated. I can sweeten the deal if you like," I continued, lowering my voice and slowing my speech down.

"Oh? How?"

"Invite Mina to the shop. You can do what you want with her… and I can give you a special 'thank you' when I collect my money," I said, doing all I could not to wretch at the suggestion.

His lips parted as I smiled at him. My stomach churned and I felt my breakfast rise to my throat. I swallowed hard, maintaining my fake smile, hoping my eyes did not reveal my thoughts.

"I thought Mina was your friend," he said, lowering his voice and moving closer to me. I stood still, hoping he would stop.

"A girl's got to do what a girl's got to do," I said, touching his chest, gently pushing him away. If he got any closer, I would have had to pour chemicals down his throat there and then. That would have been messy and obvious, and if there's one thing I hate, it's being obvious.

"You know, I've always had a thing for you," he said.

"I know."

My stomach turned so violently that it may have made an audible noise. I felt as though I could collapse. Did I just offer my best friend up as bait? Did I really have the guts and guile to pull off murder? I wasn't plotting a hands-off, slow-release poisoning; I was planning to shoot him to death. I wasn't sure I could do it. My neck muscles tensed up and I feared that my right eye would start twitching. He stepped back and pottered about for a little while.

Finally, he nodded.

"I'll do it. But only because it's you," he said, as if he was giving me a discount at a clothes shop. He looked me up and down and smiled. It was the creepiest smile I've ever seen, like something from a horror film.

"Great. A week from today, my boss will be away, so it should be easier. I'll make sure Mina is there. You can come in around 9.30, and we can do this thing," I said.

He smiled again and it unnerved me. I had to keep my game face on, so I reciprocated. I turned to leave, but stopped when I heard him speaking.

"Why do you want to leave home?" he asked.

"Why not?"

I left the lab and went straight to the restroom, where I spent the remainder of the lunch break throwing up and crying. I was disgusted by him. I was disgusted at myself. I was terrified that something would go wrong and he'd rape Mina again, and it would be my fault. If that happened, the recording of his confession wouldn't make much of a difference because he would have hurt her again.

I tried not to panic. I reminded myself that I had the upper hand. He would be on my territory. I knew about the gun Mr. Pryce kept under the counter; he didn't. I knew the shop like the back of my hand; he didn't. He had a week to plan a robbery; I had one more week to plan his murder. In the grand scheme of things, if the whole situation was a stage, I was the director and he was merely an actor. He worked for me. I had all the power and he would only realise that when it was too late.

Despite reassuring myself of all those things, I couldn't shake the feeling that something would go terribly wrong. What if he didn't actually believe me? What if he told someone? What if he didn't come to the shop alone? Would I have to kill several people? What if he didn't come to the shop at all? What if I fell ill, or William tossed me down the stairs again and I couldn't go to work?

I gave serious thought to going to the police, but something held me back. That something was fear. Fear that he would get away with his crime and that I would have lost my only chance to balance the scales of justice. I girded up my loins and told myself that all I needed to do was plan carefully and leave nothing to chance.

"Penny for your thoughts."

The voice comes from behind me, making me jump. I turn around and find Kat circling round me. She settles on my left side, pulling up a chair. Upon seeing the article about the Haywoods, she remarks, "Picture-perfect family, right?"

I stare at her blankly, until she says, "I'm joking."

"I got your messages. Sorry I didn't get a chance to reply. Last night was… hectic," I say.

"No problem. We have our work cut out for us."

"What do you mean?"

"I've been here since 7 o'clock, and let me tell you, this case is less than ideal," she says.

"How so?"

"The files you requested from Haywood's previous lawyers came through—"

"And I assume you took the liberty of reading them."

"It's not pretty. This isn't the first time he's been accused of sexual misconduct," she says.

It infuriates me when people say *sexual misconduct* when they mean *rape* or 'attempted rape,' as though rape and pinching someone's bottom were comparable offences. Bum-pinching is bad enough. But to apply the term 'misconduct' to 'rape' when the latter is such a severe violation of another human being's rights, body and freedom? That's plain idiotic. It's too early in the morning for me to get worked up, so I let it slide. I pour some tea out of the flask I always bring to work.

"What did you find?" I ask, taking a sip and ignoring my thoughts.

She shakes her head and sighs. "In 2013, he was accused of raping one Laura Norman, a waitress at a private members' club. She waited three days to report it and there was a dearth of evidence. Still, the case was settled out of court. The same year, Neha Sharma, an employee at one of his casinos, accused him of verbally harassing her on several occasions, before one day cornering her in a room and groping her. She quit and received settlement money, but not before signing a non-disclosure agreement. Three years later, his sons' tennis instructor, Ren Yoshida, quit, after which she accused him of attempted rape. She eventually withdrew her accusation."

"No settlement?"

"Nope. He claimed they had a consensual relationship and she was bitter because he wouldn't leave his wife for her."

"A likely story," I say.

She shakes her head again. "These are serious accusations."

"Yes, they are… at least he's not a racist, right?" I say in a weary tone.

She smiles, massaging her sinuses. "So how do you want to play this?"

I stop and think. "Obviously, the easiest way to get him off the hook would be to push for an out-of-court settlement."

"And if the prosecution resist?"

"We'll have to block any attempts to get Laura and Ren to testify, that's for sure. Neha probably couldn't even if she wanted to. No sane jury would stay impartial if they knew what he'd done before."

"You mean what he'd *allegedly* done before."

I wave her correction away. "Yes, yes, allegedly."

"Cool. Meanwhile, I'll see what I can find out about Aisha Thompson," she says.

"Oh before you go, do you know who's leading the prosecution?"

"Zachary Parsons."

She winks and leaves the files on my desk.

That would explain the speed with which they charged Haywood. If Zach is the solicitor in charge of prosecuting him, getting justice might not be as hard as I thought. Getting through this case unscathed will be much harder.

***

Two hours later, I'm sitting in a meeting with the team and the partners. Once again, we're in Sanders' office. It seems that this case is extremely important to said partners, and they want all meetings to take place far away from prying eyes and pricked up ears. Today, Staunton is staring me down like I stole her lunch money and she wants payback. I'm doing my best to be proactive and professional, but the pressure of having her here is… distracting, to say the least. I feel like a target and that makes me feel very uneasy.

"Given the accusations previously levied against Mr. Haywood, I believe it's in his best interest to settle out of court," I say.

"You always want to settle out of court. You really need to get over your fear of losing. You're not even a barrister," Daryl says, pouting and flaring his nostrils.

I look at Daryl's sad little duck face and resist the urge to smile. I suppose he's still feeling the sting of not heading up this case. While I hate that I'm leading the defence of a degenerate, knowing that this upsets Daryl soothes my soul. I could take the bait and respond with an equally childish comment but I'm better than that. I'm better than he is. I'm better than he will ever be at anything that's worth doing. So, I'll be the bigger person and ignore him.

"Zachary Parsons is the lead prosecutor, so it's highly unlikely that we'll be allowed to settle," I say.

"Parsons, the Piranha? As in the guy you used to sleep with?" Daryl says.

The room suddenly feels eerily quiet. In truth, Zach and I never had a relationship of that nature, not for lack of trying on his part. The fact that Daryl would say something that inappropriate in front of his superiors reveals how petty and entitled he is. I take a deep breath, thinking about all the ways in which I could belittle and humiliate this pathetic little man, but then I remember that I'm the bigger person. I visualize being a duck and having water slide off my back.

"Your point, Daryl?" I ask, looking directly at him, undeterred by his weak attempts to throw me.

"Maybe you could rekindle your relationship, soften him up a bit. It could help our case," he says, with a knowing smirk.

I feel my jaw tighten without my permission. His blatant efforts to annoy me are starting to annoy me. In my mind's eye, I can very vividly see myself reach for the bottle of whiskey perched precariously on Mr. Sanders' desk and smash it across Daryl's face. I could tell you that this was the first time I'd imagined such a thing, but that would be a lie.

I shake my head and chuckle. "I know you're not used to earning things on merit, Daryl, but that's exactly what we're going to do here. Should we go to court, we will win the case fair and square. No honey-potting necessary."

His mouth moves as if he wants to say something, but then he changes his mind. He looks away from me and to Sanders. Old Bill doesn't say or do anything.

I continue. "As we know, Parsons will never miss an opportunity to send a case to court, so we need to talk to anyone that can corroborate Mr. Haywood's story and find out if they'd be willing to testify."

"Is there any chance we can convince the accuser to rescind? It's happened before," Shane says.

"We can try, but if there's enough evidence, it won't matter," I say.

"The father, Clifton, is a tube driver and the mother, Vicky, is a nurse. Aisha is at the school on scholarship. From what I've gathered, they're just about getting by financially. I'm sure a few extra thousands wouldn't go unappreciated," Kat says.

"Ok, then we should do our best to push for a settlement. If the parents agree to it, there's nothing Parsons can do," Shane says.

"Right," I say.

"We should get Haywood on the phone and find out what he's willing to pay," he says.

This is Shane's modus operandi – he hears someone else's idea, jumps on it and talks about it so much that you forget he didn't originate it. He does it all the time and we all let him. Why? I honestly can't say. Unfortunately for him, I'm a few steps ahead today.

"£500000," I say.

"Excuse me?" Shane asks.

"I called him an hour ago. That was his initial offer – half a million pounds."

Shane tilts his head. It has not escaped my attention that neither of the partners has said anything. The whole meeting feels strangely like an assessment day. From the corner of my eye, I see the makings of a smile on Staunton's face.

"Why didn't you say that before?" he asks, sounding like his airwaves are constricted. Ha, I think I've irritated him!

"If you had let me finish what I was saying, I would have. Also, it's on the print-out you're holding."

He scans his copy of the sheet of paper that I handed to them at the start of the meeting, and I watch as his eyes go wide.

"I see," he says.

He shoots a glance in Sanders' direction, then Staunton's, and then he sinks into his seat. Shane is nothing to me and though I do despise him, he's not Daryl. I'll be pleasant. I smile at him.

"When I spoke to him, Mr. Haywood gave me the names of his two alibis," I say, motioning to them to inspect the printouts.

"His wife and his son," Staunton says. She looks at me and holds my gaze. If she's trying to communicate something to me, I don't know what it is. Maybe she's just checking for a reaction.

"The younger son, Noah... the one that wasn't drunk at the time," I say.

"He's a little young for that, no?" Kat says.

So is the older one.

We exchange a knowing look, the sort that says, 'in an ideal world.'

"So how do you want to play this?" Sanders says. I was beginning to think he'd lost his voice. Judging by how bored he sounds, he's probably only lost the will to live. Ordinarily, I wouldn't blame him for being bored. Daryl drones on and it can be soul-destroying. But I'm the one who's been leading this meeting. I've done the most talking. He's not just bored, he's bored *of me*. If I'm boring him on a case he deems to be very important, I'm in trouble.

"Kat and I will go to the parents and make the offer, while Daryl and Donna can interview the witnesses," Shane says.

There he goes again, trying to control the flow of things. If I hadn't been here for as long as I have, I'd be shocked at this behaviour. Alas, I've become inured to it.

"Actually, I was thinking that Kat—"

"That's a good idea, Shane. Start with the mother, see if she's flexible. You two, try not to kill each other," Old Bill says, interrupting me quite rudely while referring to me and Daryl.

I nod at him. We all nod at him, after which we leave his office. On my way out, Staunton looks at me, and then shakes her head slightly. It's such a small movement that it's almost imperceptible. I guess I failed her. If this was indeed an assessment, I didn't just fail her, I failed myself. I should have known better than to let Shane finish a sentence. He's such a disrespectful ass.

Under normal circumstances, I'd be worried about the safety of my job, but under these special circumstances, I'm more worried about the safety of Daryl's life. His recent, shameless displays of hostility threaten to disrupt my relative state of calm. If he is even half as rude to me for the rest of the day as he was in the meeting, there's a good chance that he won't see the end of the day.

I hope, for my sake, that it doesn't come to that.

XVI

IVY

I prayed longer than usual last night. Thanked God for restraining Donna, because only He could. Thanked Him for letting her agree to help Mina. Gave thanks for the ability to help anyone. Prayed for all my painful memories to fade. I don't know how long I've been praying about that. They go and then they come back. I want to be free from them forever.

Despite the relative success of last evening, I had a hard time falling asleep. Every time I shut my eyes, vivid images of dad hitting me came to mind. It happens every now and again, and I shouldn't be surprised it happened last night. He was, after all, the star of the show. The only time mum ever makes a fuss in the kitchen is on his anniversary and at Christmas. I don't understand how even after so many years, she's still so bound to him.

He wasn't always terrible but he was terrible enough that I would have expected her to have moved on by now. Maybe it's not that simple. She always said he was the love of her life. I remember her telling us about how they met. They were at the same university and one day he spotted her studying on the grass. He'd seen her around campus but had never spoken to her before. He was too shy, according to what he told her. That day, though, he went over to talk to her and found out that, like him, she loved Sade.

The next day he showed up at her dorm with a Sade-heavy mixtape in hand. Those were the days. He asked her out, she said yes. Within two years they were married and a little over a year later, Donna was born. Mum never did tell me when the violence started, but I'm sure the signs were there. She probably loved him too much to see them for what they were.

He had his good points, so I can see how she'd focus on them instead of his shortcomings. He was a hard worker and a good provider. He always encouraged us in our academic and extra-curricular pursuits. It was his idea for me to take up piano lessons, and he was so proud when it turned out that I not only loved playing, but was good at it. He never shot down Donna's scientific interest. The day she told us she wanted to be a doctor, he practically lit up. And then he took us on a day trip to the coast and allowed us to eat as much chocolate and ice cream as we wanted. I don't have many fond memories of him, but that was a nice day. That day, he was kind to us.

When he was sober, he had a way of making us feel special, to the point where I sometimes found myself believing that he loved us. Though good days were few and far between towards the end, they made the bad days harder. It was like, *I know you can be nice, so why must you be cruel?* Questions with no answers...

This morning, I'm tired and groggy and my thoughts are in disarray. I have a mother and toddlers' group to prepare for. Even though it's at lunch time, I don't think I have the strength for it. Oh well, it's my job. I pray for strength in addition to a million other things. While praying, I hear the front door shutting. It's not loud but I tend to detect even the subtlest of noises. I think it's a survival instinct I picked up when growing up.

Once I'm done praying, I open my Bible to a random page and read a verse:
"You will keep him in perfect peace
Whose mind is stayed on You,
Because he trusts in You.
Trust in the Lord forever,

For in YAH, the Lord, is everlasting strength."

I sigh, thinking about trust. I sometimes wonder if I have what it takes to trust people. I may not keep people at a distance the way Donna does, but I don't make the greatest effort to bring them closer either. I wonder if I treat God the same way. What I do know is that I need all the strength I can get, and I'm glad that God is willing to provide it. For now, that'll have to do.

I flip onto my side, preparing to leave my bed. I pause, mulling over the things I have to do today, but my concentration is broken by a noise coming from the kitchen. Mum doesn't eat this early. My best guess is that Mina is awake. And hungry. I climb out of bed, put my dressing gown on, and leave my room.

In the kitchen, Mina carefully opens the fridge. She closes it and yelps when she sees me. She stumbles backwards and knocks the box of cereal that was on the worktop onto the ground. The cereal spills all over the floor.

Good morning to you too, Mina.

Clearly rattled, she drops to her hands and knees and starts picking the little pieces up. "I'm so sorry, Ivy, so, so sorry."

"It's ok," I say, joining her to pick the cereal up. "Did you sleep well?"

"Oh, best sleep I've had in… a very long time."

I smile. "That's great."

We pick up as much as we can, and I get a brush and sweep the residue away. I grab a glass and fill it with warm water from the tap.

"What are your plans for the day?" I ask.

"Um, I've been looking for a job for the past few weeks. I figured I'd carry on."

I nod at her, taking a gulp of the water. "Well, mum will probably be in all day. If you don't think she'll disturb you, you can do your search here."

She raises her brows. "You mean that?"

"Of course I do. You can stay here for as long as you need to… or want to," I say.

She bites her lower lip. "Is that your decision or…?"

I smile. "Donna is happy to help you, Mina. We all are. Don't worry about her."

She nods but doesn't speak.

"Also, if it's any help, there's a job clinic at the church where I work. It's on Mondays. You can come with me and they can help you out... look at your CV, assess your skills and interests, that sort of thing," I say, before finishing up my water.

"That would be amazing." Her quiet response melts my heart. I put the glass down.

"I know you've been having a hard time, but it happens to everyone. You don't have to let your past dictate your future. Things can get better if you want them to, and they will get better if you let them."

Why do I sound like Dr. Phil?

She closes her eyes and tears slip down her face. Oh, I didn't mean to make her cry.

"You don't know how much this means to me," she says, opening her eyes.

"What are friends for?"

XVII

DONNA

The journey to the Haywood Mansion was quiet and uneventful. I thought about all the things I ought to have said in the meeting. I thought about all the things I could have said to Daryl since we were alone together. Unpleasant but true words came to mind, but I pushed them aside in favour of silence. I was surprised that he didn't speak either. He was probably still too busy nursing his bruised ego, and since we were alone there was no one for him to try and embarrass me in front of.

As one would expect, the mansion is big, and that's putting it mildly. The driveway is so long that I could have showered in the time it took for us to get from the gate to the front door. The grounds are sprawling and well-kept. I shudder to think how much it must cost to keep the place looking this pristine. And I haven't even seen the inside.

Jeremy Haywood is an entrepreneur and in addition to his clubs and casinos, he currently owns a thriving clothing brand. It's the sort that sells outfits that make the wearer look cheap, even though said outfits cost a pretty penny and are peddled as having been made with *luxurious materials* and fair labour. That's one of their selling points. They also give 10% of all their revenue to children's charities. It's all very 21st century-ethical on the outside, but I can imagine that it's a money-laundering scam. For where there are clubs and casinos, there must be drugs, prostitution and other illegal activities.

Once we're at the front door, Daryl rings the doorbell and from inside the house, I hear a sample of Beethoven's Moonlight sonata – one of the songs Ivy used to play in the old days. How very pretentious. The door opens and we are led through the very large entrance hall by a maid who neither tells us her name nor speaks to us. She looks about 22 or 23, with light brown hair and pale, freckled skin. She's wearing a hideous tent-like uniform, but even then, I can tell that she has a slim, curvy figure. Daryl notices this as well, as I see his eyes light up when she turns around.

This wasteman.

In the hallway, there are two staircases leading upstairs. The floor is marble throughout and the walls are desecrated— I mean, decorated by large portraits of the family. The maid leads us into a reception room and finally tells us that Mrs. Haywood will be with us shortly. From her accent, I'd guess that she's from Eastern Europe.

"Would you like something to drink?" she asks.

"I'll have water, please."

She looks at Daryl.

"Water is fine, thank you," Daryl says. He smiles at her and she curtseys.

As she leaves us, I can't help but notice how steadfastly he stares at her retreating backside. I open my mouth to offer a sharp rebuke but decide it's not worth my while.

I wonder how easy it would be to get in and out of the house undetected. The gate is manned by armed security guards, and the distance between it and the front door might very well be longer than that between Pluto and The Sun. I could find a way to get myself invited in and then go about lacing Haywood's drink with poison. Old habits and all that. That's an option, but would suspicion fall on me? I should think about that later. Right now, I have to keep my wits about me or else Daryl might outshine me.

Judging by the furnishings in this room alone, the Haywoods are very rich and they like to keep their money in view. To describe the room we're in, the word 'opulent' springs to mind, even as 'tacky' follows dangerously close behind. I like chandeliers as much as the next person, but I don't think they need to be golden, and I really don't think a single room needs more than one.

Daryl surveys the room and lets out one of his mindless whistles, before saying "Now this is the life, don't you think?"

I shrug at him and sit on the sofa with the best vantage point – I can see the door and no one can sneak up behind me. He gives me a disapproving look, as if I'd spilt red wine on the lily-white rug.

"Don't tell me you wouldn't give an arm and a leg to live like this," he says, plopping down on the sofa opposite me. A glass coffee table separates us.

"I won't tell you that then," I say, straining to smile at him.

He looks at me with narrowed eyes. "So all the hours you put in at the office, all the hard work you do, you vying for team leader – you're telling me it's not for this kind of life?"

The tone of his voice has shifted from one of disbelief to one of curiosity. He raises an eyebrow, like he's impersonating James Bond. I can't quite tell whether or not he's trying to flirt with me or trick me into saying something he can use against me at his convenience. There's a good chance he's doing both. Either way, he's getting on my nerves and I have to remind myself to stay professional.

I smile again. "I like my work, Daryl. It is its own reward."

He wrinkles his nose. I can't bring myself to care about his thoughts. Just as he starts to say something else – no doubt something ridiculous – the glamorous, yet frail-looking Audrey Haywood walks into the room. Daryl's silly questions distracted me and I didn't see her coming. A few seconds ago, I got a whiff of her very strong perfume. Had I been focused, I would have recognised that she was close by.

She looks as she did in the profile I read this morning – about 5ft 7, hair bleached blonde, face touched by a surgeon. It's not even noon, yet she's wearing a blue cap-sleeved cocktail dress. Dress to impress? Perhaps. She looks tired, with heavy eyes, as though she is seconds away from crying or falling asleep or both. I assume that she's already been at the bottle and is soon to feel the full effects of that poor choice. Maybe the perfume is to mask the smell of booze. Or maybe she, like the house, can be summed up with the word *loud*.

I stand up, and Daryl follows suit.

"Please," she says, "sit, sit."

I hesitate, and instead extend my hand and introduce myself.

"Mrs. Haywood, I'm Donna Palmer and this is my associate, Daryl Blake," I say. She takes my hand. Her grip is delicate, or more accurately, weak. I fear that if I close my palm even a little, I'll break her hand, maybe even her entire arm. She smiles faintly and then moves to shake Daryl's hand.

"It's a pleasure to meet you both," she says in a languid manner. "Please, sit."

We take our seats this time, with Daryl moving to share the sofa I'm on. Thankfully, he doesn't sit too close to me. Audrey sits on the sofa that he just vacated. The maid comes in with a tray and places it on the table in between us. There are three empty glasses, a bottle of cucumber-infused water, and a second bottle which contains lemon slices, cucumber slices and a clear liquid that I suspect isn't water.

She pours the water into two of the glasses and hands one to me and the other to Daryl. We dutifully thank her as she pours the mysterious contents of the other bottle into the remaining glass. Audrey picks the glass up and without looking at her, waves the maid away. She curtseys again and leaves.

As Audrey lifts the glass to her lips, I interrupt her. "How are you holding up, Ma'am?"

She appears to force herself to smile, and takes a sip from her glass before answering.

"I've been... better," she says, forcing another smile.

"We want you to know that we will do everything we can to exonerate your husband, Ma'am," Daryl says.

She nods but her expression does not change. "You can call me Audrey."

Daryl gives his signature 'am-I-or-aren't-I-coming-on-to-you' look. He holds her gaze for a moment longer than is appropriate, until she finally looks away from him, blushing slightly. This man is a bold-faced dirt bag. I really wish I was here with Kat. I'd take her tragic whining about Daryl over his presence any day.

"When can we talk to Noah?" I ask.

She clears her throat as her eyes make contact with everything in the room but me. "He won't be back for a few hours, and then he and Jerry have their tennis lesson."

Daryl and I look at each other, baffled.

"Right after school, on a Friday?" Daryl says.

"Jeremy doesn't want them wasting their afternoons. He likes them to have structure…"

Her voice trails off and she takes a much bigger sip – a gulp, really – of her drink. She exhales afterwards, and I get a faint whiff of vodka. William's favourite. It always triggers memories of him, and this time is no different.

I remember closing the basement door and leaving the house… leaving him to die, instead of calling the police.

This is not the time or place for such thoughts. I keep talking, hoping the memory will disappear, or at least park itself in the back of my mind.

"Will we be able to speak to Noah today?" I ask.

She hesitates. Another swig of vodka before she answers.

"I don't think so. He has homework he needs to catch up on."

Daryl sits back on the sofa and looks at me. I keep my eyes on Audrey, who lightly traces the circumference of her glass with her finger. Her hand shakes, but not enough that she risks spilling her drink.

"Alright. We'll speak to him some other time," I say, getting my notepad and a tape recorder out of my bag.

"For now, we'd like to know what you saw two nights ago," I say.

She sighs and downs what's left in her glass. She refills the glass and sips some more.

"I had a headache, so I went to bed early—"

"Around what time?" Daryl asks.

"Maybe 8 o' clock. I woke up maybe a couple of hours later and went to check on Noah. I thought that Jerry was at Eddie's party—"

"That's Edward Smith, your son's classmate?" Daryl says.

"Yes, that's him. Jerry had gone to his 17th and I wasn't expecting him back before midnight. Eddie lives down the road, about 10 minutes away and the neighbourhood is pretty safe," she says.

"And what time did you check on Noah?" I say.

She takes a sip of her drink and looks up.

Stuttering, she says, "Um, I think it was around… 10pm… maybe a little before that. Noah was asleep. He woke up when we heard a noise coming from outside. We looked out the window and got a glimpse of a girl running. Jeremy was coming towards her, and she bumped into him. He tried to talk to her, but she ran off."

"What was the noise?" I say.

"I think it was the front door slamming," she says, pursing her lips.

"Ok," Daryl says.

"So she was running away from the house?" I ask.

"I can't be sure. We heard a noise, looked out the window, and she was running. That's all I remember," she says, looking into her glass.

I notice that Daryl has started gently tapping his left foot. He does that when he knows someone is lying and he's trying to decide whether to confront them about it. For a man who sneaks around behind his wife's back, apparently undetected, his body language is worryingly easy to read. Looking at his face, though, you'd think he believed every word that came out of her mouth.

"What did you do afterwards?" I ask.

"I, um, I kissed Noah goodnight, and went and had a bath. I needed to relax."

There's a pause. I scribble some notes in my pad, and refrain from doodling the word 'LIAR' in the margins. Even if I couldn't already tell that she was lying, her story doesn't square with her husband's story of how he got the scar on his face. Has her brain been so compromised by alcohol abuse that she can't remember what he told her to say? Am I giving him too much credit? Maybe he's the one who doesn't remember what he told me. Maybe he forgot his lies and gave her a new story to tell. Or maybe she's faking this whole alcoholic damsel act and wants him out of her hair.

Daryl remains silent, so I continue.

"Audrey, when is your police interview?"

She looks up and sighs. "I'm due to visit the station later today. Why?"

"How much wine had you drunk that night?" I ask bluntly.

Her mouth opens as she tightly grips her glass. "What are you implying?"

I've hit a nerve.

"Your husband strongly hinted that you have... an unhealthy relationship with alcohol. Besides, you've been drinking vodka since we got here and it's barely gone noon. That and your shaky hands give it away."

Her face turns bright red. She puts the glass down and holds her head in her hands.

"Audrey, anything you tell us is confidential. You know that, right?" Daryl says. His voice sounds soothing and comforting.

She nods and lifts her head, looking at us.

"I've told you everything I remember," she says. She reaches for the glass, but changes her mind, choosing instead to clasp her hands.

"We're going to defend your husband no matter what. That's our job. Nothing you say here will stop us from doing our job. It's obvious you're lying... that won't help your husband's case," I say.

"Who do you think you are calling me a liar? Who the hell do you—?"

"How did your husband get that scar on his face?"

"Scar? What scar?" she asks. She sounds bewildered. I reckon if her forehead wasn't overflowing with Botox, it would look wrinkled at this point. Has she not seen the man lately? Don't they live in the same house?

"When I met him yesterday, there was a scar on his face. He said that you were asleep when he got home and you broke a bottle of wine on his head after he scared you awake. That's a very different story from the one you just told us.

I don't think that the discrepancy will make your husband look innocent in the eyes of the law."

She exhales loudly and slouches in the sofa. She looks off into the distance, at what, I cannot say.

"Audrey—"

She lifts her hand to quiet me.

Eventually, she sits up and retrieves her trusty glass. She sips some more of her drink. And then she speaks. "I love my husband. He's not a perfect man, but he's better than some other men. I married him because I loved him and I thought he loved me."

"Do you no longer think that?" I ask.

"I don't know if he loves anyone but himself, or anything but his pleasure. The first time that girl accused him—"

"*Which* girl?" Daryl asks.

"The waitress. I can't remember her name."

"Her name is Laura Norman," I say.

She nods in acknowledgement.

"That girl. When she accused him, I didn't believe it. How could I? What kind of person does that?"

She drinks up what's left in her glass and continues, "There was the girl from the casino, but he didn't hurt her... not really. I told myself that it wasn't a big deal."

"I'm sure Miss Sharma disagreed," I say. Sometimes I can't help myself.

She nods slowly. "And then Ren said he tried to rape her... and I thought maybe there was some truth to it. He's always been on the aggressive side – he's an Alpha. That's why he's so successful in his work. I'd seen the way he looked at her, leering. I just never thought that he could hurt anyone like that. And if he did, then what does that say about me? How could I marry a man like that? How could I even fall in love with him?"

Tears start rolling down her face. I can't be sure whether this is all an act, so I carry on questioning her.

"What happened two nights ago?"

"I don't know. I drank a bottle of wine and fell asleep around 9 o' clock. I didn't wake up till late the next morning."

"And Noah, did he see anything?" Daryl asks.

"He says he didn't."

He says he didn't. That's not exactly a vote of confidence.

"You don't believe him," I say.

"I'm not sure I'm in a fit state to make sound judgments about anything," she says, taking hold of the tissues that Daryl hands to her. She dabs her eyes and looks directly at me and continues, "Jeremy told me what to say to you. He said Noah and I should tell that to the police. The truth is I have no idea what happened that night. Only he and the girl do, as far as I know."

We pause as she blows her nose with one tissue and cleans her eyes with another. When she composes herself, Daryl says, "It's very brave of you to stand by your husband like this. Most women don't have that sort of strength."

Is he serious?

She smiles. "I don't know if I'd call this strength."

He leans forward and covers her hands with his… and she lets him. My eyes roll so hard you'd think they were snooker balls. Is he making a pass at a client's wife, at such a vulnerable moment, in front of his colleague? I've never known him to be this indiscreet. I clear my throat. He turns to me and I bend my head to one the side, look at their hands and then back at him. Audrey pulls her hands away. Interesting how he doesn't drop them – she pulls away.

"At what point can we talk to Noah?" I ask, returning my gaze to her.

"Probably not today. After tennis, he has Russian lessons. His days are very full," she says.

"What about Jerry?" I ask.

She shakes her head. "He doesn't remember anything about that night. Like mother, like son."

"We'd still like to hear his side of the story, to get a fuller picture of the night," I say.

She looks at me blankly.

"That way, we can plan our defence more robustly," I say. I muster a smile. I realize this might be the first time I've smiled since she started talking.

She sits still, her eyes moving slowly from one side of the room to the other.

"He has Spanish lessons after tennis, and then we're going to the police station. I don't think he'll have any time before then."

So she fully intends to take her sons to the police and give them this half-baked, ill-thought out, poor excuse for an alibi. I'm beginning to think that Audrey wants to see Jeremy behind bars more than anyone else.

"What time?" Daryl asks.

"When the boys are ready, I suppose we'll leave. Probably around 6 o' clock," she says.

I look at Daryl. He seems to be struggling to find his words.

"Well, Audrey… it would be in your best interest for one of us to be with you at the station. We wouldn't want you and your sons to be questioned without a counsellor present," he says, turning to look at me.

I stop for a moment and think.

"Would you excuse us, Audrey?" I say, standing up. She nods and Daryl follows my lead. We step into the hallway.

"I guess you want to go with her," I say, lowering my voice so she can't hear me.

"I *ought* to go with *them*."

"Right, same difference."

He rolls his eyes. "I don't know why Staunton has you leading this case, but I know what I'm doing, and I don't need your permission to do my job."

At last, he's got that off his chest.

"True. You also don't need me to tell you to stop flirting with a client's wife, but here I am, telling you to stop flirting with a client's wife. That's not part of your job, and it never will be," I say. Even to my hearing, the words sound like a threat.

He steps back and shakes his head.

136

"It's hardly been a day and you're already drunk on power," he smirks.

"If you think this is power, you're an even sadder man than I realized."

He blinks like he's been slapped, most likely because I've never spoken to him like that before. What can I say? The mask slipped. Stress does that to me. Ideally, I would just have smiled at him and told him to be kind to Audrey, but the pressure of the situation is getting to me. In the old days, all I had to worry about was keeping my grades up and avoiding being beaten. But now, I'm finding it hard to keep up my appearance of normalcy and lead the team while also trying to ruin Mr. Haywood's defence and/or plan his murder. Being an adult can be so exhausting.

I try to recover by smiling at him.

"I'm joking. Can't you tell," I say, raising the pitch of my voice, so that I sound like a harmless child. I've seen the way he reacts to Kat when she does that. Her eyes go wide and she twirls her hair. I can't bring myself to go that far. I refuse. He'll have to be content to watch me bat my eyelids, which I do, slowly and deliberately.

I think it works, because he runs his hands through his hair and smiles at me. I've seen him smile at Kat that way before. It might be that all is forgiven.

"You can be difficult to read sometimes," he says, still smiling.

I find it hard to accept that he's this easy to manipulate, but now isn't the time to analyse him.

"Just keeping you on your toes," I say, dropping my pitch a little lower. He smiles again. I'm not sure how far to go in my attempt to pacify him. He's still smiling at me. I decide to push a little further, saying, "You know what us girls are like."

I smile and narrow my eyes, tilting my head and moving my shoulder forward so that it almost brushes my cheek. For a moment, he looks flustered. I can hardly believe that worked. Ivy always says that the carrot can be more effective than the stick. Maybe she's right.

Finally, he regains his composure. "So, uh, I'll stay here with Audrey, wait for the children and accompany them to the police station. What will you do?"

"I'll call Kat and see if there's progress with Thompson's mother. Take it from there."

"Alright," he says.

He starts walking back to the reception room, when I stop him. "If you could help her polish off her version of events before you see the police, that would be great."

"I plan to do that."

We'll see how that works.

***

I bid Audrey goodbye. She told me that 'the maid' would see me out. After I called for a taxi, I thought it best to use the facilities. The maid led me to a restroom that was so large that it could probably have housed an entire football team, reserves included. As I expected, the room was gaudy and loud, but on the plus side, the toilet paper was very soft. It was the sort that has some mammal embossed on it. I personally find that strange and unnecessary, considering the fate of all toilet paper...

It smelt really nice in there, too. I think it was a combination of orange and neroli oils in the diffuser. Maybe there were other oils as well, but of the smell, I approved. It was subtle and relaxing, like walking through a field of flowers on a summer's evening. The scent was at odds with the over-the-top gold-plated taps and seat, which agitated me, quite possibly because they looked ugly. I've never understood this sort of ostentation, but like I said, some people like to see their money.

The hand wash and lotion were from some high-end beauty peddler. They were from the Rose and Aloe line. Never mind that of the nearly twenty ingredients, rose and aloe were listed in the last four. Forget all that, just hand over your money. Ignoring the shoddy marketing, the products had a pleasant feel. Were it possible, I would move into this toilet, despite the garish appearance.

I'm yet to work out if there's a way I can get in and out of this house undetected, but I have a feeling that it's impossible. Poisoning any alcohol during a visit will probably just result in Audrey's death, or maybe even Jerry's. I haven't spent enough time with either of them to know if it's worth having collateral damage. I assume Noah is too young to be a drunk, but I cannot say for certain at this time. Aisha's statement made mention of a shortcut, and I don't think she wrote anything about guards. If I can work out where that shortcut is, there's a chance I can flesh out my backup plan.

On my way from the restroom, I check for potential gaps in security. There are no guards working inside the house, only the maid. When I get back to the hallway, I notice that there is a staircase leading down. I suppose that's where the cellar, a.k.a., the crime scene is. I see the maid waiting near the door and decide to talk to her.

"Hi," I say.

She curtseys. This is the third time I've seen her do that today.

"What's your name?"

"Ksenia," she says, looking down.

"Hi Ksenia, where're you from?"

"Russia," she says, still looking down.

Ah, she's Russian. I lived with a Russian girl in university – Yulia. She was crazy, but in a good way. When she caught her boyfriend (now her ex) cheating on her, she poured vodka all over his furniture and set it on fire. It was wild! Everyone thought she'd lost her mind, but I understood. Love and Hate are two sides of the same coin, the coin called Passion.

The university tried to expel her, but her father donated a large sum of money to them, and they softened their stance. Money is the best friend to have. It seems that it can buy you anything. I would have liked to keep in touch with her, regardless of how reckless and unpredictable she was, but Mina sullied that relationship for me.

Ksenia keeps her eyes on the ground, as if she fears that looking any higher will result in permanent loss of sight. I wonder if this is a household rule or if she's just shy.

"Is there somewhere we can talk in private?" I ask.

"I don't think Mrs. Haywood will like that," she says, keeping her gaze low.

If Mrs. Haywood doesn't want me talking to the staff, well I simply must talk to the staff.

"Oh, it's fine. I'm one of her husband's lawyers and I just need some more information," I say, smiling. I don't know why I'm smiling when she refuses to look up.

She says nothing.

"I don't have to tell her anything you say," I say, hoping to persuade her.

Finally, she looks at me.

"I cannot talk to you here," she says quietly, "but when I finish my shift, I can meet you somewhere else."

I nod. I fish my business card out of my bag and hand it to her. She looks at it briefly, and then stuffs it down her top. At that moment, an older lady (also wearing a tent) comes out from… some room, holding a vacuum cleaner. She stops suddenly, like we've startled her.

"Is everything alright, Ksenia?" she asks.

"Yes, Irene, I was just showing the lady out," she says, rushing her speech. Irene nods and goes into another room. How many rooms are there?

Ksenia opens the door, and I turn to her. "Call me as soon as you can, ok?"

She nods and I leave the house. I get into the taxi that's waiting. As it coasts through the long driveway, I notice security cameras all through. I wish I'd seen them earlier and asked to view their contents. I hastily send Daryl a text, asking him to get the security tapes and bring them to the office. I hope that there's something useful on them.

***

In the cab, I call Kat to find out how she and Shane are progressing. We speak for less than a minute before she tells me to meet them at a café a while away from the office. The cab driver isn't pleased to be rerouted. The fact that we're meeting outside the office piques my interest. I can only assume that the visit with Mrs. Thompson didn't go too well.

The café is one that Kat is particularly fond of. She's enamoured with their banana bread. She also had a long-standing crush on one of the guys who works there, but I suspect that crush has receded since her dalliance with Daryl. Ugh, I really hope Daryl isn't planning to seduce Mrs. Haywood. That would be in such poor taste.

As I walk past the café window, a rapping noise catches my attention. I turn to find the source of the noise and see that Shane and Kat are sitting near the window, with Shane knocking on it. I smile faintly and hurry inside.

"Hey guys, how did it go?"

Shane shakes his head while Kat sips her coffee. She's got a plate in front of her, and on it is a half-eaten piece of banana bread. So predictable.

"Vicky Thompson was not happy with our offer," he says.

"In her defence, though, we interrupted her very long shift," says Kat.

"What did she say, exactly?"

"She wasn't happy at all. She's hell bent on taking it to court, said there's no way she'd take Haywood's 'dirty' money, said he deserves to rot in prison for ever, said they should bring back the noose—"

I can get behind that.

"Said we should be ashamed of ourselves for representing a 'pervert,'" adds Shane, shrugging.

"Well that's no good," I say.

It is, though. In the taxi, I thought long and hard about how realistic it would be for me to quietly kill Jeremy Haywood. I'm not certain it's something I can do on my own. I'd probably need an accomplice, and the last thing I need is an accomplice. I've seen it time and again – someone outsources their crime and lives to regret it when the accomplice snitches on them. It's a disaster waiting to happen. I don't like disasters. If I can't kill the man, sabotage is the safest way to go.

"Daryl will be happy for us not to settle," Kat says. She takes a big gulp of her coffee. "Where is he anyway?"

"Mrs. Haywood and her sons have an appointment with the police, which Daryl will attend with them," I say. She looks at Shane from the corner of her eye. He looks at me.

"Was that his idea?" she asks, stroking the side of the coffee cup with her thumb.

I shrug. This is not the time to indulge her misplaced jealousy.

"What did the alibis say?" Shane asks.

I sigh involuntarily. Where to begin!

"The wife's story is… evolving. We didn't get to talk to the son. Well, we didn't talk to either son, actually," I say, reclining into the seat.

They look at me quizzically.

"It's a long story, one I'll tell you later. Did you try the father, what was his name?"

"Clifton. His shift ends around midnight, so we won't get him anytime soon," Shane says.

I furrow my brow, thinking about how to convey this news to the partners.

"Where to now, Batman?" Kat asks.

I wish I knew.

***

To the surprise of no one, the partners were unhappy with the news. Old Bill was especially displeased to hear that I'd left Daryl alone with Mrs. Haywood.

"You should have stayed with her," he snarled.

I didn't bother asking why. I just nodded and said, "In hindsight, perhaps."

Hours later, Daryl returned to the office, visibly distressed. Audrey chose to go to the police station early, cancelling her sons' tennis and language lessons and taking them along. Despite talking her through a believable version of the events of the night in question, Audrey had told the police a story so full of holes, it could double as knitwear.

According to him, he repeatedly attempted to pause the interview, but Audrey refused, choosing instead to plough on. All he could do was watch in horror as she initially claimed to not have seen or heard anything unusual, and then revised her statement, claiming to have slept through the night. She said she had no idea what happened, but that she believes her husband's story. In other words, she did not provide an alibi.

As if that wasn't enough, Noah told the police that he was awake but because he was playing video games, he heard nothing and never actually looked out the window, so he doesn't know what went on that night. It was a stitch-up. Jerry's version of events lined up perfectly with Aisha's, ending with him passing out and not waking up for three hours. They pretty much burnt Jeremy's already toasty defence to ash.

"She screwed us hard," Daryl says.

"Ok, ok." I place my hands on my head and pace about.

I'm torn. On the one hand, I'm thrilled to know that Jeremy's days of freedom are most likely numbered. I won't have to risk my freedom and safety trying to bring him to justice. On the other hand, I am acutely aware that the security of my job may depend on the outcome of this case. I don't know whether I can fight against Jeremy's interests without fighting against my own. With Zach prosecuting, it's almost certain that no matter how well we defend him, he's going to jail.

That should console me, but it doesn't. He deserves something more permanent than jail. Knowing how the system works, he'll be sentenced to around 7 years in prison (if that) and he'll serve less than half. All he did was try to rape someone. Had he evaded taxes, you can be sure he'd die in prison.

"I didn't get the CCTV tapes either – apparently the cameras haven't worked all week," he says.

I shake my head and exhale loudly. "Maybe that's a blessing. If they don't let us see it, there's no way the prosecution will... Is there anything else?"

He nods and looks at the ceiling. "She called her divorce lawyer on the way out of the station."

I drop my hands and raise my brows. That is some juicy information.

"I suppose we can't count on her as a witness," Shane says.

Daryl shakes his head.

"If she leaves him, spousal privilege is out the window. We can't let her testify for the prosecution," he says, looking knowingly at me.

I know. *I know!*

"It might be time to pay your friend a visit," Kat says.

I sigh and nod. She's probably right.

***

Zachary Parsons seems to be a decent man. I say seems to be because one never really knows what people are like. As far as I know, he's thoughtful, kind, generous. An all-round good guy, it would appear. The fact that he would not look out of place in a perfume advert doesn't hurt his cause. He's got lovely dark hair and a sweet smile that makes you think that he thinks the world of you.

We met at university – I was in my first year, he in his final one – where he decided he had a crush on me after I defeated him in a mock court case at a party. It was endearing at first, but it steadily got irritating. He's like a puppy, and I happen to not really like puppies. They're so… eager. For some reason, the thought of being with someone like Zach worried me. Perhaps I didn't want a man who seemed so upright to be saddled with a murderess such as myself. Besides, I had more important things to do, like get a degree.

There was no way I could tell him the things I'd done, and if I had told him, there was no way he would have let it slide. He loved justice and order as much as I did. He still does. The difference between us is that he trusts the system even though it is clearly broken. He would have tried to make me confess. I would have had to kill him. For a relationship to work, it needs trust and honesty as its foundation. That's one reason why we could never have had a serious relationship, which is what he wanted. Also, at no point in the relationship should either partner be willing to resort to murdering the other. That's Basic Common Sense, but it still needs to be noted.

Regardless of my past actions, had I had chosen to date him we would never have made it as a couple. We were on different trajectories. He was disappointed when I told him I wouldn't rule out becoming a defence lawyer. I didn't really want to be one; I just really didn't want to be broke.

Between our accommodation, Ivy's and my education, the money William bequeathed us has dwindled significantly. I don't have rich parents; I have to fend for myself and my family. I can't afford to be a prosecutor, or more accurately, the prosecution service can't afford me. I made the right choice for my finances, even if it was not necessarily the right choice for my conscience.

Though I haven't seen him for a little over a year, I know that he has gained a reputation as a fierce lawyer who relentlessly pursues justice at any cost, hence the nickname Piranha. He climbed the ranks of the prosecutor's office faster than expected, and with good reason: every case he's worked on has resulted in a conviction. I hope his winning streak continues.

I called Zach's office before leaving the Sanders et al building, and was lucky enough to get an appointment. I suspect that he made room on his calendar for me. I arrive a little nervous about seeing him. His secretary, Marcus, tells me he's waiting and lets me go in. I take a deep breath, trying to prepare myself for what's coming.

The office is simple, not unlike the man himself. There's more to it than Staunton's office, but it's still on the bare side. Zach stands up, smiling warily. He looks more or less the same as he used to, except for the line that is now permanently etched into the centre of his forehead. This job can age a person faster than junk food.

"Miss Palmer, how are you today?" he asks.

"Miss Palmer? Since when were you so formal?"

He smiles again and comes round to give me a hug. I'm not too fond of hugs. I was expecting a handshake, but for him I can make an exception. It helps that it's a brief and friendly hug, as opposed to the over-long, over-familiar, creepy hugs some people insist on giving out.

Aside from the subtle evidence of aging, Zach looks well. Good, even. His shirt is crisp and white, and he has the sleeves rolled up to reveal his toned forearms. He's still wearing the ancient watch that his father gave him when he turned 21. Apparently, it once belonged to his grandfather. From all he told me, his is an ordinary, close-knit family that love one another very much. It's a nice story.

"What do you want, Donna?" he asks, squinting at me.

"What do I want? Why does that sound so bad coming from you?"

I play with a loose strand of hair, twirling the ends between my fingers. He smiles and shrugs, motioning for me to sit down, as he returns to his seat.

"I know this isn't a social call. What does your client want?" he says, reclining in the chair.

"He wants to settle out of court, if possible."

"You know that won't happen on my watch," he says, swivelling his chair a little.

"If you don't ask, you can't receive."

"Have you seen the evidence against him? There's no way he didn't do this. He's got away with it before; I won't let that happen again."

"Oh, I see. It's a vendetta and you're on the warpath."

"I'm doing my job, Donna. He's going to court, then he's going to jail, and there's no way we're giving him a plea deal."

His blue-green eyes light up as he speaks.

"I never said anything about a plea," I say, also leaning back.

"That's always the next step. It's also a no."

"You can't stop the accuser from accepting money."

"They don't want money. If they did, you wouldn't be here. They want justice, recompense, balanced scales. As you are aware, all the money in the world can't buy that," he says.

I nod. We quietly look at each other. Gradually, he starts frowning.

"Have you read Aisha's statement?"

"Yes."

"Do you really think money is what she needs?"

I shrug. "What I think doesn't matter."

"How do you sleep at night, defending people like him?" he says, his voice low. His eyes examine mine.

I don't.

I place my elbow on the chair's arm, resting my chin on my fist. "I have to do what I have to do."

He looks away from me and nods. "You know you can always switch sides…"

I laugh. "I don't think the Crown Prosecution can afford me. Besides, the courts never hand out appropriate sentences. How is what I do any worse?"

He smiles a little. "I don't know. You're a good lawyer. It'd be nice if we could… collaborate on something."

I look down. Without meaning to, I start stroking the back of my neck. I can feel his eyes on me. I wonder what he's thinking.

"How's your family?" he asks.

I look at him again and straighten up. "They're fine. Yours?"

"Good, good. Everything is good," he says, rocking back and forth in the chair.

I always get the sense that Zach wants to say more to me. I have that sense now, but this is not the time or place to ask about it. I stand up and smile.

"Thanks for seeing me on such short notice. I'll let you get back to work."

He stands as well, leads me to the door.

"We should catch up," he says, "Are you free this weekend?"

"Working. You know how it is."

He nods and smiles. He looks at his shoes, and then at my face.

"Maybe we can get a drink when this is over. You know, to celebrate my victory," he says, grinning.

I let out a laugh. "Maybe."

***

Before leaving Zach's building, I take a detour to the ladies' room. In there, my phone starts ringing. I don't recognize the number and consider letting it go to answer phone. On the off chance that it's important, I answer the call.

"Hello? Is this Donna Palmer?" the female voice says. She speaks in an Eastern European accent, and I realise who she is.

"Yes. Is this Ksenia?"

I can't believe I forgot she said she'd call.

"Yes, you remember my name," she says.

"I do. Thank you for calling me."

I hate phone calls. I never know what to say. I especially hate work-related phone calls. Do you engage in small talk? Ask about their family? Jump right into the reason for the call?

Thankfully, she cuts to the chase. "I cannot meet you today, but I can meet you tomorrow if you like."

"Absolutely. Where and when?"

She gives me an address and says she'll be available anytime from ten in the morning. Over the phone she sounds calm, which makes a change from when I met her earlier in the day. Perhaps hers is a stressful work environment. I know all about that. She hangs up and I put the phone in my bag before washing my hands. As I dry them, a vibration from my handbag draws my attention. I see that the phone is ringing again.

I hurriedly wipe my hands and look at the phone. It's Kat. When I take the call, she's practically gasping for breath.

"Kat, are you ok?" I ask. She sounds panicked.

"You need to get to Haywood's office right now," she says. From the sound of her breathing, I can tell that she's smoking.

"What's wrong? What's happened?" I ask.

I feel a knot form in my stomach. Sometimes I wish that knot would disappear forever. It's like there are ribbons in there and they take every opportunity to tie themselves into a bow.

"Reporters are camped outside his building. I don't know how, but they've got wind of the accusations and he can't leave quietly. The boys and I are on our way there, but the partners want you front and centre," she says in a rush.

"Front and centre of what?"

"Of his legal team! What else?! Just get there ASAP."

She hangs up, denying me a chance to fully understand what I'm getting myself into. The knot in my belly tightens and for the first time in a long time, I wish it was around my neck instead. I can't think like that. I have to think about my career, my future. I have to think of Ivy. I need to focus on the goal.

I leave the restroom and then leave the building. In the cold light of day, I have an eerie feeling that my life is about to change forever, though I cannot determine whether for better or worse.

XVIII

IVY

As usual, I get home much earlier than Donna. Mum and Mina seem to be having a whale of a time playing scrabble. They invite me to join them, but I decline. I've been working with noisy children and though I love it, I need to rest. I go to my room and collapse on the bed. I pray, thanking God for keeping me safe throughout the day. A million terrible things could have happened to me, but He protected me from them.

I want to take a nap since mum and Mina are getting along, and I don't need to be a buffer between them. I could sleep for an hour, or I could surf the web and find something for us to do tomorrow. With Mina's arrival, I haven't yet organised a weekend activity for me and mum, and Donna if she's not working. Mum doesn't like being at home on Saturdays. Dad didn't particularly like us leaving the house on weekends and now he's gone, I guess she's making up for lost time by visiting interesting places.

Donna has no desire to spend her free time near mum, so it's usually just the two of us. I imagine that Mina will be happy to tag along. I'll look for something that we can all enjoy.

I move onto my side and grab my phone from the bedside table. After searching the web for things to do on the weekend, I come across an affordable exhibition of the creations of Karl Lagerfeld. I remember that Mina used to love fashion and photography when we were younger. Maybe this is something she'd like.

I jump off the bed and go to the living room where I hear mum shout, "That's a good word!"

"What word?" I ask.

"Saturnine," Mina says, smiling.

"I've never heard it before. What does it mean?"

"Glum, grumpy, moody," Mina says.

I nod. "Mina, do you have any plans tomorrow?"

"No, not yet."

"There's a fashion exhibition at the Design Museum. I thought we could all go."

"That sounds lovely," mum says, reaching for the remote control.

Mina nods. "Yeah, sure."

She looks down at the board as her smile gradually fades.

"How much are the tickets?" she asks, looking up at me.

"Doesn't matter, it's on me," I say.

"You don't have—"

"I know. I want to."

She smiles. "Thank you."

"Great, I'll book them right away."

I turn to go back to my room as the TV comes on. I'm almost at my door when mum calls out to me. "Ivy, your sister is on T.V!"

I rush back to the living room and peer at the television. It is in fact Donna, walking with a colleague of hers (I think he's Daryl, the one she says slept his way to a promotion) and another man, maybe in his fifties, who looks vaguely familiar. He's got on a very nice suit, probably Gucci. The shaky camera follows them as a voice yells out, "Is it true that you've been charged with sexual assault?"

"No comment," Daryl says.

"We have it on good authority that this is the fourth time you've been accused of a sexual offence. What do you say to that, Mr. Haywood?"

"My client has nothing to say. The veracity of these allegations will be decided in the court of law, not the court of public opinion," Donna says.

"Is it true that the accuser is underage?"

"There is no truth to that statement," Donna says. "Please stop harassing our client."

They pick up the pace and she and the two men enter a car and are driven away. The feed cuts to the newsroom where the newsreader tells us that the millionaire businessman, Jeremy Haywood, has been accused of and charged with sexual assault, among other things. I thought he looked familiar. Loads of girls at uni used to wear clothes from his shop. My legs start to wobble and I have to sit down.

Donna literally killed someone because he tried to rape her friend, and now she's defending someone who's been accused of a similar crime? I can't believe she signed up to be a lawyer. I wonder how long she's been on the case, but I'm distracted by a strange noise. I look up and realise that Mina is hyperventilating.

"Are you ok?" mum asks.

Mina starts shaking. I move closer to her and put my hand on her shoulder.

"Mina, what's wrong?"

She hugs her knees into her body and wraps her arms around them, crying loudly. I know that she's sensitive because of what happened at the shop, but I would never have expected such a strong reaction. I reach for a box of tissues and sit next to her.

"Mina, are you ok?"

She says nothing, simply cries. I wrap my arms around her, and then mum wraps her arms around us and we stay there as the crying continues.

XIX

DONNA

By the time I get home, the news story has aired. Mine is now the face of Jeremy Haywood's legal defence team. Were there ever a day I was glad to be smartly dressed, today was it. The media, vulture-like as is their way, did their best to intimidate me, but I refused to be intimidated. A bunch of clowns with cameras, looking for gossip to make themselves feel better about their miserable lives – that's what reporters are, for the most part. In this situation however, I can forgive their interest. A crime has 'allegedly' been committed, after all.

I'm still not sure how anyone got wind of the accusations against Mr. Haywood, but I suspect that his wife is behind the leak. It could be that a loose-lipped police officer spilled the beans. There's also a chance that Daryl leaked the information, in an attempt to undermine me. I think it's most likely my first thought, though. The woman is going to destroy him anyway she can.

I had hoped to tell Ivy – and to a lesser degree, mum and Mina – about my part in Mr. Haywood's case, but I was too late. They'd already watched the news. I enter the flat quietly because it's late, but everyone is still up. No rushing to bed on a Friday night. The first thing I hear walking through the door is Mina and

152

Ivy talking.

Ivy sighs. "I'm sure she had no choice; it's her job."

"It's just not like her," Mina says.

I surmise that they're talking about me. Once I get within view, they go quiet. I try to smile but only half of my face moves. Mina stares at me as Ivy gets up to greet me. Mum smiles sheepishly. Ivy hugs me cautiously and then steps back. She looks tense, with her shoulders slightly lifted. I nod at mum and Mina and say hello.

"Hey, how was work?" Ivy says.

I shrug. "Did you see the news report?"

I know the answer, but I've never let that stop me from asking a question. Ivy's eyes quickly dart from me to mum and Mina.

She looks down and then back at me. "Uhhhh, yes, we did. It was interesting. You came across very well, very professional."

It never ceases to amaze me how much she tries to find the good in every situation. She smiles and I follow her into the living room, where she plops down on the sofa, sitting upright. Mum and Mina say nothing.

"I have to admit, I was surprised to hear you were involved in this. You didn't mention anything about it," she continues.

"It was all a bit sudden. I would have told you yesterday, but… it slipped my mind," I say, looking at Mina. That's pretty much true.

"So you defend rapists now?" Mina says. The terse tone with which she speaks is doing her no favours. And by the way, is she serious? I come home from a long day at work and the first words out of her mouth are an accusation.

"He's an *alleged* rapist. Innocent until proven guilty," I say, echoing Kat, and the law.

"There was a time when you wouldn't have gone near someone like him, even if he's only allegedly a rapist," she says. Her voice is thick, like she's trying to stop herself from crying. She sounds hurt and offended, as though I've personally done her harm. I understand. Really, I do. That doesn't stop my patience from slowly waning.

"Well, that was before I had bills to pay," I say sarcastically.

"That's your excuse? You've got bills to pay, so you're going to defend someone like that? Have him out on the streets ready to hurt more people," she says, close to tears.

"It's my job, I have to do it. Responsible adults sometimes have to do things they don't like, in order to survive. If you'd ever spent enough time away from jail to have responsibilities in your life, you'd know that. You'd understand that I'm doing what I have to do."

Her jaw drops and she looks stunned, as if I pulled my observation out of thin air. Naturally, Ivy stands up and steps in.

"Ladies, it's ok," she says.

"Go on, Donna, tell us what you really think," Mina says.

"Mina, please—"

"Don't hold back," she cuts Ivy off.

"Jeremy Haywood's case has nothing to do with you, Mina. Not everything in the world revolves around you and your— your pain. At some point, you're going to have to accept that and get over what happened to you," I say. I don't know if I genuinely believe that, but I've said it now and there's no going back.

"Donna, please—"

"I should get over what happened to me?" she says, sounding shocked. "You say that like I haven't already tried."

The tears start to fall.

"You call snorting and smoking everything in sight *trying*? It's not; you need to try – actually try – harder. Look, I know what you went through—"

"You don't know what I went through. You don't know what it was like. You have no idea how horrific it was for me," she yells at me.

Ivy steps back and sits down again, seemingly defeated. I'm startled by how loud Mina's voice is. It reminds me of William. Still, I maintain composure.

"Maybe so, but I did everything I could to help you. I did so much more for you than you will ever fully understand. You're welcome to hold yourself back over something that happened a decade ago, but I won't let you hold me back. I was given the case and winning it will further my career. If you don't like it: tough. Your opinion on the matter is irrelevant anyway."

Sobbing, she turns to Ivy and mum. "Thank you for letting me stay here. It's been nice spending time with you, but I think I should go."

Mum, who until now has said nothing (because that's what she's like) stands up. "No, darling, you don't have to leave."

She holds onto Mina's shoulders and hugs her.

"I know you're upset, but it's too late for you to be out on the streets," Ivy adds in soft tone.

"I've lived on the streets, remember? You know, when I'm not in jail," Mina says, wiping tears from her eyes.

"Honey, we don't want you to leave—"

"I want to leave," she says, interrupting mum's plea.

"Ok. That's fine. Just, please stay here tonight and you can leave tomorrow," mum says.

My heart sinks as I watch Mina wipe more tears away. I can't remember the last time I felt so bad. She keeps crying as Ivy leads her to her room. Tears make their way to my eyes, but I will them to retreat. I hold my breath until I feel steady in myself.

I want to apologize, but I don't know how to. I'm not even sure I should. She attacked me for doing my job. And without knowing all the facts, she's wrong to jump to conclusions about Haywood's guilt. It's wrong of her to make that call without having more information. Unlike me, she hasn't looked him in the eye and seen him for what he is. She hasn't read Aisha's statement. She hasn't heard his worthless, poorly-thought-out alibi.

It would be easy to say she's getting herself worked up over nothing, if I didn't know what I know about her. I wonder if mum and Ivy have figured out that Alan assaulted Mina, or if they still think we're just talking about his thwarted attempt. Either way, I didn't deserve to be in the receiving end of such aggression. Not after what I've done for her. Not after what I've done for all of them.

Mum stares at me silently.

"Is there something you want to say, mum?" I ask, as if it matters.

She shakes her head. "You don't have to be so cruel to her."

"If you wanted a kinder child, you should have married a kinder man," I say. That was unnecessary, but all I see when I look at her is a woman who was too weak or stupid or self-hating to choose a husband wisely. And I resent her for it. I *greatly* resent her for it. Half of the suffering I've endured in my short life has been her fault, at least in part.

She looks away from me and frowns. "Even after all this time, you can't forgive your father for his mistakes."

I have nothing to add. I glare and walk past her to get to my room, but stop when she speaks again.

"Mina has suffered enough. She needs help not criticism."

I want to say something, but the words escape me. I look at her and nod, then go to my room.

XX

IVY

After seeing Donna on T.V, Mina eventually stopped crying and then fell asleep in my room. She didn't speak, didn't say why the news upset her so much, but I know that Alan Ellis's attempt to rape her is something that still haunts her. It must – why else would she take drugs and cut herself? Mum and I made dinner, after which I woke Mina up.

We had a quiet meal and cleaned up, leaving Donna's portion of food in the fridge. I had considered calling her to ask what was going on, and to tell her about Mina's reaction to seeing her on the news, but I decided against it for no particular reason. I... wasn't sure it would accomplish anything.

I didn't get to take a nap, and I'm tired. I want to go to bed but I also want to be here when Donna comes home. Mum, Mina and I sit around the living room, talking about Donna's involvement in the case. The clip has played on the news every half hour since we first saw it, and I think I know it by heart now. Whoever invented the 24-hour news cycle has a lot to answer for.

"I can't believe she'd do something like this," Mina insists. She's wearing a mustard jumper that I lent her; it really complements her skin tone. I was going to give it away because I hadn't worn it for over a year. I had it bagged up with a bunch of other clothes, ready to make my donation. Mina didn't bring many things with her, so I gave her the bag of clothes, even if some of them are too big for her. She's not sure she'll keep any, but she's happy to wear them while she's here.

"She's not in charge of the firm, she doesn't get to cherry-pick her cases," I say. Mum nods. "She's not at that level yet."

Mina shakes her head. "It makes no sense." She bites her lower lip, looking morose.

"I'm sure she had no choice; it's her job," I say

"It's just not like her," Mina says.

I know that it's hard for her to accept, but I don't know why she seems so shocked that Donna is doing the job she was given. From the corner of my eye, I see Donna standing on the periphery. It seems that mum and Mina see her at the same time. We stop talking. I didn't hear her come in. I wonder how much she heard. I leap up and say hi to her, giving her a hug. She says hello to us, and I ask her how work was. She shrugs – her favourite move.

"Did you see the news report?" she asks. I guess she heard our discussion. I'm not certain, though. I think about what to say, whether to tell her that we not only saw it, but that it reduced Mina to tears. That would be a silly thing to do.

"Yes, we did. It was interesting. You came across very well, very professional."

I sound like an idiot, but I don't want to tread on any toes. Despite the anniversary and Mina's surprise stay, things have been calm this week. By that I mean Donna has been calm this week. I don't want to mess that up. And yet, after I sit down I can't help but say, "I have to admit, I was surprised to hear you were involved in this. You didn't mention anything about it."

She tells us that it was sudden, she meant to tell us yesterday but didn't get around to it. I suppose that would be because she was taken aback by Mina's visit. In short, that's my fault. I want to say something, but Mina jumps in.

"So you defend rapists now?"

Woah, steady on, girl!

"He's an alleged rapist. Innocent until proven guilty," Donna says. That's such a lawyer-y thing to say.

"There was a time when you wouldn't have gone near someone like him, even if he's only allegedly a rapist."

If I didn't know better, I'd say that Mina felt betrayed. I look at her, trying to think of something to say to diffuse the situation but I don't think fast enough.

"Well, that was before I had bills to pay," Donna says in a withering tone.

Oh no, this can only get worse.

"That's your excuse? You've got bills to pay, so you're going to defend someone like that? Have him out on the streets ready to hurt more people?"

I need to intervene, get them to relax but they're moving too fast.

"It's my job, I have to do it. Responsible adults sometimes have to do things they don't like, in order to survive. If you'd ever spent enough time away from jail to have responsibilities in your life, you'd know that. You'd understand that I'm doing what I have to do!"

That's a low blow.

Oh Lord, help!

I stand up.

"Ladies," I say, freaking out internally, "it's ok."

"Go on, Donna, tell us what you really think," Mina says.

This whole time mum has said nothing. She's just sat there, watching the whole thing erupt. I guess that's who she is through and through.

I try to reason. "Mina, please—"

"Don't hold back," Mina says.

Once I hear those words, I know that it's over. Donna is the worst person anyone can say something like that to. The absolute worst.

"Jeremy Haywood's case has nothing to do with you, Mina. Not everything in the world revolves around you and your pain. At some point, you're going to have to accept that and get over what happened to you."

I try again. "Donna, please—"

"I should get over what happened to me? You say that like I haven't already tried!"

I fail again. Mina starts to cry. There has to be something I can do or say. I look at Donna, trying to catch her eye, get her to back down, but she ploughs forward.

"You call snorting and smoking everything in sight trying? It's not; you need to try harder," she says, raising her voice a little. "Look, I know what you went through—"

"You don't know what I went through. You don't know what it was like. You have no idea how horrific it was for me," Mina yells. The tears come in thick and fast and I give up.

I step away from them and sit down. I'm tired. I've been tired for hours and now I just want to block everything out. I want to disappear.

"Maybe so," Donna says, "but I did everything I could to help you. I did so much more for you than you will ever fully understand. You're welcome to hold yourself back over something that happened a decade ago, but I won't let you hold me back. I was given the case and winning it will further my career. If you don't like it: tough. Your opinion on the matter is irrelevant anyway."

Oh, that was so cold. I wish I hadn't been here to witness this. Things like this are better heard about. Only after Mina announces that she's leaving does mum finally speak, telling her to stay the night because it's too late to be out.

"I've lived on the streets, remember? You know, when I'm not in jail," Mina says.

It upsets me to hear her say that... I just want to hug her. Despite mum's pleas, she insists on leaving. Mum tells her to at least stay the night. She agrees to that, crying profusely. I put my arms around her and lead her to my room. It's a bad idea to leave mum and Donna together without supervision, but I can't be in two places at once.

In my room, Mina's tears flow quicker than she can wipe them away.

"You know she doesn't mean any of those things, Mina. She's under a lot of stress. She's really, really stressed."

She shakes her head, wiping the tears from her cheeks.

"Please stop crying."

She doesn't.

"Mina, please, I don't want to see you—"

"Why do you care? I'm just a charity case to you, aren't I?"

I step back, stunned by the sudden and unwarranted accusation.

"No, you're not. How can you say that?"

"Why else would you help me? You think I'm some washed up druggie who you can take in for brownie points from Jesus. That I'm hopeless and tragic and pathetic, don't you?"

Hurt by her words, I feel my throat muscles tighten. Still, I speak to her the way I would want someone to speak to me. I owe her that much.

"I don't think any of those things, Mina. I think… I think that you've done bad things to yourself and other people, but that doesn't have to define you. You took a wrong turn somewhere, drove into a dead end – you don't have to stay there. You're still alive. You can make changes," I say, shrugging.

She wails some more, putting her face in her hands. "I don't know if I can."

"I do," I say, holding her by both shoulders. "I know you can change. It won't be easy, but nothing worth doing ever is. Except breathing… for most people."

She takes her hands away from her face and looks at me, still sobbing. Her eyes are so red that she may as well be crying blood.

"How can you be so calm with everything that's going on? How can you be so nice to me?"

I shrug again. "Trust me, I've seen worse."

Her face crumbles and tears slip down her cheeks.

I take my hands off her and she wipes her eyes.

"I don't know what to do with my life. All I've ever done is steal things and sell drugs," she says in a sober manner, sniffing.

"It's not all you've ever done – you just don't remember what your life was like before this. Don't let that stop you from doing something good. That dude from Catch Me If You Can was a con artist and a thief, and then he became a consultant for the FBI. Where there's a will, there's a way."

She exhales and rubs her forehead. "DiCaprio was so pretty in that film."

"Wasn't he?"

She laughs a little. Thank God for that.

"You can sleep in my room tonight. I'll take the sofa."

"You don't have to do that."

"I know, but I will."

She smiles and sniffs. "Thank you."

***

I leave Mina lying down in my room and take my beddings to the living room. Mum has abandoned the place and Donna isn't here either. I drop the beddings on the sofa and go to Donna's room, knocking on the door. She opens it quickly and without saying hello, I ask if we can talk. She doesn't respond, probably because she knows the question was rhetorical. I walk in and sit on the floor, leaning against the door. She sits next to me, leaving space between us. There's always space between us.

"Donna, you know I love you, right?"

"I know," she says nodding.

"Ok. You know that I'm with you all the way. I have your back."

I grab her hand and squeeze it hard.

"What are you getting at?"

I've been thinking about this for a while – a few years, actually – but I've never said it because I know it'll upset her. But after what happened tonight, I think it needs to be said. I hesitate, and then sigh, finally letting it out.

"Sometimes, you're more like dad than I think you mean to be."

I pause, holding my breath. She snatches her hand away from mine. Was that the right thing to say? Should I have worded it differently?

"I know you're in a difficult position, but Mina didn't deserve that."

She asks me if she deserves to be insulted in her own home, as if she is the only person under this roof who mattered.

"No, you don't, but—"

"Please, if you're going to talk about second chances, spare me. I've given her

162

too many second chances. Like when I let her drug-addled self stay with me and she robbed my housemates. Yulia never forgave me for that, not that I blame her."

"Yeah, and you called the police and had her sent to jail. Doesn't that comfort you?"

"Why would it, Ivy? Why would it comfort me?"

I throw my hands up, exasperated with the whole situation. That was a senseless thing to say – there's no way she'd be happy to send her friend to prison. Oh, I hate when I make things worse. But I have to do something.

Lord help!

"I know she's hurt you, Donna, but we've all made mistakes. If you could give her another chance—"

She leans away from me with her eyes wide. "What do you think this is? She is here, staying in my home rent-free, for an unspecified amount of time. I think that counts as another chance."

She's right. I'm being short-sighted and insensitive. I know deep down that Donna cares about Mina and what happens to her. I guess she hasn't fully dealt with all the past... disappointments that Mina has visited on her. I see how that could lead to frustration.

"Does she even have a plan to get on her feet, or is she just going to spend the rest of her life railing against those of us who are doing our best to make a decent living?"

I tell her that Mina is looking for a job, but it's hard for her. I tell her that Mina has agreed to attend the church's job clinic. I ignore her cruel jab in which she refers to Mina as a criminal. I mean, it's technically true but it doesn't need to be stated.

To this revelation, she does not respond. We sit quietly next to each other, each with her thoughts. I replay the bust-up in my mind, each time pausing when Donna said that Mina didn't fully understand what she'd done for her. She said it with such ardour. What does that even mean? I know she stopped Alan from violating Mina, but... that's easy to grasp.

"What did you mean when you said you'd done more for Mina than she could fully understand?" I ask.

Maybe it's a dumb question, or maybe it isn't.

She hesitates, and then says, "I saved her when Alan tried to attack her."

"I know you did. But she knows that too. Why would you say she couldn't understand that?"

I'm facing her now.

"I guess I was being dramatic in the heat of the moment. It's a figure of speech."

She smiles and pats my hand.

I lean against the door again, wondering whether it's worth my while to say anything else. Should I invite her to the museum tomorrow? Maybe not after what just happened.

"I'm sorry I lost my temper tonight… I don't want to be like dad," she says, looking sober.

Her voice gets quieter as she gets to the last word, like the significance of the comparison weighs on her.

"Then don't be. You don't have to poison everything you touch," I say.

It's that simple. I get up to leave.

"Is she still into photography?" Donna asks.

"Who? Mina?"

She nods and I tell her I think she is, though I'm not sure.

"Why do you ask?"

"It might help her find work. You never know," she says.

"So you do care."

Of course she does. She says nothing and watches me smile as I leave her bedroom. I don't know if I achieved anything by talking to her tonight, but I live in hope. And I hope that the sofa doesn't prevent me from getting a good night's sleep.

XXI

DONNA

Once in my room, I go through my leg-lifting routine. As is my way, I go over the events of the day in my mind, trying to find useful connections between them and work out if any information might help me achieve my goals. I put the argument with Mina out of my mind and focus my thoughts on the Haywood situation.

Ksenia and I will be meeting tomorrow. I have a feeling that she'll be useful to me. I resist accomplices, but I might be forced to make an exception in this case. Daryl's hostility subsided once I flirted with him. It's off-putting but I'll have to keep that as an option, if only to make things easier for myself.

Kat is doing her job as well as she can. She always does. Zach is… as determined as he ever was. He'll do everything in his power to ensure that Haywood sees the inside of a prison. If I can find a way to secretly feed him damning information about Haywood, without knowing it he may be the best accomplice yet.

In spite of myself, thinking about Zach makes me smile. I think about the warm hug he gave me earlier, about his smile, about his grit. My lips part gently as I exhale. I close my eyes, picturing his face. It's not wise to think about him this way.

A knock on my bedroom door interrupts my reflections. I swing my legs down and get on my feet. I open the door, see Ivy on the other side.

"Can we talk?" she says.

I don't want to talk, particularly because I'm sure I know what she wants to talk about. I let her in anyway. When I close the door, she sits on the floor with her back to it. I follow suit, sitting next to her.

"Donna, you know I love you, right?" she says.

This can't be good.

I nod. "I know."

"Ok. You know that I'm with you all the way. I have your back," she says, grabbing my hand and squeezing it.

"What are you getting at?" I hate it when people mince their words. Patience is a virtue, but it isn't one of mine – not when listening to people waffle.

She hesitates, sighing. After a beat, she shifts to face me and looks directly at me. "Sometimes, you're more like dad than I think you mean to be."

I withdraw my hand from hers. She may be right but it's not something I want to hear.

"I know you're in a difficult position, but Mina didn't deserve that."

"And I deserve to be insulted in my own home; by a guest I didn't invite, no less?" I say, doing my best not to raise my voice.

"No, you don't, but—"

"Please, if you're going to talk about second chances, spare me. I've given her so many second chances. Like when I let her drug-addled self stay with me and she robbed my housemates. Yulia never forgave me for that, not that I blame her."

"Yeah, and you called the police and had her sent to jail. Doesn't that comfort you?" she asks.

"Why would it, Ivy? Why would it comfort me?"

She throws her hands up lets out a sigh. "I know she's hurt you, Donna, but we've all made mistakes. If you could give her another chance—"

I can't believe this!

"What do you think this is? She is here, staying in my home rent-free, for an unspecified amount of time. I think that counts as another chance."

Ivy looks at her hands, pursing her lips.

"Does she even have a plan to get on her feet, or is she just going to spend the rest of her life railing against those of us who are doing our best to make a decent living?" I ask.

Ivy shakes her head. "She's looking for a job, but it's hard for people in… in her position."

"Criminals?"

That was malicious.

I shouldn't have said that.

Ivy ignores my comment and continues.

"On Monday, I'm taking her to the job clinic. Hopefully the crew will be able to help her."

She turns away from me, resting her back against the door again. We sit quietly for a few minutes.

I wonder what she's thinking, whether my outburst reminded her of a specific incident with William or just gave her a general sense of unease. It hurts me to think that I'm like him, but if I'm like him, it's because of him. I'll never understand how it is that Ivy turned out so well-adjusted after growing up in that environment. If I asked her, she'd probably say something about Jesus or the Holy Spirit. I roll my eyes just thinking about that. She's so into that Bible stuff, I'm surprised she hasn't gone off to live in a convent. Maybe *devout* is the word I'm looking for.

"What did you mean when you said you'd done more for Mina than she could fully understand?" she asks.

There have been times in my life when I've wanted to tell someone about Alan, about William, about Beth. Fleeting moments, usually few and far between. They were more frequent when I was friends with Zach. He always seemed so caring and trustworthy that I felt like I could tell him anything. I let those moments go by because I'm too smart to confide in anyone.

Ivy already knows I killed Alan – everyone does. I don't know why she'd ask such an obvious question. Killing Alan is my legacy. When I got back to school the week after I shot him, I had achieved celebrity status. Who knew murder was all it took? Beth and her mindless cronies reviled and bullied me. That lasted until I ended her useless life, too.

A few students, mostly girls he'd attacked (confirming that Mina wasn't the first) and friends of theirs covertly thanked me for being brave enough to defend myself and my friend. The teachers let me know that they knew people whom I could talk to, if I so desired. Most students avoided me or never openly spoke about what I'd done. But that one act made me infamous.

Suzanne Zhou in particular shamelessly declared me a hero among young women. We'd always been friendly but after Alan died, she and I grew closer. It was like she saw me in a new light, and I'd gained her respect. We drifted apart when we started our careers, but I know she works in a private investigation firm now.

"I saved her when Alan tried to attack her."

"I know you did. But she knows that too. Why would you say she couldn't understand that?" she asks, facing me now. I realize that either my choice of words or my tone of voice provoked her interest.

"I guess I was being dramatic in the heat of the moment," I say, half-smiling. I pat her hand and continue, "It's a figure of speech."

She nods and leans back.

"I'm sorry I lost my temper tonight," I say, "I don't want to be like dad."

"Then don't be. You don't have to poison everything you touch," she says in a manner that is uncharacteristically blunt.

She stands up.

"Is she still into photography?" I ask before she leaves.

"Who? Mina?"

I nod.

"I think so but I'm not sure. Why do you ask?"

"It might help her find work. You never know."

"So you do care." She smiles warmly at me and the room.

I think I've eased her mind for now. She's certainly helped me more than I could have hoped. Because of her, I've come to see that I have an untapped resource in the fight against Jeremy Haywood.

And if all goes to plan, Mina could be useful to me as well.

XXII

MINA

In Ivy's room, I try to fall asleep but can't. My mind is too busy to shut down. Seeing Donna on the news was like a hard punch to the gut. I never thought I'd see the day when she'd defend someone accused of rape. She's never ever been the sort of person to excuse abusive or misogynistic behaviour, and to think that she would do that for money hurts so much… it feels like treachery even if she's only doing what she's paid to do.

I take a deep breath, inhaling the smell of Ivy's sheets. They smell of jasmine and rose, I think. Everything about her is beautifully fragranced. Her bed is sturdy and comfortable, with four pillows. The room is full of pictures – on the bedside table, stuck to the walls, on the dressing table mirror – mostly of her and Donna, but also of people I assume she counts as friends. The bedside table is decorated with seashells.

I flip onto my back, looking at the ceiling. An image of Alan sitting on top of me forces its way into my mind. I turn back onto my side, hoping it goes away. It does for now. I agreed to leave tomorrow, but now I'm regretting that I ever offered to leave at all. That was such a stupid thing to say. I was so angry that I forgot how nice it is to have somewhere safe to sleep. I shouldn't be so desperate to sleep indoors that I accept abuse, but sadly I am.

Is it fair to call it abuse? Donna said unkind things to me but now that I'm thinking more clearly, I can see how I came across as rude and ungrateful. That was wrong of me but her spiteful reaction tells me that we're not out of the woods yet. I thought that because she let me stay here, she'd forgiven me. Perhaps I was wrong.

She's always been very good at holding grudges. I reckon that had Alan not turned his hand to armed robbery, Donna would have found a way to cause him serious harm. I think she was thrilled to find that he was the one wearing the mask. Days before the incident, we walked past him in the corridor at school. He smiled at her and she visibly tensed up. Her fists were in balls and when she released them, her palms were bleeding.

"He should be behind bars," she said.

I knew that she was trying to get me to tell the police, but I ignored her. After she killed him, I regretted that. Had I gone to the police she wouldn't have had to get blood on her hands. He would have been under investigation and unable to rob anyone.

The investigation would probably have revealed that I was not his first victim. No, not even close. The link that Suzanne gave me showed that he had raped at least four other girls, and tried to rape two more. The ones that got away only did so because people heard them scream for help. He fled before anyone but the victim could recognise him. It seems that after those failed attempts, he adapted his methods and started committing his crimes at parties where the music was too loud for anyone to hear their own thoughts. Why he decided to add robbery to his repertoire is still a mystery.

Some months after he died, I started cutting myself. I didn't know what else to do. With him gone, I had no closure and I never would. Donna had suddenly become unreachable. I noticed the changes after she killed him, but they escalated after her dad died. She withdrew almost completely. It was like the girl I'd known my whole life had died as well. I had no one to talk to. I mean, even if she wasn't dealing with her own drama, I'm not sure she would have been much help. But not having the option of talking to her made things worse.

The cutting is now more sporadic than the drug use. The last time I took a razor to my arm was two months ago, and that was because I had to do something to ease the desperate cravings I was having for cocaine. The relief was immediate; the regret took a little longer to show up. I haven't felt the overwhelming urge to hurt myself since then.

After the first few months, the cutting wasn't cutting it in terms of relief. I needed something stronger. That was when Beth's boyfriend, Michael, offered me some weed because, as usual, I was at the wrong place at the wrong time. It helped for a while, and then it didn't. I needed something stronger. Michael introduced me to Martin who introduced me to cocaine. And cocaine has been with me ever since.

I've begged, borrowed and stolen to keep it in my life even though I know it'll kill me eventually. I've even introduced others to it, for a small fee. Just thinking about it makes me want some. I need to stop. Replace each bad thought with a good one, Salome says. She always advises me to think about something I'm grateful for. Well, I'm grateful for a comfortable bed and a warm house to sleep in.

Tomorrow, I'll go to the museum with Ivy and Mama Selene. When we get back, I'll pack my things and leave. I've made my metaphorical bed, it's only right that I lie in it.

Meanwhile, I feel myself drifting off to sleep.

XXIII

NOVEMBER 23ᴿᴰ, 2019

DONNA

I don't like working on Saturdays. Most times I have no say in the matter. At least today, it's my choice. Ksenia and I are set to meet at a coffee shop in East London. I searched the internet for information about her, and found nothing. She appears to have no social media accounts. She's either very smart, or she's a criminal. She could also be on the run or an illegal immigrant. None of that concerns me. I hope she has good information about the Haywoods.

The coffee shop is an independent one, not the sort that has a branch at every exit of every major train station in every town across the globe. When I arrive there, I expect to find Ksenia sitting around waiting for me. I'm surprised to see her working behind the counter.

I walk to the counter and say hello to her. She smiles confidently and asks if I want to order something before we talk. I don't, but in order to make her feel comfortable I request a blackcurrant tea.

She prepares the tea in a take-away cup and tells her colleague to cover for her. She leads me to a table in a corner of the shop, and sets the tea on it.

"Thank you for agreeing to meet me," I say, smiling.

"No problem," she says. She seems much more relaxed than she did yesterday. One might even say she had swag.

I uncap the cup in the hopes that the tea will cool a bit faster.

"You work two jobs."

She nods. "I am here every Saturday."

"What's your arrangement with the Haywoods?"

"I live with them during the week, but most weekends I stay with a friend. He runs this shop and I'm helping him with it. It's nice to get away from that place sometimes."

I nod, noting that she called the house *that place*.

"And Irene?"

"She lives there with her son, Emilio. She's been with them for… ever since they got married, I think. I don't remember." She shrugs.

I take a sip of the tea. It's still hotter than I'd like it to be, so I fan it.

"So… what do you want to ask me?" she asks, speaking slowly and looking carefully around the shop. She suddenly seems uneasy.

"I wanted to know if you were in the house on Wednesday night, and if you saw anything."

She shifts in her seat and looks away from me.

"It doesn't matter what you tell me, I won't tell Mr. or Mrs. Haywood. I just need to know what you saw, or if you heard anything interesting or… unusual," I say, hoping that she hasn't got cold feet.

She wiggles her jaw left and right, exhaling.

"I've been working there for about 3 years. Mrs. Haywood drinks a lot. Too much, really. That night, she went to bed close to 8 o' clock. I helped Noah with his Maths homework. He had been playing sports all afternoon. He really wanted to get the assignment done even though it wasn't due for a week. He said he didn't want it hanging over his head."

I can tell she's fond of Noah. Her eyes light up as if she was talking about her son or brother. Maybe he's the reason she still works there.

"Is that normal?" I ask.

"Is what normal?"

"You helping him with his homework."

She nods and smiles. "He was almost nine when I first started there. Mrs. Haywood had been struggling for some time and Mr. Haywood isn't always around, so I help the boys with things like that. Noah asks for help more than Jerry does, I think because he's younger."

"What happened next?" I take another sip of the tea. It's a good temperature now. I start drinking.

"We finished homework around 9.30, I think. I left him in the upstairs living room. He said he would go to sleep. I went to the kitchen, to make sure everything was in order. There were a few clothes to wash, so I took them to the laundry room, which is further in from the kitchen," she says.

That house is massive. I feel bad for her and Irene. The maintenance must be a pain.

"That's when I heard a girl's voice, when I was in the laundry room. It sounded like it was coming from the kitchen. By the time I got out, no one was there. Then I heard Mr. Haywood talking to her, and then nothing. I came out of the kitchen and they were gone. I went back into the kitchen, made sure I'd done all my work, and then I went to my room. I don't know what happened after that."

I'm halfway through my cup of tea and my brain is working overtime. Haywood said that he ran into Aisha outside the house. Ksenia confirms that they met inside. My gut never lies to me; the man is guilty as sin. I am going to ruin him. He will regret the day he thought it was ok to touch anyone without their permission. I can feel blood rushing to my heart as it beats faster, I can almost hear the flow increase. I put my cup down and gently take a deep breath.

"Did you hear anything else? Did Irene?" I ask, trying to sound calm.

"I didn't. Irene hasn't told me anything if she did."

"Is there anyone else who might have seen something?"

"I don't know. But I know that... Mr. Haywood can be very, eh, well... he likes young women a lot. I've heard him and his wife arguing. She tells me not to look at him," she says.

175

"Has he ever tried anything with you?"

She sits straighter in her seat, and looks around. She shakes her head, lowering her voice. "I've never been alone with him. Irene told me not to."

In the three years she's worked in that house, she's never been alone with him? I don't know if I believe her, but that's her story.

"Do you think he did it?" I ask. I carry on drinking the tea.

She pauses briefly before answering. She looks at my face, as if trying to determine whether or not she can confide her opinion in me. Finally, she says, "I know he did. Like with Ms. Yoshida. They were having an affair and she broke it off. That's when he tried to— to force her."

I lean forward, surprised by her statement. "Did she tell you that?"

I take another sip as she answers. "No, I saw the whole thing."

I almost spit out my tea upon hearing that.

"What?" I ask, "Why didn't you say anything?"

She bats her eyelids and bites her lower lip. "I was afraid. I need that job. Mr. and Mrs. Haywood are terrible people, but I need the money and they pay well… and the boys are kind. I should have said something. I know that."

"Does he know you saw him and Ms. Yoshida?"

"No. I was cleaning Jerry's room and I looked out the window when I heard their voices coming from the garden. I saw them together. It was… horrible," she concludes, shuddering as if the memory sent chills down her spine.

I sit back in disbelief.

"Do you think you can defend him? Do you think he'll go to jail?" she asks, looking at me. Her facial expression is blank, and I can't tell if she hopes for a guilty verdict.

"I have to do my best."

Her face falls. "Will you?"

She doesn't need to know the answer to that question.

***

Suzanne Zhou is the closest thing I've ever had to a kindred spirit. Bold, fearless, unapologetic – she's everything I would want to be if I wasn't me. The main difference between us is that she's not interested in lying to people. She displays her hatred, disdain, irritation, and such like with pride. I keep those things to myself. This could be down to her being higher up on the racial pecking order (her mother is European, her dad is Asian), but I can't afford to have people see me for what I really am. Or maybe I don't want them to. Maybe I get a kick out of fooling them. I'm not sure. I am sure that if people saw my real self, it would most likely hinder my progress in life. I can't have that.

Suzanne's parents moved here from France, and she's fluent in Mandarin, French and English. Once upon a time she thought she'd be a teacher, but she decided she "couldn't deal with those recalcitrant brats." I'm sure you can guess that the *brats* she referenced were the students she would have had to teach.

She has little patience for time-wasters, and all the stories she heard about teaching convinced her that the profession would be the fastest route to misery. She said that she'd found her calling and 'babysitting' wasn't it. Being a detective was. Once she left university, she found work in a small private investigations company. I thought she was crazy at the time, but now I'm grateful to have someone to call on.

I haven't seen her for a couple of years, and she hasn't worked for Sanders Staunton & Co since I've been there, but I hear she's basically in charge of the firm now. She's great at what she does and I know that she'll be willing to help me. It will mean revealing my intentions to her, but I don't think I have other alternatives.

Her office building is so dingy that from the outside, I thought it was abandoned. There are five stories as far as I can tell, and the windows on just about every floor look like they were installed before the First World War. I'm an advocate for saving money, but this is ridiculous. Double-glazing never killed anyone.

Because I'm certain that I have the right address, I ring the intercom bell. There's no answer. It's possible that she doesn't work on Saturdays, or isn't in at the moment. I could have called first, but I don't want any traces of communications with her on my phone. There's no telling what could happen if the phone fell into the wrong hands.

I wait for a few seconds and then ring again. Almost immediately, I hear a buzzing noise, and the door is released. *Someone* is home. The building's internals aren't as worn out as its external, but it's old and smells musty. There is an unpleasant-smelling, aged-looking lift – the sort that one can imagine getting stabbed to death in – but I decide to take the steep, creaky steps all the way to the third floor. That lift looks like a death trap and I could use the exercise.

On the third floor, I see a door with a sign that reads 'Veritas Investigations.' The sign looks like something from a 1950s noir film. Perhaps that's deliberate. I knock on the door and right away, it swings open. I am greeted by Suzanne herself. She looks somewhat dishevelled, wearing a baggy hoodie and track suit bottoms. If I had to guess, I'd say that these were her night clothes and I've woken her up. Her thick, black hair looks messy and tangled. I can hardly believe that she answered the door looking like this, but this is Suzanne – she does whatever she wants and never apologises for it.

She smiles at me as her eyes widen. "Donna? What are you doing here?"

She goes in for a hug. I let her, lightly tapping her shoulder blade when I've had enough. I'm relieved to find that, despite its appearance, her hair smells like it was recently washed.

"I thought I'd see this place for myself. I have to say, it's a dive."

She laughs heartily and steps out of the way. "Come in, come in."

I walk into the office and she shuts the door.

The place doesn't look as neglected or unkempt as the building's exterior – and Suzanne's current appearance – had led me to expect. It's neat and organized. There's a desk with a stack of books on it – all fiction; a door leading to an inner room; and a couple of comfortable-looking chairs opposite the desk. There are even paintings of landscapes hanging on the walls. It's very pleasant.

"Perhaps I was wrong to call this place a dive," I say, turning to her.

"Yes, well, you've always been quick to judge."

She's right about that. On the bright side, my judgments are rarely wrong. This is one of those rare times.

"Do you live here?" I ask.

"On occasion. Can I get you anything to drink?"

"Tea, please."

"No milk, no sugar?"

"Always," I say.

"Constant as the Northern Star," she smiles, going into the inner room.

I follow her to the door and wait there. There's a sofa bed, a kitchenette and further in, a shower room. There's also a tub chair in the corner of the room. The place looks cosy and tidy. It is also very, very cold, which can most likely be blamed on the dreadful windows. She puts the kettle on and turns to face me.

"Why are you really here, Donna?"

"I can't drop by to see a friend?"

I don't know why I'm hesitating.

Actually, I do. What I'm about to do is illegal. As a rule, that doesn't bother me when my motives are sound. But I've never attempted to break a client's confidence before and this could cost me my career. Accomplices are always dangerous to have and I'm putting myself in a very precarious position by being here. I'm scared that I'm making the wrong choice. Sadly, it might be the only choice, or at least the best of some bad options.

"No, you can't. Other people can, but not you. You don't do things for reasons so simple. So what's the deal?" she says.

It's nice that she's so forthright.

"Did you see the news yesterday?"

"You mean did I see *you* on the news yesterday? Why yes, yes, I did," she says, smiling. "You were very... believable. I'd have told everyone I know that I know you, but that case of yours—" she shakes her hand from side to side, as though trying to move a drop of oil all over the back of it, "it's tricky. Can't be alienating my friends now, can I?"

I nod in her direction. The kettle comes to a boil, and she pours the water over the teabag which she'd already placed in the mug. I walk towards her and she hands the mug to me.

"Thanks."

"No problem. Shall I assume that the illustrious Sanders Staunton & Co need my assistance?" she says, propping up the sofa bed.

"Actually, I'm the one who needs your assistance." My voice gets quiet, dropping just above a whisper.

She stops what she's doing and turns to face me.

"Could you speak up? I thought I heard you say you need my assistance," she says. She looks at me sideways and folds her arms.

"You heard right. I need your help with this case."

"I don't understand. If you need my help, that means your firm needs my help."

"I need to prove Haywood is guilty. And for that, I need your help."

"I'm sorry, wouldn't that defeat the object of defending him?" she says, raising an eyebrow.

"I shouldn't be defending him. No one should. He did it. I know he did. If he goes free, he'll do it again. He needs to be punished for his crime," I say.

"Oh, you're serious."

We stay quiet for a little while, while her eyes move 360 degrees around her head. She looks like she's trying to find the right words to say to me. Eventually, she speaks again.

"You realize that I'll need you to tell me everything you know about the case. You'll probably have to break that pesky client-attorney confidentiality clause at some point."

"I know that."

"Are you willing to jeopardise your career to send this guy down?"

"My career is no good to anyone if I can't send this guy down," I say.

"Wow. Well, alrighty then. You're taking a huge risk by doing this. You do understand that, right?"

"I do, I understand perfectly. So are you in?" I ask.

She smiles. "When do we start?"

***

It's early afternoon and the day has been so productive. I told Suzanne everything I know about the case, giving her a copy of Aisha's statement, as well as her and Ksenia's contact details. I even went as far as suggesting that she hire Mina for her photography skills, if necessary. I might not be able to make up for my behaviour last night, but I can try to help her get work. Suzanne already has a photographer that she works with, but agreed to give Mina a chance. Now, all I have to do is tell Mina.

I don't particularly want to go home but I hate being out on Saturdays. It's always so crowded. People go on about how great London is, but those people tend to be tourists. They come here with loads of money to have fun. Anywhere can seem great when you have a lot of money and you're there to have fun, and London is no exception. But the truth is that this city is wretched.

Apart from the centre, which is effectively a giant tourist attraction, it's falling apart. Well, that's not strictly true. There are a number of building projects in the works. However, every 'regeneration' scheme is a thinly veiled attempt to drive poor people out of the city and bring in wealthy 'investors.' New, tiny homes are built and sold at extortionate prices. The homeless are piling up on the streets. Nothing ever changes because people are lousy – greedy, selfish, corrupt, always taking, never giving. I hate this world.

Ivy says that I'm too harsh – humans are born degenerates, says she, and it's only by God's grace that we're not living in a reality akin to Mad Max or The Road. I'm inclined to believe her but I would be. I used to think I was a sceptic, but sceptics are happy to be proven wrong. I'm just happy to believe the worst. There's little else to do. The worst is all around us, and it's all there is. Even babies only care about themselves. Feed me, burp me, clean me, rock me to sleep. People are self-centred from the cradle to the grave. If an asteroid hit this god-forsaken planet and destroyed it entirely, that would be by the grace of God.

A girl walks past me, yelling obnoxiously into her phone. Despite her anti-social speaking volume, the only thing I hear her say is the name *Beth*. Ugh, Beth. I hate that name, thanks to Beth Meyer. What an awful person she was. She did her best to make my life unbearable after I dispatched her miserable boyfriend to the land of the dead. Almost as soon as I got back to school, she cornered me and told me that she knew that I'd lured him to the newsagent because he'd told her about it. Naturally, I denied everything. And when she insisted that I was lying, I asked her why she didn't go to the police, since she was so sure. That shut her up. I still denied it, though. Strongly.

Her inability to report me to the police without implicating herself must have made her feel like it was her duty to punish me. She tried her best to do that. Her bullying would have been painful and upsetting if I hadn't already endured worse at the hands of my so-called father and if I hadn't already decided to kill her as well.

Once again, I did the world a service by removing her from it. Any normal person would have been mortified to find that their boyfriend was a rapist but from all I could surmise, she encouraged him. She, at the very least, did not discourage him. I couldn't believe it when Mina told me how Beth had set her up. I couldn't understand how anyone could bring themselves to do something like that.

Truthfully, I didn't need to understand, all I needed to do was make things right. And I did, but I took my time. Three kills in the same year seemed a bit much to me back then. I feared I would get careless and (worse yet) get caught, so I took a break. But I didn't simply sit around for a year, doing nothing. No, I prepared like I always do.

I had other things to do – adjust to a William-free life, stay on top of my school work, keep out of trouble, attend therapy sessions in the aftermath of Alan's demise, and so on – but that didn't stop me from making plans. And when the moment came, as I had done before, I struck like a rattlesnake. I did not hesitate to put a stop to her pointless life.

It wasn't hard. The wheels in my head started turning the second Mina told me about the drugs in Beth's bathroom. That was all I needed to know. I did my research, found out what herbs I could use to poison her. With cash, I bought a train ticket to Brighton (I could do things like that after William died) and acquired the necessary ingredients.

I stalked her a little, for almost a year – it wasn't an obsessive, daily thing – and found that there was no easy way to access her home unnoticed. I realized the only way I could get into her house was through the front door, so that's what I did. On her 17th birthday, I strode in there (without a personal invitation, I might add) and at some point in the evening, walked right up to her bedroom undetected and spiked her weed with my own brew. It was so easy that it wasn't even exciting. It was more challenging rolling out of bed early on a Sunday morning.

The evening wasn't without incident. When she noticed me at the party, she tried to kick up a fuss but her new boyfriend, Michael, reminded her that she'd called it an open party. Alan's body wasn't cold in the grave when they started dating, not that I cared. He seemed less criminally inclined than his predecessor, which was a step in the right direction. It was, however, too little too late for her. Her fate had already been sealed.

Within a month of her birthday, Beth Meyer got so high that she threw herself out of her bedroom window. She might have survived the fall had she not smashed her head on a marble statue – cracked the thing wide open. I wasn't there and I didn't see any pictures.

The authorities decided that her batch of weed was contaminated, though they couldn't pinpoint how that had happened. They figured the weedman messed up. It's not unheard of. I was in the clear; no one ever suspected my involvement. She became the poster girl for a local anti-drugs campaign – run by her father – that aimed to educate youngsters on the detriments of drug use. She was more useful in death than she was in life.

I had no regrets. It's not my fault she did drugs – a senseless decision by any measure – and I didn't put the marble statue in her parents' garden. I also had no hands in her being an accomplice to sexual assault. That was her choice. She chose her action; I chose her consequence. Sometimes, that's the way life goes.

Anyhow, after that hat-trick, I reckoned it was time to concentrate on making something of my life. I'd been doing well at school and had quite quickly adjusted to life without William. I was still having nightmares about him being alive, and occasionally, in the daytime, I'd have panic attacks because I'd forgotten he was dead. For me, that subsided within the first year.

For Ivy, it took a little longer. But Ivy's never had the same focus and drive that I do. We've always been different – she's gentler, more sensitive. She never lost that, even with all William put us through. Her positive traits leave her at a disadvantage in life.

My phone starts ringing. I get it out of my pocket and see that the call is from Jeremy Haywood. Why is he calling me on a Saturday? I watch as the ringing continues, wondering whether to ignore him. I against that.

"Mr. Haywood?"

"Miss Palmer, thank God you picked up."

He sounds breathless, like he's been running.

"Mr. Haywood, is everything ok?"

"I have to see you," he says in a hurry.

"Has there been a new development with your case, Mr. Haywood?"

"I need you to come to the house right now. Something has happened," he says, and then he hangs up the phone.

I stand on the pavement, confused. I quickly call Kat. There's no way I'm going to a rapist's home on my own. Not in this life. Kat's phone rings until it goes to answer phone. I hastily leave her a message: "*Hi Kat, I know it's a Saturday and you have a life, but I need you to take me to The Haywood Mansion. I should be at your place in 20 minutes. Please call me when you get this.*"

Had I known this would happen, I may have driven to see Ksenia and Suzanne. Oh well. I start towards the tube station, but pause. Should I call Daryl as well? They say keep your enemies closer than your friends... I want to say it couldn't hurt to call him, but that might not be true. And if I call him, will I have to call Shane? I ought to call at least one of them. It's smart to have a man around.

Though there's no guarantee they'll show up, I conclude it would be best to call both Shane and Daryl. As I call Daryl, the thought of having to work on a Saturday threatens to depress me but then I remember that it's part of the job. Also, I get paid double for my effort. I guess it could be worse.

***

On my way to Kat's place, she calls me back.

"What's happening? Why are you going to the mansion?"

"Haywood called me, said I had to come over."

"Where are you now?"

"About 10 minutes away from your place, near that little café you like."

"Ok, stay there and I'll come and pick you up," she says.

With that, she drops the phone. She sounded as perplexed by all this as I am.

I stop outside the café and look at the menu. I've been around here a few times, usually on a weekend when Kat and I have to go somewhere for work. They sell nice cakes and sandwiches, but I'm not hungry. I am a little thirsty. I'll buy one of their hippie juices. Probably something green. Green is good.

I step inside the café and my phone starts ringing. This time it's Daryl.

"Hello Daryl."

"Hey Donna, I got your message. Are you at Haywood's place yet?"

"Not yet. Kat and I will be leaving soon," I say.

"Ok then, I'll meet you at his house."

The call ends there, which is strange. Usually, Daryl would have kept me on the phone for at least five minutes, trying to glean as much information as he could from me. He must be tired.

I order a green juice which claims that it will 'revitalise, rejuvenate and renew' me. Promises, promises. Within 2 minutes of collecting it, Kat pulls up in her car and sounds her horn. I thank the boy who served me and leave the café, jumping into Kat's car.

"No rest for the wicked, right?" she greets me.

"No rest indeed."

***

We arrive at Casa Haywood close to an hour after I spoke to him. Shane isn't coming. He wisely made plans to visit friends in Wales and won't be back till Sunday evening. Lucky git. Daryl arrives mere seconds after we do. He and Kat exchange an awkward greeting. I'm too preoccupied with our reason for being here to roll my eyes at their drama.

We ring the doorbell and Irene lets us in. Her face looks like it's been drained

185

of blood, vampire-style. She avoids eye contact, and ushers us through the entrance hall, stopping near the kitchen.

She points at the staircase leading down, saying with a lilt, "He is waiting for you in the cellar."

"What is—?"

Daryl stops talking when he sees that she's left. She just walked away, into the kitchen, leaving us standing at the top of the stairs. Whatever is going on, it must be serious. I feel my stomach turn. It's not the turning I'm used to. It's deeper than that, the sort of fear that comes on you when you're certain your life is about to end. The sort of fear I haven't felt for years and years. The discomfort is so palpable that I have to put my hand on my belly to soothe it.

We look at one another.

"Ladies first," Daryl says.

I step in front of him, taking slow, careful steps as I descend the staircase. The basement is large and dimly-lit. A room on my left has its door slightly ajar. I walk past it, noting the large, comfortable-looking seats. That must be the cinema room. I keep walking and see another door further down the corridor. I stop abruptly when I realize that Haywood is sitting in the doorway.

His face is in his hands. His hands are stained with blood. My stomach turns again and my throat feels dry. I clear it as best I can before speaking.

"Mr. Haywood?"

He looks up at me. Blood-shot eyes, tear-stained cheeks – a combination that speaks of very bad things.

"What took you so long?" he says. His voice is quiet, low and hoarse.

I look at the cellar door. Kat comes up next to me, and Daryl catches up.

"Mr. Haywood, are you ok? What happened?" Daryl says when he sees him. He kneels next to him, as Kat stands still for a few seconds, taking it all in. Eventually, she rummages through her bag and gets out some tissue paper. I don't know why she's bothered – the blood on his hands is dry. Perhaps it's the thought that counts.

She starts to say something, but I can't hear her. I can't hear anything anymore. Only the sound of my heartbeat. I move towards the door, as everything else gradually seems to get darker. I push the door open, but am jolted back to my surroundings by someone grabbing my leg. I look down to see one of Haywood's bloody palms on my ankle. I look at his face, trying to think of a polite way to tell him to get his filthy hand off my person.

He shakes his head. "Please... don't go—"

Too late! I shake his hand off, and march into the cellar. Kat comes in after me and we're treated to the sight of Mrs. Haywood's dead body, lying in a pool of blood. There's so much blood, she may as well be floating in it. Kat screams a scream which, were such a thing possible, would raise Mrs. Haywood from the dead. It draws Daryl into the room. He gasps a little when he sees Audrey. He puts his arm around Kat as she stands there, shaking. It must be her first dead body. His eyes flash with pain, horror, disgust. Regret?

I walk closer to Audrey, as the sound of Kat's sobbing gets louder and louder. I wish she would be quiet.

"Donna, what are you doing?" Daryl asks.

I ignore him and get as close as I can to Audrey without disturbing the scene. My thoughts are manic. This is the room where Haywood tried to rape Aisha. Snatches of her statement tear through my mind. I look around the room. I can picture him hitting her and pushing himself against her. I can hear her yelling for him to stop. And now I can see his wife's corpse, wrists slashed, lying in the middle of the room. If these walls could talk, what would they say?

I crouch near her body, making sure to avoid stepping in any blood – a difficult task, given how much of it there is. Her eyes are wide open. I touch her neck. She's still warm, but barely. She stares at me as if begging me to help her, but I'm too late. I'm always too late. I close her eyes, not knowing what else to do. I stand up and turn to Daryl and Kat, who is still sobbing.

"I'm calling the police," I say.

"Wait!"

Mr. Haywood calls from outside. He enters the cellar and looks at me.

"Did you do this?" I ask. "Did you kill your wife?"

He shakes his head. "She killed herself."

"The day after she talked to a divorce lawyer. How convenient," I say.

I whip my phone out. The reception is bad. I start to leave the cellar, but Haywood blocks the exit.

"I know how this looks. I know what the police will think. Maybe we should discuss my side of the story before you call them," he says.

I look at him, trying with all my might not to dig my fingers into his jugular and carve it out.

"I'm calling the police right now. You can discuss your story with Daryl and…" I lose my words.

I turn to look at the other two and see that, although she still looks shaken up, Kat has stopped crying for now.

"…with Daryl and Kat."

I push past him and go upstairs, where I call the police. When I get off the phone, Irene is standing at the entrance to the kitchen, staring at me intently. I wonder how much she knows and how much she's willing to admit she knows.

"Irene, right?" I say.

She nods.

"Is Madam alright?" she asks, her voice wobbling. She speaks in a thick Irish accent that makes it hard for me to believe she's been living in this country for more than a week. It's funny how that happens.

"Why do you ask?"

She looks at the ground and shrugs. "I haven't seen her for a little while. She would have asked for lunch by now."

"Where are the children?"

She lifts her eyes. "They are out with their friends."

My heart sinks. When the poor boys left their home at some point today, their mother was alive. Did she kiss them before they left? Wave them goodbye? Did she expect to be alive when they got back? I know they certainly expected her to be. A lump starts to grow in my throat and I'm taken aback by the fact that I feel anything at all. I swallow hard, though it doesn't help much.

"When will they be back?" I ask Irene. I wish my voice wouldn't shake. If she didn't know Audrey was dead, she's surely starting to suspect that something awful has happened.

"Tomorrow evening. It's a weekend sleepover."

I nod and spontaneously exhale.

"Did she— did she hurt herself?" she stutters, with a frown.

I assume that she neither saw nor heard anything out of the ordinary. But I have to be sure. "Why would you say that? Did something unusual happen?"

The words pour out of my mouth so fast that I'm not sure she hears them all. She shakes her head and turns away from me. I go up to her and put my hand on her shoulder. She turns to look at me and I drop my hand.

I slow my speech down; I soften my tone. "Please, Irene. If you know anything, I need you to tell me. Please."

"Madam called Mrs. Smith yesterday, told her to take the boys for the weekend—"

"By Mrs. Smith, you mean Raquel Smith, Edward's mother?"

"Yes. They talked on the phone for a long time and Mrs. Smith came to pick the boys up last night."

"Then what happened?" I ask.

"She drank all evening like always. When sir came home, they had a big fight," she says, her hands making a shape like that of a large exercise ball.

"About what?"

"I don't know," she says, "their voices were muffled, but they were shouting and she was crying very loudly. They slept in separate bedrooms."

"How do you know that?"

She hesitates for a moment, but then carries on with gusto. "When Madam called me to her room this morning, for me to bring her some drinks, I saw sir leaving one of the guest rooms. He told me not to tidy it because he would be there for a few more nights."

This is a mess. I can't imagine how stressful it must be working for a rapist and an alcoholic. It must feel cathartic for Irene to get some of it off her chest.

"What happened this afternoon? Is there anything you can tell me?" I ask.

"I don't know. After sir left the house, she told me to take the afternoon off. I took my son to the park. sir phoned me, told me to come back. When I got here, he seemed very worried."

Even though I'm inclined to believe that Haywood killed Audrey, nothing I've heard thus far convinces me of that.

"When did he call you?" I ask.

"About an hour ago. Please, is Madam alright?" she asks. Her brow is furrowed, her words frantic. There's no point putting it off.

"I'm sorry to tell you this, Irene. Mrs. Haywood is dead."

***

At times like this, I consider taking up smoking. I can feel the strain of the situation bearing down on my bones. My breathing exercises can only do so much. The police are here now. I think one of the officers recognised me from yesterday's news. He did a double take, before giving me the dirtiest look I've seen in years. I was pleasantly surprised by that. In my experience, the police force is adept at attracting racists, bullies, rape apologists and other sorts of thugs and deviants. I suppose this man isn't one of those. How reassuring.

I waited outside for the police to arrive, didn't want to go back to the cellar… or rather the *crime scene*. There was nothing I could do there. I have no idea what cock-and-bull story Haywood and the others came up with, but I hear that Kat threw up in the corridor. It's to be expected – not everyone can stand the sight of blood.

She and Daryl, along with Haywood, are currently sitting in the reception room that Daryl and I were in with Audrey only a day ago. She looked so frail and miserable. From our meeting, I'd assumed she was another bored, whiny rich woman with too much time on her hands, no ambition to do good and no desire to be happy. Now, I don't know what to think. She couldn't drink herself to death fast enough, so she slit her wrists? Or did Haywood lend her a hand? Even if he isn't the immediate cause of her death, he's almost certainly the remote cause.

As two homicide detectives, Lawson and Miller, take Haywood's statement, an officer questions Irene. She tells him everything she told me. She adds that Haywood sounded scared when he called her, and that when she got home, he didn't tell her anything was wrong. He only said that he was expecting his lawyers, and he didn't want to be alone when we arrived.

This death reminds me of Alan, and I hate that. I hate that so much. I think about him too often. It upsets me. It's funny that I killed him, and yet he lives on in my mind. Some days, I feel like I still have his blood on my hands. I wipe my dry hands against my jeans just thinking about it. I wish I could kill him from my memory.

When he showed up at the shop that day, I couldn't believe how into it he was. He robbed the till with such glee that I forgot the whole charade was my idea. And when he turned to Mina, my blood may well have turned to ice. He had every intention of hurting her again. It was not an act. He was not pretending. He enjoyed causing pain. That's who he was.

While his attention was fully on Mina, I pulled Mr. Pryce's gun out from under the counter and fired it. Unfortunately, the gun jammed. Never in my whole life have I been as terrified as I was in that moment. Not even any of the times William went loco. It was a different kind of fear, one I'd never experienced before or since.

Despite all my planning, I had neglected to check the gun and for that reason, my plan fell to pieces. It's not that I hadn't thought about it. I had. But I didn't think it wise to check the gun – I knew it would be caught on camera and since I'd never done it before, it would make me look suspicious. The police don't accept 'woman's intuition' as a valid reason for doing something like that, even if it is the reason. I hoped and assumed that the gun was loaded and working properly. To my horror, I was wrong.

I froze. Everything went into slow motion as Mina got closer to Alan. He leered at her as she cried and whimpered. I knew that it was my fault that she was in that situation. I'd invited him there, laid her out as bait. It took me so long to convince her to spend time with me at work, but I did it in the end, and for what? So she could suffer through being attacked again? I didn't know what else to do. I threw the gun at his head. I hit my target and knocked him down.

The adrenaline kicked in and with it, courage or something like it. I leaped over the counter and ran towards Alan. I was too slow because by the time I got to him, he'd got his bearings. I tried to get the gun instead, but he hit me and dragged me to the floor. He hit me repeatedly, though not as hard or as viciously as William had done at times. Then he wrapped his hands around my neck and started squeezing it hard. I scratched and clawed at him as best I could. I thought he was going to kill me, and for a moment, I didn't particularly mind.

I didn't know why I was fighting to stay alive. I had nothing to live for. My life was one of pain and misery. Why bother holding on to it? But then images of Ivy came to my mind, and I started to think about her. Ivy's heart would break if I died. And if I died, who would keep poisoning William? Would mum have the strength to leave him or would she stay until he beat them to death?

If Alan killed me, would Mina take the chance to escape unharmed? Would she tell the police that he'd raped her? Would it make a difference? Did any of it even matter at all? And then I wondered – what if hell was real and my lousy life on earth was better than what was waiting for me after death? My vision got blurry and I felt like I was losing consciousness. I considered giving in, letting go.

And so I did. I stopped fighting. It was time to let him win. Then suddenly, he fell off me. I took a deep breath in and opened my eyes. Mina was standing over Alan with Mr Pryce's gun in her hand. Air filled my lungs afresh, and my first thought was that she had to get out of there, go somewhere safe, call for help. I turned over onto my side and yelled at her to leave, but he grabbed her before she could move. He dragged her to the ground, and then he turned his attention back to me.

This time, he didn't want to choke me. He climbed on top of me and tugged at my trousers, but I wasn't afraid. In the seconds that he took his eyes off me, I got my hands on his gun. He didn't know that until it was too late. That is to say, until he felt the nozzle on his chest, the split second before I shot him.

One bullet is all I needed. He slid off me. I lay still, gasping for air, trying my best to breathe normally again. I blinked and looked up to find Mina standing over me. The look on her face is difficult to describe, but it's forever etched into my memory. It's funny how my proudest achievement is also the source of my greatest shame. I'd won, but at what cost? In that moment, I knew that I'd compounded Mina's damage. She stared at Alan, watching him wriggle around in pain.

I had to act fast. There was a chance that in his dying moments, Alan would blurt out the truth of our arrangement. I got up as fast as I could, told Mina to go to Mr. Pryce's house and call the police. I could tell she was in a state of shock, but it was time to put myself first. Getting caught was not part of the plan. I got her out of there immediately, and locked the door behind her. Then it was just me and Alan. At last.

I rushed to Alan's side knowing there was no time to waste. He had approximately four minutes to live, six at best. There was no way I was going to let him die without gloating first. I couldn't believe that I'd almost given up, that I'd almost let him kill me. I'd brought him here for a reason, and when things got out of control, I forgot what that reason was. For that, I felt embarrassed. I was the only person who had the guts and acumen to do what needed to be done, and I almost gave up at the first sign of resistance. I knew that I needed to work on that, on pushing past the pain. I had to learn to persevere at all costs.

I knelt next to him, placing my hand on his chest. I snatched off his balaclava, and then shuffled back, feigning surprise. For a week, I'd pictured doing that. The cameras were watching and I needed to not look… smug. I furrowed my brow as I pretended to try and stop the bleeding. But there was no stopping the bleeding. I knew that. He probably knew that, too. Still, I had to make it look good.

"Don't touch me you bit—"

"Shhh, shhh. Calling me names can't help you now. Nothing can."

William had called me that word too many times. I really wasn't in the mood to hear it on what was shaping up to be such a victorious occasion.

"You set me up." He coughed up blood as he struggled to speak. Perhaps the sight of it should have disgusted me. The thick clot only fascinated me. Who would have ever thought that something as small as a bullet could do so much damage? Besides, I was no stranger to the odd blood splatter. On his worst days,

William didn't stop until he had drawn some.

I rolled his shirt up and used it to try to plug the hole in his chest. It didn't work very well.

"Did you really think I'd let you get away with rape? Do you think I'm corrupt like you?" With my hand on his chest, I could feel his breathing slowing down.

"Damn you," he said, "I should have shot you, you stupid whore."

Ugh, he was knocking on death's door and still being so salty. What a cad. And why is it that whether you sleep with a guy or not, they call you a whore? Salty and dumb.

I pressed his shirt into his chest, this time with malice. He shouted loudly in pain. I confess that that made me feel good.

"You deserve so much worse than this, Alan. I could have cut you open and set your organs on fire and it would still be less than you deserve."

I put more pressure on him until he started to cry. The tears slid down his cheeks, and I surprised myself by feeling sorry for him. I took the pressure off, and he kept crying, sobbing quite loudly.

I was baffled. I looked at the shop door, and no one was around. I turned back to him and it dawned on me that he might not have been crying because he was in pain.

"Please, Donna, don't do this. Help me, I swear I'll turn myself in," he said, his voice getting quieter, his eyes widening.

"It's too late, Alan. You're dying. There's nothing I can do."

He grabbed my hand and squeezed it. His grip was firmer than what I would have expected from one who was dying. He looked in my eyes and with tears said, "Please."

And then his hand dropped and his eyes rolled into the back of his head. And like that, he was dead. I sat back onto my heels and looked at my hands. They were covered in blood, to the point where it had seeped under my nails. My stomach churned. Pride and shame wrestled inside me, each trying to get the upper hand. I couldn't stop myself from crying. Things had worked out as I'd hoped and planned, and for that I was grateful. At the same time, what I'd done was irreversible and in that moment I wasn't sure whether it was right. I hadn't accounted for his plea for help. I never thought he'd seem so human.

That was what had made the whole thing easier. In my head, he was less than human – an animal, even – and his refusal to go to the police when I asked him to told me all I needed to know. He was incapable of feeling shame or remorse. He had no dignity. He did not respect people. He would only continue to do evil, and for that he needed to die.

As I cried, I wondered if by, taking his life, I'd also taken away any chance he might have had to do the right thing. But then I came to my senses. He'd had a chance – probably hundreds – not only to stop doing ill, but also to confess his crimes and face the consequences. He didn't do that because he was a coward and a sadist. Moments earlier he'd tried to attack me too. It was foolish of me to forget that so quickly.

I dried my tears with my arms and I closed his eyes. I couldn't take them staring at me – it was unsettling. I stood up and took a deep breath. All there was left to do was wait for the police. Murder is messy, destructive business but on some occasions, it's a necessary ill. I told myself that Alan was a menace, and I did what needed to be done. I let that thought ease my mind; I let it comfort me. Had he lived even a day longer, he may have done far more damage before truly changing his ways, assuming he ever did change. I couldn't have allowed that. It would have been irresponsible.

I pushed all my doubts aside, knowing that the hard part was yet to come. I had to convince the police that the murder happened by chance, the unfortunate result of a failed robbery. I wasn't sure I had what it took to do that, but I had to try. First time for everything. Besides, I'd gone too far to fail. I stood at the door, feeling drained and dejected, and waited for the police. I hoped Mina was safe. She never had to see Alan again and I desperately hoped she'd be able to move past the rape. I know now that that hope was vain.

My thoughts jump to Mina and I remember that I'm yet to tell her about my meeting with Suzanne. Haywood's problems have hijacked my afternoon.

The male detective, Miller, leaves the reception room and comes over to me.

Here we go again. It's show time.

***

After the police took my statement, Kat, Daryl and I left the house. Daryl got into his car as Kat and I waited in hers for Mr. Haywood. The police didn't take Jeremy into custody. At some point after he was questioned, he called the Smiths and told them what had happened. I watched him squirt out some crocodile tears while talking on the phone. I can't wait to break his neck.

He asked us for a lift to the Smiths' house, even though it's apparently a 10 or so minute walk away from his. Kat agreed. He packed an overnight bag and hopped in the back of her car. Daryl followed close behind as we drove 2 minutes down the road, but not through the mansion gates.

When Kat's car gets through the gates of the Smith house – a very grand residence – Raquel Smith, another glam-bot, is waiting in the driveway for Haywood. No husband in sight, but I assume he exists. Maybe he's inside the house with the children. Maybe he's at a mistress's house. Maybe he's out with friends. Who knows?

As Haywood leaves the car, he thanks us for our help. I restrain myself from reminding him that we're not doing him a favour, we're doing out jobs.

"If you need anything else, feel free to call us," Kat says, sincerely. She looks crestfallen. It's obvious that she's been deeply, negatively affected by today's events, so I don't correct her by telling him to *call her, not me.*

He nods and goes over to Raquel. She hugs him as he cries into her nice-looking hair. It's a rich deep brown colour, very thick, like a curtain of shiny silk. It looks like it smells of vanilla and amber. I sort of wish I had an excuse to cry into her hair. He lifts his head to speak to her, but I'm too far away to hear what he says. I do, however, see the tears streaming down her plump, wrinkle-free face. I'll have to give her details to Suzanne. She may be a useful source of information about the Haywoods.

Mr. Haywood waves us away, as though we're his servants. Kat drives out of the compound and in the side mirror, I see Mrs. Smith lead Haywood into the house. Once we exit the gate, Kat parks her car behind Daryl's, which is on the side of the road. And then she cries. Loudly, messily, like someone she loved had died. I want to comfort her, but I don't really know how to.

Daryl comes over from his car and climbs into the backseat. He puts his hand on Kat's shoulder, and strokes it. She grabs his hand and rests her face on it, still crying. Had I brought my car, I wouldn't have had to witness this. She keeps sobbing as they hold hands. If they haven't rekindled their illicit relationship, they will soon. These two don't know how to live.

***

It seemed like an eternity passed before Kat got her act together. Once she dried her eyes and cleaned her face, Daryl left and she kindly offered to drive me home. I accepted.

For most of the drive, the car was quiet. I did very little to console her during her crying-fest, and am in no mood to talk. I am mildly curious about her relationship with Daryl, but then I remember that I don't care.

Still, I can never be sure what information I'll need when, and for what purpose… so I decide to speak.

"You ok now?" I ask.

She nods.

"My father hanged himself when I was seven," she blurts out, adding, "I found his body."

She lets out a heavy sigh, and then frowns. This is news to me. Kat and I have known each other for a while, and given how much she enjoys gossiping, I'm surprised that she's never told me this before. I suppose everyone has something that they hold back. Well, that explains her reaction *and* her dreadful taste in men.

"I'm sorry… I didn't know that."

"It's not really something I tell people," she says, glancing at me.

Understandable. If she craved the sympathy of strangers, she'd have solde her story to a magazine by now. I consider probing her but I can't be sure that she won't lose control of the car and drive us into a tree, or off the side of a bridge. Still, as the car slows down in the traffic, I do my best to appear understanding and relatable.

"My father died when I was 17," I say.

She looks at me with a wrinkled forehead. She shouldn't look so surprised – she's never asked and I'm nowhere near as chatty as she is.

"I had no idea. What happened?" she asks. The concern in her voice can't be faked.

"He got drunk. Fell down the stairs. The paramedics said that if he'd got to a phone in time, called for help, he might have survived…"

"That's awful. It's so hard losing someone you love," she says

I wouldn't know.

I nod and frown. The cars ahead of us move a few metres, and then stop again. Only now do I notice we're at a makeshift traffic light, and it may take us another 10 minutes to move five paces

Knowing we'll be stuck here for a while longer, I change the subject.

"Are you and Daryl sleeping together again?"

Her body tenses up as she looks at me. Her face is flushed.

"I— I—"

"I'll take that stuttering as a 'yes' then?"

She shakes her head and slumps in the seat. The light goes green and we move forward ever so slightly. Within 15 seconds, it's red again. I look over at the bus on our left. I hope no one on it has anywhere important to be.

I look back at Kat, waiting for an answer.

"It's not what you think."

"What do I think?"

"It was a mistake. We're not back together. There can't be a 'we' unless he leaves his wife, and… he won't now that she's pregnant," she says, frowning.

Oh, that poor woman. Another child with that jackass? I suppose she has no idea that he cheats on her. Or maybe she knows and she doesn't care. I gather that some people want a family more than they want peace of mind.

"I see. Was that planned?"

"I didn't ask," she says.

She shakes her head, looking weary and disappointed. Imagine how Veronica would feel. The light changes again and the cars in front of us speed away. By the time it's red again, we're at the front of the queue. Slow and steady.

"Girl or boy?"

"I didn't ask," she says gruffly. She sighs, runs her fingers along her hairline. "It's probably too early to tell anyway."

I reckon she's right about that. I could take the opportunity to gloat, however I'm too tired to say anything.

"You were right," she says, tapping her fingers on the back of her head, as her hand rests against the window.

Though I don't need her confirmation, those words are music to my ears.

"I was stupid to think I could find love with a taken man," she continues.

She's right, she was stupid.

"You slept with him, didn't you?"

"After you left last night, we went for a friendly drink near mine, you know, 'cos we're both mature adults. He walked me home… you know the rest."

The light turns green and at last we're free to continue our journey.

"We spent the morning together. He was in the shower and I saw a message from her. He must have told her that he was working all night—"

"And she believed him?"

"I guess she did. She wanted him to pick up some prenatal vitamins because, and I quote, 'baby needs to be strong and healthy, like daddy.'"

Kat shakes her head ever so slightly. She bites her lower lip, as though full of regret. I actually feel bad for her… a little.

"You kicked him out?"

"No, I didn't because I'm an idiot. He came out of the shower and we argued, which is why I missed your call. He said it didn't matter that she was pregnant because he loves me. Then he said we can still see each other until she gives birth, after which he would leave her and his two children under the age of three. For some reason, I didn't believe him this time."

"They say the best predictor for future behaviour is past behaviour. She's his job security; he won't leave her for anything. He's wants power and position, and you can't provide either of those things for him. You need to cut him loose, for good," I say. I surprise myself by giving her such heartfelt advice.

She nods emphatically, eyes on the road. "That's the plan."

For the rest of the drive, neither of us says a word. The silence is pleasant and comforting, and I like to think that Kat is using it to make sensible resolutions. Of course, I've known her long enough to know that that's probably not the case, but it's a nice thought.

Because there is indeed no rest for the wicked, images of Audrey Haywood's body stream through my mind. I try to work out whether there were any subtle signs of foul play that I missed. I wonder how her children took the news. Will they believe that she killed herself? Will they suspect their father? It's hard for children when a parent dies. Such violent circumstances must complicate the situation.

Ivy seemed quite upset when William died, though I'm sure there was a part of her that felt pure joy. A week after his funeral, she asked me if I was happy that he was gone. I shrugged, said nothing. She said that the night before his fall, she'd prayed that God would 'set us free.'

"I was just so sad and tired of him being so cruel to us. I didn't think he'd die!" she said, tears streaming down her face.

I didn't know what to say.

"Is this my fault? Am I responsible for dad's death?" she asked.

I watched her as she cried. I wanted to hug her, but I didn't. I just looked at her as she sank to the floor, cradling herself against the bedroom door.

A part of me wanted to confide in her, tell her how I'd taken matters into my own hands, how I'd saved the day... but I knew that would be a foolish thing to do. Ivy is pure and good and unblemished, as evidenced by her sadness over the death of a man who hated her. There was no way she'd be able – or even willing – to keep my secret. And deep down, I didn't want her to. She's a good person and I didn't want to change that, didn't want to soil her with my filth. I didn't want her to be like me. So as usual, I said nothing that would incriminate me.

I walked over to her, sat by her side, and put my arm around her shoulders like a good sister would.

"You can't make God do anything He doesn't want to," I said, racking my brain for any theological information I may have picked up at the abysmal church we used to attend. The pastor was more like a failed actor than an actual Bible scholar, so my search came up empty. In lieu of solid Biblical encouragement, I went for sentimentality.

"I know that you're feeling sad right now, and that's ok. You didn't do this. Everybody has to die at some point. It was just his time to go."

Still, she cried.

And then it came to me! Ecclesiastes 3! We'd memorised it as children.

"To every thing there is a season, and a time to every purpose under the heaven:

A time to be born, and a time to die; a time to plant, and a time to pluck up that which is planted; A time to kill, and a time to heal; a time to break down, and a time to build up; A time to weep, and a time to laugh; a time to mourn, and a time to dance; A time to cast away stones, and a time to gather stones together; a time to embrace, and a time to refrain from embracing; A time to get, and a time to lose; a time to keep, and a time to cast away; A time to rend, and a time to sew; a time to keep silence, and a time to speak; A time to love, and a time to hate; a time of war, and a time of peace."

She looked at me, mouth agape, as I said the words. When I got to 'a time to heal,' she cried even harder, and I thought she wouldn't stop. At the end of my little speech, she rested her head on my shoulder.

I placed my hand on her head and patted it. Had I been ambivalent about my decision, that moment showed me that killing William was the right thing to do. Were he still alive, there was no way that Ivy and I would have felt free to sit together, knowing there were no surprise beatings in store. For the first time, we had a semblance of peace.

I wonder if Audrey's death will leave a void in the boys' lives, or if they're better off without her. She was a miserable drunk, and I doubt she was a competent parent, but there's a chance that she was kind to them. There's a chance that despite her self-centred addiction, she loved her sons. If she did, it's a shame that they have to grow up without her. And if she didn't love them, I hope they can allow themselves to feel good about her absence. She may have been their mother, but that doesn't necessarily make her death a tragedy.

Kat parks outside my building. She sighs loudly, as is her way and leans into the seat, letting her head rest. She turns to me.

"Do you think those children will be ok? You think they'll be able to move past this?" she asks.

"Did you move past your father's death?"

I know this will come across as an attempt to forge a deeper bond with Kat, and though that's not my intention, I'm curious to know the answer to my question.

Her head wobbles as her gaze moves from my face to the grass outside the car.

"I'm not sure. Sometimes I think so, but other times…"

She looks back at me and shrugs, half-smiling.

"Do you really think she killed herself?"

She sits upright.

"Wait, you don't think he killed her, do you?" she says in a way that implies that the thought hadn't crossed her mind.

"Who slits their wrists in a cellar when there are bathtubs available? No one…"

She stares at the steering wheel, mouth ajar.

"It doesn't make sense. His life is under a microscope, it wouldn't be smart for him to kill her… I think you're barking up the wrong tree here."

I shrug. "You're probably right. I'm sure the autopsy will make things clearer."

She nods in agreement.

I pop the door open and hear her say, "How about you?"

I turn to her, shaking my head.

"Did you get over your dad's death?"

Ha! Did I ever!

"I had to. There was no alternative."

She smiles at me and lifts her head. "That makes sense. You're a fighter."

I smile back. "You live for the fight when it's all that you've got."

We exchange goodbyes and I leave her car. It seems right that I stand around and wave her off, so I do that. Once her vehicle disappears in the distance, I turn to the apartment building and brace myself for whatever is coming next. Assuming she hasn't left yet, Mina is probably still upset about last night. I hope she can accept my olive branch and work with Suzanne. It would be for the greater good.

The flat is empty when I get inside, which is a pleasant surprise. The only time it's ever guaranteed to be empty when I get home is the last Friday of the month. I have the whole place to myself for an entire night. That's the best night of the month. It's less than a week till the next one or (as I like to think of it) my next date with myself. On one such occasion a few months ago, I splashed out and went to a spa to get a massage. It was a nice way to spend the evening, knowing I'd return to a quiet, peaceful home. Unfortunately, with all that's happening at work, I might not get that alone time this month. I should be grateful to have some today, even though I am at a loss as to what to do.

My phone buzzes. It's a text from Ivy. The message says that they're at a museum and I can join them if I'm interested. Although I wouldn't mind seeing an exhibition, the day has already been long enough. I need to rest. And think. And plan. But first, I must rest.

***

I wake up and after a few minutes of tossing about on my bed, I check the time. It's 7pm. I hear a noise coming from the kitchen. And then I hear another one. It sounds like the fridge door opening and shutting. They must be back. I'd like to stay here for as long as possible, gathering strength for the remainder of the evening. Sadly, within moments there's a knock on my door.

No point ignoring it. I drag myself out of bed, shuffling to the door.

"Donna, are you in?"

I open the door and light streams in and hurts my eyes. When my vision adjusts, I am greeted by Ivy's smiling face.

I smile back. "Yeah, I'm in."

203

"Oh, sorry, did I wake you?"

"I'm not sure," I say.

I can still hear noises coming from the kitchen. The clanging sound of crockery and pots. Dinner preparations, no doubt.

"What's up?"

"I just wanted to check on you. How was your meeting?" she says.

Though I hardly ever tell Ivy anything about my work, she's too polite not to inquire. I'd never reveal details about my meeting with Suzanne but considering the high-profile nature of Jeremy Haywood's case, I'll probably have to tell her about Audrey's death. At some point.

Instead of answering her question, I shrug. She nods. Always so understanding. I move out of her way and she enters the room. We sit on the ground, with our backs against the door, as usual.

"How was the exhibition?"

"It was nice. Would have been nicer if you'd been there," she says, being sincere.

"No, it wouldn't." I'm being honest.

She smiles. She knows I'm right, even if she doesn't want to believe it.

"Mina's making us dinner before she leaves. Her way of saying thank you."

I nod slowly, wondering whether to say what I'm thinking.

Ivy leans closer to me, nudging me with her elbow. "Don't even think it."

"Think what?"

"She's not going to drug us!"

I laugh cheerily, pleasantly surprised that Ivy has read my mind.

"How can you be sure?" I ask.

"Well, for one thing, she's clean now. And I trust her. You should try it sometime."

"Trust is overrated. You should withhold it from time to time."

"She wants to get well, Donna. She just needs people in her corner. She needs you in her corner. She *wants* yo—"

"I get it, Ivy, she needs support. You don't have to go on about it."

"Uh, yes I do. I never know if you're paying attention!"

"To you, I'm always paying attention."

She smiles and rests her head on my shoulder. I think about the night she thought she was responsible for dad's death. I clasp her hand in mine and we sit in silence for a little while.

"I convinced her to stay tonight. She's thinking about leaving after church tomorrow, but I don't want her to. I don't think it'll be good for her."

I have a feeling I know what's coming next. She lifts her head and looks at me.

"She'll stay if you ask her to. Your approval… it means so much to her."

I look at her. Her eyes sweep across my face, presumably looking for any indication that I'm on-board.

"What if I don't want her to stay?" I ask.

"I know you do."

***

My mother isn't great at many things, but she is an outstanding cook – a fact underscored by Mina's attempt to make us dinner. It's not that the meal was bad, it was just, eh, underwhelming. If she chooses to stay, I hope the only time she sets foot in the kitchen is to wash up, or learn from mum.

Once we are done eating, Mina starts clearing the table. Ivy volunteers to wash up and invites mum to help her. I suppose that's my cue. I move from my side of the table to Mina's and accidentally reach for the same plate she does. She withdraws her hand but doesn't make eye contact.

Ugh, this is going to be awkward.

I pick the plate up and start speaking. "Ivy tells me that you're thinking of leaving tomorrow."

"Does she tell you everything?"

"Not that I'm aware. She tells me things that are important. Or things she thinks are important… to her and me."

She looks at me and folds her arms. It looks like she's trying to protect herself.

"Where will you go?"

"I don't know. I have a few people I could call. Maybe Graham—"

"Oh man, not him."

Bad news, he's such bad news.

"He's a good guy and I trust him," she says, in a defensive manner.

"I trust him to supply you with—"

"That's not what he does. You've got the wrong idea about him, but— you know what, it doesn't matter." She looks at her feet as they shuffle back and forth.

I realize that I've gone off script. Time to rein it in.

"Look, Mina, I'm sorry about last night. I was so far out of line and I should never have spoken to you that way."

She nods, arms still folded, eyes still down, feet still shuffling.

She looks up at me. "I've disappointed you before. I can't blame you for being upset about that."

It's nice that she's not so far gone that she can't admit her wrongdoings. That's a good sign. My next words, I must choose with care.

"You don't have to leave tomorrow, you know. You can stay with us for a little longer."

I'd rather she didn't think she's moving in. Her arms loosen slightly. Her eyes move around slowly, like she can see her options in the four corners of the room. I say *options* as if she has many.

"I don't want to be here if you don't want me here," she says.

"I got you a job— that is, if you want it."

Her arms drop and she furrows her brow.

"I should probably have started with that. I gave Suzanne your number and—"

"Suzanne? Zhou?"

"Yes. She'll call you tomorrow. If you're interested in helping her out, it would be more convenient for you to stay here," I say.

"Donna, I don't know what to say. Thank you."

I smile and take another plate.

"You're welcome," I say, before quickly adding, "and you were right last night. Everything you said was true."

"Everything?" she asks.

"Everything."

***

After speaking to Mina, I retire to my room. I've barely made it in when Ivy knocks on my door, even though it's slightly ajar. She sees me through the crack, and smiles.

"May I?"

I nod. "Twice in one night?"

She walks in, holding a stress ball, and jumps on to my bed. She sits in the centre of it, with her legs crossed.

"What's this job you got Mina?" she asks.

News sure travels fast.

I turn to face her. "You should ask her."

Ivy looks down. "Sometimes I wonder if you'll ever trust me." Her voice is low. She lightly taps the stress ball.

"What's trust got to do with this?"

She shrugs, looking at me. "I don't know. Sometimes I... I get tired of you being a lawyer all the time. I miss the days when you were just my sister."

"And when was that?"

She shrugs again and looks at the stress ball, as I walk over to the bed. I sit close to her.

"Before you— before the *thing* at the newsagent's," she says, looking up from the ball.

I say nothing.

"Like that time when— do you remember that day that dad took us to the beach? He drove us down there for mum's birthday. And he helped us make a sandcastle, and pick pretty seashells..."

"I remember the day that dad beat mum and called her a whore because she had the nerve to let Uncle Kwame hug her." I speak with no emotion.

She sucks her cheeks in. I'm confused when tears fill her eyes.

"What is going on, Ivy?"

She inhales and bats her eyelids rapidly, blinking back the tears.

"I have this feeling that you're... you're on a dark road, Donna. And I'm worried about you." She squeezes the ball, rocking slightly.

"Where is this feeling coming from?" I'm genuinely curious.

She shakes her head. "I don't know – it's just a feeling. But it's been... growing for a few weeks now." She holds my gaze and for the first time in a decade, I worry that she knows my secrets. But there's no way she could know, right?

"Feelings come and go. This too shall pass," I say.

"Feelings only go if you let them. It's pretty obvious that you've got still some anger and resentment that you need to release."

I feel my back straighten and my jaw tighten.

"Release?" I say. "That's what my workouts are for."

"A temporary fix."

She drops the stress ball on her thighs. She clasps her hands and places them over her mouth, letting a few moments pass before she drops them, with a loud exhale. She places her hands on her knees and continues.

"I think you need to give all the negativity you feel to Jesus. He's been through far worse than either of us ever have, and if you come to Him, He'll help you and save you and—"

"Save me? Like He saved me from dad? How many times did He do that, exactly?"

"Donna, you know it's not that simple—"

"No, Ivy, I don't. You think you were the only one praying for a miracle? You think it was just you asking God to get us out of there? If I wanted to talk to someone who didn't care about me, I'd go to work or download a dating app. I'm not wasting my free time on that."

I surprise myself by staying calm the whole time.

"Life isn't that simple. God didn't *make* dad do hurt us," she continues.

Sometimes, she just doesn't know when to quit. That is one of her flaws.

"Yes, well, He didn't stop him either, so as far as I'm concerned, He's complicit."

"He's given us the ability to do whatever we want because He doesn't want slaves. It's not His fault if we choose to do the wrong thing. And yes, maybe our prayers went unanswered, but His timing—"

I can feel my heart rate increasing, and I'm scared that if she says one more word, I'll lose control and tell her that I killed William. I can't afford to do that. She has to stop talking.

"Enough, Ivy! Please, stop." Without meaning to, I glare at her.

She looks at me like a wounded animal, but she's quiet now. I get off the bed and compose myself. She doesn't say anything. I look at her and then up at the ceiling, my hands clasped behind my neck. I look back at her and shake my head.

"You don't have to worry about me, Ivy; after all, all things work together—"

"Oh please, Donna. We both know you don't believe that. You never have," she says.

"Once upon a time, I did. But life has changed that."

Her face falls.

I sigh. "I guess you'll have to believe it for both of us."

PART II

I

NOVEMBER 25TH, 2019

DONNA

I don't care for Mondays. But today, I wake up feeling somewhat… alive. The ball has started rolling in a direction that pleases me. Yes, I will have to deal with worms and rats at work but all in all, things are looking up.

Leaving the bathroom, I run into Mina in the corridor, who at 6.15 is awake and ready for the day ahead. I'm impressed by her desire to progress. She tells me that she'll be meeting Suzanne at 7 o' clock and the two will discuss how to stalk Jeremy Haywood without raising suspicion. I wish Mina the best of luck.

She creeps out of the house, doing her best not to wake Ivy up. I go back to my room and proceed to get dressed. I don the clothes that I picked out last night – a charcoal trouser suit and a white shirt. I tie my hair into a bun and fasten it with my favourite hair sticks (a gift from Ivy). I complete the look with a pair of low-heeled black shoes. This is my look in a nutshell – simple, safe, hassle-free.

The bus ride to work was uneventful, exactly how I like it. I manage to get to the office before the rest of the team, which is unusual but not unwelcome. I use my alone time to check my emails – nothing interesting there. The barrister, Solomon Mensah, likes to have things far in advance so it would be wise for me to start preparing the paperwork for Mr. Haywood's case. I wonder how his children took the news of Audrey's death. I wonder if the official verdict will be suicide. I let out a heavy sigh as I open my notebook.

"That's quite the sigh."

I grab my flask and spin around in my chair, stunned. As far as I knew, I was alone in this corner of the office. I don't recognize the man's voice, but it is smooth as silk. I am taken aback when I see that the voice belongs to Detective Miller.

"I didn't mean to startle you, Miss Palmer," he says.

"How did you get in here?" I ask, unconcerned that I might come across as rude.

"I charmed my way in. It's what police detectives do, right?"

He probably flashed his badge downstairs, and they let him through. I'm sure it doesn't hurt that he's good-looking and well-dressed. I'm no expert, but if that suit isn't bespoke, I'll eat my hat. What does he earn? His coat looks like it belongs to someone whose salary is far above what I assume his pay grade is.

"What are you doing here?"

I set the flask down on the desk, keeping my hand on it

"Just like that, right to business," he says. He looks around the room. I see his nose wrinkle when he catches sight of Shane's unsightly desk. It's the only reasonable reaction.

"I assume you came here to do work, not avoid it."

He smiles and looks at my hand that remains on the flask.

"I wanted to ask you some questions about Audrey Haywood."

"I already told you; I wasn't there when she died and I didn't see anything."

"I know what you said, but I wanted to ask you what you thought."

"What I thought about what?"

"The crime scene. When you arrived, what was your first thought?" he says.

Our eyes lock for a few seconds, as I try to determine his real reason for being here. He looks at my hand again and smiles.

"Nice flask, by the way. Are you planning to club me with it?"

"When I saw the crime scene, all I could think about was what a bloody mess it was."

"Did Mr. Haywood seem—"

"I don't think talking about my client is worthwhile. You know the rules," I say.

He nods and raises his hands, as if in defeat. "You're right, I do know the rules. The trouble is, even though you say you were there as Mr. Haywood's lawyer, to us – the police – you're a witness, and a potential suspect."

"Excuse me?"

"For all we know, the four of you beat the woman to death and staged the scene. We have to investigate every avenue."

Beat the woman to death – like I would ever be so sloppy!

"Are you saying it wasn't a suicide?" I ask.

"I'm saying we have to investigate every avenue."

I open my mouth to say something, but can't think of what to say. He asked me if I was going to club him. Who does that?

"This is absurd. I didn't kill Mrs. Haywood. I had no reason to. I literally met her once before she died. I respect that you're doing your job, but this isn't an avenue – it's a close."

He smiles again and nods. "I should leave. Thank you for your time."

He starts towards the exit, then turns back to me.

"What are you doing for lunch?" he says.

What a needless and random question. I hate it when men do this. They seem to think they have the right to ask every woman they meet out. My gut reaction is to tell him to go to hell and never return, but Ivy says you can catch more flies with honey than with vinegar, so I won't do that.

"Probably working," I say. I even muster a smile.

At that moment, Kat walks into the office, coughing loudly. She stops as soon as she sees Miller.

"Detective, what are you doing here?"

"Leaving," he says.

He smiles at me and leaves the office.

"What was that all about?" Kat asks.

I have no idea.

***

I and the team spend the morning working on strategy. We aim to use Audrey Haywood's apparent suicide to eke sympathy out of the jury. The man couldn't be a rapist when his wife was suicidal, or some such illogical rubbish. In addition to that, we've proposed that the trial be delayed, in order to give the family time to bury and mourn their wife and mother.

Of course, I've been tasked with convincing Zach that delaying the trial is the humane thing to do. I get all the fun jobs around here. No one has yet been able to tell me how the children are faring. I wish I didn't care about that.

At lunch time, I decide to step out for some air. I am fortunate enough to elude Kat on my way out. The only thing she ever wants to talk about is Daryl, and I'm sick of hearing about him. She refuses to accept that he's wasting her time. Worse yet, she's enabling him – damn shame, too. If she could see her worth, she wouldn't be fooling with him. Their relationship might kill her long before the cigarettes do.

In the crisp November air, it dawns on me that Christmas is on the way and I've almost been too busy to prepare. There are baubles, trees and lights all over the land, and everywhere I go, I'm treated to Christmas songs, most of which annoy me to no end. Cranberries and chestnuts have materialised in the supermarkets, making me wonder where they hid all year. I spend so much time working that I always leave my shopping till the last minute. Well, I say 'last minute' but I mean 'end of November.'

I'm usually more organized than that but I find Christmas quite depressing. I try to ignore it for as long as possible. Between the aggressive marketing of charities and the aggressive marketing of perfumes and toys, at a time when the only thing that should be remembered is the birth of God, this time of year makes me hate the world more than usual.

Perhaps I shouldn't be so harsh. After all, I am part of the problem. I am a shameless money-chaser, willing to sell my soul in order to care for my body. Deep

216

down, I would love to be working with Zach, prosecuting criminals, making the world a fairer, somewhat safer place. But I'm a greedy coward, and I chose the wrong side. Maybe when I'm done with this case, I'll quit and do something more meaningful with my life.

I'm about to turn into the park when I see a face I recognize. Detective Miller is walking towards me, with a coffee cup in hand and a big smile on his face. This can't be a coincidence.

What does he want now?

"Lovely day for a walk, Miss Palmer," he says, still smiling.

I want to punch the smile off his face.

"Don't you have a job to do? Or do they pay you to waste time?"

"Ouch. Police officers do have lunch breaks."

I start turning into the park when he speaks again.

"Aren't you curious as to why I'm here, Miss Palmer?" he asks, looking above my head.

It takes all my willpower not to roll my eyes. Am I curious? Maybe a little, but not enough to care. I had nothing to do with Audrey's death, thus I have nothing to worry about. That said, it might worth knowing why he's taken an interest in me.

"You're taking a walk on your lunch break," I say, smiling.

He chuckles.

"Fine, why are you here, Detective?"

"Please call me Ken."

"I'd rather not."

His eyes briefly dart away from me before he carries on. "I was struck by how composed you were on Saturday. Your colleagues said you got close enough to Mrs. Haywood's body to confirm that she was dead. Not many people can stay so calm in such situations. And when we questioned you... cool under pressure. I was impressed."

Now I roll my eyes. "I'm glad I impressed you – that was my goal."

"In my experience, there are only two sorts of people who would be that unmoved by such a tragedy – seasoned police officers and cold-blooded killers," he says, narrowing his eyes at the word 'killers.'

"Two subsets of psychopath," I say, smiling.

He blinks rapidly, his ears moving backwards.

"I'm not sure what you're doing here or what you hope to achieve by cornering me like this, but here's what I know: Audrey Haywood's corpse isn't the first one I've seen and knowing my luck, it probably won't be that last. I'm sorry that I didn't cry and throw up like you'd have wanted or expected me to. If my reaction wasn't to your taste, that's too bad. Now I have to go – you're eating into my lunch time."

I walk down the pathway to the park, but hear his footsteps. I toss him a look over my shoulder.

"Seriously, are you following me?" I ask, still walking briskly.

"Your lack of emotion made such an impact on me that I looked into your background."

I slow down and let him catch up with me.

Where is he going with this?

We're walking side-by-side now. "Don't you have any real work to do?"

"I wasn't completely surprised to find that you're a killer," he says.

It's been a long time since anyone called me that. I thought I was done with that after Beth died.

At first, I don't know what to say to that but the lawyer in me comes alive. "My past is none of your business."

"I'm a police—"

"You're using your position to access information that doesn't concern you or this case. I will be talking to your superiors about this," I say, facing him squarely. He's tall, quite a bit taller than I am – maybe 7 inches – but I feel like I'm looking down at him since I am in fact metaphorically standing on higher ground.

"I think you misunderstand me. I was amazed by your grit and fortitude. I couldn't understand how that girl grew up to defend criminals," he says.

"And you never will. My life, my motives, nothing to do with me has anything to do with you. If you show up near my place of work again, I will inform your superiors. Your first warning is your only warning."

He nods and instead of walking further into the park, I leave it altogether. Lunch is ruined.

I'm going to see Zach.

II

MINA

I t took me by surprise that Donna went out of her way to help me find work. Ivy had promised to take me to the job lab today, but Donna took charge. I'm amazed and grateful. I'm glad I let Ivy and Mama talk me into staying, despite how hurt I was by the things Donna said. It seems like it's all worked out. Well, maybe I should say it's working out.

I've never done anything like this before – all this cloak and dagger detective stuff – but I'm willing to try. That's half the battle won. As a teenager, I was into photography. Not like anything major but people seemed to think I was gifted, or close enough to that. I loved the feeling of being able to capture beautiful moments forever. Now I get to capture ugly ones. All for a good cause, obviously. If we can prove this Haywood man is guilty, I'll feel like I've done at least one good thing in my life.

Yesterday, I met with Suzanne and she took me to town to buy a fancy camera. We eventually found one that felt… right. I don't know how to explain it. It felt like it was an extension of me. I didn't have a chance to follow anyone, but today I'm ready to do whatever needs doing. Bring it on.

Today, I was the first to leave the flat. Ivy let me spend the night in her room again, while she slept on the couch. I felt a bit bad, but she insisted that she didn't mind. I got up early, showered and got dressed. I did my best to look ordinary. I put on a pair of black jeans, a black tank top, a dark blue jumper and a black hoodie – all Ivy's things. I don't think I'll stand out looking like this.

I meet Suzanne in a run-down-looking building in a run-down part of town, half-expecting to get mugged somewhere between the entrance and her office. I take the lift to the third floor and almost instantly regret it, as it makes a scary noise that makes me think it is moments away from plummeting through the building's foundations. Thankfully, my fear is unfounded and I get to Suzanne's office in one piece.

I move to knock on the door, but she opens it before I get the chance. She looks me up and down and smiles. Aside from her hairstyle – it's a bob, which is in a real mess at the moment – Suzanne's appearance hasn't changed much since we left secondary school. I guess it wasn't that long ago.

"You're early," she says.

"Actually, I'm on time."

She looks at her watch and moves out of the way, letting me into the office.

"Well, I was expecting you to be late, so in my head you're early."

I suppose in some way, that makes sense.

"I wanted to make a good impression," I say. Why did I say that? I shouldn't have said that. That makes me sound pathetic and desperate. I've barely been here a minute and I'm already grovelling. Between this and yesterday's show of keenness, she must think I'm tragic.

"There's no need for that. You're here primarily to take pictures. As long as you can get a clear shot, I'm happy."

I nod at her and walk further into the office. "Is that all we're doing today?"

"Probably. Would you like a drink?" she asks, walking into another room. I follow her and look through the door. She picks up a brush and runs it quickly through her hair.

"I'm fine, thanks. It's a little early in the day for that." As she turns to reply, I realise I've misunderstood her question.

"Early in the day? I meant tea or coffee. Duh," she says.

"Oh, I knew that." I feel embarrassed as my cheeks warm up.

She looks at me and scrunches up her nose. She darts out of view and comes back a few seconds later with a backpack slung over her shoulder.

"You've got your camera?"

"Yes."

"Ok, let's go."

She walks out in front of me and I follow her out of the office. We take the stairs, leave the building and go to her car. It's a small, metallic-silver hatchback – rather common and non-descript. Excellent for her work, I imagine. We enter the car, and she reaches into her jeans pocket and pulls out a wad of cash, which she then hands me.

"I almost forgot – in case we need to split up in a hurry, here's some money for taxis and such."

As I take the money, I start to mumble. "Oh, um… I don't think—"

"It's £250 in 5s, I thought it'd be easier to work with than five 50s, you know?"

I nod.

She smiles. "Right, let's get this party started."

She starts the engine and the car roars into motion. The money is still in my hand. My hand shakes a little, but not from the car's movement.

***

Suzanne drives like she's practicing for a future in Formula One. After a perilous journey made at break-neck speed, we park outside Jeremy Haywood's neighbour's house. Forget what I said about her car being common – in this area, the hatchback sticks out like a sore thumb. The only cars around here cost more than some people's homes. If it could, the road would smell like money.

Speaking of money, I considered giving some of the cash back to Suzanne, so I wouldn't be tempted to waste it on my vices. Worried though I was, I eventually decided to give myself a chance to practice self-control. I can't pass a test I never take. I don't have to buy drugs. I haven't even been around any dealers since I got out so, all things being equal, I should be fine.

As for booze, as long as I stay hydrated and well-fed, I won't think about it too much. In short, I kept the money. If I do wind up needing a taxi or having some other unavoidable expense, I'll give any change back to Suzanne. That should keep me accountable.

The gates of the house open, and a car drives out. Three teenage boys are in the backseat. We don't get a good look at them – only a fleeting glimpse – but I assume they are the Haywood boys and the Smith one, and that they're on their way to school. The only adult in the car is the driver. I assume Jeremy Haywood is still in the house.

"Really? They're going to school two days after their mother dies?"

Suzanne shrugs. "Maybe they really like learning."

That seems unlikely, given the circumstances.

Suzanne's research has revealed that James and Raquel Smith have been married for 20 years and have a son, Edward, who is in Jerry Haywood's year at school. Mr. Smith is a property developer and Mrs. Smith is a cardiologist. She's more like a consultant now, and spends most of her time home-making.

From the pictures that Suzanne gave me, James has kind eyes and his wife's aura radiates warmth and care. Their son looks like a responsible young man, despite being the only child of a very wealthy couple. I expect that he's been spoiled rotten all his life, but it's possible that the Smiths are normal, decent people with money. If that turns out to be true, it will be a relief.

"So, what's the plan?" I ask.

"Wait and watch. Maybe watch and wait."

"Ok."

Suzanne reaches over to the backseat, picking up her backpack and placing it on her lap. She opens it. As far as I can see it doesn't contain anything but snacks. A lot of snacks.

"Crisps?" she offers.

"Is that the best choice of food for a stakeout? I mean, they make you thirsty…"

"That's true, but they also taste nice."

"I'm fine, thanks."

She shrugs and rips open a pack of crisps and starts chomping. The crunching noise is fine at first, but as she makes her way through the packet, it starts to grate. I try to distract myself by surveying the area. A young man is out jogging, with his dog on a leash. He looks over at the car as he goes by. Our eyes meet and I smile. He smiles back and keeps moving until he's out of view. It's a nice little moment, the sort I rarely have and tend to savour.

And then I hear a crunch.

"He's got a nice butt," she says, with her mouth full.

This is going to be a long morning.

***

Three packets of crisps, one litre of water and an hour later, a large black BMW pulls up in front of the Smith house. I snap a picture of the license plate and Suzanne searches the internet for registration information. The gates swing open and the car goes through.

"Any hits?" I ask.

"I'm not a musician," she says.

I stare blankly at her, trying to work out what she means. She looks up at me, and then blinks in realisation.

"You meant the license plate. Sorry, I thought we'd reached the life catch-up portion of the day. I will know in a moment."

I narrow my eyes as she looks back at the screen.

"Ah, here we go. The car is registered to a William Sanders, 65 years of age, lives in the city."

She looks at me, brow furrowed. I think we're having the same thought.

"One of the partners at Donna's firm is named Sanders," I say.

Suzanne returns to her laptop, typing furiously. "Yes, that would be the same one."

"What's he doing here? This isn't his case," I say, looking out to the gate of the house.

"Maybe they're friends."

"If only we could hear what they're saying."

"Don't worry about that. Ksenia will hook us up in no time, although it looks like you'll be using that money after all," she says.

Now is as good a time as any.

DONNA

I show up at Zach's office without an appointment. I am fortunate enough that he's there and he's not busy. He greets me as he did the last time we met – warmly.

"I apologise for coming here without warning. It's urgent," I say.

"You know I'm always happy to see you."

"I know you say that," I reply, sitting in the chair he offers. He sits back in his chair and fiddles with his pen. It seems like he's trying to avoid looking at me.

"So, how can I help?" he asks, looking at the pen.

Ordinarily I would get right to business, but I'm still heated after my encounter with Detective Miller. It's left me a bit shaken. I tried to put my annoyance aside on the trip over here. I failed.

"Would you say I was cold-blooded?" I ask. My voice sounds mousy and small.

I don't know why I'm asking. I know I am. If I wasn't, I wouldn't be able to live with myself or sleep at night. I don't sleep that much but I get a few hours in.

"What? Cold-blooded? No, I wouldn't. I'd say you were determined, though," he says, finally looking at me.

I sit back in the chair. *Determined.* That's a good word. I must remember to put that on my CV.

"Why do you ask?"

"Some detective, Ken Miller, thinks I'm cold-blooded because I didn't cry when I saw Audrey Haywood's body. I'm not sure why that has… irritated me."

"Since when do you care about the opinions of strangers?" he says, smiling broadly.

I smile and shake my head. "I'm not getting enough sleep. This case is… challenging."

"Should I presume that you want a delay in the hearing?"

He's been doing this long enough to know how the game goes.

I nod.

"Do it for the children. Please," I say, "they could use a break." My voice is soft and quiet. Our eyes meet for a brief time which feels longer than it is. He breaks eye contact and nods.

"One month. That's the best I can do," he says.

"Thank you."

He smiles and stands up. "You should probably go. I've got… things to do."

"Of course. I'll let you be."

He walks to the door and holds it open. As I walk towards it, he looks me up and down and smiles. "For what it's worth, Miller is an ass. He makes it his business to get on people's nerves. Don't let him get to you."

"Thanks. You always know what to say to me."

"Oh, in that case, maybe we should get a drink later this week. How's Thursday?"

I already know that there's no point – this will end badly. I know because we've done this before. Neither of us has changed, so the outcome will be the same. Stir in the fact that we're on opposite sides of the same case – of the legal system, even – and there's nothing but a mess to be made. Nevertheless, it's been a while since we really talked, and Zach is a good guy.

"I don't know, it's a school night…"

He laughs and looks away, then looks back at me. "If memory serves right, you don't like going out on Friday nights – something about too many drunk people… Come on, it's one drink."

I sigh. I hate it when people use my words against me.

"Sure, Thursday sounds great."

"Thank you," he says.

He smiles again as I leave his office. I know I will live to regret this.

***

I'm at the train station about to go underground, still thinking about my meeting with Zach, when I get a call from Suzanne.

"What's up?"

"Do you really think it's a good idea to go for drinks with your ex?" she says.

I stop and look around. There are so many people coming and going that even if she is one of them, I can't see her.

"He's not my ex. You have superpowers now?" I say, still scanning the crowds for her.

"Oh, if only," she says, "My methods are far less spectacular."

I can hear her smirking.

"I'd ask you to elaborate, but I have a feeling that will complicate my life."

"You're probably right. Anyway, that's not why I called. I thought you should know that your boss, Mr. Sanders, just paid Haywood a visit," she says.

"What?"

"Yup. He came over to the Smith house. Didn't leave for almost an hour."

"Why?"

"No idea, but our girl is following him – Sanders, that is. We'll see if anything comes of that," she says.

Instinctively I move to lean against the wall, then tense up and stand straight when I remember that it's filthy.

"Any progress with Thompson?" I ask.

"Patience, Donna. I will keep you informed."

"Ok, thanks. I've got to go," I say.

"Later."

We hang up the phone as I try to work out what Old Bill might have been doing with Haywood. It's possible that he was merely extending his condolences, but that seems unlikely. Until now, I'd thought that Bill's interest in this case was purely monetary. Perhaps I was mistaken. Maybe the two have history that I'm not aware of. It might be time to do a bit more digging.

I'm sure Kat will be a good source of information.

IV

MINA

Suzanne and I split up and now I'm pacing the establishment outside Sanders Staunton & Co. It's weird to think that Donna and I went to same school, grew up in the same neighbourhood, and knew a lot of the same people and she wound up here, while I ended up in jail. I guess that's life. Two people can have the same starting point yet find themselves in different places.

Another thing that feels strange is how I've been up for hours now, and I've been moving but I feel like I've got nothing done. Sitting in a car aimlessly, while listening to someone eat isn't exactly how I'd envisioned spending the morning. And I didn't think I'd spend another hour waiting outside a building. The taxi I was following Mr. Sanders in got stuck at a red light. We lost him and since I didn't know what else to do, I came here.

Will he ever return to work? Does he even do any work? Sometimes it seems like the higher up people go, the less they do. It's possible that he's a gentleman of leisure. I don't even know why I'm bothering to follow him. Oh right, 'follow all leads' as Suzanne put it. Whatever. I hope he comes back soon so I can bug his phone and car and get out of here. Being out in the cold is making me hungry and I can't afford to get hungry.

I am startled by a vibration coming from my hoodie. The phone Suzanne gave me is ringing. I get it out of the hoodie, and answer the call.

"Hello?"

"Mina, we have a slight hiccup," she says.

"What's wrong?" Judging by how nonplussed she sounds, I don't immediately think we're in big trouble.

"I just spoke to Ksenia. She paid Haywood a visit at the Smith house. Tried to get the spyware onto his phone, but it didn't work."

"Uh oh," I say.

"I know – we have to find another way to hack his devices."

At that moment, Sanders' BMW drives up and whizzes into an underground car park.

"He's here now. I have to go."

"Call me when you're done. I have an idea."

I end the call and run up to the car park. It doesn't appear to require any special credentials for people to get in. That's good to know. I keep my hand on my phone and retreat from the car park, making my way to the office building. I wait near the entrance and after a minute or two, the man I now know to be William Sanders emerges.

I start walking towards him, looking at my phone. I activate the spyware as I brush past him. It's the faintest bit of physical contact, but he bristles. He looks me up and down and says, "Excuse me."

The words drip with derision. Hiding my phone from his sight, I smile and keep walking. I can feel his eyes trailing me as I cross the street. When I turn around, I see his back as he enters the building. I look at my phone. It worked! I now have access to every application on his phone. All we care about are his communications, and the camera and microphone.

I cross the street again, this time to get to the car park. I can't assume that he'll always have his phone on him, so I'll put a tracker on his car. Once I've done that, I'll call Suzanne and we'll discuss our next step. Finally, I get to do something today!

***

Suzanne comes to pick me up outside the firm's building. We drive to a nearby car park that lets us park for free for up to one hour. We may not need that much time. There, as she tears open another packet of crisps, Suzanne tells me her idea.

"Aisha Thompson," she says.

Crunch, crunch, crunch.

She could be eating a salad. It would be healthier and certainly wouldn't be noisier. I guess I should get used to this.

"Instead of following her around, we should get her on board," she says. She has not stopped eating.

"Get her on board how?"

"I don't know. Maybe get her to confront Jeremy."

"I don't understand what you're saying."

"We know that we can't hack his phone because he's careful, but if we can get Aisha to talk to him," she says, waving a crisp around and widening her round, hazel eyes, "we can use her phone to record their discussion."

She looks at me as if this is the obvious answer, but she doesn't know what she's saying. She doesn't know what she's asking of Aisha. The thought of confronting Alan after what he did to me... If Aisha is anything like me, she won't have the strength for that. It'll be too traumatic. She'll crumble.

"I don't think that's a good idea," I say, leaning against the dashboard, resting my head in my hands.

"Why not?"

She doesn't need to know what happened to me. In all the years since the rape, Donna is the only one I've ever told. I never told my parents. I never even told Salome, despite how much she's done for me, how supportive she's been. I've been open about everything, but not that.

"Bringing her face-to-face with the man who attacked her seems like a waste of time," I say. "After what he put her through, what he did to her, you don't really think she'll be able to face him, do you?"

232

"She had the strength and presence of mind to go to the police pretty much right away. If you ask me, she's got a steel backbone. I think we should at least try."

She's right. Aisha did go to the police. She also fought to get away from him and she was lucky enough to succeed. She wasn't intimidated by his position in society. She just did what she thought was right. I shouldn't assume she's scared of him. She's probably nothing like me.

"You're right. Trying won't hurt," I say.

She starts the car and a thought crosses my mind.

"Wait, Suzanne. I have another idea."

I hope it's a good one.

V

DONNA

Back at the office, Kat greets me with a worried look on her face – the sort that hints at terrible things on the horizon. She ushers me into a meeting room before I can get to my desk. She shuts the door behind us and looks at me like she's about to tell me I've lost my job.

"What now?" I say.

"That detective that was here earlier, he and his partner came back. They've 'invited' us to the station."

"What, like for drinks?"

"If you would let me finish—"

"Well, finish. What did they want?" I ask. My exasperation must be evident.

"They think that Haywood may have killed his wife," she says slowly. The words sink in and I almost can't believe them.

"Seriously?"

"Well they didn't spell it out, but they want us to bring him in for question-ing," she says. "They took our statements again. I got the feeling they think we were involved."

"What? Why?"

"I don't know, but they wanted to know where we'd been all Saturday morning, who could verify, that sort of thing."

"Alibis? For real?"

She nods.

"Did you tell them the truth," I ask, lowering my voice.

"Not the whole truth. I told them I was in my apartment, which is true. That's all. Daryl said he was at work all night, same thing he told his wife, I think."

"How long do you think it'll be before you have to come clean?"

"You should be more worried about yourself. The dude, Miller, was especially interested in where you spent Saturday morning," she says.

"What? Why?"

"You're the one who called me and Daryl. I think he thinks you were there when it happened, when she died, or you at least know more than you're saying. I got the feeling that he thinks you're hiding something."

I hold my hands to my temples and shake my head.

"This is insane," I say, "I was nowhere near that house."

"Yeah well, I don't think he believes that."

My breath gets shorter and shorter. If they find out that I went to see Suzanne, my job, nay, my life is over. I'll be disbarred. Haywood will probably get away with his crimes and I'll be left unemployed and unemployable. My heart rate increases and I feel my throat muscles tightening. I try to calm down, start breathing normally again. I can't have a meltdown at work.

Breathe. Breathe.

I feel the air travel through my nostrils, down my throat, into my lungs. My chest expands until there's room for nothing else.

Breathe out.

I let the air out. My breathing is jagged, but I continue until the exhales get longer… I can feel my heart beating normally again. Given all I've gone through, the poor thing has done well not to give way.

"Why do they think she was killed?" I ask. I suddenly feel a little dizzy. I lean on a desk to steady myself. My stomach is in knots.

"Something about her head being dented," she says.

"Those surely weren't the exact words."

"Yeah, I'm not quoting verbatim here, but that's the gist of it."

She leans against the wall and shakes her head.

"This is insane," I say again.

"I know. It's not every day your client is accused of a different crime while you're defending him. But you should be fine. Just tell them where you were, and they'll let you be."

"Yeah, you're right," I say, trying to think up some version of the truth (or as it is commonly known, 'a lie') that won't end my career.

"You need me to come to the station with you?" she asks.

"No, no. I'll be fine. We've still got a lot of work to do. Speaking of which, have you found anything on the victim?"

As Kat starts to reply, it occurs to me that I've tipped my hand a little.

"Do you mean the 'accuser'?" she says, giving me a serious look, as if to remind me of which side I'm on. I nod and wave my hand for her to continue.

"Not a single blemish on her record. She's a good student, quiet, responsible, and all-round credible witness/accuser/human being. No one said a bad word about her at all. I mean, she fluffed her lines in a play once—"

"Poor baby—"

"And she doesn't smoke weed, which some kids seemed to think was a bad thing… but other than that, clean as a whistle," she says, shrugging nonchalantly.

"So… we have a defendant who on more than one occasion has been accused of sexual crimes and an accuser—" I say, looking at her face as she nods in approval, "whose reputation is essentially untainted."

"She did go to a party, and then follow a random boy to his house… to make out, and maybe more. There's that."

"Of course, I forgot those are crimes in some circles."

"Oh, and she's considering going vegan," Kat says, frowning.

My stomach feels alright now, but I've had enough of life for one day.

"I should have been a doctor."

I sit on a chair, resting my elbows on the desk as I cradle my head in my hands. I lift my head when I hear Kat chuckle softly.

"You'd have made a terrible doctor."

"Is that so?"

"Your bedside manner leaves much to be desired."

"I beg to differ."

Her right hand starts twitching.

"You don't have the patience for patients." She makes a silly cartoon-like face.

I groan. "I see what you did there."

She lifts her index and middle fingers to her mouth. "Anyway, I need to take a break."

"Sure."

As she starts towards the door, I interrupt her. "Kat, do you know anything about Old Bill and Haywood's relationship?"

"What do you mean?"

I shrug. "I don't know – are they actually friends? Is this personal for Bill?"

With one hand on the doorknob, she bobs her head about and frowns. "I've not heard anything specific. I think they run with the same crowd, members of the same clubs, that sort of thing. I don't know if they're *really* friends, like us."

I nod. "Ok."

"If it's personal for Bill, it's because it affects his bank account and reputation."

"Yeah… that makes sense."

She winks at me and leaves the room. Through the glass door, I watch her go to the lift. As she gets into it, I wonder if she sincerely believes we're friends. She has a history of deluding herself, so it's entirely possible. For the first time in a little while, I genuinely feel bad for her.

The lift doors shut, and I'm left to weigh up my options. If Jeremy killed Audrey as the police now suspect, I would very much like him to go down for that crime, as well as his attempt to rape Aisha. It's looking more and more likely that I won't kill him. Yes, I know I'd already decided not to, but sometimes I change my mind. Not this time, though.

Between Detective Miller's sudden and unreasonable interest in me and my whereabouts, and my place on Jeremy's defence team, there's no way I could get away with murder again. I'll let Suzanne and Mina carry on their investigation, and we'll feed whatever damning information they come across to Zach or the police.

Ah, the police. I suppose I should pay them a visit. Back into the cold I go.

VI

MINA

I feel like such a creep, hanging out outside a school, watching and waiting. It doesn't matter that my intentions are good – I still feel weird and wrong about this. We've been sitting here for an hour. There is more than an hour left until lessons end. Suzanne asked around and for a small fee, the security guard was happy to tell her that Aisha stays late on Mondays to attend drama club. There's a man who doesn't mind losing his job.

The car is quite cold, so she turns the heater on. She reaches for her backpack again and I sink into my seat, expecting another round of crisp-chomping. Instead, she brings out a pair of fingerless thermal gloves, and puts them on. They look warm and comfortable and I wish I had a pair. I mean, I have a pair of gloves but they're old and frayed and were never that warm. They were a gift from a stranger… more like a donation, really.

Just as I settle back into my previous seating position, Suzanne surprises me by pulling out another packet of crisps.

"You eat a lot," I say.

Her brow furrows slightly as she looks at me, packet in hand.

"You could stand to eat more. What diet are you on?" Her voice is cool and monotonous. It's actually kind of unsettling. I lean away from her, taken aback by the question.

She blinks at me, licking her front teeth. "Sorry, was that insensitive?"

"It's fine. You— you didn't mean any harm."

She nods. "I take it it's been difficult adjusting since you left your previous residence."

"It comes with the territory. I'm sure I'll get used to things eventually."

She looks at the packet. "Are you? Sure, I mean."

She looks up at me and our eyes meet. I look away.

"No, I'm not. Some days I wake up and I think I'll be ok. You know – as long as I put one foot in front of the other, things will work out. Then other mornings I know it'll take a miracle to get through the day without screwing up."

She fondles the packet of crisps, and it makes a loud, cracking sound. I face her, wondering if I've over-shared. She stares at me for what must be a good 20 seconds, not blinking once.

"What?" I finally ask.

"I don't know. I've never noticed that your eyes are so big."

"What?"

"You have big eyes. And they're a nice shade of brown. They're pretty," she says. She rips open the packet of crisps and starts eating, still looking at my eyes. I look away, back to the school gate.

"You're uncomfortable with my observation."

Crunch. Chomp. Smack.

I sigh.

"It— it's a bit random, that's all," I stay focussed on the school gate.

"Well, it's the first time I noticed, so I thought I should say something. People tend to like compliments."

She rummages through the packet, almost like she's looking for a specific crisp. I hear her take another bite. I close my eyes and wait till the chewing stops.

"Your life will get back to normal sooner or later. And I'm sorry that you don't like my eating, but this is how I roll. When you make enough money, you can get a car and then you won't have to put up with me."

Clear, precise, emotionless… not a single word minced. I turn to look at her, but her eyes are buried in the packet of crisps. She looks up and smiles. I don't know what else to do – I smile back.

"Patience is a virtue," she says.

"So I've heard."

***

At last, the students start pouring out of the school. There are so many of them and, at first, it's hard to tell one from another. Suzanne and I are watching from the car. I've studied Aisha's picture closely. It wasn't hard to find – all her social media profiles were public. She seems less vapid and self-obsessed than most of her peers, and it looked like she knew all of her 'friends' in real life. She has dark brown hair (which, from her social media pictures, might be in braids or an afro depending on the week), mahogany skin, eyes the colour of midnight. Slim build, average height. Given that most of the students are white, she should be easy enough to spot.

A girl matching her description walks out, flanked by two other students – a mixed-race redheaded girl and a white girl with hair that's dyed blue. Blue hair dye? She'll regret that one day. Aisha looks down as she walks arm-in-arm with her companions.

"That's her," Suzanne says, opening her door and leaping out of the car.

I sit still, watching her stride over to the edge of the school's property. I give no thought to the safety of her car as I jump out of it and hurry after her. She stands around next to a wall, looking at her phone, (I assume) to give off a carefree vibe. The three girls walk past her and she watches them go by. As I approach, I hear her call Aisha by name.

The girls stop and Aisha faces Suzanne. The other two look suspiciously at her, eyeing her up and down. By now, I'm next to Suzanne.

"Who are you?" the redhead asks. She disengages from Aisha and steps forward.

"Someone who can help your friend," Suzanne replies. She lowers her phone and walks closer to them as I stand against the wall.

"Oh? And how is that?" the same girl says. The other girl keeps her arm in Aisha's, as Aisha stares at Suzanne.

"It's confidential. For her ears only."

"Are you a lawyer?" Aisha says, softly.

"Do I look like a lawyer?" Suzanne asks. I'm not sure if it's rhetorical.

"Is she a lawyer?" Aisha asks, pointing at me.

I shake my head; though that's the best compliment I've received in years.

"We work for a lawyer who needs your help with a delicate case," I say.

"What case?" her outspoken friend asks.

The blue-haired friend tugs her arm. "Let's go, Aisha."

"What case?" Aisha asks. Her voice gets quieter as she walks closer to Suzanne. She fixes her eyes on Suzanne's face, like she's trying to read her mind. Good luck with that.

"Aisha, they might be crazy or—"

"Niamh, chill," she says, cutting our interrogator off. She looks from Suzanne to me.

"What case?" she asks again.

"We can't talk about it here. But we can buy you lunch," Suzanne says.

"You're not going anywhere with these weirdos," her other friend says.

"Can they come, too?" Aisha says.

Suzanne shrugs. "Uh… sure, why not?"

"See Claire, you get a free lunch," she says.

The girls look at each other and then at Aisha.

"Mum says there's no such thing as a free lunch," Claire says.

People still say that?

"Aisha, are you sure about this?" Niamh asks. "What would your parents say?"

Claire nods. "Yeah, this seems like a dumb idea."

"It's ok," Aisha says. "I think we'll be fine."

***

"You girls aren't very smart."

Claire lifts her chin towards us like it was a weapon, chicken burger in hand, and smacks her lips at Suzanne. "And you're not very nice."

Suzanne smiles. "Thank you."

We're sitting in a booth in the chicken shop a short drive away from the school. The sidekicks, Claire and Niamh, have ordered chicken burgers while Aisha ordered a two-piece meal which she is yet to eat. She's been staring out the window, absentmindedly pushing her chips around the plate.

Niamh lifts her hands. "What are you on about?"

"I'm just saying, getting in a car with two strangers isn't the smartest thing to do. You're old enough to know that. Don't you listen to true crime podcasts? We could have kidnapped you," Suzanne says.

Well, that's one way to start a conversation.

"Women don't do stuff like that," Niamh says.

"Some do, and you need to be aware of that so you don't get victimised by crazy people."

I sigh.

"Is this why you brought us here? To lecture us on safety?" Claire asks. She chews her food violently as the words leave her mouth.

"Clearly someone has to!"

I clear my throat. Suzanne looks at me and nods.

"Aisha, if we could talk to you in private, that would be a great help," she says. Aisha looks away from the window.

She points at an empty booth further away from the one we're in. "We can move over there."

Niamh and Claire exchange a look.

"I don't think you—"

"It's ok, Niamh. I won't be long," she says.

Claire glares at Suzanne as we leave our side of the booth. She and Niamh then make way for Aisha to follow us. They sit back down and keep eating as we walk across to the empty booth.

"So who are you, then?" Aisha asks as she takes her seat opposite us.

"You can call me Suzy. I'm a private investigator. This is my associate, Mina." I smile at her. She smiles back tentatively.

"What do you want?" She looks at me. I look at Suzanne.

"We work for someone who needs evidence – concrete evidence – that Jeremy Haywood attacked you," Suzanne says.

When she hears his name, Aisha flinches, eyes wide. Almost unconsciously, she holds onto her elbows and swallows hard.

"So, you work for the prosecution," she says with quiet concern.

A smile creeps onto Suzanne's face, and she nods. "We'll go with that."

"I told the police everything that happened, and Mr. Parsons, too," Aisha says.

"Yes. The thing is, we were hoping that you could help us elicit a confession from that obnoxious criminal," Suzanne says.

Aisha's hands drop to her lap as she stares at Suzanne. "What? I don't understand."

"It's your word against his, Aisha, and he has some very good lawyers working very hard to make sure he doesn't go to prison for what he did to you," I say, speaking for the first time since we got here.

"What can I do? Against him and his lawyers?"

"You can talk to Jerry. Ask him to talk his dad into confessing," I say.

"Jerry?" She throws her hands up. "He hasn't even looked me in the eye since I got back to school. I tried to talk to him today and he just blanked me. He didn't even ask if I was ok."

"For what it's worth, he'd probably have done that even if his dad hadn't attacked you... and *especially* if you'd slept with him," Suzanne says.

"What?"

"His reaction to you is not uncommon for boys his age... or even boys twice his age. It's likely a genetic defect, something to do with that Y chromosome..." Suzanne's voice trails off as her eyes move around the room. The absence of inflection in her voice is at once calming and unnerving.

"Anyway," she carries on, "his mother died a couple of days ago, so his defences will almost certainly be low. He won't be in a fit state to consistently ignore you."

"His mother is dead?" Aisha says, her voice trembling. "How? When?"

It's obvious she cares for the boy, although I'm not sure how well knows him. Suzanne looks at me, as if to say, "Young people, eh?"

"Did he not say?" I ask, turning to Aisha.

"Well it's not like he would tell me, but I've not heard anything about that."

"In that case, don't spread that around," Suzanne says.

"What happened to her?"

"It's best we don't say," I say.

She sinks into the seat and her eyes wander around aimlessly. "You want me to take advantage of him."

"N—"

"Yes, that's exactly what we want you to do. But it's for the greater good, so it's ok," Suzanne says.

"I can't do that. That would be wrong."

"Look, all we're asking you to do is talk to him; get him to talk to his dad. That's it," I say.

"This is insane. I have to go home."

She gets up and leaves the booth, but Suzanne leaps up after her and grabs her hand. "Are you really going to let this man get away with hurting you because you have a silly little crush? Come on, you're smarter than that."

"Get away from me," Aisha says, raising her voice as she snatches her hand away. Thankfully, she's not loud enough to draw the staff's attention.

"You know I'm right," Suzanne says, folding her arms.

Aisha stomps over to our previous booth and within a couple of seconds she and her friends leave the shop.

"What was that?" I ask.

Suzanne shrugs.

We watch as the girls cross the street.

"You know what this reminds me of?"

I shake my head.

"Uni," she says.

"Huh?"

"I once dated a guy who looked like melted cheese, not a crime in and of itself, but highly inconvenient. I was trying to make his friend jealous – we'd been flirting for months and I thought I could motivate him to ask me out."

"What?"

"I know. It was ridiculous. Anyway, melt-man took me to a place not too dissimilar from this one. That was his idea of a first date. The food was terrible, and it turned out he had no personality or… honour. Perfectly good waste of time."

It's dawning on me that not everything Suzanne says is worth hearing.

"Did his friend ask you out?"

"Only after I stopped flirting with him. He was one of those guys who's allergic to happiness."

"Uh huh."

When the girls disappear round a bend, we walk over to the other booth and see that Aisha's meal sits on the table, untouched.

"That's your lunch if you want it."

She turns to me, smiling. I think I might be working with a crazy person.

"Yeah, I'll have it."

She sighs and looks around at nothing in particular. "Come on, we'll go to her house. Maybe her parents can talk some sense into her."

"We really should have started there…"

"Yeah, yeah."

I pack up Aisha's meal and follow Suzanne out of the shop. I really hope we're not speeding to a dead end.

***

Like a pair of stalkers, we find our way to the Thompson residence. Parked outside the modest-looking mid-terrace house, Suzanne decides our best course of action is to march into the home and convince Aisha's parents to talk her into helping us.

"I'm not sure that's the smartest way to go about it. That didn't work with her, why do you think it would work with her parents?"

I've tried my best not to call Suzanne out on her unusual way of dealing with situations and people, but I feel protective of Aisha.

"Time is ticking, Mina. What do you suggest we do?"

"Let me do the talking this time."

She pauses for a moment, then shrugs. "Ok. If all else fails, we'll move on to Plan C."

"What's Plan C?"

"You don't need to know that."

We get out of the car and walk to the door of the house. I ring the doorbell. Suzanne stands behind me and I can feel her fidgeting. The door opens and we are met by a short, rotund woman. I'd say she is in her mid-to-late forties. She looks at us with brows furrowed and eyes narrowed.

"Mrs. Thompson?" I say.

"Who are you two?"

From the house I hear Aisha's voice calling out, "That's them, mum. They're the ones who stopped us outside school."

I look around and see Aisha's face in a window next to the front door. I assume that's the living room. When I look back at her mother, her eyes are wide and her nostrils flared. She starts closing the door, but I put my foot in it.

"Remove your foot from the door or I will break it," she shouts.

"Please, ma'am, we need your daughter's help to send Mr. Haywood to jail." I push against the door as she tries to force it shut.

"She already said no."

A tall, angry-looking man emerges from another room and stands behind Mrs. Thompson. Slightly wrinkly, most likely in his early fifties, with what's left of his hair turning grey. I suppose this is Mr. Thompson. Have they coordinated their work shifts?

"Do you want us to call the police?" he asks.

"Please, sir—"

"If that's a no, you'd better leave."

"Sir, all we're asking is that your daughter talks to Jerry. What if her help is the only thing we need to defeat the man who tried to—?"

"Don't say it!" he yells.

His wife leaves the door and goes into the adjacent room. I remove my foot from the door.

"She's suffered enough," he says. "It's not her job to put him away."

From behind me, Suzanne speaks. I'd almost forgotten she was here.

"You couldn't stop what happened to your daughter, sir, but do you really want to deny her a chance to have justice, because of your guilt? Maybe you couldn't protect her that night, but you can help her make things right now," she says.

That's the sanest thing I've heard her say all day… maybe even ever.

He looks down and swallows hard. He walks away from the door, leaving it open. Suzanne and I look at each other.

"So, are you letting us in?" she asks, raising her voice.

***

Records show that Clifton and Vicky Thompson have been married for 19 years and they've lived in this house for 12 of those. Suzanne and I sit next to each other at the table in the open-plan living and dining area. Aisha sits opposite us, and her father sits at the head of the table. His expression has softened, although he still seems wary of us. Vicky brings a pot of tea in from the kitchen and serves it to us.

"Thank you," Suzanne and I say at the same time.

Vicky grimaces and takes a seat next to Aisha. They hold hands as Aisha stares intently at her tea.

"Ok, what do you want?" Clifton asks.

"All we're asking is for your daughter to talk to Jerry, and ask him a few questions," Suzanne says.

"And how do you think this will help your case?" he asks.

"Human nature," Suzanne says.

The three of them look puzzled.

"I think what Suzanne is saying is that by confronting Jerry with his father's actions, Aisha would stir up curiosity in him that he won't be able to ignore. He'll talk to his dad, and perhaps get him to confess. From what we've gathered, he seems like a decent boy. He's not dangerous. There's no way he's happy with what's going on," I say.

Clifton nods. His calloused hands grip his mug tightly.

"All she has to do is talk to the boy," Vicky says.

"Yes. We'll give you some pointers about what to say, but yes, that's all," Suzanne says, smiling as she turns her attention to Aisha.

Vicky puts her arm around Aisha's shoulder, as the girl sits still.

"The past few days have been hellish," Vicky says.

"You have no idea how hard it's been for her," Clifton says.

Unfortunately, I do. In my mind, I see Alan's face. I feel his hands on my hips. I physically shake myself, just to get the picture out of my head. I take a gulp of tea. For the first time today, I think about how helpful a drink might be … and how some drugs would relax me.

"So, will you help us?" I ask.

The desire for relief starts to rise, but I focus my attention on Aisha. I think about her bravery, and how I need to be brave, too. I need to be brave enough to deny my desires.

Aisha looks at her parents, first her father, then her mother.

"You'll be close by the whole time?" Clifton asks.

"The whole time," Suzanne confirms.

"I think you should do it," Clifton says.

Aisha looks at her mother, who nods.

"Alright. What's the best time for—?"

"We can do it now," Aisha says. Suzanne's mouth hangs.

"When you say now, you mean…"

"I mean now. He's at football practice. I can talk to him at the end. No time like the present, right?" Aisha says.

"No time like the present," Suzanne echoes. She smiles and takes a sip of tea.

I guess it's game on.

VII

DONNA

By now it must have caught your attention that I hate a wide variety of things. Police stations also make the list. This particular station has an air of gloom and despair. It's haunting and dull and everyone here looks hopeless and downcast, almost like they're contemplating ending their lives. If I worked in such a wretched environment, I would most likely look the same way.

It is here that I meet Detective Miller, and his partner Detective Lawson. Lawson is tall, average build, wearing a nice enough trouser suit. Her curly brown hair is in a bun and her light brown eyes look weary. Her shoulders are slumped, like she physically feels weighed down by all the paperwork she has piling up on her untidy desk (which we walk past as they lead me to an interrogation room). I take a seat and Lawson sits opposite me, while Miller stands with his back against the wall behind her. This room is similar to the one Kat and I met Haywood in less than a week ago.

Miller took me by surprise earlier today – both times – and I was so startled by Audrey's apparent suicide that I did not at any point take the time to study his features. He has brown eyes that look like they conceal a world of secrets, the kind of secrets that people would kill to know. Unlike his partner, there's a sense of purpose in his eyes, and perhaps a hint of decadence. He towers over Lawson and me, but I do not find his size or manner intimidating.

As he opens a packet of chewing gum and takes a stick to his mouth, my gaze is drawn to his lips. They look soft and inviting. I feel my lips part instinctively but am quick to rein myself in. I turn my attention from Miller's face to Lawson's, lest I give the wrong impression. It's too late though. From the corner of my eye, I see him smirk. He's probably used to such reactions. Between his appearance and his voice, it seems that he's in the wrong profession. I breathe slowly, quietly reminding myself of why I'm here.

"Thank you for coming, Miss Palmer," Lawson says. She smiles at me, wearily. Her politeness just about hides the tiredness that threatens to knock her out.

"It's no trouble," I say. I glance quickly at Miller. He doesn't move, just stares at me. Perhaps he intends to make me uncomfortable.

"We just need to go over your statement again," she says.

"My colleague tells me you suspect foul play."

She nods, fiddling with papers and pictures in a file that sits between us. "The victim had swelling on her skull, implying that she endured a blunt force trauma that most likely killed her. Preliminary results show that her wrists were probably slashed very soon after she died."

My mind goes to the Haywood children. I wonder how they'll fare when they find that in addition to being a rapist, their father murdered their mother. I wonder how they'll feel if he gets killed. Will they be grateful? Will they be better or worse off without him? Emotions can be complex, there's probably no way of knowing with certainty.

"That's awful."

"It is," says Miller.

I look at him and he comes closer, taking a seat next to Lawson.

"Tell us again what happened on Saturday," Lawson says.

I sigh and look at the ceiling. I move my hand to my neck and start massaging it.

"I got up early, left the house… got some coffee," I say, looking from one detective to the other and back again.

"And then?" Miller says.

"And then I went for a walk. I don't see how any of this is relevant."

He taps the desk lightly.

"I was thinking about going to the park when Mr. Haywood called me. You know the rest," I say, placing my hands on the table and reclining in the chair.

"What do you think happened that day?" he asks. He keeps his eyes fixed on my face, and I hold his gaze. Neither of us looks away, each trying to figure the other out. It feels like an hour before Lawson clears her throat.

Her interruption forces me to turn to her. "I have no idea."

"You have no idea what you think, or you have no idea what happened?" Miller asks.

I'm starting to feel like a suspect.

"You're the detective – work it out."

"Miss Palmer—"

I cut him off before he can irritate me further. "I was nowhere near the house when Mrs. Haywood died and I don't know what happened between her and her husband. If he killed her, he didn't tell me about it."

"And had he told you…?" Lawson probes.

"I wouldn't be legally able to tell you, as you know. But he didn't make any sort of confession to me."

"Why did he call you and not one of your colleagues?" Lawson asks. Miller looks quietly at me. His eyes move from my face to my hands. They linger there for a moment and then return to my face.

"I can only assume it's because I'm the lead on his defence. You'd have to ask him."

"And why did you call your colleagues?" Miller asks, lifting his fingers to his lips. He touches them gently. It's… distracting.

I find myself unsure of how to answer the question. Should I tell them about my reservations about being alone with a man like Haywood? Should I carry on playing the part of the loyal lawyer?

"I thought it would be unprofessional to go to his house alone. I prefer things to be above board."

He grunts. "Well that makes sense."

"You're welcome to check the location data on my phone if you want further proof of my whereabouts that afternoon."

"I don't think that will be necessary," Lawson says.

Miller sits up and straightens his jacket, looking at Lawson. She nods with her eyes.

"That will be all for now, Miss Palmer," he says.

"Great."

I stand up, gather my things and leave the room. I weave through the station and to the exit. As I step into the freezing cold, I hear Miller's voice.

"Miss Palmer."

I turn around, surprised to see him a few feet away from me. I should have noticed him following me. I should have scanned my surroundings. I'm not usually so careless.

"You think he killed her, don't you?"

"Why are you so interested in what I think?"

"I think you're interesting," he says, shrugging slowly. The words hang in the air, leaving me unsure of their meaning or my response.

"If he killed her, I'm sure you'll bring him to justice," I say with a hint of sarcasm in my voice. That was unintentional. He smiles and puts his hands in his pockets. We stand there, looking at each other. I should leave but for some reason, I don't.

Finally, he runs his fingers through his hair and says, "How are you getting back to work?"

"The same way I got here."

He smiles. "When can I see you again?"

The question surprises me. It seems to have come out of nowhere. In my head, I run through a list of possible reasons he might want to see me – he thinks

I'm an accomplice and wants to entrap me; he wants me to spy on Haywood; he wants to use me to get a confession out of the man; his interest in me is not work-related.

I can't deny that he's attractive, but once upon a time my mother thought my father was attractive and I'm sure you're sick of hearing about how that turned out. Besides, this is so unprofessional that he's probably terrible in every arena of life.

Yet, I don't immediately say no.

"Why would you want to see me again?" I ask, softening my tone.

Honey… not vinegar.

"I don't know. To talk, maybe. We could go for a drink. Dinner, if you like."

His eyes move from mine to my lips and back again.

I cross my hands in front of me. "I'm not sure that's professional."

"It's unprofessional to eat and drink?"

I pause and think of what I could lose by taking him up on his offer. As long as we're in a public place and I don't tell him too much about myself, I should come out on top. I may even get a free meal out of this.

"I'm really busy," I say.

Still, it's nice to play the game sometimes.

"So am I, but I still have to eat."

"Ok… how's Wednesday lunch time?"

He smiles. "Unless someone gets killed, it should be fine."

I nod and turn around, leaving the premises.

Was that a mistake?

I suppose I won't know until it all goes to hell.

As I walk to the train station, my phone starts ringing. It's Suzanne again. I pick it up. I've not yet said a word, but I hear her talking excitedly.

"Donna! We have to see you tonight. You'll never believe what we've got."

Let's hope it's something good.

VIII

MINA

Today, I reckon I've done more sitting than is healthy. Here I am again, in Suzanne's car. We're back at the school, waiting for Aisha. She's been inside for about 10 minutes; football practice has been over for 5 of them. She said she'd wait for Jerry outside the boys' changing room. With her permission, we've linked Suzanne's phone to Aisha's in order to listen to her conversation with Jerry. Suzanne's phone sits on the dashboard as we wait.

"You think she'll stick to the script?" Suzanne asks.

"She'll be alright."

"I hope so. This is all so sudden; I hope she has what it takes."

"Are you nervous?"

"No, I just don't want to have to move on to Plan C."

"What *is* Plan C?"

"Plausible deniability," she says.

"That's not a plan, that's a legal term."

Over the phone we hear Aisha calling Jerry's name. It sounds like she's jogging.

"Jerry, please wait!"

"Stay away from me."

"I heard about your mother... I wanted to say I'm sorry."

There's quiet, like she's paused, and then Jerry speaks. "How do you know about my mother?"

"It doesn't matter. I'm sorry. She always seemed nice."

"What do you want?"

"To talk. About what your dad—"

"Liar! You're such a liar. My dad didn't— you know what, leave me alone!"

His voice sounds shaky. Suzanne and I stare at the phone, riveted.

Once again, Aisha sounds like she's moving.

"*Your dad* is the liar!" she yells.

"You're lying about him because you want money."

Ugh, straight out of The Rapists' Defence Manual: Moneyed Man's Edition.

"I don't want your filthy money! Did you even ask him what happened that night? He didn't care that you were drunk. You could have choked on your vomit. You could have died and it didn't matter to him! All he wanted to do was hurt me! He's disgusting!" she shouts.

Her voice breaks a little and the pain in it is too familiar. I've felt it more times than I wanted to. Knowing that you're not even human to someone, being treated worse than an animal... I swallow hard, holding back tears.

"He would never do something like that. He's not like that."

"You're wrong about him. If I hadn't fought him off, he would have raped me!"

"Shut up," he yells, "you're a liar!"

"Ask him then," she raises her voice again, "Ask him! If you know him like you think you do, you'll know if he's lying."

Another male voice says, "Hey what's going on?"

Aisha starts moving again. I think she's walking away. Suzanne looks at me, but I avoid making eye contact. I try to wipe the tear that's falling down my cheek without her seeing.

"She free-styled a little, but that's cool."

"Yeah, I guess." I finally look at her.

"You're up," Suzanne says, her head motioning to the school gates.

I look towards the gates, waiting for Aisha to come through them. Once she does, I get out of the car and walk past her. She goes to the car and gets in. I get closer to the school, loitering near the gates, pretending to wait for someone.

Within a couple of minutes, Jerry comes out of the school. I stay where I am and reach for my phone, waiting for him to walk past me. As he does, I say, "Nice shoes."

He looks me up and down, and smiles sheepishly, still walking.

"Thank you," he says. His voice is slightly hoarse, and he looks distracted. He keeps walking until he gets into a car. I see that the driver from the morning is the only one inside. I suppose little brother and the Smith boy are already at home.

Seeing Jerry up close, my heart goes out to him. He really does look like a genuine, good-natured young man. It's such a shame that his life is falling apart. I wish I could help him, but I can't. Instead, I install spyware on his phone. He's not as careful as his father. That's good for us. Jeremy Haywood has done awful things, and for them he will pay.

***

Evening has fallen, night is not far behind. I'm in a taxi outside a pretty townhouse in an upscale neighbourhood populated with pretty townhouses. I would have asked the taxi driver to leave, but this is not the sort of place that I can hang around on foot. I would draw attention to myself. I've paid the taxi driver to stay until I'm ready to leave. He was more than happy to do that, and has spent his time listening to something on his phone. Music? Podcast? I didn't ask. I'm doing some listening of my own.

Once we finished at the school, Suzanne and I took Aisha home. En route, she stopped at a petrol station to refuel. Sadly, apart from buying petrol, she bought more snacks. The only saving grace was that I got to talk to Aisha on her own while Suzanne made her purchase.

I turned to her in the back, where she sat with her arms folded and her head resting on the window.

"How're you feeling?"

She shrugged. I nodded at her.

"I don't know if you know this, but you're very brave," I said, with a half-smile.

She looked at my face, and then looked down. "I don't feel brave."

"What do you feel?"

She sighed and spoke softly. It was almost like she was scared someone would hear us and disapprove. "I don't feel anything. I don't know what I'm supposed to feel."

"I get it. Sometimes something so bad happens to you and you don't know what to do about it. There is no textbook on how to react to being assaulted."

She sat up and nodded. "Yeah, I guess."

"The most important thing you can do now is take care of yourself. Don't rush the healing process. Some days, you'll feel worse than others. You'll be tempted to self-medicate, to bury your feelings, to act like you're fine when you're not. Don't do that. It won't help. Don't let anyone push you into saying you feel good when you don't, ok?"

She nodded again. "Thank you."

"You're lucky. You have family and friends who care about you, and there are helplines you can call if you ever need them. And it doesn't hurt that you're resilient."

She kept nodding. I wanted to stop talking but I felt like I couldn't. I felt like there were all these things I needed to tell her.

"It doesn't matter what Jerry's dad did to you – you're an amazing young woman who is worthy of love and protection and respect. Nothing that happens in your life can or will ever change that. You're a queen and you deserve the very best that life has to offer," I said, feeling a lump grow in my throat.

She started crying. "Thank you so much. Thank you."

At that moment, Suzanne opened the door and tossed a carrier bag full of crisps in the backseat next to Aisha. That's when she saw her tears.

"Now what?"

I didn't bother explaining. We dropped Aisha off, and I followed William Sanders' trail to this location. I can't see what's going on in the room, but due to my efforts earlier in the day, I can hear. And I'm so glad that I have earphones, because what I'm hearing could make anyone blush.

William Sanders is currently meeting with not one, but two young ladies who I would guess are prostitutes. The services they're providing are definitely nothing to crow about. I hope I won't have to be here for much longer. I feel like a voyeur, albeit a blind one.

As I listen to Mr. Sanders and his guests, my mind wanders. It wanders to the usual places, the wrong places. I try to refocus my thoughts, think about something other than my misfortune but... I can't. This listening material doesn't help either. Mr. Sanders has some strange predilections. The girls he's with sound young, too young for him. I doubt that they grew up dreaming of trading their bodies for money. No one dreams of being used and abused. Well, no one in their right mind.

The unpleasant noises stop. I think they're done. I really hope so. Sanders gives them money for their trouble. I sit up and watch the door of the house. It takes close to 20 minutes, but the two ladies leave the building. They get into a car that's been parked outside since I got here.

In a split second, I have to decide whether to follow them, or to stick around and follow Sanders. I decide to follow them. I can catch up with him whenever I want to. They will prove more elusive.

The driver of their car starts the engine.

"Hey, mate," I say.

The cab driver doesn't respond. I tap his shoulder. The car is starting to pull out of the parking space.

He turns to me. "Yes, Miss?"

"Follow that car," I say, pointing at it.

He switches the taxi on and does as I ask.

We'll see where this leads.

IX

DONNA

The hours fly by and it's officially time to leave work. Because I'm seeing Suzanne tonight, I leave at a sensible time. Kat invites me to the pub, but I tell her that I'm meeting an old friend. We arrange to go tomorrow. I even offer to pay for a round. I notice that almost as soon as she leaves, Daryl does as well. Good luck to them both.

Suzanne and I meet at an Asian fusion curry house equidistant from our respective places of work. When I get there, she's already waiting for me. She sits at a table at the far end of the restaurant. It's far enough away from the door that it's warm, and she can see everyone that comes in and out. A waiter leads me over to her and hands me a menu.

"Tonight's special is the beef curry," he says.

"Thank you," I reply.

He smiles and leaves us.

"You really should try the lamb, it's far better," Suzanne says.

"You've been here before?"

"Once or twice. I try to switch it up. Can't risk getting predictable, you know?"

She speaks with a twinkle in her eye, and I feel like she's about to tell me she's won the lottery.

"Mina's running late, but she'll be here," she continues.

"What did you want to talk about?" I ask.

The waiter returns with a jug of water, an empty glass and a glass of orange juice. He places them all on the table, the empty glass in front of me, the juice-filled one in front Suzanne. He pours some water into my glass.

"Would you like to order any starters?" he asks.

I look at Suzanne and she shakes her head.

"Not yet," I say.

He nods. "Please, take your time."

They always say that but they never mean it. He smiles and leaves us. I decide to look at the menu this time.

"I figured you'd want water," she says.

"You figured right."

As I inspect my options, she carries on. "We met Aisha Thompson and her parents."

"And…?"

"She agreed to help us."

"Seriously?"

"Yup. With her parents' consent she helped our investigation."

I put the menu down. "Help how? What are you doing, Suzanne?"

"What you're paying me to do. Aisha agreed to help us get a confession out of Jeremy. Albeit in a roundabout way," she says, beaming with pride.

"I don't understand anything you're saying. How is she going to get him to confess?"

She opens her mouth to say something but stops as she looks past me. I turn around and see the waiter coming towards us, with Mina shuffling behind him. She looks tired, but not as bad as she did last week. Despite her fragile exterior, her shoulders are pushed back and she walks with her head up. There is dignity in honest work.

She sits next to me, and the waiter puts a menu in front of her, retreating with a smile.

"Sorry I'm late," she says.

"Actually, you're right on time," Suzanne says.

Suzanne takes a gulp of her juice and smiles at me.

"So what is this magic confession and how are we going to get it?" I ask.

The waiter returns with another empty glass and pours water into it. He gives it to Mina with a smile. She smiles back.

"Thank you," she says.

He leaves, but not for long I'm sure.

"The special is the beef curry, but I recommend the lamb," Suzanne tells Mina.

"Wow, this place is nice," Mina says.

I can feel my patience starting to wear thin. Yes, we have to eat. Yes, the waiter's job is to make us feel welcome. Yes, it's nice to know that lamb is greater than beef, but for the love of the little that is good in the world, I want to know how our plan is progressing!

"I'm sure we can admire it later. What's the status?" I ask. My tone is brusque, and Suzanne knows I mean business.

She clears her throat and rummages through her jacket, which is draped on the back of her seat. "Get your headphones out."

She pulls a phone out of the pocket, taps around it a few times and shows it to me. There's an audio file saved on the phone. I'm not sure what I'm supposed to get from this.

"What is this?" I say.

"Get your headphones out!" she repeats.

I fumble around my bag until I find my earphones. I look at her and she eggs me on. I plug the earphones into her phone, and she presses play.

I hear what sounds like movement, a rustling noise as if the phone was in someone's pocket as they paced around. It lasts for about 30 seconds before the voice starts speaking.

"Dad, I need to talk to you," the voice says. It comes from a young male, I'd guess between the ages of 14 and 17. His voice sounds like it wants to break, but hasn't quite got enough hormones to make it happen yet.

"Sure, son. What's up? How was school?" says a voice, that of an older male. But not just any older male – Jeremy Haywood.

"Did you attack Aisha?" the young male says. I suppose this is the voice of Jerry. Well this should be interesting.

"What? Jerry, what are you saying?"

"Dad, please tell me the truth. Did you— did you try to rape her?"

"Don't be ridiculous, Jerry. That girl wants a payday. This is what happens when you're an important man. People always try to bring you down. She probably saw the house and figured she could make some easy money by telling lies about me. I respect that you were trying to get some action but you should never have brought her here."

"Wouldn't it have been easier for her to accuse me? And what 16-year old is looking for a payday? That doesn't make any sense."

"People will always try to hurt you when you have money. Never forget that, son. It doesn't matter how old they are. Maybe her parents put her up to it. Who knows?"

There's a brief pause, and then, *"You haven't said no, Dad. All you've done is make excuses."*

The boy is paying attention…

"What kind of man do you think I am, Jerry? You really think I would try to do something so careless under my own roof? While my wife and children were asleep? How can you think such things about me? I'm your father!"

Jeremy has that 'I'm such a victim' tone down pat.

"No smoke without fire, Dad. This is the fourth time!"

Jerry sounds agitated. He's losing his patience, it would seem.

"What do you—?"

"Do you think we're stupid? Or deaf? Do you really think we never heard you and Mum fighting? Is that why you killed her? Because she couldn't take the lies any longer? Because she didn't want to have to cover for you for the rest of her life?"

Ok, I wasn't expecting that. I lean forward on the table, pressing the earphones into my ears. There's a brief silence before the recording continues.

"You have no right to talk to me like this!"

Deflection. Of course. Standard operating practice.

"And yet you don't deny killing her! You don't deny any of it!"

Jerry is loud, his voice bellows as if it has chosen this point in time to break. This is the moment he becomes a man.

"Your mother was a very sick woman, so sick in fact that she took her own life. You're young, so it's difficult for you to understand—"

"The only thing I understand is that you're a rapist and a murderer!"

I hear a smack. Once. And again. I suppose Jeremy struck his son across the face. This is… eventful.

*"You're pathetic, just like your mother. You couldn't even follow through when you brought that little slut to the house. She practically offered herself to you, but you're a dumb drunk **exactly** like your mother. She didn't follow you home for nothing. She wanted it, even if she said no."*

"Dad, for the love of God – 'no' means 'no.'"

Jerry yells really loudly. I imagine him doubled over in pain, realising that his father is shameless and depraved. The poor boy must be crushed. However sad he may feel, it's nice that he ever thought his father was a man to be admired. Some of us never had that luxury.

"Not for men like us. But like I said, you're stupid and weak, like your mother."

"You tried to rape my friend," Jerry says, crying, *"You wanted to hurt her. You didn't care that it's wrong. You didn't care that we were home. You didn't even care that I was unconscious. Did you even think to check on me? What if I had died, Dad? What if I had died?"*

His voice crumbles and all I hear are sobs.

"Oh Jerry, it's a shame you turned out to be so weak," Jeremy says matter-of-factly.

Through his sobs, his son says, *"Why did you kill Mum? Why?"*

There's a rustling noise and then another smack. In my mind's eye, I see Jerry rushing to his father, only to be batted away like a fly.

"She wanted to leave. She threatened to expose me. She stepped out of line."

"You're evil. You're the devil. I hate you."

He lets out a little noise that makes him sound like he's in pain, as if Jeremy yanked his head up or something equally unpleasant.

"I know you won't say anything about this to anyone. Even you aren't that stupid."

"And what if I do?" Jerry asks, still sobbing.

"I will kill you like I did your worthless mother."

Jeremy says the words like he is ordering a pizza. It's as though murder means nothing to him. Despite having killed several people myself, I have always considered murder to be a weighty thing, not something to be taken lightly. Jeremy Haywood sounds like he doesn't feel the same way. He's willing to kill his own son if he can't control him.

The boy runs out of the room – I can tell by the sound of rapid footsteps. I hear a door slam and then a squeak, maybe of a bed... and then the sound of seemingly endless weeping before the recording cuts off.

I look at Suzanne, and then at Mina. I realise that my mouth is open. I close it. They both nod at me.

"We got him," Suzanne says.

Yes, yes, we have.

***

It turns out that Suzanne was right – the lamb was good. Very good, actually. Was it better than the beef? I don't know. I'll have to work that out another day. I am in such a good mood that I order dessert, something I rarely do considering the rate at which I purchase ice cream. Mina and Suzanne join in, each opting for a slice of cake.

While waiting for our orders, we weigh up our options.

"I could send this to Zach – anonymously, of course. It would arrive in his email from an untraceable account," Suzanne says, in between sips of water.

"I don't know..."

"What don't you know? We have a recorded confession. Why the hesitation?" Mina asks.

Suzanne nods. "This is a slam dunk."

"We have to do this carefully, legally. I... I need to sleep on this. The last thing we want is for this to get thrown out because of some silly loophole. Give me a couple of days to think it through, ok?"

Mina sits back, pouting.

"That's cool," Suzanne says.

I nod. "Thank you."

Leaning forward again, Mina says, "Well, I have news about your boss."

"Sanders? What did you find?" I ask.

Suzanne smirks as she carries on drinking.

"He has a thing for strippers," she says, reaching into her backpack to get her camera.

"Strippers? As in paint strippers...?" I ask. I know the answer, but you just never know. There is a chance that in his free time, he ingests paint stripper. People do the strangest things in private.

"I'll bet his wife would prefer that," Suzanne says.

Mina leans into me and shows me pictures on her camera screen.

"This lady goes by the name Rain, last name Storm—"

"Naturally," I say.

"It could have been Forest," Suzanne says with a wink.

True, true.

"—and this one—" she clicks to the next picture "—goes by the name Tempest," she says.

"No last name?" I ask.

"Not that I could find, no. They work at the fine establishment known as The Naked Truth," she says.

"I can't say I've heard of it."

"I have," Suzanne offers.

Mina and I look at her. She shrugs and pours more water into her glass. The waiter comes around with our desserts and Mina quickly puts the camera away. He places the plates in front of us and walks away. Almost immediately, Suzanne picks up her spoon and starts on her cake. Mina continues her update.

"They met in the middle of the day at a house in West London. I had no visual, but plenty audio," she says, retrieving her phone and showing it to me, "You might want to listen to that on your own. It's a bit... explicit."

She raises her eyebrows as she taps her phone screen.

"There. I've sent it to you. Enjoy at your leisure."

I've heard enough. I don't think I want to hear what's on this, but it pays to be thorough. To be honest, I'm not sure if following Old Bill is worthwhile, but one can never be sure that seemingly useless knowledge will not one day turn into life-changing information. Had I not paid attention at school, there's no telling what my life would be like now.

"We have copies of those pictures, as well as Haywood's confession and your boss's afternoon activities on a server," Suzanne says. She slides a small piece of paper to me and continues, "Should you ever need to access any of it, use that."

I unravel the paper and see that Suzanne has scribbled a server address, a username and password on it. Her handwriting is terrible, but I can just about make out the details.

"1-2-3-4... really?" I say.

"You can change it if you like," she says, in a sing-songy voice.

"Your penmanship could use some work," I say, smiling.

Suzanne rolls her eyes. Mina laughs and starts on her dessert. I fold the piece of paper and tuck it into a compartment in my money purse. I now feel ready to eat.

"You know what? This is probably the first time that I've had so many breakthroughs on the first day of a case," Suzanne says.

"Lucky me."

"Lucky us," Mina says, admiring the piece of cake on her fork.

Like Suzanne, I can hardly believe that we've had this much success on day 1. It seems a little too good to be true.

"Since we've got a confession, I don't know if there's much point in following Haywood around," I say.

Suzanne nods.

"What about your boss?" Mina asks. She looks my way with her brow furrowed. If I didn't know any better, I'd say she wanted to keep an eye on him.

"You guys can stay on him, at least for the rest of the week."

She nods, and sighs as she turns back to her plate. I guess this is the first 'real' job she's had in a while and she'd like it to last for longer than a day.

"Cool. We can do that, right?" Suzanne says to Mina.

"Absolutely," Mina says, smiling.

We complete our desserts without speaking. I am feeling generous and slightly euphoric, so I decide to pay the bill. We leave the restaurant and Suzanne offers Mina and me a lift home.

I look at Mina, who shrugs. "Your call."

"Why not?" I say.

Really, it's probably best for me not to be seen in public with Suzanne, but I'm in no mood for public transportation. Also, I feel like her presence creates a nice barrier between me and Mina. We pile into her car – me in the back seat, Mina in the passenger's – and she starts the engine. It's late enough that the traffic isn't dire.

There is still much to accomplish, but good things are on the way. I can feel it.

X

NOVEMBER 29TH, 2019

DONNA

The past three days have been ordinary. I lived like a normal person – gone to work, sat in meetings, attended boxing classes. Suzanne and Mina kept following Old Bill, informing me that he met the two prostitutes again. Twice in the same week, what a greedy old goat. This time, they were able to get a visual recording and pictures. When I asked how, Suzanne was kind enough to tell me that, "Plausible deniability is your friend."

Mina appears to be relishing her role as a detective. It's good that she has something productive to do. They've sent some of the video and sound clips to me, in addition to uploading them to the Suzanne's server. All this knowledge has done is lay waste to the little respect I had for Sanders.

I'm yet to firmly decide what to do with Jeremy Haywood's confession of guilt. I know the recording won't be admissible in court because it was obtained in a less than legal fashion, so there's no point sending it to Zachary. He'd know the truth, but to what end? I'm inclined to suggest that we give it to Suzanne's journalist source but she's not independent and may not be allowed to publish it.

Aside from all that, a part of me feels strangely protective of Jerry and Noah.

Their mother hasn't even been buried yet and if we release this recording, everyone will know that their father killed her *and* that he's a rapist. Jerry already knows but if the whole world knows, how much worse will he feel? The destruction of their father's reputation and the exposure of his true nature will probably do those boys no favours. Despite myself, I'm worried about them.

Going back to Zachary, I called him and Detective Miller and cancelled my *appointments* with them. I used work as an excuse – big case, blah, blah, blah. They were very reasonable. I got the sense that Zach knew I got cold feet. He didn't push to reschedule. Miller, on the other hand, suggested we go to dinner another night. I politely declined, telling him that I had other plans.

Today started badly. Once again, I didn't get enough sleep. I had a nightmare. I don't remember all the details, but I know that I was in a park. It seemed like the one near work, but different. You know what dreams are like. A puppy ran up to me. It looked cute and harmless. Then out of nowhere, it turned into a huge wolf and tried to eat me. I was trying to climb a tree to get away from it, but it got hold of my leg. Suddenly, there was a bright light in the sky and the wolf was blinded. I picked up a tree branch and beat it to death.

When I woke up, my heart was beating so fast that I thought it would give way. It was eerie and frightening. It took me 3 hours to get back to sleep, and when I got up again – surprise – it was too late to catch the bus. So here I am, on the train, squished against a wall near the door. I stand still, trying to shake the feeling that something bad is going to happen to me.

I was so unsettled by the dream that I opened a Bible. It was probably the first time in more than a decade that I read it outside church. I liked psalm 23 when I was a child. It made me feel… safe. So that was what I read. And yes, I felt safe. I also felt guilty. Some might say that I've done more than enough to warrant being eaten by a wolf, yet I want comfort. Is that right?

The train stops and as many people leave as those that board. I'm pushed closer to the wall, wishing I wasn't here. Five more stops. I'll be there soon enough. My eyes wander across the carriage to a man who stands near the opposite door. He's tall, well-dressed, carrying a medium-sized briefcase. He looks about 35, full head of brown hair, not a grey in sight. We briefly make eye contact. As I draw my eyes away, I see the makings of a smile on his face.

The train stops again and the man moves forward, weaving through the mass of passengers, as though he's about to disembark. He stops at the wall opposite me and stays there, watching people pile into the carriage. The doors shut and the train keeps moving.

He looks at me, stares more like. He looks me up and down with his hooded eyes, as though he were trying to picture me undressed. He's not being subtle, not even a little. I narrow my eyes and curl my lips in disgust, but he smiles again. There's never a good time to deal with harassment, but it's definitely too early in the day for this. I look away from him.

When people get off at the next stop, the man takes the chance to move closer to me. I try to move but have nowhere to go as he squishes right in front of me. The feeling of revulsion rises inside me. The door closes and he's looking down at me. I should have left at that stop, waited for the next train. Why didn't I think to do that?

He presses his body against me and I feel parts of it that I have no business with or interest in. My stomach churns. I look around to see if anyone notices what's happening. Everyone's in their own world. He pushes himself closer to me, firmly but stealthily moving up and down.

I could yell something like, "This man is a degenerate pervert!" to the hearing of all in the carriage, but will anyone care? People are so apathetic; they'd probably shrug and ignore me. Well, the ones that hear me – most of them are listening to headphones. I suppose it doesn't help that there's not much room for movement.

As disgusted and sick as I feel, I do not feel afraid. It's sad that I'm so resigned to the possibility of being abused that I'm not even scared that he might try to do anything worse to me. He continues slowly dragging himself along my thigh as I avoid making eye contact. Thank God I'm wearing trousers. I keep telling myself there are only three stops left. Three more stops. Three more stops.

The longer he grinds on me, the angrier I feel. That's bad for me, but worse for him. I might follow him off the train and smash his head in with his briefcase. I like the thought of that but then I remember that there's CCTV everywhere – that won't work. He'd feel pain and I'd feel vindicated, but for how long? He carries on doing his thing until the train pulls up at the next stop. He backs away slightly, and I think for a moment that he's about to leave. No such luck. The doors close, and he starts shuffling forward again. I decide I've tolerated enough. If no one can see what he's doing, no one will see what I'm doing.

When he comes closer this time, I'm ready. I feel him on my upper thigh. Good, this means I won't have to move my hand far. I grab his crotch, and he stiffens. I think I've startled him. Good. I squeeze and twist as hard as I can, digging my nails in as well, hoping that despite his clothing, he feels pain and a lot of it. From the look on his face, he feels enough. He tries to move away from me, but the train is so packed that he has nowhere to go. I let go and punch him sharply in the groin. I hurt my elbow in the process but it's ok. No pain, no gain. He doubles over a little, and his face is so close to mine that I'm able to whisper in his ear, "You like that?"

He coughs and I punch him once more, moving my head away from his. He tries again to move away from me, but he's trapped. He starts groaning as I apply more pressure. I look around and another man seems to hear the groans. He looks towards us and our eyes meet.

His eyes ask, "What's wrong?"

I shrug, as if to say, "Who knows?"

The man looks away, retreating to his thoughts. The harasser stays doubled over. As the train pulls into the station, I punch him one more time, just for fun, before the train stops. Like a shot, he's first out of the carriage, staggering onto the platform. Other passengers leave, nearly rushing him off his feet. He goes to the wall and steadies himself. New passengers board the train and he turns to look at me, wincing and holding on to his groin. I smile triumphantly while the doors shut. As the train pulls away, I wave.

I hope he has a rotten day.

***

This morning's edition of Sexual Harassment on the Tube has brought me to a conclusion regarding Haywood. We have to release his confession to the media, the public, the internet, whoever. Darkness is the soil in which secrets grow. If we put the recording on the web, there will be nowhere for Haywood to hide and nowhere for his evil to flourish. Everyone will know about his depravity, everyone will know what he did to Aisha, and everyone will know what he did to Audrey. There isn't a court in the land that would let him go free, no matter how good his defence or how corrupt the judge. His life will be over and his reputation, destroyed. Even that is not enough but it'll have to do.

I walk from the train station to the office, looking over my shoulders. There's no telling what other maniac creep is on the loose today. On the approach to the building, I glance across the street and see a familiar car – Suzanne's, to be precise. She's in the driver's seat, and Mina is next to her. She spent the night on Suzanne's sofa because they were working late, from what they told me.

I cross the street and walk over to the car. I tap on the window and Suzanne winds it down.

"Morning Sunshine," she says.

"What are you doing here?"

"Hop in."

There's a popping noise as the backseat door releases. I enter the car and she winds her window up.

"Hey Donna," Mina says. I smile at her.

She looks tired. I don't blame her. I wonder how long she's been up.

"Been following your boss for a few hours," Suzanne says.

"It's not even 9 o' clock," I say.

"Yes, but he was up at 4 for a personal training session—"

"—totally legit, above board," Mina offers.

"—then off to the massage parlour for some… *recovery*," Suzanne says.

I look at Mina. She shakes her head. "Not at all legit, 100% below board."

"Are you positive?"

"I know that place. It's a front for organised crime and half the workers have been trafficked in. From the look of things, he's a regular there," Suzanne says.

Is Sanders serious? His affair with the strippers is sleazy and immoral, sure, but this massage parlour business definitely falls foul of the law. He must know that.

"Wow. Ok." There's not much else for me to say.

"Oh, and last night, I followed him to a hotel where he met with a young woman he called Sarah. I got some pictures of her," Mina says.

"Researched her and found that she's both his friend's wife and his daughter's friend," Suzanne says.

Mina reaches into her bag and gets her camera out. As she loads it up, I shake my head, trying to understand how this man juggles work and so much debauchery. Where does he get the energy? And then it hits me.

"Wait… it's not Sarah Matheson?" I ask, leaning forward.

Suzanne nods, smiling as though I'd impressed her. "Yes. You know her?"

Mina shows me a photo.

I bite my lip. "I've heard of her."

"I've heard her. And now I need therapy," Mina says.

I rest my head in my hands. Perhaps I'm in too deep. I now know more about Bill than I ever wanted to. And this knowledge seems dangerous. The information about the massage parlour should be handed over to the police. I should turn him in but… I don't know who his friends are. I'm not interested in risking my job but I can't sit around and let him exploit people, especially when it's illegal. I shake my head. Now's not the time to think about that. There are more pressing issues at hand.

"I thought you'd be here earlier," Suzanne says.

I look at her and throw my hands up. "I woke up late."

"Lucky you," she says.

If only.

"I've been thinking about Haywood," I say.

"And…?" Mina looks at me, sitting up. I think she's keen to see him sent down. This probably means more to her than to anyone who isn't Aisha or a member of her family.

275

"Send it to your reporter friend, and to Zach… put it on the internet. Let the whole world see who Jeremy Haywood really is. But do it slowly."

"Slowly?" Suzanne asks.

"Yeah. Leak the Aisha bit first, then the bit about Audrey later," I say.

"How much later is later?" Mina asks.

"A few hours. I'll let you to decide."

Mina smiles widely. Suzanne nods.

"Aye, aye, captain. That man is about to have a very bad day," Suzanne says.

It couldn't have happened to a nicer guy.

***

The day is shaping up to be productive. Knowing what's coming in the next few hours, I mentally prepare to work late and to feign stress and agitation. It's all good, though, I'm no stranger to pretending. The police are still trying to poke holes in Haywood's story about his wife's death. They'll get their man before the day is out.

As I enter the building, I see *the* Veronica Blake-Sanders walking to one of the lifts. She comes into the office once in a while to see Daryl and Old Bill. At first, I thought she was keeping tabs on them for some reason, but now I think she's idle and possibly lonely.

She's wearing a multi-coloured wrap dress and a pair of shoes with heels so high that they could double as weapons. Her chocolate-brown hair is in a messy bun. Her handbag matches her shoes. If Ivy was here, she would tell me whether or not they were designer, and which designer to boot. Veronica looks happy and carefree. It seems that the truth of her situation is a mystery to her.

Oh, the joy of being in the dark.

I consider hanging back until the lift doors close but I'm already late enough. I run after her and get into the lift just in time. It's such a drag being around people's family members; they always feel the need to engage in Meaningless Small Talk.

"Hi Dana!" she says.

It doesn't help that she always gets my name wrong.

"Hello Veronica."

I've stopped correcting her. It's wasteful.

"How's life?"

I smile and nod, but say nothing.

"You've got that big case, I hear," she says, sporting a big grin.

I smile and nod, but say nothing.

"How are you finding it?"

She won't shut up, will she?

"They're all challenging but the team is doing a great job." Generic non-answers are best for people like her.

Still smiling, she nods and rubs her belly absentmindedly. Ah yes, she's carrying another one of Daryl's progeny. How sad for her. The little one is probably less than 12 weeks old, so she's unlikely to admit it to me. Still, I like testing people.

"How're things with you? How's the baby?"

"Baby?" Her eyes go wide as she drops her hand. Her smile vanishes.

I smile and raise the pitch of my voice, bobbing my head a bit. "Carla. How is she?"

"Oh, yes, Carla." She smiles, exhaling quietly. She tucks an errant lock of hair behind her ear. "She's great. Not a baby anymore, though. She's over a year old now, walking, talking."

"If they're under 5, they're babies to me."

We both laugh. You know – the polite 'it's not that funny but I'll laugh anyway' sort of laughter. The lift stops at our floor.

"After you," I say. She smiles and steps out. I follow her.

Shane, Daryl and Kat are at their respective desks. Veronica walks ahead of me into the office, and I see Kat stiffen when she sees her. Oblivious, Veronica goes to Daryl and leans over his desk, planting a big kiss on his mouth. He seems surprised to see her, but smiles warmly as they hug. I watch as his eyes dart over to Kat, whom I suppose he spent the night with.

"Excuse me," Kat says. She gets up and walks past me without saying hello. I assume she's off to cry in the restroom. That woman needs to get a grip on reality. I take my seat and prepare my desk for the day ahead. Veronica and Daryl disappear into a private meeting room.

I settle down at my desk and turn my computer on. While it loads up, I pour out some tea for myself and take a sip. A short while later, Daryl and Veronica come back into the office. They kiss and she waves at me and Shane before she leaves. She keeps smiling, like she has not a care in the world.

***

The morning went by without incident. Lunch time came and went, and I took a walk. Not to the park, though, because the dream scared me too much. I went to a shop and bought some fruit. Ivy called on my way back to work, reminding me that she'd be spending the evening with some church member who's recently had a baby.

Along with others from the church, she's cooking a meal for the new parents and taking it to them. This means they have one less thing to do now there's a baby in their midst. More importantly, it means that until she leaves for tonight's prayer meeting, I'll be alone with mum. That is, assuming I don't have to work late and Mina does. It was good of Ivy to let me know. It gives me a chance to prepare myself or make other arrangements. I didn't bring my workout clothes with me today but at this rate, I may have to hastily buy some new ones and find a class, any class, to attend.

That all takes a back seat once I return to the office. It has begun – a portion of Mr. Haywood's confession has been leaked online and the team is going bananas. It seems that while I was at lunch, a reporter (Suzanne's contact, Jen) called to ask for a comment. Kat told her she'd get back to her, and then tried to call me after listening to the audio herself. I missed Kat's call because I was speaking to Ivy. Externally, I'm relatively calm and composed. Internally, I'm having a party.

"What's the plan?" Kat says.

"Plan? What's on the audio?" I say.

"Short version – Aisha's name is redacted, but he admits he tried to rape her. It gets worse, though," she says.

"How can it be worse than that?"

"The boy seems to think that Haywood killed Audrey… and Haywood doesn't deny it."

"Oh my goodness, this is bad," I say.

"We're still not sure it's him. The whole thing is kind of choppy. It's obviously been edited," Shane says.

I look at Shane, nodding slowly. "You think it's a fake?"

"No way," Daryl says, "It's him. His son set him up."

"Why would he—?"

"Does it matter if his son did this? The guy confessed! Our case is blown!" Kat says, interrupting my sentence. It's clear to me that her problem is not with me. Shane puts his hands on his head, the way football players do when they miss a chance to score. Yes, it's that bad.

Daryl and Kat stare at each other for a moment, she narrowing her eyes and shaking her head ever so slightly.

Now is not the time, guys.

"So we're done for. That's the summary of this, right?" I say.

"We might sti—"

"Right," Kat says. Daryl stops speaking and looks at Shane, who is still reeling.

"We're still not 100% sure it's Haywood on the audio," Shane insists.

Rebecca Staunton storms into the office and stares at each one of us as silence falls.

"What is this I'm hearing about a confession?" she asks. Her arms are folded, her jaw is so tightly clenched that I fear she'll break some teeth.

No one answers her.

"Are you all deaf or mute?" she says, raising her voice. Well, if we were deaf that wouldn't help.

"Ma'am, we're still trying to piece together what exactly is happening here," I say, trying to sound like I'm in control.

"Sort this mess out, immediately!"

She turns and leaves, and we all stand there, watching as she does so.

After standing in silence for a little while, Daryl pipes up, "You heard her.

Let's sort this mess out."

"I'll call Haywood, find out what he has to say for himself," I say.

I need to focus. I hesitated for a moment, and now Daryl is subtly trying to wrest control from me again. I can't let that happen. My hard work is starting to pay off and I need it to pay off in every area, not just in Haywood's case. I need to stay sharp.

"Daryl, Shane: get the tech guys to see if they can trace the origin of the file, or find any evidence of manipulation, or whatever it is they do!" I say.

Shane nods. "On it."

He and Daryl leave.

"Kat…"

She looks longingly at Daryl, gulping as he and Shane exit the office. "Hmm?"

I soften my tone. "Kat, you need to get a grip. He's not yours and he never will be."

She curls her tongue and breathes heavily as her eyes grow damp. She looks at me, frowning. "Have you ever been in love?"

I don't believe this.

"Kat, this isn't love. It isn't smart and it isn't right. Seriously, does it seem fair to you that you and Veronica get half a man, and he gets two women? Does it?"

Her eyes widen and start leaking as she shakes her head.

"I need you to focus right now, ok? We have work to do. If you can track Jerry down and try to find out what he's got to do with this, it might help us."

She wipes her eyes. "Ok, ok. What a day this is turning out to be, huh?"

I nod. She takes her bag and leaves. Now it's time for me to talk to Haywood. I can't wait to hear what he has to say for himself.

Justice is on its way.

***

Jeremy Haywood is distraught, as expected. I'm speaking to him, and he sounds like a desperate man. So far, he has denied that the voice on the tape is his. I am in the process of reminding him that I'm his lawyer and whatever he tells me is in confidence.

"I'm telling you, that's not me," he says.

"So what, you're saying it's a sound-alike? Deepfake for voices?"

"I don't know, but it's not me."

Why pay so much for a lawyer only to lie to them about everything?

"Mr. Haywood, I'm your lawyer. If you won't be honest with me, I can't properly defend you."

"William and I have an understanding, Miss Palmer, and you will defend me, no matter what."

He drops the phone. I didn't even get a chance to ask about his son's involvement, or what the boy has to say for himself. I put the phone down, thinking about calling him back, when it rings. I pick it up. It's Zachary.

"Miss Palmer, how's your day going?" he asks. His voice has a wry tone to it, so I surmise that he isn't calling for a friendly chat.

I sigh loudly down the phone. "I've had better days, but I've also had worse ones."

"You must have heard that recording that's floating around the web."

I nod though I don't know why – he can't see me.

"I've not had the pleasure, but I've heard about it."

"Are you still on the case or should I be talking to someone else?"

"It's still me."

"Ok. I don't have to tell you that your client's days as a free man are numbered," he says.

"Are you calling to offer him a deal?"

"Not at all. I'm calling to gloat, and to let you know that Jeremy Haywood will spend a significant chunk of his future behind bars."

"What a charmer!"

He laughs. He sounds very happy. I know how he feels.

"We should get a drink tonight – to celebrate my victory. Say didn't I predict that?" he says. I can hear him grinning like a clown.

"You've not won the case yet, Mr. Parsons."

"Maybe not officially, but it'd still be nice to spend time with you." He speaks in a soft, dulcet tone that has me rethinking my life choices. I thought I was done with this after cancelling drinks with him but here he is, back for more.

"Ah, Zach… I don't know if I have the time…"

"Here's an idea – I'll be with some friends at the pub from 7 o' clock tonight. We probably won't leave until after midnight. If you're free, you can swing by. No pressure. How does that sound?"

I close my eyes, trying to think of a way to turn him down, and then it occurs to me that I'd rather while away the evening with him than go home. What a beautiful coincidence.

"You know, that could work," I say.

He sighs. "Great. That's great."

"I should get back to work, Zach."

"Yeah, of course. Ok, I'll let you go. I'll text you the details. Good luck, Donna."

"Thanks."

I drop the phone and take a moment to bask in the warmth of the day's events. It feels so good to have done something so good and despite my reservations, it feels very good to know I might be seeing Zach tonight.

My moment-savouring is cut short by another call, this one originating in the building. I'm really sick of talking to people I work with. I pick the phone up and it's Old Bill.

"Miss Palmer—"

"Sir—"

"I've just had a chat with Jeremy Haywood, and he seems to be under the impression that we're considering dropping him as a client," he says.

"Sir, I never said—"

"You didn't have to. He's a very dear friend and nothing he said in that recording – assuming it's of him – is admissible in court."

"Yes, sir."

"We're in this for the long haul, right to the bitter end."

"Yes, sir," I say.

He ends the call.

I can't believe he's not ready to cut his losses. It makes me wonder if those two dogs really are friends, or if Haywood knows things about Old Bill that the rest of us don't. If it's the latter, I hope Mina and Suzanne can unearth it.

***

Late afternoon and it's looking like I will have to work late into the night. Though Jeremy denies being the man on the tape, the police have invited us to come in for an interview tomorrow. I'll go and pick him up and drive him to the station. Hurray for me, I get to work on another Saturday *and* I get to babysit.

While Shane and Daryl work on some poppycock defence in light of the new, damning evidence, Kat and I discuss her waylaying of Jerry at his school.

"He seemed really worried. He thinks he's been bugged," she says.

"Bugged? What, like in *Enemy of the State*?"

"*Enemy of the State*? What is this 1998?"

I shrug. "It's a classic."

"Anyway, he was really alarmed when I told him about the audio. He was almost... terrified."

"Did he say why?"

"Perhaps because his father threatened to kill him if he talked," a voice that comes from behind me says.

I turn around and see Silas Bradshaw, who works in the tech department, walking towards us while adjusting his glasses.

"What did you say?" I ask.

"Oh, have you guys not heard? The full audio dropped about 15 minutes ago," he says. His dark brown eyes twinkle, as if he's delivered pizza to the happiest customer.

"It's not a mixtape, Silas," Kat says.

Daryl rushes to his computer and finds the site hosting the first file. Sure enough, there's a new upload. He presses play on the new recording. For as long as the file streams, we all stand there, transfixed by the awful, callous nature in which Haywood admits his guilt to his defenceless son. Well, all of us except Silas, who sits around stroking his beard. Like me, he's already heard this. Unlike me, it appears that he's not as troubled by it.

Rather than the bits and pieces solely to do with Aisha, which is what the initial release contained, this file is the entire conversation between father and son. The one where he calls his son pathetic for not approving of rape. The one where he admits that he killed his wife. When it's over, Daryl speaks for all of us.

"Ok... he's screwed."

And not a moment too soon.

***

The plan has changed. With the release of the latest bit of information, the police are on their way to Haywood's house. He called to tell us as much, sounding frantic, talking about how people were out to get him and how 'his enemies' were trying to bring him down. He sounded like a proper crazy person. I couldn't believe that he would keep denying that his was the voice on the recording. So convincing was he that, were I not privy to the truth, I would have taken him at his word.

"I've analysed samples of his voice and compared it to the one on the audio. It's a match," Silas confirms. He runs his hands over his low afro, brushing his hair forward.

"So, it really is him," Shane says.

"Well, that or it's his evil twin brother, separated at birth," Silas says.

"So, it really is him," I say.

"As for where the file came from, I haven't been able to get to the bottom of that yet. Whoever uploaded it is not an amateur," he says.

"Probably some 12-year old with too much time on his hands," Daryl says.

"Or her hands," Kat retorts.

"Of course. It could be a girl," he says.

"Or it could be little Jerry himself. If my daddy killed my mummy, I'd want him to pay," Silas says, in a high-pitched, whiny voice.

"It doesn't matter how it got on the web. All that matters is what we do about it. We're not dropping Haywood as a client," I say.

Shane throws his hands up. "Are you kidding? This is a losing battle if ever there was one."

"This cometh down from on high," I say, lowering my voice.

With that, Shane, Daryl, Kat and I all hop in Kat's car and head to meet Mr. Haywood in his house. We hope to get there before the police do so we can give him some rubbish story to tell… or at least stop him from saying anything at all. The drive is surprisingly quiet. Everyone seems to be in their own world. I think the confession has rattled my colleagues.

I, on the other hand, am doing my utmost to not look pleased, because this development pleases me almost as much as the deaths of my enemies did. It's not over yet, though, and they say there's many a slip between the cup and the lip. I hope everything goes according to plan. I hope Jeremy dies in prison.

As we pull into the driveway, my phone starts ringing. I forgot to call mum and tell her that I'd be home late. I hope this isn't her. I look at the phone, and it's the office. When I answer it, Old Bill is on the line.

"Miss Palmer," he says.

"Yes, sir," I say.

What does he want now?

"I see that you and your team aren't on seat."

Kat parks the car and the men get out. She sits there and watches me on the phone.

"We've just arrived at Mr. Haywood's house, sir. We'll be prepping him for his interview with the police."

"About that… Mrs. Staunton and I have had a long chat. We've decided that it would be in the firm's best interest to refer Mr. Haywood to another firm."

I pause briefly, wondering if my comprehension skills are failing me.

"I'm sorry, sir, I don't think I—"

"Tell Haywood that Sanders Staunton & Co will no longer represent him in any capacity. We will be in touch with a final bill and we will recommend him to another firm. Is that clear?"

His voice is cold and stern. I wonder whose decision this was.

"Yes, sir, very," I say.

He ends the call and I stare blankly at my phone. It's all happening so fast. I can hardly keep up.

"What now?" Kat asks.

"I don't believe this."

As I prepare to deliver the news to Kat, I imagine that it's times like this that she's grateful for expense claims on fuel.

***

Along with Haywood, Shane and Daryl are waiting in the room where we first met Audrey. Kat stays in the car. I walk into the room and look at Haywood. He stands up, starts flailing his arms. The other two stay seated behind him.

"Well, what took you so long? The police will be here any minute," he bellows.

"Sir, I'm afraid I have some bad news," I say.

Just beyond him, I see Shane and Daryl look quizzically at me. I clear my throat slightly and maintain eye contact with Haywood.

"Bad news? The whole day has been full of it," he yells, like a politician whining in parliament.

"It is with regret, sir, that I must inform you that Sanders Staunton & Co will no longer be representing any of your legal interests."

"What?" All three men speak in unison.

"What the hell do you mean?" Haywood says. He starts towards me, with a scowl on his face and his fists clenched.

I take a step back. "Sir, please: control yourself."

"What do you—?"

"We will be in touch within the next week with your final bill, and we will refer you to another legal firm," I say.

His eyes widen and he turns to look at Daryl and Shane. Shane adjusts his tie and Daryl looks away, with his mouth open.

Turning back to me, he says, "So this is what Bill does to his friends?"

"We wish you the best of luck with your defence," I say.

I look over to the other two and beckon to them with my head. They get up and leave the room without speaking to Haywood. In the distance, I hear police sirens and wonder if they're coming this way. He sits on the couch, eyes bouncing around his head, mouth trembling.

I turn to leave but stop when he says, "What's going to happen to me now?"

I turn back to him, only slightly. "You'll probably spend the rest of your life in jail. It's only fair, since you're a rapist and a murderer."

He looks up at me, narrowing his eyes. I turn away and walk quickly out of the room and, with Daryl and Shane, exit the house. I get into the car where Kat smiles mirthlessly at me. She starts the engine once we're all strapped in and puts the car in gear. The sound of the sirens gets louder. As she manoeuvres the vehicle out of the driveway, we hear a loud bang. She slams the brakes and we look at one another.

Shane is first out of the car, with Daryl not far behind. A couple of police cars pull into the driveway. I know what that noise was, but I don't know what has happened. Curiosity seizes me. I run back into the house.

I get to the room we just left and find Shane kneeling next to, and Daryl standing over, what appears to be Jeremy Haywood's lifeless body. There's a gun in his hand and a hole in his bloody head. Shane checks his pulse.

"He's still alive!" Shane yells.

"We need an ambulance," Daryl says equally loudly.

Detective Miller hurries into the room with Detective Lawson and some uniformed police officers.

"What happened here?" Lawson asks, her eyes shifting from Shane to Daryl, and then, to me.

"I think he tried to kill himself," I say.

An officer radios for an ambulance.

Miller turns to me and cocks his head. "We really have to stop meeting like this."

***

They wheeled Haywood out on a stretcher and took him to the hospital. It's doubtful that he will survive but stranger things have happened. Kat was inconsolable. Of course, Daryl took it upon himself to try to calm her down. When the police were done questioning them, he drove her home in her car. I can guess how that will end. Those two are the worst. As for Shane, I've never seen him so sombre before. He seemed both sad and shaken. I'll be surprised if he makes it to work on Monday.

It turns out that neither Jerry nor Noah was at home when the excitement took place. They were at an after-school tennis lesson. When they got back, they were immediately ushered to the Smith house. Shane and I walked over there with a police officer, watched him give them the 'bad' news. It's all relative, I guess. Noah cried. The poor lamb.

Jerry, on the other hand, put on a brave face and didn't shed a single tear. Instead, he comforted his brother. He must feel rather conflicted. In light of recent revelations, he might be both relieved and hurt by his father's suicide attempt. He might even feel like it was his fault. I wonder if he's worked out how their private discourse wound up online. I hope for Aisha's sake that he never does.

As for Aisha, I wonder how she will take the news when it finally reaches her. Will she feel vindicated? Happy? Disappointed? Is this the sort of justice she hoped for, or was she eager to see him incarcerated? I'm curious, but I have enough to deal with for now. Like the way Detective Miller has been staring me down, like he thinks I have something to do with this. I can't wait to be rid of him and his suspicions.

Shane and I leave the Smith house, letting Raquel and her son attend to the boys. Outside, Shane calls a cab and sits on the pavement, waiting.

"This case is so messed up," he says. He stares into the distance, his eye line perched on a tree.

"What part of it?" I say, sitting next to him.

"The whole thing. He tries to rape someone – a child, as if it wasn't bad enough – and we defend him. And then he kills his wife and here we are. What kind of people are we?"

He shakes his head, clenches his fists.

"We didn't know he was guilty, not for sure."

"Maybe not at first, but we did our homework. It's like the kid said on the tape – no smoke without fire. And we were going to help him get away with it, all of it. What does that make us? Accomplices, that's what," he says, his voice trailing off, fists still clenched. He slumps a little, lifting one fist to his chin.

"We're doing our jobs. That's not a crime."

I stop talking and sit quietly next to him, taking it all in. Everything he's said is true, though I never would have thought he was capable of such… introspection. Maybe I've misjudged him. I look ahead at the tree that he seems to be studying. It's tall and looks old, older than most of the houses in this neighbourhood. When the houses and their occupants are all gone, that tree will probably still be here. People spend so much time hurting and betraying one another, fighting over insignificant, fleeting things. How many of us think about what it's all for? Why even bother when our destiny is dust?

"I think I'm going to quit," he says.

"What?"

"This isn't what I signed up for. I don't want to help criminals cover their tracks. There isn't enough money in the world that'll make that ok."

"I thought you always wanted to be a lawyer," I say.

"I did— I do, but I don't want to do *this*."

I shrug. Not my problem, though I am impressed by this newfound disdain for the sort of work we tend to do. All this time, I thought I was the only one who hated the duplicity of being a defence lawyer, and now I find that Shane, of all people, feels the same way. I guess we only see the outside.

"Well, whatever you decide, I hope you find something that's worth your while," I say.

"Thanks, that really means a lot to me."

I think he's being sincere. There really is a first time for everything.

"Miss Palmer…"

The voice comes from a distance away. Shane straightens up, releases his fists, rests his palms on his knees. I look around and see Detective Miller walking towards us from the direction of the Haywood house. Here we go, time to put one of my game faces on.

"Detective, how can I help you?" I ask. I smile sweetly, the sort of smile that comes naturally when you see someone you like, someone you're happy to be around.

"Do either of you need a lift?" he asks, looking only at me.

The cab arrives in time to save me from what might be an awkward exchange.

"This is ours," Shane says.

"But thanks for the offer," I say.

"Oh, I wasn't offering. I was just asking," he says, winking.

I laugh despite myself.

Shane nods at Miller and gets into the cab, leaving the door open for me.

"Any word on Mr. Haywood?" I ask.

His expression turns serious, and he shakes his head. "Not yet, but I wouldn't hold my breath for any good news."

I nod. That's what I want to hear.

From inside the cab, I hear a cough.

"Well, thanks for the update. See you."

He smiles and moves quickly to hold the door open for me as I climb into the car. Once I'm in, he shuts it and waves as the car pulls away. I wave back. As I put on my seatbelt, I notice Shane roll his eyes a little while shaking his head.

The cab driver asks for confirmation of our destination address and Shane gives him the office's postcode. It's been such a long and eventful day that I'd rather go home now, but the thought of being alone with mum irritates me.

It's best to go back to the office. I'll be more productive there.

XI

MINA

Donna called to tell us about Haywood's suicide attempt. I've always found her to be inscrutable, but not this time. This time, she sounded satisfied.

"You both did a great job," she said, relishing this victory.

She said that I should be proud of myself. I don't know if I am – a man literally tried to end his life and that seems like a tragedy. At the same time, he was evil and I know that I've made her proud so that makes me feel good. I don't know if she knows how much that means to me. She's always been in my corner, even when she left my life. I know that she left because she couldn't stand to see me hurting myself. She actually said that to me once – the one and only time she came to visit me in prison. I appreciate her concern now more than I did then.

Back then, I felt like she'd betrayed me by turning me in. I told her as much, accused her of sucking up to her Russian friend. She didn't react, even though I wanted her to. I wanted her to tell me she hated me. Instead, she told me that she hoped that jail would help me get my life in order. For years I wished I could take back the stupid things I said. I finally feel like I'm on the road to making things right. Considering that she went out of her way to get me this job, it feels amazing that I didn't let her down. *I feel amazing not to have let her down.*

Rather than celebrate, Suzanne went to the hospital to see what she could find out about Haywood's chances of survival – a grim but essential task, as she put it. We left her office together and parted ways at the station. I decided I would sleep at Donna's place tonight, though I forgot to mention it to Donna. I'm sure she won't mind. Ordinarily I'd go out drinking, but Salome helped me realise that when I drink, I'm more likely to take drugs. Once my inhibitions are low, there's no telling what could happen. I can't afford to fall off the wagon again.

But I need to do something to commemorate the occasion. It's only right to mark an important event with a celebration. What to do…? I could go back to the flat, but there's not much to do there. Ivy and Mama Selene are probably tired of seeing my face. And then they'll be going to church together and I'll be on my own till Donna gets back.

I could call Graham, but… that may not be a smart thing to do. I can feel this longing rising in my heart. For what, I don't know. It's like I feel hungry but instead of in my belly, it's in my chest. Some sort of craving. You know what? Graham might not always be the safest company, but he knows how to make me feel good. I'll call him, we'll kick it, chat, have fun. If he offers me anything dodgy, I'll decline. I need to exercise my 'no' muscle anyway. That's it, I'll call Graham. It beats doing nothing for hours.

I call him, and he answers with that mischievous tone of his. He calls me 'babe', a term which both irritates and flatters me at the same time. My first boyfriend, Hugh, used to call me that, usually when he was trying to pacify me after having been an ass. But coming from Graham, it's a term of endearment. I guess I can't blame him for my past experience with the word. He's always treated me well and been considerate of me. If he didn't love drugs so much, he'd make an ideal boyfriend.

He says he didn't know I was *in town*, a.k.a. out of prison. He says that we need to catch up, and it's my lucky day because he's around all weekend. We can hang out and have some fun, maybe watch a film or something. It isn't the most exciting plan, but it sounds better than the alternative. We agree to meet at a bar near his place. Apparently, he'll be with some of his friends. Sounds cool to me.

I first met him when I was eighteen. My then-dealer, Martin, was having a guys' night, which I inadvertently crashed because I was desperate for a fix. Graham answered the door. In the heat of my cravings, I wasn't expecting to be greeted with a handsome, smiling face. Martin was always so gloomy and irascible that I was taken aback by Graham's friendly demeanour.

I wasn't surprised when I heard that one of Martin's clients killed him in a fit of PCP-induced madness. He could really get under a person's skin. But Graham... Charming and Disarming is what he is. That first night, I bought my weed and we left together – went back to his place and got high, among other things. We've been friends ever since.

He's one of those 'disciplined' addicts, as I think of them. He only smokes marijuana, and only smokes it on weekends. He never did graduate to anything harder. Lucky guy. In my experience, people like him are few and far between. Most addicts I know have every other part of their lives eclipsed by the habit. They chase The High and nothing matters except getting it. Maybe they do it because they're damaged, as opposed to bored or idle or something along those lines. I know I do. I mean, I did. That's behind me now.

That said, even some of the more disciplined addicts I know eventually slid deeper into depravity, until, like me, it was all they knew. I wonder if or when Graham's day will come. There's a chance that he's changed. Today is a Friday, so if he hasn't, he'll be getting high. It's ok, I'm not into that anymore. If he offers me anything shady, I'll turn it down. Easy. I might even be able to talk him out of it.

I arrive at the bar at 8pm sharp. It turns out to be one of those new-fangled hipster-type ones that have popped up everywhere in the years I was away. There were a few when I was last around but now, it's commonplace. I make my way to the bar and spot a couple eating chips and a salad from a chopping board. Yup, seems about right. How do people not feel conned by these establishments?

As I approach the bar, Graham sees me and leaps off the stool. He opens his arms wide and walks to me with a huge grin on his face. A grin that could brighten even the darkest mood. It's such a pleasure to see. He looks as I remember him, but a tad more handsome. I guess he's lucky enough to be getting better-looking with age.

Since I last saw him, he's let his thick, dark hair grow to the point where it's at the base of his neck. It looks wavier than it used to. He looks like he's been spending time working out, as his shoulders are broader than I remember. His dark eyes look the same as they always have – pretty, happy and welcoming. They're representative of his being. I hurry into his arms and we hug. He smells like a mixture of after-shave and alcohol. Not altogether inviting, not altogether off-putting.

While still hugging me tightly, he says, "Babe, babe, babe, where've you been?"

Ah, his voice! Smooth, strong, full of vigour. We separate and I shrug.

"You know me," I say, "always ducking in and out."

I don't have to say anything else. He knows what that means.

He nods. "Cool, cool. Well, you're here now, so let's get you a drink."

"Oh, I'm not drinking tonight. Doctor's orders."

"Wait… you're not…" His eyes widen as he makes the shape of a circle around his belly.

I shake my head vehemently. "No, I just need a break from that stuff."

"Hey, that's fine by me. Come on; let me introduce you to everyone."

XII

DONNA

Being summoned into Mr. Sanders' office like this makes me nervous. It doesn't help that it's after hours. If I was a normal person, I wouldn't even be here. But no, I just *had to* work overtime today. I wish I'd left with Shane... I could have avoided this. Then again, maybe I would merely have delayed the inevitable.

He called me himself, no minions involved. He didn't tell me why he wanted to talk to me but I think I can guess. Since Haywood shot himself, Old Bill probably wants to send me over to the hospital with flowers and good wishes, or something along those lines. Some gesture of kindness will be extended by the firm, with me posing as the arm. Maybe he feels guilty for abandoning his friend in his time of need.

Once at The Top, I note that Mrs. Staunton is not in her office. Maria's desk is clear and her bag is gone. I assume she's left for the day. Sanders' assistant, Charlene is still here, however.

She smiles at me. "He's waiting for you."

"Thanks," I say. Usually, she walks guests into his office and closes the door.

Not this time, though. She stays seated, returns to her computer and carries on typing.

I stand at Sanders' door, hesitating to go in unannounced. I feel a rising sense of unease, but I tell myself that I have nothing to worry about. I knock on the door.

"Come in," I hear him say.

I walk into the office, hoping for the best. He looks up from his desk and beckons to me. The words of the 23rd Psalm bounce around my head for reasons I don't quite know. I struggle to quiet my mind as I walk closer to his desk.

"Please, sit," he says.

I do as I'm told, trying my best to appear professional, yet relaxed. Shoulders down, hands on my lap, legs crossed at the ankles.

I sit as comfortably as I can, and smile. "You wanted to see me, sir."

He doesn't smile back. "Jeremy Haywood. How's he doing?"

"Last I heard, he was out of surgery. They managed to remove the bullet. As for when or if he comes out of the coma, they can't say... but he's stable for now," I say, doing my utmost to sound like I care. Thinking about how delicious Haywood's comeuppance has been makes me want to dance. But this is neither the time nor place for that.

"He got lucky," Sanders says, sighing. He leans back into his chair and looks out the window. There's a spectacular view of the skyline from here. I've never been here at night, so I never noticed. Twinkling lights illuminate the buildings in the distance like thousands of stars in a clear, moonlit sky. Despite how much I dislike this city, I have to admit it has its moments.

"How do you think his confession got onto the internet?" he asks, sitting up again.

"I have no idea."

"You think it was his son?"

"I can't say for certain..."

Poor Jerry was simply a pawn.

"Did you have anything to do with this?" he asks. He looks directly at me, waiting for an answer.

Why would he say that?

"Me? That's a wild accusation!"

"It's not an accusation, it's a question," he says. He leans on his desk, frowning. "Did you leak the audio online?"

I shake my head vigorously, wondering why he'd suspect me of being involved.

"I had nothing to do with this, sir. I don't even know how their conversation was recorded in the first place! Why would you think I was involved in something so underhanded?" I say, quickly. Maybe too quickly. I speak so fast that if I were Old Bill, I'd know I was lying. Ugh, I was not prepared for this.

"Silas worked his magic, tracked down the device that uploaded the audio. He even managed to trace its GPS history, and he tells me that the device was in this building's vicinity this morning."

Damn you, Silas!

The one time I need a colleague to be incompetent, they fail me.

"I assure you, sir; that has nothing to do with me. I would never try to sabotage my own case. That's… insane. Besides, there must be thousands of devices in the building's vicinity on a daily basis!"

I keep flexing and pointing my right foot, hoping to keep any tension away from my face and upper body. I try to keep from clenching my fists. I put my hands on the desk and lean forward.

"I would never do anything to bring disrepute to a client, or to this firm, sir. I don't know how any of this happened, but—"

He lifts his hand to silence me. "Miss Palmer. Daryl told me how reluctant you've been to defend Jeremy and how vocal you've been about your disdain for him."

I shake my head, sincerely surprised by the accusation.

He continues. "You despise him; you think he's a criminal. I understand… you have some sort of moral compass that you feel obligated to follow. Please, you don't have to lie to me."

His voice is calm and soothing. He must think me a fool if he thinks he can fool me. As for Daryl, if he lies to his wife, it's no surprise that he'd lie about me. One of these days he's going to get his!

"Whatever Daryl said is untrue. I'm telling you that I didn't upload that audio and I never said a bad word about Mr. Haywood. I may not have been his biggest fan but I would never let that negatively affect my work. I wouldn't do anything to jeopardise this job."

I think I'm about to be arrested. My breaths are getting rougher, shorter. It feels like a snake has coiled itself around me and is steadily crushing my life away. I remind myself that I've gone about this the smart way and there really is nothing to tie me to this leak. I sit back in the chair as my mouth gets drier.

"Daryl isn't very clever. And he tells lies, but he's not the only one. You're lying to me and I don't appreciate it. I don't appreciate it one bit."

"Sir—"

"I'm terminating your employment with the firm, effective immediately," he says.

He sits back in his chair and looks at me, smirking. He can't be serious. I've worked too hard for this to happen. What about Ivy and mum? I know I can't stay here forever, but if he sacks me now, like this, I probably won't get a good reference.

"Excuse me?"

"Go and clean out your desk – you're fired."

I look at him in stunned silence. This can't be happening.

"Are you deaf? I said go!" he says, raising his voice.

I nod and stand up. "Sir, with all due respect—"

He rises to his feet as he raises his voice further, pointing his long finger at me.

"Don't talk to me about respect. I don't know how you did it, but I know in my gut that you're responsible for Jeremy's current state, and for damaging our case. Once I have enough concrete evidence, I will call the police and have you thrown in jail. And I will see to it that you never practice law in the developed world again," he says.

I step back. The words and the way he says them hit me hard. His threatening stance scares me. The overall effect sends my mind spinning back to the night Alan raped Mina, and the beating William gave me for sneaking out to meet her. In my mind's eye, I see him kicking me even though I was already on the floor. After he died, I promised myself I would never let anyone overpower me again. I must keep that promise.

I step back again as Old Bill stands still. His eyes brighten. Clearly, this is a part of his job that he enjoys. Unfortunately for him, Suzanne and Mina have excelled at their jobs and provided my ace. I close my eyes and take a deep breath. I've ended lives before – ending a career pales in comparison.

"May I say one thing, sir?" I ask, looking down. When I look back up, I see him shrug.

"Make it brief."

I promise no such thing.

I reach into my trouser pocket and get my phone.

"I don't think it's in your interest to sack me, sir." I speak slowly, giving him time to think about what I might be implying.

He doesn't think, though. He just speaks. "My interest? What do you know about my interest?"

I take a slow, deep breath. "I know that there are things you do, and places you go that you don't want anyone to know about. By anyone, I mean your wife and daughter. Maybe even some of your employees. Maybe even the law."

He narrows his eyes. "What are you talking about?"

I step forward, slowly and carefully, keeping my eyes on him.

"I know that there are people you associate with in private that you wouldn't dream of being seen in public with. People like the dancer who goes by the name Rain Storm, real name Lena Murphy. I have a video of her right here," I say, handing him my phone. "It should help jog your memory."

He takes the phone from me, brow furrowed. And then his eyelids peel back when he sees the video's thumbnail.

"You can press play, unless you remember the events of the evening," I say.

He says nothing. Instead he stands there, staring at the screen with his hand shaking.

"Ah of course," I say, "nights like that are quite difficult to forget. I imagine Rain and her friend… Tempest was it? I imagine all the narcotics in the world can't erase their memories."

I might be rubbing it in a little, but it's not every day I have a man like this where I want him. He keeps staring at the screen, doesn't press play.

"Where did you get this?" he asks. There's a slight tremble in his voice. That's enough. That's all I need to know – he's mine.

"That's beside the point. The point, as I'm sure you are now fully aware, is that I like working here and would very much like to continue doing so."

"Where did you get this?" he asks again. He speaks slowly now. It sounds like there's a lump in his throat.

"All you need to know is that I have copies and photographs in a safe place, and I know about your sordid relationship with Sarah Matheson—"

He throws the phone at me, but I duck. It flies across the room and hits the door. He starts coming out from behind his desk, moving towards me, but I stand my ground. I will not be cowed.

He's right in my face now. "Who the hell do you think you are, little girl? You think you can threaten me?"

"I know I can destroy you. Help you destroy yourself, more like. And now you know that, too. In my opinion, it would be in both our best interest for me to keep working here… unless, of course, in addition to having to endure being married to a man as degenerate as her father, you want your beloved Veronica to endure the heartache that will no doubt follow your public disgrace. Not to mention that she would be so hurt to find that you're sleeping with her friend. And disgusted, she and your wife would be thoroughly disgusted. Add to this your frequent visits to that massage parlour in Chinatown, and I'd say that you're in a very unpleasant situation."

He takes a couple of steps back, blinking rapidly. He holds his head in his hands for a moment, and then looks at me. At first his eyes widen, and then there's a gradual dimming until he's squinting. It's almost like he's seeing me for the first time. And from where he's standing, I must look as cold as the hand of death.

"I'm not judging you; I'm just trying to stay employed…"

I take another slow, deep breath in, waiting for his next move.

"Fine, fine. You can keep your job," he says. He goes back behind his desk and sits down. His shoulders slump while he looks vacantly at the papers in front of him. He thinks we're done, but he's wrong. I've come this far and I'm going all the way.

"The thing is… I don't want to keep my job. I want a promotion. Daryl has outlived whatever little usefulness he had. I want his job, starting in a month," I say.

He looks up, mouth open. "What? I can't fire Daryl."

I smile, raise an eyebrow. "Then don't. I don't care what happens to him. All I want is to head up the team, and I want to earn what Daryl earns, plus half. A month should give you more than enough time to make it happen and figure out what to do with your treacherous son-in-law."

He reclines in his chair and shakes his head.

"I always suspected there was more to you than you let on. I could never have guessed you would stoop to blackmail," he says with a wry smile on his face. He almost looks impressed.

"Oh Bill, don't think of it as blackmail. This is merely a negotiation. You get something you want, I get something I want. Everybody wins."

"Daryl doesn't," he says.

"We don't really care about him, so that's not a problem."

He laughs. For the first time all night, he laughs. I don't know if that's good. I've never been this close to him when he's laughed. I've been at work parties and, from a distance, seen him laughing. I look at him as his head goes back and his mouth flies open. His laugh is loud, the sort that wouldn't be out of place in a pub or some other alcohol-soaked location.

When he stops laughing, he looks at me with a very serious expression on his face. "Daryl is useless. Getting rid of him would be a pleasure."

Well, he changed his mind fast.

"You have no idea how heartbroken I was when Veronica told me she was pregnant for that low life. I wanted so much more for her than to be with one so… unworthy. The saddest day of my life," he says, shaking his head.

I'm a bit surprised by his candour. Perhaps since I know more about him than his family do, there's no point hiding his feelings. What's one more secret between us?

"I believe every word."

His face falls. Even now, I can sense his disappointment. For a split second, I feel sorry for him, but then I remember the video I showed him a moment ago and all traces of sympathy evaporate.

"So," he says, clearing his throat, "if I give you Daryl's job and the other perks you requested, you'll lose the videos?"

"I won't share them."

"And I suppose anytime you want a raise or a promotion or a birthday cake, you'll remind me of their existence."

"That's not really my style, Bill. I don't like cake. And I don't ask for much. Between me and you, I'll probably leave the firm in a couple of years – with a glowing reference, of course – and you won't have to think of this situation ever again," I say, smiling.

He nods and sighs. "Fine."

A moment of awkward silence follows, as we look at each other. I didn't think it would be this easy, but now the negotiation is over, I'm not sure what to do. And how will I explain this to my colleagues?

"Well, I still have some work to do. You should probably go home," he says.

"And Mr. Haywood?"

"He's no longer our problem."

I nod. "Alright. Have a good weekend."

"And you."

I walk to the door and pick up my phone, putting it back in my pocket. I glance at him over my shoulder. He's looking at his own phone. I leave his office and shut the door behind me. I lean against the door and let out a loud sigh. It feels like I've been holding my breath this whole time. My heart beats rapidly as I try to get my bearings.

"That kind of meeting?" Charlene says.

I step away from the door and walk past her.

"You don't know the half of it."

XIII

IVY

Another week draws to a close. My friend Ayo had her first child ten days ago – a girl she and her husband, Remi, have named Adeola. I've made a meal for them and will be driving a group of us over to their house later this evening, taking it along. I called to tell Donna that. She sounded concerned when I told her there *might* be a few hours between her coming home and mum going to church later tonight.

"Thanks for letting me know," she said. The words were simple enough, but her tone... oh, the shift was subtle but I knew what she was thinking.

It's like she doesn't trust herself not to be cruel to mum if no one else is around. I know that mum has put us through— I know that we've endured a lot of nasty experiences because of mum's mistakes, but everyone makes mistakes. If after all this time Donna still can't be alone with her, she needs more serious help than I realised.

I pray for her like my life depends on it but still, nothing happens. Sometimes I feel like I'm wasting my time, but I'm too scared to stop. What if one of these days she comes to her senses and realises that despite all the bad things that have happened to her – to us – she can move forward and have a good life? She doesn't have to stay angry, she doesn't have to keep on hating our parents for the stupid and wicked things they've done. He's been dead for so long, but she still hates dad. Why bother?

I say 'so long' but sometimes it feels like only a few months have passed since he died. It helps that we moved house and left that area altogether, but some days I wake up and I don't know where I am, and I'm suddenly seized by this fear that I've somehow disappointed my father and I'm going to be beaten for it.

Other days, I catch a glimpse of my reflection and see the scar near my left shoulder blade. He gave me that when I was 12, the one and only time I ever talked back to him. He was cussing at mum, closing in on her, obviously going to slap her around because she went swimming without his consent. I called him a bully and a coward. I thought it was smart and brave. I soon realised that there was a price to be paid for such conduct. I had seen Donna get beaten time and again for defending mum or herself or even me but in the heat of the moment, I forgot all of that.

How offended he was that I told him the truth about himself! He told me he expected such disrespectful behaviour from my 'unruly sister' and was appalled that I would dare to emulate her. In his fit of rage, he cracked a bottle of vodka on the table and jammed the half he was holding into my back. Suffice it to say, I did not enjoy that. Mum did nothing, save take care of the wound, as usual. The scar is still with me... it never completely faded.

I do my best to avoid thinking about the bad times but there are times that I can't help it. Once, at university, I tried counselling at the church I attended. It might have worked if I'd ever been able to bring myself to talk about the violence that I suffered at the hands of someone who was supposed to love and protect me. I ended up talking about not knowing what to do after graduation.

I'd met the counsellor, Iona, a few times. She seemed nice enough. I was depressed and confused about what to do with the future, but also about what to do with the past. I got so low that I considered drinking alcohol. That was when I knew I needed help. I told one of the pastors that I thought I could benefit from counselling (which they were always talking about on the pulpit), and he arranged a meeting between me and Iona.

We talked briefly about my degree and my concerns, and then she moved on to my family life. I told her the truth – my father was dead, and I had a mother and sister. It didn't take long for her to work out that there was more to my life than that, because I refused to talk about what effect his death had had on me.

I shrugged, "I'm not sure that has anything to do with this."

She nodded knowingly, chewing on her the top of her pen. That habit made me squirm. *Does she know how many germs live in the mouth?* I often wondered to myself. When she was done chewing, she let out a heavy sigh and said, "I think your lack of direction has something to do with your father, or perhaps his absence."

"Maybe it does, or maybe it doesn't. Will finding the answer get me a good job?" I asked, channelling Donna in all her hostility.

"It's something to prayerfully explore."

I went back to see her two more times. The penultimate time, she told me that she'd prayed about my 'predicament' and knew that I needed to forgive my dad for anything he'd done to hurt me, including but not limited to dying young.

"I'm not sure that was his choice," I said.

"You told me his death was alcohol-related," she said.

I nodded. That much I had divulged.

"Then in a way his death was his choice, even if it wasn't what he wanted. His actions led to his early death, and for that you need to forgive him."

I quietly pondered her words for a minute. Maybe she was on to something. Even if he hadn't woken up that morning thinking 'goodbye cruel world,' for years he'd drunk himself so senseless that it was only a matter of time before his liver gave way. It's bizarre that it didn't. And though he didn't die from alcohol poisoning, had he been sober he might have got down the stairs unscathed. The thought may have filled someone else with sadness, but I was ambivalent.

"That's an interesting point," I said.

We prayed that I would release all the hurt, anger, unforgiveness and resentment into Christ's loving hand and know God as my Father. I cried so much that we ended the session early, and then I went home and cried for the rest of the evening. For as long as I could remember, I knew I had a bad father. Some people who grow up in abusive households say they think that's how it is in every household. I don't know why, but I never did. I knew that what went on in my family – how my dad treated us – couldn't be normal or right. I knew the drunkenness didn't make him a different person; it just amplified who he really was, gave him licence to be his truest self.

But for some reason, after that meeting with Iona, I felt the pain more acutely than ever before. It was like before that, it had been buried, not too deeply, but deeply enough that it wasn't something I thought about or felt all the time... then she prayed and it all came to the surface, and it kept on coming and it wouldn't stop. I couldn't get out of bed the next day, missed all my lectures. My housemates thought I'd been dumped by a boyfriend I didn't even have. They offered to take me to the hospital, which was endearing.

I wanted to call Donna and weep with her, but I knew she'd shut me down. She never wanted to talk about dad. To her, his death was a gift, a turning point in her life – one that meant that her life could be good, that she could be important and influential. She didn't want any reminders that there was ever a time when that seemed impossible.

I cried on my own. I didn't talk to anyone. Right or wrong, I thought no one would understand or be able to help me. I didn't know Iona well enough to bare my soul to her, the way I felt I needed to. In the end, I poured my heart out to Jesus and He got me through. And I accepted that I had to forgive dad in order to be free. It was hard, but worth it for my peace of mind.

I wish Donna could see God as He is and let Him help her as well. But she's too stubborn and proud, and she blames Him. I can't say I never blamed Him... He got me past that, too. I have so much to be grateful for.

Donna not only ignores God's pleas to let Him heal her, she makes no attempt to get human help. If she doesn't let anyone help her, what will become of her? How will she ever be healthy? How will she ever be free? I spend so much time thinking about her you'd think I was her mother. I do wonder if mum cares for us that way, and if she will ever understand how much damage we've accrued. On many occasions I've considered talking to her about dad but I'm not sure it's worth the trouble. There's nothing she can do to change the past. I've forgiven her for her mistakes and I owe it to her and God to love her, no matter what.

Donna, on the other hand, has a different view of... well, everything. For the two years after she finished her degree, while I was still at university and living on campus, she hardly spent any time at home. If living at home hadn't been more convenient for her, I'm sure she'd have moved out. Instead, she studied and worked from the crack of dawn till late at night in an attempt to avoid spending time with mum. On weekends, she'd go away on her own, where to she didn't always say. She's not quite broken the habit, though in the summer she sometimes finds her way home before dark. I don't know how she lives with all the much anger and resentment.

Done with the food, I wash my hands and place the containers into a large carrier bag. I may have overdone it a little. There are eight containers... well, that's what refrigerators are for, right? If there's altogether more food than the couple can handle, I can always bring some back home.

"Mum, I'm off to pick the others up," I say raising my voice so she can hear me from the living room.

"Ok, send them my love."

She comes to the kitchen as I sling my bag over my shoulder. She's smiling.

I take hold of the carrier bag. "I will."

I leave the flat and walk to the car. When I get there, a strange, cold feeling comes over me. The hairs on the back of my neck stand on end and I almost feel like I'm being watched. I look around but see nothing out of the ordinary. The feeling subsides and I get into the car and lock it. I start the engine and without warning, burst into tears. That's not something that happens for no reason. I don't know what's happening, but I know what to do about it.

I start praying for mum and Donna, for Ayo and Remi, for Mina and Suzanne, for Lottie and everyone else I can think of. I pray that God sends His angels to protect them. I pray for angels to direct them away from evil and violence, and to protect our neighbourhood and children and schools.

As I pray, my thoughts keep going back to Donna, so I focus on her. I pray that God will give her the grace to forgive our parents. I pray that He'll help her leave the past behind and get over killing Alan. I pray that she'll see Jesus for who He really is. I pray until the tears stop coming and I feel a sense of calm.

I turn the engine off and catch my breath. After composing myself, I start the car again and drive off. It's good that I'll be praying all night tonight.

Something bad is on the horizon. I can sense it.

XIV

DONNA

I was at the tail end of writing a report when Old Bill called for me. When I get back to my desk, I finish it and leave the building. I can't decide whether to go home or meet up with Zach and his friends. I reckon I should at least go to the bus stop since it services buses to both destinations.

While walking, I get a call from Suzanne.

"What's up?" I ask.

"The man is still comatose, unlikely to wake up tonight, so I'm clocking out."

"Cool, thank you."

"Do you need anything else from me?"

"I.T. traced the leak to your phone – you might want to get rid of it."

I hear nothing for a moment.

"Good to know, I'll do that. Any impact on you?" she asks. She sounds as she always does – unflustered.

"No, I handled it."

"I'd expect nothing less."

I can hear her smiling.

"Call me if anything changes."

"That'll be tomorrow. Have a good night," she says.

She hangs up as I get to the bus stop. I look up into the night sky. It's clear and the full moon illuminates it, amplifying its beauty. The stars glimmer in the distance and I wonder if what I've done makes any difference in a universe so vast and complex. In the grand scheme of things, does it matter that Jeremy Haywood is on his death bed? And if it does, are my methods deplorable? How are Jerry and Noah doing?

No, no. I need to stop thinking like that. It matters. It matters to Aisha that the whole world has heard the man who attacked her confess to it. She may never forget what he did to her, but she has a better chance of moving on. Wrongs have been righted. I've done a good thing.

I'm also consoled by the fact that I didn't even have to kill anyone to get what I wanted. That shows growth, if you ask me. I'm disappointed that I had to resort to tactics as blatant as, yes, *blackmail* in order to stay employed, but I had no choice. I was in a corner. I hate that I showed Bill my true face, but it had to be done. There's no going back now.

I look at the bus routes, wondering whether to go to the pub, or to go home. If Ivy and mum haven't left yet, they soon will, so I have nothing to worry about. As much as I am looking forward to spending the night home alone, Zach's offer is tempting.

I check my watch. It's 10:35.

Deep down, I know that seeing Zach will be more trouble than it's worth. If I ever decide to spend time with him, I can do that on another occasion. Tonight only rolls round once a month. I should take the chance to be by myself.

I whip out my phone and text him, telling him I won't be meeting him tonight. Within a minute, he replies with a sad-faced smiley. That makes me smile a little. I feel bad for letting him down again. Still, he'll get over it.

My thoughts turn to the victories I've secured. I helped Aisha and got a promotion in the space of a fortnight. All in all, this week is ending on a high note. The only way is up. I look up and, in the distance, see the bus that'll take me home. I smile to myself.

Everything will be fine.

XV

MINA

couple of hours have passed and even though I've not had any al-cohol, I feel pretty good. I managed to dodge Ivy's prayer meeting which she called to invite me to. I felt a little bad at the time, but I don't know how it's supposed to help me. Maybe tomorrow I'll ask her about it some more. I've spent so little time around her this week that it'll be nice to hang with her over the weekend. I invited Donna to the bar. She turned me down.

As it stands now, a total of six times I've had to repeat my story that, for health reasons other than pregnancy, my doctor has told me to abstain from drinking. It's weird – despite how much I knew it was hurting me, I was one of those people who always asked why someone wasn't drinking.

Are these people like me? Are they so hell-bent on erasing bad memories that they'd risk erasing good ones too? They'd even risk creating more bad memories to later attempt to erase with more alcohol. It's a never-ending cycle: Regret – Drink to Forget – Repeat. People would jeopardise their very lives for a moment of escape. I should stop thinking about this. All this thinking is stressing me out, and that makes me want to drink. That's another thing I realised: over-thinking leads to drinking. I'm still learning my triggers, but at least I know that one.

Graham is as delightful as ever, the life of the party. I can tell that a particular girl, Natalie, is quite interested in him. She's taken every opportunity to touch his arm, whisper in his ear, that sort of thing. He doesn't seem too responsive. I can't figure out why, though. She's pretty enough – petite, blonde, large boobs that are half-exposed. She's wearing a sleeveless blush-pink mini-dress (or as Donna would call it, a rag) that has a window over her cleavage. The dress is mid-way up her thigh, and her strappy heels are so high that she totters when she walks. I don't think she wants to leave here alone.

She also has a lovely face. Light brown eyes which are emphasized by her false lashes and light blue eye shadow; well-applied makeup; a cute little mouth. I'm not sure why Graham wouldn't be attracted to her. Maybe the fact that they work together has put him off.

As Natalie turns to the bar to order more drinks, Graham looks at me and asks, "Where're you staying tonight?"

I hesitate. I look over at Natalie. Her body stiffens and her head tilts slightly, as if she's furtively trying to hear my answer. He smiles at me, reaching over to gently stroke my arm. He knows what that does to me. I smile and look away, playing with my hair.

Finally, I reply, "With a friend."

His eyes narrow.

"Oh," he says, "is that so? What kind of friend?"

He looks from my eyes to my mouth. I smile, shaking my head.

Natalie returns with the drinks and looks at me, smiling.

"I'm off to powder my nose. Would you come with me, Mina?" she asks, still smiling.

This is only the second time tonight that she's spoken to me. She has a strong accent and would place her in the 'posh bird' category. I'm pretty sure that she wants to separate me from the group and warn me off Graham. It's her right. I agree to go with her. Graham smiles, brows raised, as we leave him.

In keeping with the bar's hipster feel, the toilets are labelled *Dudes* and

Dudettes, rather than the traditional *Male/Female* or *Ladies/Gents* combination. The walls in the corridor are made of exposed bricks, making the building look incomplete. As soon as we get into the toilet, Natalie places her handbag on the counter and pulls out an eyeshadow palette.

She looks at her reflection in the mirror. "Are you having fun?"

Her tone is light and flirtatious. She sounds like she's trying to put me at ease.

"Yeah. Are you?" I reply, in a similar upbeat manner. I don't know why I'm trying to match her tone.

"Absolutely. Graham knows how to have a good time," she says, applying more eyeshadow. I don't say anything. Instead I hang around, inspecting the facilities. They've got swanky hand dryers in here, in addition to baskets housing paper towels, and a quick peek into a stall reveals that the flush mechanism is motion-activated. I look back at her as she puts the finishing touches to her other eye. It's obvious that she's well-practiced. That took no time at all. Another patron comes in, and I move out of her way so she can get to a stall.

"Thanks babes," she says rather loudly.

Once Natalie's done retouching her eyeshadow, she puts the palette on the counter and moves on to mascara. She piles the make up on as though it's war paint. I can't help thinking that it's wasteful to put that much product on false lashes. At last, she pulls out her eyeliner.

At this point, she leans so far forward that I worry that she's on the brink of a wardrobe malfunction. She looks at my reflection in the mirror, and my eyes meet hers. She looks back at her reflection, paying careful attention to the eyeliner application process. In the same fun tone as before, she asks, "So... who is this friend you're staying with?"

"What do you mean?" I ask, confused by the question.

"Is it your boyfriend?"

"Oh, no," I say, shaking my head and realising that we're (sort of) talking about Graham, "it's a friend from school. I'm staying with her and her family."

"For how long?"

"I'm not sure yet. Why?"

"I was wondering if there was any chance you'd be coming over to Graham's place," she says, completing the eyeliner reapplication.

She puts the makeup away, as the other woman flushes and leaves the stall. They both wash their hands. The woman moves to use the hand drier. As it blares noisily, Natalie stares at my reflection. I hold her gaze, unsure of why it's so intense. With her hands dry, the other woman leaves. Natalie takes a paper towel and turns to me as she wipes her hands. I watch her in silence. I don't really have anything to say. I don't know why she's brought me in here.

She discards the towel and opens her handbag. From it she extracts a small, sealed plastic bag. She doesn't have to tell me what the white powder in it is. As soon as I see it, I know it's cocaine. I freeze almost instantly. The night just took a very bad turn.

"Have you ever had fun with Charlie?" she asks flightily, rattling the little bag.

My heart starts racing like a cheetah. I wasn't ready for this. It's one thing to think you might be offered a bit of weed or whisky, but cocaine is my kryptonite. And this pretty little posh princess doesn't look the sort. I guess there is no look. My throat dries up and I'm having trouble thinking. It's like all my mental faculties are shutting down at the same time. When I first started doing drugs, it was for anaesthetic purposes. Then I was doing them because I felt like I physically needed them to live. I've been clean for six months now, but... I guess I'll always be vulnerable to this stuff.

She looks me up and down, waiting for an answer. I'm too torn to say anything. On one hand, I know that I should say no but on the other hand, now it's here in front of me, it seems senseless to turn it down. I didn't go looking for cocaine, it found me. If the situation wasn't so dangerous, it would be opportune. I take a deep breath and exhale loudly.

"No?" she asks, "Well, he really is something. Wanna try?"

She's still holding the bag up.

"In public?" I finally find the words. She shrugs and turns back to the mirror. She opens the little plastic bag and sprinkles some of the coke onto the palette. I'd never have thought to do that. She stoops a little and sniffs it up. When she said she wanted to powder her nose, this is not what I thought she meant.

I can feel my resolve weakening. I want to leave but I feel like I'm rooted to the spot. She wipes her nose and looks in the mirror. She shakes her head like a dog shakes itself after a bath.

"Oh yesssss," she exclaims, breathily. I really should leave. I should have left by now. Maybe I should never have come here.

"I can tell that Graham likes you a lot. I like you too," she says. She starts swaying from side to side, looking at the ceiling.

"Thanks," I manage to squeak. I swallow hard as I feel myself starting to sweat.

"If you change your mind about staying with your friend, maybe you can come over to his place later," she says, blinking slowly at my reflection.

She seals the bag, turns to me and takes my hand. It must feel limp. She puts the bag in my open palm and closes it, winking.

"You can thank me later," she says, sporting a broad smile. She leans forward and kisses me on my cheek. And then she leaves me standing in the restroom, holding onto the drugs.

Even when I'm not chasing The High, it's chasing me. I may never outrun it.

XVI

IVY

The prayer meeting has started with praise and worship. I'm mentally settling in, focussing on Jesus and how much He loves me, trying to empty my mind of all doubt and fear and anything else that might interfere.

I stand still, eyes closed, opening myself to the Lord when I suddenly feel a stabbing pain in my side. I double over, coughing. My eyes fly open and all I see is darkness. I feel my back against a wall. My breathing speeds up as I hold onto my side, still leaning forward. I feel like someone has put their hands on me, like I'm being choked. I can't breathe properly.

In my head I start praying, "Lord Jesus, help me!"

Instantly, my vision clears and I'm once again surrounded by my fellow congregants. I stagger backwards but manage to maintain my balance. I look at mum, who seems lost in worship.

What just happened? Was that real?

It felt real, too real in fact. I disrupt mum's concentration and push past her, walking into the aisle. I pick my phone out of my pocket, intending to switch it on and call Donna. I walk to the back of the church, where the prayer team are stationed.

"Ivy, are you ok?" Christina, the head of the prayer team, asks.

I look at her, still confused.

"I'm honestly not sure."

I put the phone away.

"Is there something you'd like to pray about?" she asks.

I nod slowly.

XVII

MINA

I left the bar right after I left the restroom. Graham seemed disappointed, but I had to get out of there. Alas, I took the drugs with me. I know it sounds stupid, but as soon as that little pouch got into my hand, I couldn't let it go. Maybe I didn't want to. Either way, I left with it and I could feel it burning a hole in my pocket for the whole journey home. Home? It's not my home. It's a place I'm staying because I've spent so much money on drugs and so much time in jail that I don't have anything of my own. I know that no good will come of this, but I can't bring myself to throw this thing away.

When I get to the flat, it's way past eleven. Mama Selene and Ivy will be gone all night. Donna said she'd be working late. I don't know how late 'late' is. I have a quick look around the house to be sure that I'm alone. When I am, I get a straw from the kitchen and go to the bathroom, where I lock the door and empty my pocket. There it is, the white powder that brings despair, but not before giving you The High. I open the plastic bag and pour the contents onto the toilet seat.

This is insane.

I don't know whether I'm going to take some or not.

"Think about the consequences," Salome always said. I put my hands on my head. I'm thinking, I'm thinking.

Why the hell did I empty the plastic? What happens if Donna comes home? She'll throw me out, and then where will I stay? I could go to Graham's, but for how long? Did Natalie go home with him? Does he know she's a coke head? Have they had sex yet? That man sure attracts a type.

The more I think about things, the less stressed I feel, surprisingly. I look at the drugs, and even though they're the most basic, bland, white thing you could ever see, they're calling to me, promising me things that I know they can't deliver. At least not long-term. Every single time they promise me Peace; Euphoria; Love; The ability to forget my past. It's a lie. Every single time they lie. The High is always a lie. Getting high gets me nowhere. I know this but knowing doesn't make a difference.

My thought train is derailed by a subtle noise. It sounded like someone entering the flat. Crap! If it's Donna, my life is over. Should I check? Should I flush the drugs? I was dumb enough to empty all the damn contents. What the hell was I thinking? Have I lost my mind?

I'm stupid and disgusting. I hate myself.

I'm panicking, but I don't even know if I should. Should I see if she's back? No, I'll wait. If I hear a knock on the door, I'll know for sure and that will give me time to clean up.

I walk closer to the door. I'm not certain but I think I hear the faint sound of footsteps approaching it. Someone is creeping around. My heart is beating fast again as I tell myself that there's time for me to flush the cocaine. The footsteps stop, and then there's silence.

I sense a presence on the other side of the door. It occurs to me that if Donna was in the house, she would most likely have said something by now. That means that either no one is in the house and I'm losing my mind without having taken any drugs, or there's an intruder standing on the other side of this door. I don't know which is more frightening.

In a flash, the memory of Alan climbing on top of me whilst punching my face returns with the force of a hurricane. I double over, holding my head, hitting it, trying to get rid of the picture. What if someone *is* out there? Is it going to happen again?

Then there's another sound – the noise of the front door opening, and then shutting loudly. Oh man, is *that* Donna or am I going mad? I hear a noise in my head. I look over at the toilet seat, and the drugs are still there, quietly but forcefully calling my name. I need them. In this moment, I know that I need them. The memories are coming in thick and fast, and I stumble over to the seat. As I crouch with the intention of snorting some coke, I start to cry. Donna is outside and here I am trying to get high in her home.

I hear a dull noise all of a sudden. It sounds like an object falling over. Then I hear muffled sounds. That's not in my head, and it doesn't sound right either. I walk out of my mental prison and carefully open the bathroom door. There's no one outside it. I creep through the corridor to the living room area, and then freeze when I see it. Donna is being attacked – maybe suffocated – by a strange man.

I look around and see that a lamp has fallen on the ground. I pick it up and smash it as hard as I can on the back of the guy's head. The lamp crumbles to pieces. He releases Donna and falls on the floor. Before I can say or do anything else, he leaps up and kicks me in the stomach.

I topple over the sofa and everything goes dark.

XVIII

DONNA

The door slams behind me as I walk into the flat. I exhale. Home at last. The place is warm, and silence echoes throughout. One step. Another. With each step, my heels clatter on the ground. I stand still. Again, I hear nothing but silence. It's the sort of silence that some might find unsettling. It's the sort of silence that fills me with comfort and is indicative of peace. I feel even better to be here.

It'll be midnight soon. Mina's earlier text said she'd be spending the evening at some bar, though she didn't say with whom. Probably that dopehead, Graham. No surprises there. She invited me to join her, but I declined. Perhaps I should have gone to keep an eye on her but given the sort of evening I've had, the last thing I need is to be around people. I hope she's ok.

I hang my coat up, thinking about what a relief it is to have solitude, especially after all the drama at work. I walk through the entrance hall debating whether or not to have my ice cream right away or change my clothes first. I turn in to the kitchen where I put the shopping bag on the counter. A split-second later, I catch a glimpse of something from the corner of my eye. Not something, someone. A man. I don't have time to think or react before he grabs me. He covers my mouth with one hand and tries to restrain me with the other.

He doesn't get my hands in time. I push myself back from the counter and into his body. He is sturdy – he moves backwards but neither falls nor lets me go. I hear a thud as he knocks something over. I can feel my breath shortening. I start scratching his arms and trying to shout. My voice is muffled. I bite his hand and kick his shins and knees, hoping my heels are doing some damage.

I dig my nails so deeply into the skin on his forearm that I can feel the blood beneath them. His grip starts to loosen but by now I'm enjoying hurting him way too much. I hold onto his hand and bite down hard, hoping to get to the bone or rip off some flesh. He manages to snatch his hand away and hit me in the eye. The pain is intense, though the blow isn't as hard as I imagine he intended.

I suddenly hear a crashing noise. He lets go and falls over. I stumble a little, managing to stay on my feet. I turn around, and see Mina holding the remains of that hideous ceramic lamp that mum insisted on buying. A part of me is relieved that it's gone, but another part of me is upset that we'll never get that £40 back. I didn't hear Mina come in but I'm glad she's here. The man springs to his feet and kicks her in the stomach and she goes flying over a chair.

He pulls a knife out of his dirty-looking boot and turns back to me. The knife has a short, curved blade that's about four inches long. The handle is wrapped in a frayed, black cloth which looks like it's seen better days. The man shakes his head like he's dazed, yet he looks somewhat amused that I've put up a fight so far. He sneers at me, as he darts towards me with the knife. I dodge, but there's not enough room for me to escape. He moves closer, with purpose, as I take slow steps backwards. He must think I'm frightened, but he has no idea who he's dealing with. Maybe I should feel scared. I don't. I've dealt with bullies and abusers before. What's one more? I don't know who this man is or what poor decisions led him here but he has broken into the wrong home, and I will make him regret that.

This time he charges at me but I move out of his way, narrowly avoiding getting cut. I run further into the kitchen hoping to get a weapon. He follows me, and as I get my hands on a carving knife, I feel a sharp pain in my side. He twists the knife and I fall to the ground, dropping the carving knife. I scramble backwards until my back is against the wall. He towers over me, a smile creeping up on his face. For a moment, I'm 15 again, lying on the floor of my bedroom with William telling me I did this to myself. At last, I am afraid.

"Please, take whatever you want and go. I won't try to stop you." My voice shakes, though more from the pain than the fear. I pant, holding onto my side. My heart starts to beat faster and my stomach drops. I feel the terror rising. I can't let him see it. I can't let it take over. I manage to stand up, but there's no way I can get past him. I'm trapped.

The knife is still in me, and the pain is palpable. My mind is racing, trying to calculate how to get out of this situation alive. Can I jump over the countertop with a knife stuck in my side? Is Mina going to sneak up on him again? Was she knocked out? Is she even alive?

A line from The Art of War comes to me: *"Hold out baits to entice the enemy. Feign disorder, and crush him."*

He moves his head to one side, as if he's contemplating leaving, but he says nothing and he does not leave. Instead, he comes closer to me until he's mere inches from my face. A bead of sweat drips from his temple to his dark stubble, and stays there. He sniffs, as he looks from my face to my neck and then back again. One way or another, I have to get out of here alive and it looks like I can't rely on anyone but myself to make that happen. I know that he's going to try to kill me – I've seen his face. I look into his eyes. It's now or never.

Feign disorder.

"Please, don't hurt me," I say. He smirks. One of his hands starts moving. I take a deep breath, right before he puts it on my throat, squeezing hard.

"Where is it?"

Where is what?

I don't know how he expects me to answer him while I'm being choked. What I do know is that this is not how my life ends.

Crush him.

With all I have left in me, I pull the knife out of my side and jam it into his neck. I pull it out and blood gushes from him like water from a broken pipe.

His blue eyes go wide, maybe with pain, maybe with surprise, maybe with both. He didn't see it coming. They never do. He staggers away from me, grasping at his neck, trying to stem the tide. It's about as much use as trying to plug a hole in a burst dam. He's done. Damn him. Damn him straight to hell. He coughs up blood, sputters, staggers some more. At last, he crashes on the broken ceramic shards.

Silence.

I move closer to him and kick his leg. No movement. His eyes stare vacantly into space. The same eyes that moments ago spoke of murder now speak of nothing. I stand over his body, bleeding and bruised and hurt, but triumphant. Confident that he's dead, I drop the knife.

Another one bites the dust.

XIX

MINA

In my semi-conscious state, I hear a crash. I don't know if I'm dreaming, but I wake up and my head is throbbing. It takes me a few moments to remember where I am and why I'm here. My legs are on a sofa, and my torso is on the floor of Donna's living room. My back really hurts, but at least my skull hasn't been smashed open. I can't hear anything. It takes a while, but I'm able to swing my legs over and roll onto my side.

I struggle to get to my feet, and then peer into the kitchen. I see Donna standing over the intruder, who lies flat on his back. I think he's dead. I can't believe this is happening again. Suddenly, I'm back in the newsagent, watching Alan bleed all over the floor.

I back into the corner of the room and put my arms around myself. I rock back and forth slowly, tears streaming down my face. It's exactly like it was that day. Donna walks into the living room and stares at me. She calls my name. Her voice is hoarse. I look at her but can't bring myself to speak. Her hands are soaked in blood and her eye looks like it's starting to swell. I want to say something, ask her if she's ok, but the words won't come out.

327

When she slinks away, probably exasperated, I know that I will have to say something, for she's headed in the direction of the bathroom. There's no way for me to get the cocaine out of there before she sees it. I excel at making bad choices and for that, my goose is cooked. I run up to her though I know there's no point. I'm done.

"Please, Donna, don't go in there."

My voice is soft, but the plea goes ignored. She looks at my face, and then realisation covers hers. She moves resolutely towards the bathroom, and I follow her. I try to cut her off but I fail.

They should write that on my epitaph: *'She Tried and She Failed, Repeatedly.'*

She opens the door and sees the powder on the seat. She spins around, looking at me with tears in her eyes. I've let her down once again.

I have done this to myself.

It's time to face the music.

XX

DONNA

I've never killed without first making the necessary preparations. My most recent victim caught me unawares but, despite that, I overcame. For that, I am grateful. Here I thought I'd spend the evening relaxing. To my disappointment, life has once again dumped a truckload of lemons on me, and I'm scrambling to make something palatable out of them.

In the kitchen, standing over the corpse of the stranger, I try to organise my thoughts. I don't know why he broke in. He wanted something from me... he didn't say what. My hands are covered in blood, a combination of his and mine, and my side hurts so badly that I think I might have cracked some ribs. Or maybe the stab wound is deeper than I thought. Maybe he punctured an organ. I sincerely hope that knife was sterilized. I can barely stand straight because of the searing pain. As if that wasn't enough, my throat hurts from the aborted strangulation.

Blood seeps from his body and spreads itself out on the kitchen floor. This will be a drag to clean up. I don't remember there being as much blood the first time, but then again that was a decade ago. Time has started chipping away at the finer details. And come to think of it, this is a big guy. Maybe he has a lot more blood than Ellis did. I do recall that the blood dried on my hands and was ordeal to wash off... and I remember how much the incident further traumatised Mina.

Mina! Suddenly, I remember that she's in the flat. There's nothing like almost getting choked to death to make you lose focus. I hurry, as much as I can, to the living room and find Mina standing in the corner, cradling herself. I wonder how long she's been conscious. Did she see what happened?

"Mina." My voice is hoarse, but not inaudible. I get no response.

She stands still. I want to shake her, but I'm aware that my hands are blood-stained. I'm also aware that I should call the police. Before I do that, I have to clean myself up. I feel revolting. I turn to go to the bathroom when Mina starts walking towards me. I'm startled by the speed with which she does so. She was practically comatose mere seconds ago.

She looks at me with a pained expression on her face, and whispers, "Please, Donna, don't go in there."

I pause for a moment, trying to read her, trying to guess why she'd say that.

"What have you done, Mina?"

I bound to the bathroom, ignoring all the pain I'm in, and she follows me, trying to cut me off. I still get there before she does. Then I see what she was hiding. Drugs. A lot of drugs spilled onto the top of the toilet seat. I feel the muscles in my throat tighten more as I realise that she not only fell off the wagon, but she brought these filthy drugs into my flat. After all the promising and pleading, she goes and does this. Tears well up in my eyes, tears which take me by surprise. I didn't realise how invested I was in her recovery. I can't believe I ever thought that she'd get over her addiction. I turn to look at her, and she starts to mutter something about explaining.

Without thinking, I lunge at her, grabbing her by the collar of her jumper. This is turning out to be a very bad evening.

"What the hell is this?" I ask, with my voice strained and my hands still on her. It upsets me that I've stained her clothing, but I suddenly can't control myself. She doesn't answer me, just looks away.

I ask her again, "What is this, Mina? Tell me."

"Please let me go, Donna."

The words sound more like a squeak, and my mind goes back to the day she told me what Ellis had done to her. She sounded the same way – fragile, helpless, frightened. It occurs to me that putting my messy hands on her was a mistake.

I look in her eyes, and she looks at me like she did after I shot Ellis. She looks like she doesn't recognise me. She looks like she's afraid of me. I've never wanted her to be afraid of me. I drop my hands and step away from her. She sinks down to the ground and cries quietly. I've hurt her, reduced her to tears. Am I any better than any of the people I've killed?

"I'm going to wash my hands and see about this wound. And then, I'm calling the police."

"Donna, please. You know they'll send me back if they find me with drugs."

"Well maybe you shouldn't have had any in the first place!"

I manage to keep my voice low and even this time, trying to avoid putting further strain on my vocal cords. I look at her and think of how badly she's failed herself – and me, and mum and Ivy – again. I walk to the sink and start washing my hands. The blood is almost dry so I have to scrub harder than I'd like, and use a lot more soap. I already know that cleaning my hands won't wash the stains off my soul. I've been here before. I know what to expect. In my defence, this time I was just trying to stay alive. That is my right.

Clean hands now. I rinse my face with very cold water, paying special attention to my eye. The water's coolness soothes my eye, though only temporarily. I look at my reflection and notice that it is starting to swell. I look like mum did on one of the more awful nights. Thanks to the colour of my skin, though, my neck isn't visibly bruised.

I grab my trusty face towel, rinse it in hot water, then apply it to my side. I don't know if this is hygienic, but I need to stop the bleeding. My top is already soaked in that spot. The towel does nothing to ease the pain. I turn back to Mina, holding the towel in place, and notice the blood stains on her collar. Evidence that she was here. I point to the drugs.

"Get rid of— of this and get out of here."

"What?" she asks, finally standing up.

"I said trash this stuff and leave. Change your clothes and hide that jumper under my bed. I'll deal with it later. By the time the police get here, you need to be gone."

She doesn't say anything. She doesn't have to – she slowly nods and looks down, and then sighs loudly. She brushes past me and scoops up the drugs, then lifts the toilet seat and tosses them in the bowl. She flushes them down and waits to make sure they're gone.

Who knows how many times she's done this before!

Afterwards, she sprays soap into one of the cloths that Ivy leaves lying around the bathroom and cleans the seat. Very professional.

I walk to the living room and peer out of the window. What if this guy has an accomplice or a getaway driver? I don't remember seeing anything suspicious on my way in, but that doesn't mean much. I survey the street outside. I don't see any cars – or people – I don't recognise. I head back to the kitchen where the body (thankfully or otherwise) still lies, and carefully manoeuvre around it, so that I can get to the paper towels. I retrieve one, and rifle through the dead man's trouser pockets, looking for any clues as to who he is.

If my suspicion is right, he came here for Mina and/or those drugs, but he ran into bad luck instead. When he left his house this morning, did he know that this would be the last day of his life? I think about things like that. I wake up and think, 'Is this the day it all ends?' Did he think like that? Or did he just think he'd live to kill another day?

In one of his pockets, I find a wallet. He's got some cash – twenty pounds in 5-pound notes – and a couple of loyalty cards. One of the cards is for a chocolate shop, and the other is for a restaurant. I suppose criminals need to eat. Apparently, he's two purchases away from a free bag of truffles, and seven away from a free chicken meal. There's nothing else in the wallet. No identification of any kind, not even a bank card. I return the wallet to the pocket I found it in, fighting the urge to take the contents for myself. He won't be using them after all. Before I have a chance to investigate further, I hear Mina approaching.

She goes to the living room and calls to me. Moving as quickly as I can under the circumstances, I dart across the corridor to meet her, and lean against a beam.

"What now?" she asks, wringing her hands.

"Well, first of all, don't look so nervous. It's probably best if you go to the prayer meeting."

She moves her head from one side to the other, and her mouth hangs open. "You're kidding."

"Fine, go wherever you want. But the church would be a safe place and it's only a few minutes away. You can say you spent the evening with your friends, and then had the urge to pray. I'm sure they'll believe you."

She stays quiet, so I continue.

"Don't tell anyone you were here. I'm calling the police. You should go."

As I pick up the house phone, she leaves. I take a deep breath, trying to prepare mentally for what will no doubt be a gruelling rest-of-the-night. When I feel sufficiently ready, I dial the number.

The lady on the phone says officers will be with me 'as soon as possible' and that an ambulance is on its way. She asks me for details of the incident. I give her a quick summary of what happened, leaving Mina out of the story.

When the police arrive, I expect I'll have to recount my version of events. They'll ask questions and then ask them again to see if I'm lying. I remember how this works. I've been through it twice now. I didn't think I'd ever have to go through this again.

I hear a vibration. It sounds like that of a phone. I know it's not from my phone and I saw Mina leave with hers. I look over to the mad man's corpse and wonder if the sound came from his device. I end the call after the woman assures me that a unit is 'on its way.'

I walk to the kitchen. I want to search the body but I'm having difficulty moving without wincing. The pain I'm in grows with each passing moment.

I stand over him and get my phone out of my pocket. Ideally I'd rummage through his messages, perhaps even steal his SIM card and use the information to find out who he is… who he was… but I can't do that. I can barely stand. My

333

breathing is laboured. I snap a picture of him. I'm sure it'll come in handy at some point. I slither into the hallway, taking a seat a short distance away from the door.

To think that I was coming home to celebrate my promotion… it's true when they say that man proposes and God disposes.

I shouldn't be so despondent. After all, the circumstances could be far worse. I could be the one who got stabbed to death but I'm not. I'm a survivor. I'm *the* survivor.

I feel tired and light-headed. My vision is getting blurry. That's never a good sign.

I think I might pass out.

I'm probably in big trouble.

XXI

MINA

When I leave the building, I'm still reeling from what happened. I can hardly believe it. Tonight makes the second time that someone has tried to rob Donna (and me), and wound up dead. Why am I such a magnet for bad luck? I agreed to go to the prayer meeting, but now more than ever, all I want to do is curl up into a ball and snort some coke. I need something to make me feel better and I know church isn't it. I don't have any more drugs on me and though I know that I have to stay away from them, I want them so badly. I don't know how much longer I can resist.

I need to focus. I could go to Graham's place. Oh no, what if Natalie's there? What if he's doing harder drugs now? I can't take that risk. Donna's given me a way out tonight; I have to make it worth her while. I can't let it be for nothing. I should go to the church. It's the best, safest alibi I can currently think of. When I was there last Sunday, people were crying with abandon. I could use a bit of that.

As I start in the direction of the church, my phone rings. It's Graham. I shouldn't have given him my number. I pause on the pavement, trying to decide whether or not to answer. I picture him lounging around, calling because he cares about me and wants me to know that. The thought fills me with warmth, displacing some of my anxiety.

"Hello," I say. My voice sounds shaky.

"Hey, babe, are you ok?"

"What do you mean?"

There's no way he can know what just happened, is there?

"You left the bar so fast, I wasn't sure if I'd done something to upset you."

"No, I was tired, like I said," I say, stifling the tears that are trying their best to come through.

"Ok, I just wanted to be sure. If you need anything, or you ever need to talk, I'm here for you. You know that, right?"

I tell myself not to cry. Given what's happened tonight, I know that I need some comfort, and here he is, calling to offer it or something close enough.

"Yeah, thanks," I say, exhaling to stop myself from sobbing. "Are you alone, Graham?"

"Yeah, I am."

"Can I come over?"

"I'd love that."

"Cool. I'll see you soon."

"Can't wait," he says. I hang up the phone. If Donna... When Donna finds out, she'll be disappointed that I didn't stick to the plan. But I can't go through with it. I want to see Graham. I *need* to see him.

I turn in the opposite direction of the church and head for the station.

XXII

IVY

Christina and Micah, another member of the prayer team, prayed for and with me. Though I felt better afterwards, I couldn't concentrate for very long. My mind kept wandering back to the vision I had. Nothing like that has ever happened to me before. My side felt fine and there were no visible signs of harm, but the memory of the pain stayed with me. I left my seat again and went to the restroom to call Donna. Her phone was off. I called the home phone as well. No answer.

I told myself not to worry. She was probably in the bath. She liked taking baths sometimes. Yes, of course – it's her night off, as she says. There is nothing to worry about. Besides, I told myself, we'd prayed and that was the most important thing.

Despite all that, I could neither relax nor focus, so I did the only thing I could. Around 1 o' clock, I decided to go home and check on Donna.

Christina saw me leaving with my stuff and stopped me. "Is something wrong, Ivy?"

"I… I think I need to go home," I said.

She offered to drive me there, saying it wasn't wise for me to be out so late at night on my own. I aim never to turn down kindness. I took her up on her offer even though it would have been quicker to walk.

As her car pulls up to the building, I notice an ambulance driving away. My heart skips a beat. The heavy police presence and the arrival of a second ambulance do nothing to calm me down. Christina parks and tells me that she'll wait for me in the car.

I run to the building's entrance, where an officer stops me.

"What's your business here, ma'am?" she asks.

"I live here. What's going on?"

"What number?"

"Excuse me?"

"What number do you live in?"

I crane my neck, trying to look past her, though I don't know why – we live on the 3rd floor.

"3.12," I say.

She lifts her eyebrows and looks away from me. That seems like a bad sign. The night is freezing cold but that does not stop a drop of sweat from forming and sliding down my face.

"Is something wrong?" I ask.

"There was an incident in your flat."

The words make me feel limp.

"Donna… is she ok?"

"She's alive, Miss. She's been taken to the hospital."

I'm not sure if it's from fear or relief but I start shaking uncontrollably, sobbing loudly. The woman steadies me and calls for assistance. Christina must have seen the whole thing because she appears suddenly and holds onto me.

"What's going on, Ivy? Are you ok?"

I don't say anything; all I do is cry.

I'm not sure how much time goes by before the feeling passes. I remind myself that no matter what has happened, Donna is in the hospital and not the morgue. She's alive. When my tears dry up, Christina and I lean on the boot of a police car. The officer, Reynolds, explains that a man broke into the flat and that, in an apparent act of self-defence, Donna somehow overpowered and killed him. I listen, stunned by the details. I know it's the sort of thing Donna is capable of – she's done this before. Still, my blood runs cold and not because of the weather.

I can't believe that someone broke into our home. I know it happens all the time, but you never think things like that will happen to you. I've lived with an abuser, didn't worry too much about the ones from the outside. While Officer Reynolds talks to us, I see the intruder's body being wheeled into the nearby ambulance. A chill runs from the top of my head to the base of my spine.

I finally muster the courage to ask the question. "What did she do to him? I mean... how did he die?"

Officer Reynolds looks at the ambulance as the paramedic shuts the door.

"Stabbed him in the neck," she says.

"Oh my goodness," Christina says, crossing herself. "That's awful. Your poor sister."

"She'll be fine," Reynolds says. "The fighters always are."

She salutes us and walks away.

Sadly, this is too familiar. The night that Alan died, the police came to our house and told us what had happened. I'd already seen on TV that a burglar had been killed in Mr. Pryce's store, and I knew right away that Donna had done the killing. I just knew. I sat and watched the news, with all its ridiculous sensationalism, and hoped she hadn't been hurt.

As I watched the footage of the crime scene, I imagined what the burglar's corpse looked like. I pictured it being bloody and broken. For no real reason, I imagined that she'd beaten him half to death, before finally riddling his body with bullets. I'd always worried about what Donna might do under the wrong circumstances, and that day I knew that the worst I'd feared was not as frightening as reality. She was far more dangerous than I could have predicted.

When the police arrived, mum started crying before they told us anything. She thought Donna was dead. It was probably the first and only time I saw any indication that she cared about either of us. Yes, she took care of us – made sure we were well-fed and that we had clean clothes – but I never knew if she cared *for* us.

The police officers told us the burglar's identity and gave us the nasty details – break-in, attempted rape, attempted murder leading to murder in self-defence. Mum cried more. Dad didn't say much, told her to *calm down*, which was code for *control yourself so I don't have to*. I sat quietly, relieved that Donna had made it out alive, happy that she had saved Mina and herself, and both scared and proud of her for putting the assailant down. I couldn't understand why Alan would do something like that.

Dad's mood changed that night. He'd been somewhat belligerent earlier in the evening, but once the police broke the news to us, he seemed more subdued. I wasn't sure, but it seemed to me that he too was scared. We were taken to the hospital and he refused to go in and see Donna. He waited in the corridor while mum and I went to get her.

Mum hugged Donna when she saw her. It was a real hug, filled with a mixture of relief and apprehension. Donna sat limply, didn't make any attempt to lean into the embrace. Mum pulled away, wiping the tears from her eyes.

"I'm so glad you're ok," she said, touching Donna's face. Donna moved her head away, looked off into the distance. I think that hurt mum's feelings. I felt bad for her, though I understood Donna's position.

"Can we please go home?" Donna asked.

Mum nodded.

"First, I need to use the ladies' room, ok? I won't be long," she said.

She covered her mouth as she turned around, trying to restrain herself from crying. My eyes met hers and I could see the shame and hurt in them. I looked away, fixed my eyes on Donna's face.

After mum left the room, I walked over to Donna and hugged her. She hugged me back and we stayed like that for what felt like a long time.

"Thank God you're alright," I said to her, biting back tears.

"Yeah, thank God." Her tone was sober and her delivery, grave.

"What happened? What did you do to him?"

She blinked as her eyes got moist. "I did what I had to. It was him or us."

I stepped back, staring at her. She looked back at me and we locked eyes.

"How could you do something so brutal?"

I truly wanted to know how she could bring herself to end someone's life. She closed her eyes, sighing heavily.

"Maybe it's in my blood," she said. Her voice was low, as if she didn't want anyone to hear herself… as if it hurt her to think that.

She opened her eyes and there was not a trace of tears visible, almost like in an instant she went from feeling sad to feeling nothing. Her gaze was cold and steely.

"What's wrong, Donna? What are you thinking?"

"I'm grateful to be alive," she said. Her expression softened and she jumped off the bed.

"Me too," I said. "If anything had happened to you…"

I broke down, thinking about how differently – how terribly – the night could have ended. Had she died, I would have been alone in the world – no parents, no friends. No matter what happened in my life, I would have felt incomplete. She's the only person I'd known my whole life and the only one that I knew actually wanted me to be safe. I couldn't afford to lose her. I *can't* afford to lose her. Not now or ever. I don't know what I'd do without her.

I lean against Christina, grateful to have someone here with me. I wonder if mum is worried about me. I doubt that she would be. I've been in unpleasant situations that she's known about and done nothing to save me from. I reckon that tonight, her behaviour will be no different. She'll tell herself that wherever I am and whatever I'm doing, I'll be fine.

"Let me take you to the hospital," Christina offers.

I smile at her, weakly. "Thanks, but you don't have to. You've done enough for one night."

It's not her job to ferry me all over town, in the middle of the night for that matter. It's not her fault that any of this has happened. Why should she have to suffer for my misfortune?

"You should probably get back t—"

"I want to help you, Ivy. There's a prayer meeting every month. You can use my help now." She puts her hand on my shoulder and fixes her dark eyes on me. "Well, what say you?"

"Thank you."

XXIII

MINA

I get to Graham's swanky apartment complex within an hour of inviting myself over. It's a gorgeous place and he must be doing well for himself if he can afford to live here. A couple leaving the building are kind enough to hold the door open for me – a total stranger. Today, they're lucky it's me. I enter the lift and go to the 4th floor. My head is still hurting from the fall, and I can feel that a bump has formed. I have no intention of explaining this to Graham.

Once on his floor, I find his flat and knock on the door. He opens it within seconds, as though he had been waiting for me for a while. He's still wearing the same clothes from earlier in the evening. He smiles at me. Oh, that smile. I want nothing more than for him to touch me. I kiss him without speaking, without warning. He does not withdraw.

He pulls me into the flat and closes the door behind me. We separate for a few seconds as he locks up. He turns to me and looks me up and down. He smiles again, this time more softly. I move closer to him and kiss him again, lightly putting my hands on his chest. He holds on to my waist and pulls me closer, until there's no distance between our bodies. His hands move slowly, deliberately, gently to the small of my back, and then lower. I've been so lonely for so long; I've missed being touched.

We stop kissing, and he rests his forehead against mine. I feel his warm, gin-scented breath on my face. He kisses my neck, then moves up to my ear.

He whispers, "Are you sure about this?"

He's always so thoughtful. Am I sure about this? After the horror I've witnessed, I need something to take my mind off the pain. I can't have drugs, but I can have Graham. Perhaps I'm using him. It's not malicious – I like him. I like him a lot. I always have. Besides, he gets to use me, too. This will be good for both of us. What could go wrong?

I kiss him on the mouth again, lightly. "I want you," I say, looking into his eyes. He smiles and steps back, taking his top off. I start unbuttoning my shirt, but he stops me. He takes my hand and leads me to the bedroom.

There, he kisses me and starts unbuttoning my shirt. I let him. He takes my shirt off and carefully unzips my trousers before pulling them down. I step out of them. He takes his trousers off, and then removes his boxers. He moves closer to me and puts both his hands on my face. We start kissing again as he lifts me off the ground and plops me down on his bed.

That's when the memories interrupt. Damn them, they always interrupt. Once again, I see Ellis hitting me. Over and over, it plays back. I wish it would stop! I think this might be the first sober sexual encounter I've ever had. I'm usually too high for the visions to upset me.

Graham starts touching my body, until his hand lingers just below my navel. He looks at me and smiles as one hand goes further down, until he's stroking my thighs – softly... back and forth... up and down. He keeps this up and returns to kissing me. It feels so good, until it suddenly doesn't. As he removes my underwear, I remember how Ellis tore it off. I remember begging him to stop. I hear him calling me a filthy whore. I try to push the memories away, but I can't. They're too strong. They're always stronger than I am.

Graham takes my bra off and touches me with the tenderness of the most considerate lover. His kisses get deeper as he strokes my tongue with his. He moves away, and lifts his hand to my face. He looks at me like he doesn't know I'm a screw-up, like he thinks the world of me… like he loves me. He kisses me again, and I feel his body move into position. I can no longer control myself. I start to cry, quietly at first, but as he hovers over me, the crying gets louder.

His body freezes and he immediately stops kissing me. I can't look at him, I just keep crying.

"Hey, babe, what is it? What's wrong?" he asks, his voice filled with panic.

I shake my head. "It's nothing. I'm ok."

That couldn't be further from the truth, and he can tell. He rolls to the side and sits up. I instinctively move into foetal position, backing him. I try not to sob so loudly, but I can't stop myself.

He touches my shoulder. "Mina, are you ok? Did I hurt you?"

"No, you didn't. I just— I…"

I can't finish the sentence. All I can do is cry. He gets off the bed and puts his boxers back on. To my surprise, he climbs back into the bed, facing me.

He lifts my face in his hand and says, "Whatever it is, it's ok. I'm here for you." He kisses my forehead and hugs me tightly, stroking the back of my neck. "Everything will be ok."

I wish that was true.

PART III

I

NOVEMBER 30ᵀᴴ, 2019

MINA

Following our failed attempt at copulation last night, Graham and I fell asleep. I didn't sleep very well, had nightmares as is the way with me. You'd think that I'd be used to them by now. Last night's events did not help matters. Both the drugs and the attacker featured in my dreams.

I wake up to find that Graham isn't in bed. My head feels better than it did last night, though it still hurts. I don't think I have a concussion. I should probably have gone to a hospital when I left Donna, but I am a fountain of bad decisions. I put my clothes on and walk out of the bedroom. I'm surprised to see that Graham is in the kitchen. He's been cooking – scrambled eggs, toast, sausages, the works. The kitchen smells like oil and herbs.

"Hey babe, you're up," he says when he sees me.

"Yeah… what is this?"

He smiles widely. "I made breakfast. You like eggs, don't you?"

I nod.

"The sausages are great; they're from this farmers' market I go to sometimes. Really amazing, you'll love them!" he says.

Only Graham could be this enthusiastic about something as simple as sausages.

He pulls up a stool at the breakfast table and gestures to it. "Come on."

I walk towards him and sit down. He places a plate in front of me and then brings the pan over. He spoons the food into the plate until it's nearly full, then does the same for himself. Sitting opposite me, he smiles. I want to smile back but all I can think of is what happened last night... or rather, what didn't happen last night.

"This is really lovely, Graham. Thank you."

"It's nothing. I don't generally have people over for breakfast, and it's my favourite meal, so this is great for me."

I'm not sure if he's trying to assure me that he's not seeing anyone. I'm not sure that matters.

"Listen," I say, clearing my throat, "I'm sorry about last night. I—"

"Babe, it's ok. You don't have to explain anything to me. It's fine," he says. He shrugs and takes a bite to eat.

"I feel like maybe I let you down."

"You don't owe me anything, Mina. And sometimes, these things happen... it is what it is."

I sit silently, wondering whether he's being polite, or if this is an attempt to butter me up so he can try again. Then I remember that I threw myself at him, not the other way around. Maybe he's glad nothing happened because he's not really interested anyway. Maybe he was bored and I was a potential distraction.

"I have to ask, though," he says, sitting back in the stool, "are you ok? I mean, is everything ok with you?"

I stare at my plate. These are the best-looking eggs I've seen all year. The sausages look plump and juicy and so fresh that the pig might very well have been killed this morning. I should be thrilled to be here with him. I want to say something but I don't know if there's anything to say.

I shake my head and say, "Yeah, everything's fine."

I start eating. The food is almost as delicious as Mama Selene's. And he is not wrong about the sausages. For a man, he really is a good cook.

"Are you sure? 'Cos you say you're alright, but you're shaking your head. And you... you just seemed really... *upset* last night," he says.

I gulp down the food that's in my mouth, following it with a sip of water. I don't think I can tell him about Donna. I'm sure I shouldn't. As for Alan, I don't know if I can bring myself to tell Graham about that, even though he really seems to care...

"It was a long day yesterday," I say, nodding, my vision getting cloudy.

His hand reaches over and grasps mine.

"I don't really want to talk about it right now," I say, clutching it, breathing loudly in the hope that the tears will evaporate before they fall.

"It's ok," he says, "Whenever you're ready, you know I'm here for you."

He squeezes my hand, lifts it to his mouth and kisses it. He smiles at me and lets my hand go, returning to his meal.

When we're done eating, he clears the table and refuses to let me wash up. With nothing else to do, I turn my phone on. Seconds after it loads, I get a flurry of notifications – missed calls and voice messages. All of them are from Ivy.

I know what I'll be doing once I leave here.

DONNA

I wake up in a room that I don't recognise. I'm alone, lying in a bed, the smell of which falls just short of fresh. My heart is pounding. My head hurts. I move to touch it, but a sharp pain in my side stops me. I touch my side instead. The skin feels raised. It all comes back to me – the home invasion, the attack, the kill. More blood on my hands, not that I needed any. If only I had a carnivorous alien plant to feed these dead people to.

I realise that I'm in a hospital bed. How I got here, I don't remember. I'm sure I can fill in the blanks. Thankfully I'm not chained to the bed, so I can assume that the police don't think I'm guilty of anything untoward – well, not yet at least. For once, that's the truth.

I sit up in the bed. My throat hurts, though nowhere near as much as my side. I touch it, feeling the swelling around my neck. It's subtle but it's there. I try to clear my throat. It feels sore and tender. I suppose things could be far worse.

I look around the room, taking in my stale surroundings. I don't know what hospital I'm in, but it hardly makes a difference. You've been to one, you've been to all. I've only just woken up but I already can't wait to get out of here. Across from the bed, there is a small table upon which rests a vase containing a bunch of colourful flowers. They're the only thing giving a hint of life to the room.

The door opens and Ivy walks in, looking down. Her shoulders are slumped, and she holds a cup of *something* in one hand. From this distance I can't determine the contents. She closes the door and sighs, turning slowly towards the bed.

"What're you drinking?"

My voice is hoarse and low, but she hears me. She jumps a little, then puts the cup on the table and runs to my side.

"Oh thank God, you're awake!" she says, leaning in for a hug.

"Not too hard, please."

"Sorry." She pulls up a chair and sits next to the bed. "How do you feel?"

I wince. "Honestly? Terrible."

She frowns.

"So, what's in the cup?" I say, hoping to lighten her mood.

"Oh," she says, looking across to the cup. "I want to say tea, but there's a good chance it's poison."

I try to laugh. I fail.

A sad smile crosses her face. And then it disappears. "What happened last night?"

Her face looks wan and there are dark circles under her bloodshot eyes. I haven't seen her looking this rough for many, many years. She must have been very worried about me.

"I got home and this man came out of nowhere and... tried to kill me."

She swallows hard. I can see her holding back tears.

"You fought him off," she says, quietly.

I nod.

"And you killed him." It's almost a whisper.

I look away from her, feeling like her eyes are burning a hole in me. I nod again.

"It was him or me," I say, eyes on the bed.

That's what I told her when she asked about Ellis. It was true then and it's true now. I look back at her, see her wiping her eyes. She nods repeatedly, looking off into the distance.

"You did what you had to do. He brought it on himself," she says, biting her lower lip. I hold her hand, and she covers it with her other hand.

"The flat is a crime scene now, so we're staying at a hotel tonight."

"We?"

"Mum, me, Mina," she says, "You too, if the doctor lets you leave."

Mina. I'd almost forgotten about her and her life-taking habit. Had I been anyone else, I'd be dead now because of her. I'm going to have to find a way to send her on her way. She's done enough damage for one lifetime.

"I see," I say.

"She introduced us to a friend of hers. He brought her here," Ivy says, still holding my hand.

"Oh, who?"

"Graham... *Somebody*," she says, shrugging. "He said you've met before."

I nod and recline in the bed. I touch my throat with my other hand. So sore.

"Yeah, a couple of times. They've known each other for a few years now. He's a dopehead, by the way," I say, glancing at her briefly.

She smiles. "Jesus loves dopeheads, too."

I roll my eyes.

Sure. Of course He does.

"So did she take him to the prayer meeting?" I ask.

She frowns and shakes her head slowly. "She wasn't at the prayer meeting."

My body stiffens, and I know she detects it from my hand. Her brow furrows slightly.

"Oh, I just assumed you asked her and... she said yes, that's all."

She smiles, though her brow remains furrowed. "Well, I did ask her, but she said no. It would have been good for them to be there. They need Jesus like everyone else does."

Uh huh. You would say that.

Her brow is smooth again. I think I've managed to avoid any more questions regarding my confusion over Mina's whereabouts overnight. Ivy sucks her cheeks in as her eyes move to the right. She looks like she's considering how to say what she wants to say next. I know what she wants to say and I want to shut down the conversation before it goes any further. I want to, but I'm weak and tired and my throat hurts. I look at her, knowing what's coming.

"So if you'd died last night what would have happened to you?" she asks.

There it is.

"I would be dead."

She shakes her head.

"It's ok. We all have to die at some point. I've left all my savings to you, just so you know. I trust you'll use them wisely," I say, smiling wryly.

"That's thoughtful, but you know that's not what I'm talking about."

"My throat hurts. I don't want to talk anymore," I say, removing my hand from hers. I turn onto my side that wasn't stabbed, backing her.

"You can't outrun death," she says.

Wow, she's still talking.

"Even if you have 100 years left to live, you're going to stand face-to-face with God and He will judge you impartially. He will give you justice. What are you going to do?" she asks. Her speech is calm and frantic at the same time. Despite the even tone, there's a sense of urgency in her voice, like she *knows* that my time is running out. Everyone's time is running out. I suppose in that respect, life is fair.

I turn back to face her. "I'll tell Him I did my best in a world He wouldn't fix."

"That's not good enough."

"Then I guess I'm screwed."

"You don't have to be."

"Seriously, Ivy – I go to church once a month, I give to charity and I don't cheat on my taxes."

"Your taxes are taken from you before you get your hands on the money. You *can't* cheat on them; you don't have that chance."

She's right. Given the opportunity, I'd probably cheat on my taxes. Tax is legalised robbery. It's no different from protection money; the key distinction being that in this case not everybody gets the protection they pay for.

I shrug. "What do you want from me, Ivy? What do—?"

"It's what I want *for* you. Not everyone is trying to take things from you."

I sit up again, massaging my brows with one hand.

"I want you to have peace in your life... and even if not in every way on earth, in eternity. Do you really want to go to hell? Do you really want to spend every moment after you die suffering for everything you've ever done wrong? Do you want to be tormented and in pain forever?"

With each word she speaks, I feel heat rise in my belly. I want to tell her to shut up, to take her religion and shove it, but I look in her eyes. The fear in her eyes is real. She's afraid for me. She thinks my soul is in jeopardy. She's desperate to help me. How many people can I say that about?

The door opens and a nurse comes in, smiling widely.

"Ah, you're awake," he says.

Less than 24 hours ago, a man broke into my house and tried to kill me, and someone thinks it's a good idea to assign a male nurse to me. This thoughtlessness tells me that a man is in charge.

I don't reply. I'm not in the mood for pointless chitchat. I never am, but I am especially not in the mood at this present time.

"I'm sorry, Joe, I should have called you," Ivy says.

Joe? She's on first-name basis with the nurse?

"That's no problem. How are you feeling?" he says, approaching the bed, looking at me.

"Traumatised," I say.

He stops moving, looks from me to Ivy.

"I think a female nurse would better understand what I'm going through... thank you."

His mouth starts to move, but Ivy speaks first. "I think what my sister means to say is that she's been through a harrowing experience. She'd be more comfortable having a woman close by at the moment."

"That is completely understandable," he says. "I'll see if anyone else is available."

"Thank you so much, Joe," she says.

He leaves the room and she turns to me, clearly frustrated.

"Was that necessary? Must you always be so rude?"

I roll my eyes and slink back onto the pillow. I turn my back to her again and look at the bare wall. They'd better not send a man who thinks he's a woman in here. That would add insult to injury.

I hear her go to the door, then stop. "Detective Miller brought these flowers over earlier. I think he's coming back to question you."

"Can't wait," I say.

"I'll see you later."

The door shuts. I turn to look at it.

"Later," I say into the empty room.

MINA

Graham was kind enough to drive me to the hospital. I sit in its chapel, thinking about last night. Thinking about how I almost died. Wondering why I'm always at the wrong place at the wrong time, why my safety is always under attack. I look at the effigy of Christ – the so-called God-man, promised Messiah, Saviour of the world – hanging on a cross with His arms stretched out and eyes lifted heavenwards, and I think about all the things the Bible says He suffered before He got to this point. Is it worse to suffer for being disliked, as He was, or for being unlucky, as I am?

I drop my eyes to the floor, while the image of the statue lingers in my mind. The good news is that Donna is alive and out of surgery, even if she's under heavy sedation. The bad news is that when she wakes up, she will most likely want nothing to do with me. I know it, I know *her*. This betrayal, she will not overlook. In other bad news, Ivy told me that the police want to question me, see if I recognise the attacker. I'm not looking forward to that.

On the bright side, I didn't die last night. No matter how bad things get, I always hope they'll improve. I can't hope for anything if I'm dead. I made it out, thanks to Donna. And thankfully, my head feels fine now.

The chapel door swings open, making an uneven, creaking noise. I turn around and see Ivy coming towards me. I smile at her as she sits next to me, shoulders slouched, eyes on the statue.

"You ok?" I ask.

She huffs, "Donna's awake."

My breath shortens. I'm not sure if I should see her. I'm not even sure if she wants to see me. Judging by Ivy's demeanour, neither surgery nor sedation has interfered with Donna's knack for being disagreeable.

"Is she ok?" I say.

Ivy turns to face me squarely. "I don't know. She's as she always is."

Is that good or bad?

"Did you tell Donna you'd be at church last night?" she says.

My eyes flutter as I lean away from her. "Uh, what do you mean?"

How could she know I was there last night? Did Donna tell her? Did she tell her about the drugs? Will Ivy call the police on me? She squints and moves her head to the side, examining my face which has no doubt gone bright red. My cheeks feel warm though I do my best to act normal.

"She seemed to think you and Graham would be at the meeting," she says, still scanning my face. It feels like she's inspecting my soul.

I blink rapidly and look away. "Oh, yeah. I don't know why she'd think that."

Ivy nods. I've blown it. It's what I do best.

"Probably crossed wires," she says.

She turns back to the effigy. I feel bad for lying to her, but I feel worse for lying to her in a chapel. I'm not religious but I feel like I've sinned terribly.

"Yeah, probably," I whisper.

We sit together, looking at the statue of Jesus. I wonder what she's thinking. If He really is God, I wonder what He thinks of me. I wonder if I should see Donna.

"I should get back to the hotel, shower and change and stuff. You coming?" she asks.

"Uh, no. I'll probably hang out here for a while. Check on Donna, maybe go and see Graham."

"Ok. I'll be back later with mum. I might see you then."

She smiles, though not as warmly as usual. She definitely suspects something.

"Sure thing," I say.

She stands up and puts her hand on my shoulder. She walks away from me, leaves the chapel. I watch her go, and then the statue gets my attention again. A sudden wave of what I can only describe as peace washes over me. It's almost like the statue is calling me, telling me that things will work out. I hope that's true.

I get up as well and leave the chapel. I step outside and see that Ivy is still here, but she's not alone. A man and a woman are talking to her. She turns towards me, pointing, and then back to them. The woman comes in my direction, as the man walks away. Ivy stands still, head low.

"Mina Kaur?" the woman says.

"Yes."

"I'm detective Lawson. I have a few questions for you."

And like that, I feel the peace slip away. It may as well never have been here.

IV

IVY

Sometimes I wish I was an orphaned only child. I'm certain that those who find themselves in such circumstances are burdened with their own unique set of problems— I mean, *challenges*, but on days like this it feels like it would be easier to have no one to look out for but myself.

Donna is awake and unrepentant. I shouldn't be surprised but I am. Silly me. Another brush with death at the hands of some maniac has done nothing to bring her to her senses, nothing to help her see things as they are. She's all too aware of the fragility of life, yet she doesn't seem to understand how precious her soul is. I'm tired of caring about her, but I can't do anything but care. On days like this I want to sleep and never wake up.

Ugh. I hold my head in my hands as I fold over in the waiting area. Even though she'd spent the whole night at church, mum rushed here once she got the voicemail I'd left. It was merely a courtesy – I didn't expect her to show up. I didn't blame her when she got tired of waiting for Donna to wake up. Doctor Liu said there was no telling when she would, so I took mum to a hotel near our flat. She was falling asleep when I left her.

Earlier, the police let me collect some things from the flat but I didn't get as much as I wanted. I'm hoping that they'll let us back in tomorrow, so we can go right home after church. I'm hoping, but Donna always tells me that I hope for too much. The best one can look forward to, she says, is not a soft place to land when you fall, but a quick death. That's my sister for you – the eternal optimist.

I'm bored of sitting here. I decide to go to the chapel instead. It's quieter and I'll be able to think better in there. I hope I will anyway. I arrive at the chapel and find Mina sitting on her own. I thought she'd left with Graham. I meant to tell her that it was nice meeting him. It seems pointless to do so now.

I walk over to her and sit by her side. She looks pensive, worried even. I want to ask what about, but… I'm not sure I want to know. With Mina there's always a chance that she's done something criminal. I'd hate to know more that I need to.

She asks if I'm ok. I tell her that Donna is awake. I'm sure she can deduce what that means. Still, she asks if Donna is ok, to which I reply – she is as she always is. Mina's eyes go low, like she can't work out if that's good. I recall Donna's assumption that Mina had gone to the prayer meeting and for some reason I can't pinpoint, it bothers me.

"Did you tell Donna you'd be at church last night?" I ask.

She looks at me and her pupils dilate as she blinks. She moves back a little, asks what I mean.

Why does she seem so cagey all of a sudden?

I look at her closely. "She seemed to think you and Graham would be at the meeting."

"Oh, yeah. I don't know why she'd think that."

Her cheeks are bright red. She's acting jumpy and evasive. Something very strange is going on.

Why would she lie?

"Probably crossed wires," I say, trying not to sound suspicious.

I turn to the statue of Jesus, the only person I can depend on for truth and beauty and purity. I slowly take a long, deep breath in. *Be still and know that I am God.* I exhale. I should leave since I can't think properly in here either. And then

362

I remember that I still have things to do.

"I should get back to the hotel, shower and change and stuff. You coming?" I ask.

"Uh, no. I'll probably just hang out here for a while. Check on Donna, maybe go and see Graham," she says.

I tell her I'll come back with mum and I stand up. I pat her shoulder and walk out of the pew, and then the chapel.

Out in the corridor, I turn to go to the lifts when I'm stopped by the sight of Detectives Lawson and Miller. When I met them last night, I gathered that they knew Donna from work.

Miller walks up to me. "Miss Palmer, we were hoping you could tell us where to find your houseguest. We're yet to question her."

"Oh, she's in the chapel," I say, turning around. As I point, Mina exits the chapel, coming into view.

"That's her right there," I say, turning back to them.

"Thank you," Detective Lawson says.

She strides over to Mina, leaving me with Miller.

"Is your sister awake?" he asks. His tone is difficult for me to assess, but to me, he sounds concerned. Perhaps more than is required.

I nod.

"Thank you," he says. He walks towards her room.

I sigh and roll my neck from one ear to the other. I need some rest.

V

DONNA

I dozed off. I'm not sure how long for, but I don't think it was very long. I wake up from a dream or rather a memory of last night's events. The whole thing replayed in my mind, from when I first noticed him until I stabbed him. I awaken so suddenly that a shooting pain travels from my side to the rest of me. I try to gently sit up, but the soreness makes me think that might not be worth doing.

"You feeling ok?"

The voice comes from a corner of the room. I sit upright, startled, ignoring my discomfort. Detective Miller is standing near the window, on his own.

"What are you doing here?" He shouldn't be here by himself. This is surely inappropriate at best.

"I wanted to see how you're doing."

I stare at him, wordless and perplexed.

"I brought you flowers earlier, but you were... asleep," he says, pointing at the bunch in the vase.

"Ivy mentioned that. They're nice, thank you."

364

He walks towards the bed, putting his hands in his pockets.

"Where's your partner?"

"She's outside, with your friend," he says.

"And they let you in here on your own?"

"Do you think I want to hurt you?"

"I think you have a partner for a reason – accountability."

"She'll be here in a minute, don't worry," he says, smiling.

I look from him to the door, hoping that he's telling the truth and Detective Lawson will walk in any second now.

The silence is uncomfortable.

I wish I had something to say.

"Are you two the only detectives in town?"

He laughs. "Sometimes it feels that way."

I lift the pillow and shuffle backwards, resting my back on it. "I suppose you want to know what happened at the flat."

"Let's start with the assailant – any idea who he was?"

"No, I was hoping you'd tell me," I say. "He's not known to you?"

He shakes his head. "His DNA matched that previously found at a number of crime scenes, but he's not in the system."

"So he's a career thief?"

"We're not so sure he's a thief…"

If he's not a thief, maybe he's some kind of enforcer. Maybe Miller is fishing for clues about Mina's links to drug dealers. I know she's made a mess this time (as usual), but if I can throw them off her scent, I will.

"Then why did he break into my place? And where else did you find his DNA?"

"I'm not at liberty to answer the second question, and I don't know the answer to the first."

"You're not very useful, are you?"

He smirks, almost as if he knew I'd say something that *direct*.

"So, tell me what happened."

I stop myself from rolling my eyes, choosing to blink instead. I press my body further into the pillow, so far that I might hurt myself. Over the phone, I told the sanitized version of the incident and now I have to repeat it. I know how this works but knowing only adds to the tedium of it all.

"I woke up, went to work—"

He smiles. "Last night, please, not the whole day."

"Of course," I say. I take a deep breath and recite my script. "I got home close to midnight, went to the kitchen to put my shopping away, and a man… appeared and jumped me."

"And then what happened?"

"I fought him. He was strong, but I managed to push him off me. I don't remember all the details, but…"

I touch my throat instinctively, staring at the bed covers. The seriousness of what happened, of the fate I narrowly escaped begins to weigh on me. My eyes fill with tears. I hate crying, especially in front of people. I bite my lower lip and close my eyes, sitting up a little.

"He cornered me in the kitchen. I tried to get a knife, but he stabbed me and then— he started choking me. I didn't know what to do. I pulled the knife out and I—"

I breathe out, wiping the tears from my cheeks.

"It's ok," he says. I open my eyes when I feel him reach over to me, tissue in hand.

"I don't know how long it was before I called the police. It's kind of a blur," I say, taking the tissue from him. I blow my nose as he stands watching.

"You'd never seen him before."

I shake my head.

"And he didn't say anything to you, nothing at all?"

"Nothing."

"Alright, thanks. You'll have to repeat this when Lawson gets here," he says.

I recline in the bed, looking at the ceiling. "I'm tired of thinking about this. I'm tired of having to talk about it."

"I understand that, and I'm sorry that this happened to you, but this is the way it goes. Think of it this way: you lived to tell," he says, shrugging.

That is one way of thinking about it. I wonder where Mina is and if she knows who sent the enforcer.

"One thing that's weird, though…"

I look at him, waiting for the rest of the sentence, but he looks towards the door.

"Do you really like them?"

I follow his gaze, unsure of what he means.

"The walls?" I ask, looking back at him.

He laughs and glances at me again, meeting my eyes.

"The flowers," he says.

"Oh. Yes, they're nice. I thought I already said that."

He sits next to the bed and crosses one leg over the other. He places his hand on top of his leg.

"The man didn't have a smart phone."

I blink slowly at him. "So…? You think he's a time-traveller?"

He laughs again. That makes me smile. I like his laugh, it's hearty and infectious. My heart flutters a bit when he looks at me again. That is terrible. Even if I had any concrete interest in him, I would not be able to embrace it because he's a policeman. If he's any good at his job, it wouldn't take him too long to figure out that I'm a murderer.

That being said, I have no proof that he's good at his job.

"That would definitely complicate things… but no; I thought it was unusual. All his texts were encoded."

I look right at him. "That is strange. I'm sure you'll work it out eventually."

He smiles warmly at me, then looks down almost as if he's contemplating saying something. The half-smile on his face tells me it won't be anything worth hearing. I interrupt his thoughts.

"Did he have a car or motorcycle or some vehicle?" I ask.

"We've not identified one at this stage."

I nod. Well they certainly have their work cut out for them.

He sighs like he's about to speak but I pre-empt him.

"How's Mr. Haywood doing? Or is that something else you don't know?"

"Still in a coma. I wouldn't hold my breath."

At last, some good news.

Detective Lawson finally enters the room. I had wondered if she was really in the building. She looks at Miller and her eyes turn serious.

"Miss Palmer, how are you feeling?" she says.

"I've been better."

"I'm sure you have."

"Are you here for my statement?"

"If you don't mind," she says, pulling up a chair and sitting next to Miller. He uncrosses his legs and sits up straight. She pulls a book and tape recorder out of her pocket.

"So, what can you tell me about last night?" she asks.

***

No sooner have the detectives left than Mina comes in to see me. That's fine – I've been expecting her.

She shuts the door gently, then stands with her back to it. I sit up in the bed. We look at each other, as if we were on opposite sides of a river. She looks down, and starts walking closer to the bed.

"I'm glad you're ok," she says.

"Are you sure about that?"

She pauses and swallows hard. "I know I've let you down—"

That's her favourite way to start an apology.

"—but I swear, someone gave those drugs to me," she says very quietly.

"So, you didn't waste your hard-earned money on them, or steal them?"

She shakes her head. "I swear to you, they were a gift!"

"How many times have you lied to me before?"

She clasps her hands in front of her body. "Too many."

"I think I can be forgiven for not believing you."

"I know my word means nothing to you, but I give you my word – I did not buy or steal the drugs."

"You didn't turn them down either."

Her gaze rises above my head, as she frowns.

I look away from her. "Who gave them to you?"

"Someone that works with Graham," she says.

I should have known he'd be involved in something like this. I look back at her. "Graham. Of course! How many times have I told you—?"

"He's bad news? You keep saying that, but you don't even know him. He's not that bad. He's kind and caring and understanding. And yes, he does drugs, but that doesn't make him an awful person."

I roll my eyes and shuffle forward. "Can you hear yourself? If he's such a good guy, why are his friends giving you drugs? Why does he have friends who do cocaine?"

"Why do *you* have friends who do cocaine?"

That is a good question.

Her eyes moisten. I want to believe her, but she's burned me too many times. I'm not a masochist, yet I keep letting her back into my life when I know that she'll only bring damage with her. I want to cut her loose, once and for all, but I can't stop thinking about what she was like before Alan assaulted her. She had hope. Her future was bright. It's not my job to get her back to that… but I feel like it is. I don't even know if that's possible.

"Sometimes, I ask myself the same thing," I whisper. My throat tightens with emotion and I collapse on the bed, staring at the ceiling. Tears run down the side of my face, and I do nothing to stop them.

She walks over to me and grabs my hand.

"I know I've let you down, Donna. I know I keep letting you down, but I don't want to… I'm just… a screw-up," she says through sobs.

I grasp her hand and we stay like that for a few minutes. All I hear is the sound of her marginally restrained sobbing. She sits down and rests her head on our hands. I keep staring at the ceiling.

After a little while, I pat her head with my other hand. She lifts her head up and lets my hand go. I wipe my face and look at her. She's holding a piece of tissue to her eyes.

"Is there any chance that the guy who gave you the drugs wanted them back? Did he steal them from someone?" I ask.

"I don't think *she* did."

"But you can't be sure."

She shakes her head. "She gave them to me for no real reason. It was almost like she thought she was doing me a favour. I don't think she'd send someone after me."

"Are you sure?" I press.

"No, I'm not. I don't know her."

I pause, wondering if Mina was somehow set up. And then I remember the photo I took. "You have to find my phone. There's a picture of the attacker on it. I guess you and Suzanne could use it to work out who he is and who sent him."

She exhales. "If you let me, I will do everything in my power to get to the bottom of this."

My eyes dart between her face and the sheets. "It might be best if you stayed with Suzanne… or Graham for the foreseeable future."

She nods and looks down. "I understand. What should I tell Ivy?"

"You'll think of something."

She's always been a talented liar.

She sighs, and then looks at me. "I promise I'll do everything I can to figure this out. I won't le—"

"Don't say it, please."

"I'm sorry."

She stands up and walks to the door.

"Did the police give you any trouble?" I ask.

She shakes her head. She opens the door and pauses, like she wants to say something. Instead, she walks out, closing the door behind her.

VI

MINA

Detective Lawson is none the wiser about my presence at the flat last night. She asked me if I'd noticed anything suspicious in the time I'd been staying there. Anything or anyone. I said no. She asked if I knew of anyone who would want to hurt any of the flat's residents. I said no. She asked me if I could think of anything that might help with the investigation. I said no. Finally, she asked where I spent the night. She specifically asked where I was at the time the attack occurred. I think I kept my poker face. I think she believed me when I told her I was with Graham. I hope they don't ask him about it.

After she and her partner left, I went to see Donna. I was surprised that she didn't immediately boot me out of the room and her life. I don't know how she could give me yet another chance. It's a miracle.

I found her phone and sent a copy of the picture to myself, before deleting the original. Suzanne was in the middle of streaming a workout when I called her.

"I thought we'd wrapped this one up," she said.

"This is something else."

I told her what had happened to Donna, omitted my presence from the story.

As expected, Suzanne thought the man's death was the best possible outcome, something about there being 'one less prisoner wasting taxpayers' money.' I'm sure one day when she's bored of being a detective, she'll make a great politician.

We arranged to meet at her office. I haven't asked yet, but I think I'll stay with her tonight. I could stay with Graham, but I don't know if that would be good for me. I don't want to run into Natalie or anyone else who shares their drugs… and I don't want a repeat of last night's non-performance.

I get to Suzanne's office and find her freshly showered, drinking a smoothie or shake or… *something*. It's some sort of odd-looking brown sludge.

"It's chocolate peanut butter, got lots of protein. It tastes better than it looks," she assures me.

"Here it is," I say, placing my phone on her desk.

She stares at the picture and nods, sipping the shake. "Wow, that's nasty."

"What next?" I ask.

She grabs the phone and, with a smile, plops down on her well-worn couch. "I know a few people who might recognise this guy. I'll get a copy of that, ask around."

She very loudly and consistently sips the dregs of her drink.

"That sounds good. Is there anything I can do?"

"You can tag along, make some new friends. That'll be tomorrow. I've got other plans for today."

"Ok then." I say. "Is it ok if I crash with you tonight?"

"Sure, anytime."

I smile. "Thank you. I can't exactly afford a hotel room at the moment."

She nods. "Don't worry; you'll get paid at the end of next week."

"Oh, that's not what I meant. But thank you – that would be great."

I stand up and stretch. "Well, I'd better go and get my stuff."

"See you when you get back."

She hands the phone back to me. I get my bag and sling it over my shoulder.

"That reminds me," I say, reaching into my pocket. "Here's the change from the cab money you gave me."

I clutch the money in my hand and move to drop it on the desk, but she waves it away. "Oh, there's no need for that. Keep it – consider it a bonus for a job well done."

I look at the money in my palm and then back at her. She smiles and I smile back. The thought of having done something productive moves me. Yet I'm scared to have cash on me. I always need to be extra vigilant when I have money.

"Thank you," I say before I turn away from her. I start walking to the door when she calls to me.

"Oh, Mina."

I pause and turn to her again.

"Cash in hand, or do you have a bank account?" she asks, getting off the couch. She pulls a piece of paper from her desk drawer. She grabs a pen from the desk and puts it on the paper.

I stand still, mulling it over. If I get used to having cash, there's a very good chance that I will spend it, and not wisely. On the other hand, my back account is basically a bottomless pit. Any money going in there will never come out again. I suddenly have difficulty breathing, thinking about how trapped I am by my very nature.

I stutter. "Uh, um, cash please."

"Cool, you'll get it on Friday."

She pushes the pen and paper away. I half-smile. I leave the office and stand outside. I lean against the door and exhale. I put my hand on my chest to steady my heart, taking deep breaths in and out. One cycle. Two cycles. Once I feel better, I start down the stairs.

The struggle continues.

***

The police have cordoned off the entrance to the flat with tape. There's no one here, so I duck under it and let myself in. It's more or less as I left it last night, except for the presence of the blood stains and the absence of the corpse. There are stains on the kitchen floor and some on the carpet in the corridor. I suppose the former are from the perpetrator and the latter from the victim… or should that be the other way around?

I go to Ivy's room to check that I haven't left anything in there. When I'm sure, I leave. During the week, Ivy cleaned some of my clothes and left them in the laundry room. I head there to get my things, finding them folded neatly on the side.

I pack my stuff up. I leave the room to make my exit and am shocked to see Ivy in the living room as I walk past. I jump and let out a shout. She jumps as well.

"Oh my goodness! I'm sorry. I'm sorry," I say.

She has her hand on her chest, clearly as startled as I am. "What are you doing here?"

"I—Donna sugges— I'm going to stay with Suzanne for a little while," I say, finally getting the words out.

She raises her eyebrows, walking closer to me. "Donna asked you to leave?"

"That's not really what happened."

"She runs this place even when she's not here," Ivy says, tilting her head so she's looking away from me.

"I can't afford to stay at a hotel, Ivy. I thought I'd be better off crashing with Suzanne."

"I understand."

"What are you doing here?"

"Just getting a few more things," she says.

I nod at her and notice that she's holding a piece of the broken lamp.

She smiles at me, starts talking again. "I should let you go. If you need me, you have my number."

"Thanks."

I smile at her and leave the flat. When I get out to the street, a man who can't seem to walk in a straight line stumbles past me, smelling of weed.

Oh no, not now.

I try to blow the stench out of my nostrils, but it's like it's been burned into my nose and my mind. And it triggers something, something unfortunate within me. All I can think of as I keep walking is how much I'd like to smoke something, anything.

I stop on a street corner and try to get the thought of drugs out of my head. They go for a split second, and then come back with the fierceness of a lion hunting its terrified prey.

I am prey. I can run but I cannot hide.

I put my hand in my pocket and fumble for my phone. I look at it, try to put it away, but can't. I dial a number I've known for years, a number I know off head, one I wish I could forget. It rings once as my hand shakes. Twice as my grip on the phone tightens.

I don't have to do this.

Third ring and no answer.

It's a sign. I can turn around; I've been so good lately.

"Hello?"

Damn it. It's too late

"Hey Jeff, it's Mina."

There's no turning back now.

VII

IVY

I went back to the hotel as planned, checked that mum was ok, and then showered and changed. Only after showering did I realise that I'd packed Donna's toothbrush and forgotten my own. Typical! I don't really want to buy a new one.

Ugh, fine.

I decide to go back to our place. With stale breathe, I tell mum I'll be back soon, and I leave the hotel.

When I arrive at the flat, it's got some crime scene tapes around the door. I never thought I'd see those again. They put one such tape outside the entrance to the newsagent's. Even after they finally took it down, the shop never looked quite the same to me. I'd go past it on foot or in a car and it was always a crime scene in my mind. It was always the place where my sister took a life. That's probably going to happen here as well.

I walk into the living room and stand there. I look at what's left of mum's favourite lamp, its pieces all scattered on the floor. I squat and pick one up, thinking about how delicate everything about this life is. Had God not had mercy, I would have come home to find my sister's dead body here in addition to the shattered lamp. I feel a wave of emotion steadily coming over me. I have to avoid it, or it will drown me. I have to make it through the rest of the day. I hold my breath for a moment, then inhale deeply and exhale. I can't afford to fall apart now.

I stand up and, from the corner of my eye, see Mina walking through the corridor. She jumps and yells. Even though I know it's her, I also jump. I wasn't expecting anyone to be here. She apologises, I assume for scaring me.

"What are you doing here?"

She hesitates, starts saying something, stops. Eventually she says that she'll be staying with Suzanne for 'a little while.' I see Donna's hand over this. I ask if she told her to leave.

"That's not really what happened," she says.

I'll bet that's exactly what happened. I should never have left them alone together. She acts like she always has to be in control of everything.

Mina tells me that she can't afford to stay at a hotel and that Suzanne's place is a better option. If I could afford to pay for her stay, I would at least offer. She leaves and I stand there with the shard still in my hand. I shake myself out of the funk, drop the shard. I go to the bathroom and fetch my toothbrush. I look out of the bathroom window and see Mina paused on the street, bag slung around her shoulder. I'm about to wave at her, but I realise that she's on the phone. Her foot taps furiously as she stands there.

For some reason, I feel the urge to run out of the house and talk to her. I put my toothbrush in my bag and leave the bathroom. I slam the flat door behind me and run outside. Out in the cold, I see her put her phone in her pocket and walk away quickly, rubbing her hands together. She disappears around a corner. I chase after her. Once past the bend, I see her back. I follow her, making no effort to close the gap between us. I don't know what I'm doing but that doesn't stop me from doing it.

We'll see where this leads.

VIII

MINA

Jeff is a man of many talents. I hear that he runs several thriving businesses, including a restaurant which he uses to launder money. His real passion, though, is selling drugs. He and Martin used to work together – he was the brains and Martin was the foot soldier. I imagine he was quite upset when Martin got killed.

I arrive at one of his nightclubs, hoping to get my hands on some cocaine. Not a lot, just enough to numb the pain of being alive. He promised me a discount 'for old time's sake' but I'm sure he'll change his mind once he sees me. That doesn't stop me from going.

Night is yet to fall but the club is in full swing. I suppose this is a private event. A bouncer with a neck thicker than a brick leads me to the VIP area. The music is loud and pounding and it feels like the ground beneath me shakes with every step I take. The punters move and grind on one another, oblivious to anything but the music. In the VIP area, Jeff is dressed to the nines wearing a navy-blue suit, which makes a change from his previous hoodie-and-tracks combination. A Rolex watch hangs off his deathly pale wrist.

He presses a fist into his palm when he sees me. "Hey, there's my girl. It's been a long time."

"You look… different from the last time I saw you," I say, trying not to sound too surprised.

"That was ages ago. Things are different now. I'm a successful businessman."

Instead of nodding, my head moves about like I have a nervous tick. "Sorry to hear about Martin, I know he was a friend."

"We all have to go some time, right?"

How pragmatic.

"So," he reaches into his pocket and pulls out a sealed plastic bag – the kind Natalie's drugs were in – and dangles it in front of me.

My heart skips a beat or more. I know I'm a fool and this will destroy me, yet I start to think about how quickly I can find somewhere quiet enough for me to inhale the drugs. My heart wants this, and they always tell you to follow your heart. I get some of the change I offered Suzanne earlier, and hand it over. He notices my hand shaking as he takes the cash. With one brow raised, he smirks.

He puts the money in his breast pocket. "I don't think that's enough, sweetheart."

"It's what we agreed on. Maybe you should count it."

He shakes his head slowly, folding his palm over the little bag. My heart sinks. That's most of the money I had. I can't give him any more. I should take this as a sign, a sign that I should leave this life behind. I should.

"Come on, Jeff, don't be mean. We agreed," I say, trembling. My head feels light when I see him put the bag back into his pocket.

"I'm sorry, the price has gone up."

"That's all the money I have," I say. My throat gets tighter and I suddenly feel very thirsty.

He sits down, leaning back and spreading his legs. "Oh, honey, if you're out of cash, we can work something out."

No. No, this is bad. I can't go down this road, not again.

"Like what?"

I feel as though I've lost control of my faculties and a foreign being has hijacked my body. That being is speaking for me, saying all the wrong things.

Jeff smiles at me, looking me up and down. "I can think of a few things…"

The words hang in the space between us, filling it with heaviness. Dread seizes me as I wonder what words will come out of my mouth next.

"What do you have in mind?"

Suddenly, my phone rings and I jump, letting out a yelp.

"You ok?" he asks.

"Yeah. Excuse me." I look at the phone and see that Ivy is calling.

What does she want? Is Donna ok? Has she taken a turn for the worse?

A different kind of fear grips me and shakes me back to reality. "I have to take this."

I show myself out, through the building's entrance and walk to the street to answer the phone.

"Hey, Ivy, what's up?" I ask, trying to sound as cool as I can under the circumstances. Even then, my voice is shaky.

"Where are you?" she asks.

"Uh, what do you mean?"

"Where are you?"

'I'm trying to buy drugs' is never the right answer to any question.

"I'm with Suzanne. Why? Is something wrong? Is Donna ok?"

"Look across the street."

Her reply confuses me, but I do what she says all the same. Initially, I see nothing noteworthy, but then something catches my eye. There's movement coming from behind a couple of people walking past. It's Ivy, waving at me.

I am so busted.

I hang up and stay where I am. She starts crossing the street, coming towards me. I want to run away from her, but I don't have the power to move. So here I stand. Motionless. Exposed. Ashamed. Weak. Excuses run through my head as to why I'm here, but I know she won't believe any of them. She approaches me, and I straighten myself up, preparing for the inevitable dressing down.

She's in front of me now.

She frowns. "This isn't Suzanne's place."

I could split hairs, point out that I said I was 'with' Suzanne not 'at her place,' but she's nowhere in sight so there's no reason to try.

I shrug and look at my feet. She touches my arm gently.

"What are you doing here? How did you know I was here?" I ask. My voice is wobbly.

"I followed you."

I look up again, wondering why she would do that.

"I'm sure I can guess why you're here," she says, looking from me to the heavily-tattooed man standing at the door. I'd tried earlier to make out his facial features. Alas, the ink obscures them.

She wrinkles her nose as she surveys the area. I can't help myself. I start sobbing right there in the street. Ivy puts her arms around me and pats my back.

"It's ok. It's ok." She sounds like she's singing a lullaby to a restless child.

Is it ok? Will it ever be? Is this the rest of my life? Is this all I have to give to the world?

There's no way things will be ok. No way.

She pulls away from me and smiles at me. "Everything will be fine."

She puts her arm through mine and pats my hand. "Come on, Mina, let's go."

I let her lead me across the street like a blind dog leads its owner.

"Coffee?" she asks.

I nod.

She smiles. "Great."

We walk down the pavement for a little while, until we finally turn a corner.

***

"May I have them, please?" Ivy opens her palm and gestures with it.

I look at the cup of coffee in front of me, tired from crying. "Have what?"

"Whatever it is you bought."

"I didn't buy anything," I say.

She sighs and clasps her hands together on the table. She lifts them to her face, resting her chin on them.

"Please, Mina, I want to help you but I can't do that if you won't let me," she says, unravelling her hands and massaging her temples.

"I—I didn't buy anything. You interrupted the transaction."

She drops her hands to her side, nodding slowly. "Is that true?"

"Yes, it is. If Jeff was an honest man, it wouldn't be. I'd be sitting here with a stash of cocaine in my bag, but… he took my money and gave me nothing."

"It's kind of like a metaphor for the addiction, no? It takes important things from you and from it, you get nothing. Nothing but shame and regret, right?"

Her voice is soft and soothing. My face crumples up. I imagine I look like a badly-drawn cartoon. I sob, grabbing the coffee cup so tightly that the colour drains from my knuckles. Ivy wraps her hands around mine.

"Why do you do this, Mina? Why do you keep hurting yourself?"

I remove one hand; use it to rub my eyes. She takes her hands away, and rummages through her bag until she finds some tissue. She passes it to me. I dab my eyes, undone by everything. Were she here right now, I can't be sure that Donna would be this caring or understanding. But Ivy isn't Donna.

"I—I used to have nightmares when I was younger. I couldn't sleep very well."

"I remember that," she says, nodding. "You had to get prescription sleeping pills."

"Yeah, well, they didn't work for very long. After she died, I caught Beth Meyer's boyfriend, Michael— you remember him?"

"Um… I think so. He dropped out, became a DJ? That one?"

"Yeah, that one. He was smoking weed on school grounds, and he offered it to me, said it would help me sleep. He said it helped him deal with the pain of her death. It sort of worked at first, but then… it stopped. I needed something else, something stronger. He introduced me to some guys. Well…"

She sits back, tapping her fingers on the table. "I guess you couldn't sleep because of Alan Ellis?" She frowns as her eyes dance across my face.

I nod.

"Mina, I know that he threatened you and you saw him get shot, but you survived. You got out unscathed. He didn't get to hurt you."

"He raped me!" I blurt the words out without thinking about them or what telling Ivy might mean in the long run.

Her eyes widen and she leans forward. "What do you— what? Donna stopped him before…"

She sits back again, shuffles in the seat a little, looking at her untouched coffee, brow furrowed. She looks up at me. "What are you talking about?"

My lips tremble. "Before he attacked us, he raped me. At Beth's party, long before he tried to rob the shop."

The words echo in my head as tears instantly spring to Ivy's eyes. She would never have guessed, from the look of things. "Oh my— I didn't know. I didn't know."

She grabs both of my hands in hers. She shakes her head. The tears drop down her cheeks in crooked lines while her eyes close.

"I never told anyone. Only Donna."

Her eyes fly open and she sniffs loudly. "Donna? When— when did you tell her?"

"Right after it happened. She wanted me to go to the police, but I couldn't do it. I did drugs instead because I'm a coward."

I finally break down crying. Ivy leaves her side of the table and comes over to me, wrapping her arms around me. I want to tell her about his other victims, about the information that Suzanne led me to, but I'm too busy crying to say anything else.

"It's ok, Mina. It wasn't your fault. You don't have to keep punishing yourself. It wasn't your fault."

I really want to believe that. But I don't know if I can. I don't know if it's true. I went to that party because I wanted to be liked and accepted. I brought it on myself. I should never have gone there. I cry into her jumper. It smells of chamomile. I feel bad leaving my snot all over her clean, lovely-smelling clothes. She cradles my head and doesn't let go.

"I understand that you're in a lot of pain, Mina, but drugs won't make you feel any better. They won't set you free from the hurt or the memories."

I know that. I've been addicted for almost ten years and no good has come of it. Now that I think about it, it's a miracle I'm still alive. Before this period of abstinence, the longest I'd gone without using was 3 months. Even then, I thought about them every single day. I thought about them until I decided that I couldn't live without them, and then I relapsed. I was using whilst in jail. I'm a prisoner and I can't escape.

I want to be free but I don't know how. I've been on drugs for so long that my body is too used to them. My mind is used to them. I'm used to screwing up – it's who I am now. I don't know if I could function or live without drugs. They're the one constant thing in my life; my whole identity is wrapped up in the word 'addict.' Without cocaine, what am I?

"I know that but I can't stop using them. I've tried so many times but it doesn't matter. I need them," I say, sobbing.

"No, you don't, Mina. You need freedom from what Alan did to you and the evil and shame and misery that he inflicted on you. No drug can give you that. Counselling can't give you that, neither can discipline or self-help. Those things can help you, but they can't set you free. You need the freedom that only Christ can give."

At this point, I've tried everything else. Nothing has worked. What's one more failed attempt at healing?

"You think so?" I ask, lifting my head and looking at her.

"I know so. I've been where you are – trapped. Maybe not in the same prison, but in a prison all the same. You try your best to forget all the bad things that have happened, all the things that people did to you. The things you did nothing to deserve… but you can't forget them. They're carved into your mind, into your body, into your soul. They shape parts of your existence, colouring how you see everything, skewing your interpretation of things. And there's nothing you can do to erase them, there's no balm for those wounds. You didn't make yourself so you can't fix yourself, but Christ can. He has so much more power than we can ever fully understand, and He will never abuse it. He has so much more love for us than we can ever fully experience, and He will never withhold it. His blood will wash away all the shame and horror of every evil thing that people have done to you and that you've done to other people, and yourself. The guilt of all the sins you've committed against God and yourself and anyone else, it can all go in an instant if you let Christ in. He loves you so much more than you could ever love yourself—"

"That's really not hard," I say, laughing a little.

She smiles even as the tears slide down her face. "I can't save you from… anything, really, but I know that Jesus can. Open your heart and let Him love you."

"You make it sound so easy… How can He love me when I'm so damaged? How can anyone?" I start crying again, cupping my face in my hands. The smell of coffee on my breath threatens to give me insomnia.

"He loves you because He made you to reflect Himself. Your worth isn't based on anything that's happened to you or how you've lived. You're valuable because you're alive. You were valuable from the second you were conceived. Don't ever let anyone tell you otherwise."

As I listen to her, I feel my heart melt. The agitation, that gripping desire for The High steadily fades as every word she speaks soothes me. The things she's saying feel like aloe on my sunburnt soul. The tears start to dry up as a new sensation rises inside me. I'm not entirely sure what is it, but it feels remarkably like hope.

I look at her. "So what do I have to do? How can I— how does this work?"

"I can pray with you if you'd like."

I nod. "Yeah, that would be great."

She puts an arm around me and holds my hand with her free one. She smiles at me as if she cares about me, about what happens to me… as if she thinks I matter.

She closes her eyes and I do the same.

IX

DECEMBER 5ᵀᴴ, 2019

DONNA

Today is my first day back at work since leaving the hospital. I had to drive. I couldn't bring myself to use public transportation in my current state. The thought of being around so many people while I'm still recovering made me feel ill.

I'm working late again. I suppose I should get comfortable with that, especially since I'm on the brink of taking charge of the team. Despite my recent brush with death, I feel that it would be unwise for me to stay away from the office for long. It would make me look weak. I have to stay in control, to show them that I'm strong and capable, to go above the call of duty. I don't want anyone questioning my promotion when it finally comes to pass. So here I am, working instead of recuperating.

Old Bill is yet to send me the official paperwork regarding my new position. I'm sure he will in due time. To be fair, it hasn't been long since I got promoted and I have been away for three days. It might have seemed inappropriate, given the reason for my absence. I'm not worried about the delay – he's not foolish enough to rescind on our deal. I have enough material to keep him in line, though

I don't particularly want to waste time reminding him of that.

The stab wound is healing quite well. Apparently, it helps that I'm young and healthy. What helps more is that no muscles, tendons or blood vessels were severed during the attack. Doctor Liu said I was lucky. I feel like it has less to do with luck and more to do with the man's desire to question me. Had he wanted to kill me right away, I imagine he could have done it with one blow.

On Monday, the police finally released the flat to us. It doesn't feel like home anymore. It's been tainted, marred. What I once thought of as a relatively safe corner of the world has been infected with violence from without. I want to move, though I've not vocalised that desire. It's not that I'm afraid, I just feel like something sacred has been lost.

I don't want to have to live in another house where I was victimised, or where someone died. Or should I say *where I killed someone*? It doesn't help that I haven't slept properly since I got back there. I don't know if that is because of the attack or simply a continuation of my on/off relationship with insomnia.

Mina and Suzanne told me that they hit a wall when investigating the would-be killer, but they're trying to find a way around it. None of Suzanne's shady acquaintances recognised the man from the picture of his corpse. Perhaps they're lying for fear that they'll end up like him. As far as I know, the police haven't yet found a concrete motive for the break-in, nor have they established a link between Mina and the dead man.

She swears the drugs were a gift but lying is second nature to someone like her. She was very convincing, but I've been down this road before. It always leads to the same place – disappointment. Being her friend is more trouble than it's worth. I'm not expecting much from her, but she can at least make herself useful by helping Suzanne find out who the man was.

Before they discharged me on Tuesday, Kat paid me a visit in the hospital. She was kind enough to deliver a bouquet of flowers from 'everyone at work.' Zach had stopped by a day earlier. I thought he would cry, the way he looked at me. I fear that his crush on me will not wane anytime soon. He seemed shocked that I had it in me to kill someone. I thought that was adorable. He's called every day since to check on me. I haven't spoken to him today, though I wanted to. I couldn't find a solid reason to call him. Haywood is still comatose and since we no longer represent him, I can't use his case as an excuse. I'd like to talk to Zach, really sit down with him and—I don't know… convince him that we're not right for each other.

My navel-gazing is cut short by my phone's gentle ring. A useful thing, I suppose. I don't recognise the number. That's never a good sign. I ignore the call and get back to work. The phone stops ringing. And then it starts again within a few seconds.

"New boyfriend?" Kat asks.

"Watch this space."

I leave my desk and go to the kitchen, answering the phone when I get there.

"Hello?"

"I thought you'd never pick up," a male voice says. I'm confused for a moment, and then I realise that it's Daryl. He left work hours ago.

What does he want?

"Daryl? When did you change your number?"

"I'll explain later. I need to see you."

"What for?"

"I can't tell you over the phone. It's important, about work." He speaks with urgency in his voice. It sounds like he's looking over his shoulder.

"Is everything ok, Daryl?" I ask. Kat walks past the kitchen and steps out of the office.

"Can you meet me tonight or not? I don't want to say too much, but it's about the partners. I think it's something you should know."

The mere mention of 'the partners' stokes my interest, even though I have nary a clue what Daryl might want to tell me. I try to control it but my curiosity has got the better of me. "Where do we meet?"

"I'll text you the address. Come alone. I can't risk anyone else knowing about this."

He ends the call and I'm left standing in the kitchen wondering what could have turned Daryl against Bill. I'm assuming we'll be talking about Bill, not Rebecca. But who knows what he knows and wants to share?!

I go back to my desk and start to clear up when Kat comes back in.

"You off?" she asks.

"Yeah, I'm wiped."

"Of course you are. If I'd been through what you've been through, trust me, I wouldn't be here," she says, half-smiling.

I smile at her.

"Thanks for being so understanding," I say. "Are you leaving anytime soon?"

She sighs and folds her arms. "Daryl and I were supposed to meet later tonight…"

I look at her, slowly opening my mouth in surprise.

"I know, I know. I'm an idiot. But you don't have to worry. He cancelled, said something important came up with the family," she says, shrugging.

"You're not at his beck and call, Kat. You can do so much better for yourself."

She smiles. "You always say that."

"It's always true."

I pick my bag up. It brushes against my bandaged wound and I wince.

"Still sore?"

"Yeah… but it could be worse."

She nods and I start walking past her to leave the office. When I get close enough, she puts her hand on my shoulder. "Be safe."

I nod at her and she lets me go. As I leave the office, the text from Daryl's new number comes through. I read it while waiting for the lift. He wants to meet a few miles away at an address I don't recognise. Who knows what privileged information awaits me!

***

As the car approaches the location, I realise that the only parking spaces are in a side road behind the building. I drive round that way and find Daryl leaning against a garage door. He's smoking, puffing furiously. I didn't even know he smoked. I slow the car down and he comes towards me.

"Thanks for meeting me."

Even from this distance, the nauseating smell of nicotine hits me hard.

I move my head away. "No worries. Let me just park—"

"In here," he says. He walks away from me and pulls up the garage door. I watch as he drops the cigarette and stubs it out. A chill comes over me, but... I drive in anyway.

The garage is less of a garage and more of a wide-open space. It's almost like I've driven into a hangar. I park the car not too far from the door, and step out. He comes into the garage and pulls the shutters down.

"So what is this?" I ask.

"In its glory days, this was a nightclub. Those days are long gone," he says. He fidgets a little as he walks past me and goes further into the space.

"Useful though that information is, that's not what I was asking. I meant, what is *this*?" I say, gesturing at him and then myself. "Why am I here?"

He stops walking. He doesn't say anything, doesn't turn around. He just stands there. The back of his head leaves me uninspired.

"Daryl."

No response.

This is pointless.

I should have ignored his call and gone straight home. I'd rather be there, or even with Zach. Curse my curiosity!

"What was so important that you dragged me out here?" I ask, still hoping this trip amounts to more than a waste of fuel.

"Did you tell anyone at the office that you were meeting me?" he asks.

"No, you asked me not to."

"Did you tell anyone at all?"

The first question was reasonable. The second one makes me feel uneasy.

"No... but what if I did?"

He turns around and looks at my face. His expression is blank. His skin suddenly looks ashen. He looks away, shaking his head. "I don't know if I can do this."

The quiet way he speaks alarms me. The dream about the dog-wolf speeds to the forefront of my mind. I step back without thinking. It dawns on me that I'm alone with him in a place I'm unfamiliar with and worse yet, no one knows that I'm here.

I know better than to meet up with men, alone in strange places. How could I make such a careless decision? Did I lose some brain cells during my hospital stay?

"You know what," I say, turning back to the car, "let me know when you—"

I'm cut short by an unsettling clicking sound. I know what it is, although I hope I'm wrong.

"Turn around."

I hold my breath and do as I'm told. When I'm facing him, I see that he's pointing a gun at me. This has to be a joke.

"Daryl, what are you—"

"Don't talk. Stop talking."

His hand is a little shaky. He's scared. At least I think he is. I hope he is.

"Daryl, what are you doing? What is going on?"

"Did you really think Bill was going to give in to blackmail? Did you?"

I stare at him, searching his face, his body language for any sign that he's trying to scare me, that he's not intent on hurting me.

"I— I don't understand."

"He told me everything. Your interference with our case, how you drove Haywood to the brink—"

"Daryl, I don—"

"Shut up!!" he yells. My heart leaps and I shudder. I can't believe this is really happening. He lured me here and I let him. How did I let this happen? I swallow hard.

"Bill told me that you tried to blackmail him into giving you *my* job."

I say nothing. There's no point, he'll only yell at me again.

"You told him that I cheated on Veronica… he wasn't happy about that. I'm only alive because he gave me a choice – leave her or kill you. I'm not leaving my wife for anything," he says.

The words sink in slowly. My hands feel numb as I try to reason with him.

"Daryl, this is insane. You're not a killer."

"If the guy he'd sent had done his job right, I wouldn't be here. I'd probably be dead. Every cloud, I guess," he says, almost like he's thinking out loud.

"*What?*"

"How did you pull that off? Bill was sure his man was solid – messy but efficient, he said."

And like that, everything falls into place. All this time I blamed Mina for the attack, and it was my fault. Old Bill tried to have me killed. Wow… I can't believe I didn't work that out myself. All the head punches I've endured in my life are starting to take effect. Early onset dementia cannot be far behind.

I look at Daryl in disbelief. My mind is racing. He looks like he hasn't done this before – killed someone, that is – which means that I might be able to talk him out of it.

"Daryl, whatever choice Bill gave you, however he threatened you, it doesn't matter. You don't have to do what he says. You don't have to let him control you," I say. I'm surprised that he let me speak for that long. He looks at me, the gun still in his shaky hand, as I walk slowly, carefully towards him.

"That's enough," he says. He tightens his grip on the gun. "Don't come any closer."

I stop.

"Maybe I don't have to kill you, but I do need your leverage."

"My leverage?"

"The dirt you have on Sanders. Whatever it is, it must be special… and I want it."

I look at his hands and then his face. My breathing becomes laboured. If I give him any information about the recordings, I'll have nothing to bargain with. He'll have no reason not to kill me.

Then a thought crosses my mind: I'm reaping what I sowed. I lured Alan to his death and now the same thing is happening to me. This is what I deserve, what I've earned. Ivy always says that you get out of life what you put into it. I've put in a whole lot of death and that's why Daryl is going to kill me in cold blood.

Will they ever find my body?

No, wait. I can't think like that. If I give up in my mind, it's over for certain. Maybe I've done bad things – very bad things – and maybe I deserve to die, but I can't let him take my life. I especially can't let *him* take my life. He's not smart or clever or interesting in any way, and I don't respect him. It would be embarrassing to be murdered by Daryl. Above all else, he has no right. No one does. I have to get out of this by any and all means.

"Sanders is lying to you. He's trying to pit us against each other. He offered me the promotion!" I say.

"No, *you're* lying to me!"

"I'm telling you, he said he'd had enough of you and he was going to fire you and give me your job. I asked him not to – I knew how it would look!"

My voice remains steady, albeit a little high-pitched. He squints and blinks slowly, looking rather stern.

"Please, Daryl, you have to believe me. Do you really think I'd have the brass to blackmail one of the senior partners? Do you? And if I did, would it make sense for him to tell you? That's just crazy!"

His eyes zip from left to right, like his brain is trying to filter the lies from the truth.

"He told me that he sent an assassin to your house. Why would he do that? That's beyond incriminating."

"Did he tell you that before or after I got attacked?" I ask.

I hope it was after. Please God, let it be after.

"After," he says.

Oh, thank God!

"You see, he's playing you. He probably lied about the burglar, so you'd be terrified of him. He's trying to get you out of Veronica's life and I'm the sacrificial lamb!"

He's still holding the gun.

Seriously, isn't he tired?

"What's this got to do with Veronica?" he asks. His voice wobbles a little, as does his hand.

"He told me that you cheated on her, and that you are useless and unworthy of Veronica's love. He said you were never worthy of her and that she can do so much better. He even said that the day she told him she was pregnant with Carla was the worst day of his life. He hates you, Daryl, despises you. He thinks that if you stay with Veronica, you'll inherit everything he worked for, one way or another."

I impress myself by coming up with such believable lies under such great pressure and in such a short space of time. This yarn is golden.

Finally, he lowers the gun, his gaze on the floor. I take a small step forward. And then another one.

"The worst day of his life... he really said that?" Daryl asks.

"He said it was the saddest day, to be precise."

He laughs and strokes his chin.

"Yeah, he would say that, that old bastard," he says. "His precious little girl can do better."

That's the truth but now is not the time to point that out.

"If you kill me, Daryl, he will turn you in and you'll go to prison. You'll never see your wife or children again," I say, walking closer to him.

His expression hardens and he looks at me as I close in on him. I'm only an arm's length away when he raises the gun again. I should have tackled him the moment he let his guard down.

Why did I hesitate?

"Don't move," he says, pointing the weapon at me with a renewed sense of purpose.

I stand still.

"On your knees."

Right... I guess this is it.

I kneel. "Daryl, please... don't do this. Don't let Bill use you. Don't let him win."

"Children… you said *children*. I have only one child," he says.

I look at him and shrug.

"How did you know Veronica is expecting?"

I don't answer him. My gaze drops to his feet.

"Let me guess, Kat told you. I guess she also told you about our relationship, and you told Bill. And that's how you got the promotion. That's why he was going to demote me, right?"

"That's not true, Daryl. I told you, it was his ide—"

"I never knew you were such a committed liar."

"Ok, fine. You want to know how I know your wife is pregnant? She told me!" I say.

He shakes his head, smirking. "And why would she do that?"

"We talked in the lift when she came to see you last week. She said she hopes it's a boy. She said you'll name him Spencer, after your dad."

His eyes well up with tears and in the split second he takes them off me, I smack the gun out of his hand, leap to my feet and strike him three successive times in the throat. He loses balance and drops to the ground. I kick him twice in the side. Yes, I kick people when they're down. I consider putting my foot on his neck but that seems needlessly cruel.

As he coughs and rolls on the ground, I walk quickly to the gun and pick it up. It's like old times. I open it to check if it's loaded. It is. This lunatic really was ready to kill me. I turn to look at him.

Oh, he's going to pay!

His coughing subsides. He lies on the floor and clutches his throat. He looks at me and our eyes meet. Yeah, he didn't see that coming.

"On your knees, hands behind your head," I say, pointing the gun at him. I won't make the same mistake he did.

He obeys without resistance. I keep my distance – far enough away that he can't reach me, close enough that I won't miss, should I choose to shoot him.

"Are you going to kill me?" he asks.

"I don't know. I haven't decided."

He sneers. "You're not a killer."

"Tell that to the guy who broke into my house."

"That was self-defence. You don't have what it takes to kill someone in cold blood. That's not who you are."

I almost burst into laughter. I can't tell if he believes what he's saying or if he's trying to manipulate me. Unfortunately for him, he's wrong.

I sigh and roll my shoulders back. I can feel tension growing within me. "Who knows you're here?"

"Sanders. That's it," he says.

"He really sent you to kill me."

"And the other guy, too. At least that guy got paid. If it's any consolation, Old Bill said he respected your drive and ambition, but not your methods."

"It's no consolation," I say.

He nods. "He didn't think he could control you, couldn't risk you betraying him… even if you kill me, he'll send someone else after you. He won't stop until you're dead."

"Good to know."

For a few seconds, I look quietly at him, considering my very limited options.

"So… you really did blackmail him?"

I nod.

He smiles. "You've got some nerve."

I smile.

"You know I never knew you hated me so much," he says, almost whimsically.

"I don't hate you, Daryl. I have no reason to. I'm better than you at everything. The simple fact is that you were an obstacle and I needed you removed. It wasn't personal."

"Did Veronica really tell you about the baby?"

"Oh no, that was pure fiction. Kat did. You know what they say: loose lips sink ships."

My hand feels heavy. I lower the weapon, keeping my eyes on him.

"She told me everything – about the affair, not that she needed to. Your body language told me that, months before she ever said a word. She did, however, tell me about your wife's pregnancy," I say.

He nods. "And my dad? Did she tell you about him, too?"

"Ages ago. She said that you told her you'd leave your wife for her, and the two of you would run off together and have kids, live happily ever after, that sort of nonsense. And you'd name your first son after your dad."

"And you remembered…"

"All information may prove useful one day," I say.

"You're much smarter than I realised. I underestimated you"

"That's ok, Daryl. You're not the first to make such a grave error of judgement."

I tuck the gun into my trousers. He stays on his knees with his hands behind his head.

"You weren't really going to kill me, were you? There's no way you'd have got away with it. CCTV would have had you in cuffs in no time," I say.

"Bill owns this place. There are no cameras in the area – thanks to budget cuts, the council couldn't afford to keep them running. I was instructed to put your body in the boot of your car and leave it here. He'd have done the rest… or maybe friends of his would have. I'm not sure; he didn't give me all the details."

He speaks so frankly about 'my body' that I feel queasy.

"He probably lied to you," I say. "There's almost certainly a thousand cameras in here, and he'd have sent the car and— and my body to the police, along with the footage of the crime."

Still kneeling, he lets his hands down and shrugs. "I believed everything he told me. But yeah, he could have been lying."

I doubt Old Bill was lying. He despises Daryl but he seems to enjoy controlling people. He most likely couldn't resist an opportunity to force Daryl to do something this heinous.

"Are you going to kill me?" he asks, his eyes filling with tears

I sigh. "I don't know, Daryl. Should I?"

"I have a baby on the way. I don't want my children to grow up without a father."

My throat tightens with irritation. "Moments ago, when you pointed the gun at me, did you spare a thought for my family?"

The tears spill out of his eyes. He cups his face and cries into his hands. He sobs and sniffs, until finally, he wipes his face. Now a shade more composed, he looks at me again, still sniffing.

Before me kneels a man who has given up. No swag, no exit strategy, no dignity. This is Daryl, stripped of all his armour. His tank is empty. I'm not sure killing him would accomplish anything. It might send a message to Old Bill, but the collateral damage might be more than my conscience can bear.

Daryl is a lousy husband and probably a subpar father, but somehow I feel like it's not my place to put him in the ground. Maybe I'm going soft in my old age. Maybe I need to get my head examined. Five years ago, he'd already be dead, and his body turned to a pile of ash.

On one hand, I should kill him simply because he came so close to ending my life. But on the other hand, this is too spontaneous for me. I have no plan in place, no alibi. I don't know all the angles and I haven't thought this through. I don't like killing, and I hate killing without a plan. If it came down to it, how would I explain this to the police? Killing two people in such a short space of time would look suspicious to Detective Miller, among others.

Damn it, I have to let him go.

I remove the gun from my trousers. He flinches, whimpering a little. I disengage the magazine and hold on to it. I toss the gun at him and put the magazine in my pocket.

"It's your lucky day, Daryl. You get to go home, hug Veronica and Carla, and tell Bill that you failed. I'm feeling altruistic today. I'll give you a couple of hours before I call the police," I say.

His eyes widen as I walk past him to my car. I open the door, overwhelmed with a sense of relief. As I step into the car, I feel myself being pulled away by my shoulders. I slam onto the ground hard, face down. I cough, feeling dizzy, trying to lift myself up. A searing pain goes up my side. I think I've pulled some stitches.

My ankle hurts too much for it not to be sprained.

I'm still trying to make sense of what's happening when I feel myself being dragged across the floor by my feet. I kick violently until I'm released. I scramble to my knees and turn around in time to see the maniacal look on Daryl's face. He lurches to me and punches me. I fall on my back.

He pulls me up by my jumper and punches me again. The pain is excruciating. It's been so long since I've been subjected to this sort of treatment that I'm no longer used to it. I've forgotten how much pain I can feel. He tries to punch me a third time, but I block him and throw a left hook. He falls back, letting me go.

"What the hell, Daryl?"

I stand up but he kicks me in the shin and I'm down again.

I should have killed him when he was at my mercy.

He climbs on top of me and slaps me. I try to block him, but he forces my hand away and punches me square in the jaw. The pain goes all the way to the top of my head. I shut my eyes, trying to absorb it. I open my eyes again. Instead of Daryl's face, I see William's. He raises his hand and punches me where I was stabbed. I cry out in pain. If the stitches hadn't ripped before, they have now.

He reaches into my pocket and gets the magazine.

"There's no way I'm going to tell Sanders that I failed. No way," he says.

He jams the magazine into the gun.

I curl up into foetal position, focussed too much on how much my body aches. If this is the end, at least the pain will end too. Or maybe it won't. Maybe it will go on forever. I'll find out soon enough.

"Look at me," he barks.

Drops of crimson-coloured saliva trickle out my mouth as I slowly, painfully lift my upper body off the ground. I can feel the wound bleeding. My jaw throbs, as does my head. I manage to sit, and then I look at Daryl like he ordered me to. I feel like a deer staring down the barrel of a hunter's gun. Still, I can't help goading him. If I'm going to die, I might as well unburden myself.

"You're a coward, and an ingrate, and you're weak and pathetic. You're nothing, Daryl, worthless. And if you do this, you won't be able to live with yourself."

His eyes narrow and he sighs. "I've always liked you, Donna – you have spunk. I want you to know this isn't personal."

"That in no way comforts me."

He starts lifting the gun when his phone rings. He jumps a little, visibly startled by the noise.

This time, I don't hesitate.

The adrenaline flows through me like the blood that seeps out of my side. I leap at him and knock him off balance.

The phone rings again.

He stays on his feet, but the gun drops. The phone keeps ringing. I strike at his knee and then he falls.

Still ringing.

I get on top of him and elbow his face too many times to count. When it's bloody and my arms are tired, I get up and find the gun.

The phone stops ringing.

This time, I won't hesitate.

"Donna," he groans.

"I can't believe I was stupid enough to—"

"Don't do this."

My ankle throbs but I ignore it. He's still on the ground, trying to get his bearings. He moves slowly from his back to his side. From the corner of my eye, I see him watch as I pick the gun up. His face is covered in blood. It hurts me to look at him.

I check the gun again, because I have to be sure. I look at him as he wipes blood and tears away. He reaches into his pocket, but I wave the gun at him, indicating that he best not try it. I want to cry, and I'm not sure I know why. I steel myself for what's coming next.

I raise the gun, point it at him.

"Please Donna, don't do this. You'll regret it."

I exhale as I stifle a sob. "I'd rather regret killing you than regret letting you live."

I brace myself as I put my finger on the trigger.

"Donna, don't—"

"My name is Belladonna, and you brought this on yourself."

I pull the trigger.

The noise is loud and jarring, like I knew it would be. For a while, it echoes through the open space like trauma through a lifetime. His body slumps with a thud but afterwards, there's silence. It's the sort of silence that would bother other people. It's the sort of silence that brings me relief.

Once is all it takes. My aim is impeccable; I hit him between the eyes.

His body lies motionless and I hobble over to it. I look down at the corpse as blood streaks down his forehead. His eyes stare at me, but Daryl is no longer there. He looks as vacant in death as he was in life. I kneel next to him and close his eyes. It seems like the decent thing to do. And then I break down, wailing.

This is not how I expected the night to turn out.

***

I stumble to the garage door (limp, really) and unlock it. The police are en route. I considered abandoning the crime scene, but I knew I couldn't go home like this. There's no way I could explain my appearance to Ivy and mum. So, I called the authorities.

My head hurts. The wound in my side is bleeding, as is my nose. I sit on the ground and hang my head backwards. I pinch my nose between the nostrils and the bridge, and sniff repeatedly. The blood slides into my throat and I spit it out. This carries on until I feel the blood clot at the back of my throat. I spit that out and lean forward again, wiping my face. This reminds me of my childhood.

Daryl's body lies a short distance away, waiting to be folded into a body bag and tossed in the dirt. I still can't believe that he tried to kill me. I can't believe that he almost succeeded. Life is so fragile and awful. I can't begin to think about how terrible Ivy would have felt if I'd died tonight. Would she ever have known? Would my body ever have been found?

Oh God, thank you for sparing my life.

I hear the sirens now. I'm too weak to move. Was it Veronica that called him?

I think about her and her children. I think about how the one in her womb will never know his or her father. A part of me thinks I've done that child a favour but I can't know for certain that that's true. I start crying again. I'm in so much pain. I'm sick of living in a world where I can never expect or hope to be safe. Danger is all around me. I've lived with it, gone to school with it, worked with it. I'm tired of people trying to kill me, I just want peace and quiet.

My mind is a mangled. I'm having a hard time thinking clearly. I wonder who called him. Had his phone not rung, my life would be over. It was probably Sanders, checking that I was dead. He will pay for this. I have to finish that wretched curmudgeon off one way or another.

Police cars drive into the garage, an ambulance following close behind. I sit still and call out to them, though it takes all my strength to raise my voice. Paramedics rush to my side. As one attends to me, I see Detective Miller step out of a police car.

Why is he even here? And where is Lawson?

He comes over to me. I must look absolutely terrible, because his face looks like that blue-headed emoji that clasps its cheeks. His concern is evident. His forehead is lined and his eyes flit between my face and the large blood stain on my jumper.

"We need to stop meeting like this," I say, smiling through the pain.

"What happened here?" he asks.

"It's a long story."

Another paramedic brings a stretcher towards me, and helps me onto it.

"I'll ride in the back with her," Miller says to him. The guy nods, wheeling the stretcher into the back of the ambulance.

Miller climbs in, holds my hands gently as he sits next to me. Maybe he's trying to reassure me that things will be ok.

I'm fairly certain that they won't.

IVY

I'm home, milling around after work, doing nothing important. Mum is 'watching T.V.', which today means she is falling asleep. I haven't seen Mina since we prayed together, though we've spoken on the phone. She's with Suzanne, as far as I know. She says she's doing well and that since we prayed, she hasn't had any cravings for drugs. She also says that she hasn't had any nightmares, either. I pray that all of that is behind her forever. I know she'll need as much support as possible to rebuild her life. She knows I'm here for her. I hope she can finally start to heal.

Days have passed and I'm still shocked by Mina's revelation. In all the years that I've known her, it never once crossed my mind that something so atrocious had been done to her. I always thought that the aftermath of the armed robbery and attempted rape – the fear and helplessness she had felt – had sent her spiralling out of control. Now I know it was much worse than that.

Likewise, I'm having a hard time wrapping my head around Donna's part in this. I find it very odd that mere weeks after she learned of Alan's attack on Mina, she happened to shoot him dead. It seems too coincidental. I want to believe that it was just a coincidence but… my gut tells me otherwise.

Sitting next to mum on the sofa as she starts snoring, I try to shake the feeling that Donna executed Alan. I don't know how she could have orchestrated that. If she did, is that the worst thing she's done? Is it even really a bad thing? If she did somehow 'murder' Alan Ellis, has she actually done anything wrong? I want to tell myself that she hasn't. I'm not sure I can.

I've barely spoken to her since they let us back into the flat. I've cooked for her and encouraged her to rest but I haven't been able to bring myself to ask her about any of this. I'm afraid of what she might say, or maybe I'm afraid that everything happened like she said and she'll be hurt that I ever thought she was capable of anything so diabolical. I'm praying that these thoughts will somehow disappear and things can go back to normal.

As I try to tuck the unsettling thoughts away in some place they can't cause trouble, my phone rings. It's Donna. I shake my head, thinking about how ridiculous it is that she returned to work so soon after she was discharged. She doesn't even like being there. I grab my phone and leave the living room before answering.

"Hey Donna, how goes?"

"Hello. Is that Ivy?" a man says.

"Who is this?"

"This is Detective Ken Miller; we met a few days ago."

My heart sinks.

Why does he have Donna's phone? Oh, this can't be good.

"Detective, where's my sister?"

"She's in the hospital. I thought you'd like to know."

"Is she ok? Please, detect—"

"Donna's fine, they're treating her now but… it would be good for her family to be here," he says. His voice is firm, but beside the firmness is softness. He speaks her name in a manner that is far from professional.

"Where are you?"

God knows what has happened this time.

XI

DONNA

I didn't need surgery tonight. The doctor stitched and patched me up again – my side, my face – and checked that I hadn't lost any teeth. They are all intact, I was happy to hear. The nose bleed was nothing serious and it looks like I'll be ok. They bandaged my ankle and I can just about walk on that leg. I don't have a concussion. I feel less confused than I did earlier, so I hope my brain is in order. All in all, I think I've fared quite well.

"You're free to go, Miss," the doctor says to me.

"Thank you, doctor."

She hands me a packet of painkillers – the strongest ones available – as well as a prescription for more.

I leave the examination room and find Detective Miller sitting in the waiting room. It seems like he stayed here while I was being checked over. I don't know what to make of that. Either this guy really wants to close cases or he's got nothing interesting to do with his life.

In the ambulance, I told him everything that happened, everything except the part about the blackmail. As far as he knows, Daryl – jealous over my impending promotion – lost what was left of his mind and tried to kill me in a misguided attempt to keep his position. I told the same story to the officer who came to see me while I waited for the doctor.

It's not the whole truth, and it leaves Old Bill free to try to kill me again, but I think it's the right call for now. Whilst I won't spend the night in jail, I'm under investigation for murder. This is why I plan these things in advance. That said, I'm tired of lying and hiding. I want to tell the truth; I have to if I'm to stay sane. But before that, more than that, I want to see Bill suffer.

When he sees me, Miller stands up, walks quickly to me.

"Are you ok?" He rests his hand on my arm as he speaks. "I was worried about you."

I step away from him. "I'm ok, no broken bones."

He notes my discomfort and removes his hand. "I'm sorry. I didn't mean to—"

"Why are you here, Detective Miller?"

"Why am I—?"

"Here. I've already given you my statement, so why are you here? What do you want with me?"

He takes a step back and curls his lips. "I want to know why people keep trying to kill you, and how you always seem to overpower them."

As I think about the question, he carries on. "Alan Ellis. Gary McDonald. Now Daryl Blake. This can't be by chance."

Gary McDonald. Was that the assassin's name?

If the police found that out before Suzanne and Mina did, I might have to get some of my money back. I'd like to know more about his identity but before I can probe further, my anger charges to the fore.

"So what, you think I'm asking for it?" I spit the words with disgust, raising my voice a little.

"No, that's not what—"

"You want to know why always me, I'll tell you – it's because those men were cowards, and cowards just love bullying women. They think we're weak, and that preying on us makes them strong. If you would pay attention at work, you would have noticed that. But I guess you're too busy hassling survivors of violent crimes to do your job properly."

"Donna, please—"

"Miss Palmer. You don't get to call me by my first name. You are nothing to me."

He squints and winces subtly, but I don't let that stop me. I never would.

"And let me correct you on one more thing – I don't *seem to* overpower these criminals. I do overpower them."

He exhales sharply, runs his hands over his hair while looking at his shoes.

Relief blended with fear and annoyance. That's what I feel, apart from the dull pain in my jaw and the sharp one in my side. I didn't order this, but it's what I get for speaking from the heart. This is why I always need a plan.

"Donna! Oh, thank God!"

I look past Miller to see Ivy hurrying towards us. Miller turns around, and she brushes past him.

She moves to hug me, but I put my hands up. "I'm a little sore."

Her eyes swell when she sees my face close up. "What happened *this time?*"

"It's ok," I say, "You should see the other guy."

I've always wanted to say that. I missed my chance with Ellis and McDonald, but not this time. Miller steps away, returning to the seat he recently vacated.

"What the hell, Donna? Who did this to you?" Ivy does not say 'hell' for nothing.

"Daryl... he attacked me."

"What?"

I nod gently.

"Why would he—? Has he been arrested?" she says, nostrils flared.

I shake my head, closing my eyes.

"He's dead, Ivy," I say. "I... I killed him."

I open my eyes again; catch her blink slowly with her mouth hanging open. She turns and looks at Miller. She turns back at me. She puts her arms on my shoulders, gently leans into me. I rest my head on her shoulder, and my eyes meet Miller's. He looks away, evidently hurt by my outburst. I pull away from Ivy.

"It's like you have nine lives."

I smile at her, and then flinch as the pain in my jaw shoots up to my ear. Thanks to Daryl, I can't even smile properly. Oh well, this too shall pass.

Detective Miller comes to us again, clears his throat slightly. "How are you two getting home?"

"Where's the car, Donna?" Ivy says.

"It's in police custody for now," Miller says. "If you need a lift, I can help you out."

Ivy looks at me, waiting for me to say something. I shrug.

"Thank you, detective. That's really kind of you," she says.

"It's nothing," he says, looking directly at me, his gaze soft and sombre.

Ivy slowly glances at my face, and then watches as he leads the way.

Her voice drops to a conspiratorial whisper. "Am I missing something?"

"No, Ivy, you're not."

***

On the drive home, no one says a word. I rest my head on Ivy's shoulder the whole time, and she lets me. I don't know the last time I did that. It's usually the other way around. Her body is tense for the entirety of the journey, even as she occasionally cradles my head. The tension bothers me. I know she's probably just worried about me, but something inside tells me that things have changed. She doesn't trust me anymore.

From time to time, I catch Miller peering at me in the rear-view mirror. I don't like the way he looks at me, it makes me feel… vulnerable. Thanks to his earlier questions, I'm starting to think that he's on to me and he's now convinced that I'm no 'ordinary' victim. At this point, I'd be surprised if Ivy wasn't at least a bit suspicious of me.

There's a part of me that hopes that's the case. I'm tired of everything – lying, plotting, killing. I'm tired of life. I don't know how much more blood I will spill before I die, but I've had enough. The desire to confess and be done with it starts to rise within me. I try to suppress it but now I know it's there, I feel like it's only a matter of time before it consumes me.

A picture of Veronica smiling in the lift flashes through my mind. Soon enough she'll hear the news, if she hasn't already. I know Daryl was beneath her in every way but she loved him, proving that there is indeed no accounting for taste. I've killed the love of her life, the husband of her choice, the father of her children. I've made a widow of her. For that I feel... guilty.

On the one hand, I've freed her to move on to someone better (assuming that in this day and age, such a man exists) or no one at all if that's her wish, but on the other hand, I've trapped her in a cell made of memories and full of misery. I am directly responsible for the loss and emptiness that will most likely overshadow the rest of her life, and the lives of her children. There's a small chance that one day they will thank me. Somehow, I doubt that.

I feel less terrible that she will soon find out what a vulgar, depraved man her father is. I will be responsible for shining a light on his true nature, but I am not responsible for his true nature. I feel no guilt or shame in this instance. Who knows? I may even find it in my heart to send him to prison. Time will tell. I hope she can find solace in the thought that disgrace is better than death.

Miller parks the car outside our building. I lift my head from Ivy's shoulder for the first time since we entered the vehicle. She shuffles to the door.

"Thank you for the lift, detective," she says.

She opens the door and steps out. Miller turns around.

"Can I talk to you for a minute, Miss Palmer?"

Ivy looks at him, then at me. "I'll be right here if you need me."

She gets out of the car and shuts the door. She stands outside, leaning against the car.

"What is it?" My tone is frosty, even though I don't want it to be.

"I've never met anyone as lucky as you before, you know that?" he says.

"No, I didn't know that."

His eyes rest on the passenger seat. "I'm sorry about how I worded my question earlier. I never meant to suggest that you've done something to deserve being attacked."

He looks at my face.

"I didn't mean to insult you, or to upset you," he says in a clam tone.

"Ok."

"And... I'm sorry if my... concern for you has made you feel uncomfortable. That was not my intention."

I nod.

A brief pause, then he continues. "I've killed people before... on the job. It's not easy. It takes a toll on you."

I watch as one hand taps the dashboard.

"You've had to kill three people to stay alive, yet you seem fine. How is that?" he says.

He still wants to know. He's still poking me for evidence, probably hoping I'll say something to incriminate myself.

Not today.

"Like you said, I'm the luckiest person you've ever met."

He moves his head to one side. "There's more to it than that. I can feel it."

"Oh? What else can you feel?" I ask, leaning forward just enough to throw him, or so I hope.

He looks away from me, shifts in his seat, half-smiling as his cheeks flush with colour. "If you ever need someone to talk to, you know where to find me."

"Thank you, detective. I'll keep that in mind."

He looks up. "Don't leave town, ok?"

I nod at him and tap on the car window. Ivy moves out of the way. I open the door, mouthing 'thank you' as she helps me out of the car. The door shuts behind me, and Miller drives away.

Ivy watches as the car goes further into the distance. "Did he ask you out?"

"Of course not. That would be inappropriate," I say.

"Shame. He seems to like you."

I shrug, and we start our slow walk to the building.

We get inside, get to the flat. Mum is nowhere to be seen. I assume she's gone to bed. That's probably for the best. She's never cared about my wellbeing before, why should she start now?

"Mum was asleep when I got the call. I thought it best not to wake her," Ivy says. "She'd only worry and… that's more than I can handle right now."

"Oh, I assumed she didn't care."

Ivy frowns. "I figured you would."

"Can you blame me?"

She says nothing, just folds her arms as if for comfort.

"Water?" I ask.

She shakes her head. "I'm fine, thanks."

I limp to the kitchen, pop the painkillers on the worktop, pour myself a glass of water. I think about taking the pills on an empty stomach, but decide it's best to follow the directions. I wish I could just go to sleep, maybe never wake up. I don't think I'll make it in to work tomorrow. I don't know if I should be honest about the reason.

I feel like saying, *"Hey guys, I'd love to be there, but the police are investigating me for our colleague's murder. Later!"* might be a bit much… 'love' is not the right word. I remember that I'm yet to tell Suzanne to release the recordings of Old Bill and his lady friends. I should do that right away.

I should but instead, I rifle through the fridge looking for something easy to eat. Luckily for me, there's still food leftover from Ivy's Adventures in Cooking for Friends. Easy enough, I suppose.

"Would you like some?" I ask her.

She shakes her head. "I already ate."

My previous dose of painkillers is wearing off. My jaw hurts significantly but I reckon I can just about chew. I extract a small portion of the food from the fridge and scoop it into a plate. I place it in the microwave, watching and waiting as the plate rotates. Second after second, the rays heat the food up. The longer it stays in there, the hotter it gets.

It makes me think of all the anger I have in my heart. It's been with me for so long and I've never done anything to douse it, just heated it up mulling over

411

all the cruelty and injustice the world has to offer. I've let – even helped – the hatred grow and now every chance it gets it spills out, causing death. I am the handmaiden of death and I fear that there's nothing I can do to change that.

Death is all I have to give.

The microwave clicks and I get the food out. It's the right temperature, good enough to eat. I place the plate on the counter, and realise that the whole time, Ivy has done nothing but stand there watching me.

I look at her, puzzled. "What's up?"

She stares hard at my eyes. Her gaze moves to my hands, and then back to my face.

"What really happened tonight?" she asks. "Why did Daryl attack you?"

My lips part as warm air escapes them. "I don't know, Ivy. I think he went crazy."

She clasps her hands in front of her, placing them on the worktop. "You know you can tell me anything right?"

That's not true but I nod. "I know."

"Tell me you didn't plan this. Tell me you didn't murder him. Tell me you weren't trying to take his job." Her eyes search my face diligently.

"Why would you think I would do—?"

"I know how angry you were when you didn't get that promotion. Nepotism! Sexism! Racism! It was almost a year before you stopped complaining about it!" she says, flailing her hands above her head.

Is that how I look when I'm ranting?

"So you think I lured him to some abandoned building so I could kill him and take his job? Do you think I'm crazy or stupid or both?"

She chews the inside of her mouth before speaking. "Mina told me what Alan Ellis did to her. She told me about how you helped her, how you tried to convince her to come forward…"

I swallow hard, blinking rapidly.

"And…?" My voice is quiet. My tongue clings to the top of my mouth as I try to moderate my emotions.

"You killed him, Donna. Weeks later."

"Because he tried to—"

"I'm not stupid. All these years, I bought the story about the botched robbery and the attempted assault, but that's because I didn't know the *whole* story. I couldn't see the bigger picture. I do now, and I know you. There's no way you would let something like that go. Not you, Donna, not in this life."

I say nothing. She's right… I want to admit it but there's no reason to. I can't predict what that would mean for the future. I'm not sure what it would mean for us. She will probably hate me, despise me. She's the only reliable person in my life.

I shrug, switching to lawyer-mode. "So what are you saying? What do you think happened?"

"I don't know but I don't think it was an accident that you killed him. Somehow you knew it was Alan that night, didn't you? You knew."

She closes her eyes, breathes shallowly as water pours down her cheeks.

"Are you shedding tears for the rapist?"

She opens her eyes, slowly shakes her head. "All the tears I shed are for you, Donna. Every last one of them."

We stare at each other in complete silence. I think about the food that's getting cold again.

"What did Daryl do to you? Did he hurt you?" Her voice goes quiet. "Is that why you killed him?"

She lifts her hand to her eyes, swots teardrops away.

"I swear to you, Ivy, I only killed Daryl to stay alive. He tried to kill me. Twice in the space of, like, ten minutes. I wasn't going to wait for a third attempt."

"Twice?"

I nod.

Her jaw clenches. "And Alan?"

I pull up a stool and sit on it. I'm weak, tired, spent. I touch my side, feel the bandage. I touch my face, swollen from tonight's beating. I touch my neck, still not fully healed from the assassin's attack. What was his name? McDonald. Ellis tried to choke me, too.

"Donna, please. Tell me what really happened that night."

I look at her, still silent. Her eyes plead with me. She's desperate to know the truth, though I think she knows it already. All she wants is confirmation.

"He brought it on himself," I say.

Her mouth opens, but no words come out.

"You didn't see her, Ivy – Mina, I mean – after he violated her. She was a mess, hair messed up, clothes ripped. She called me, told me she needed help, a change of clothes. I thought Aunt Flo had done her worst, you know? Something like that, something normal… mundane. I could never have imagined…"

A stabbing pain strikes my heart at the memory of that night. My throat tightens, but I continue. "I told her to go to the police, said I'd go with her but… she refused. She— she didn't think it would make a difference, because of who his father was. She said no one would care; he'd get away with it because she didn't matter. But she did matter, by virtue of being. And she mattered to me, you know? She still does," I say, my voice cracking as I give in to the emotions.

Ivy cries quietly, same as me.

"I, uh, I cornered him, told him that I would go to the police if he didn't turn himself in, but he didn't care. He really thought he was invincible. I had evidence but I knew I couldn't use it because Mina… she wouldn't budge. I tried but she wouldn't. She was so scared and ashamed, as if she'd done something wrong."

Ivy takes a tissue, blows her nose into it, tosses it in the bin.

"What did you do, Donna?"

I slump a little in the stool. Feeling a pinch in my side, I straighten up and exhale.

"I told him I'd turn him in if he didn't help me rob the shop. I— I told him Mina would be there; he could do whatever he wanted to her. You should have seen the way his eyes lit up, Ivy." I shake my head, massage it with one hand. "I didn't know if he'd show up or not. Part of me hoped he wouldn't. But then he did, and he really had every intention of raping her again, in front of me. He had to die, Ivy. He would never have stopped. I had to kill him. There was no other way."

She folds over the worktop, gasping noisily for air. She covers her mouth with one hand, whimpers into it, more tears spilling. I don't know what to do, so I sit there, wishing I hadn't warmed the food so promptly.

For a few breaths, her breathing gets louder. Eventually, it gets closer to normal and she's upright again.

"I can't believe you never said anything," she says, practically panting.

"Like what? Oh, someone raped my best friend and I murdered him! It's not exactly dinner time conversation. Besides, you had other things to think about. We both did."

"Does Mina know?"

"Of course not! Do you think I'm insane?"

Her breathing stays audible. "How have you been able to live with yourself all these years? Ten years and you've just— you've acted like it was all a coincidence?"

"What does it matter about the circumstances? You knew I killed him. Everyone did. So I planned to – why does that make things worse?"

"Please don't pretend that you – a lawyer – don't understand why that makes things worse. You weren't simply defending yourself; you set out to kill him! You took the law into your hands!" she says, gesticulating wildly.

"Well somebody had to. Do you really think Mina would have got justice if she'd turned him in? Do you? She wouldn't have, I assure you."

My cheeks feel hot and my voice gets louder. The memories have never left me, but now that they're at the forefront of my mind and I'm talking about things, it feels so fresh.

"You don't know that."

"I do, Ivy, I really do. Like you said, I'm a lawyer. People go on and on about how it's innocent until proven guilty, but when it comes to rape, both the accused and the accuser go on trial, and even if it's clear that the man is guilty, people always blame the woman. Always. I've seen it enough times first-hand but before I ever did, I knew it – just like Mina did – because that message is everywhere, sometimes unspoken, but still woven into the fabric of *every* society. So yes, I took the law into my hands but only because I had no choice."

"You had a choice but you made the wrong one. You denied Mina justice!"

"Are you serious? I *gave* Mina justice. And not just her, either. You think she was his first victim? She wasn't. You think she would have been his last? No chance. People like him do not change and they do not stop. All they do is get smarter about it. I'm not sorry I killed him, Ivy. He had it coming, he was asking for it. He earned his fate. He would have grown up to be one of the countless men who consistently do nothing to take responsibility for their own weaknesses, the ones who hold women accountable for their refusal to control their own lust and then try to destroy those women, as though it was their right, as though it was right. He was no good to anyone and he got what he deserved. He's better off as a spectre in a bad dream. My only regret is that I can't kill him all over again."

It feels good to have got that off my chest. I glare at the thought of him, then pull the plate to myself and take a bite. The food is still warm, which is a relief. I just need something to line my stomach so the painkillers don't rip a hole in it. At least, I think that's why they tell you to eat first.

Ivy stands, mouth ajar, as I chew gently. I look at her, knowing that our relationship has changed forever, and not for the better.

She rubs her temples for a moment before she resumes speaking. "By your logic… you haven't changed either. You've just got smarter about it. So, what else have you been hiding?"

She sounds calm and reasoned, but I'm wary. She pulls up a stool and sits near me. She clasps her hands behind her neck and rests her elbows on the worktop.

"I've not been hiding—"

"The man who broke in here, who was he?"

"That I don't know," I say.

"You're lying."

"Oh, you're a human polygraph now? You can tell I'm lying without the Lasso of Truth? For years you had no idea about the circumstances surrounding Alan's death, but now you do and you think I'm lying about *everything*!"

"Your right eye twitched when you answered!"

Did it? I didn't realise that had happened. The pain and tiredness must be affecting my poker face. I see now that there's no going back. They say the truth will set you free. I'm certain that in my case, the truth will lock me up. Oh well, I did do the crimes, it's only fair that I do the time.

"I don't know who he was, but I'm sure the police are working on it. Let them do their jobs, since you trust them so much," I say.

She sighs and looks away. I imagine she's exasperated, disappointed even. She's the most honest person I know. I expect that she'll be reporting this to the police at some point in the near-future – most likely tomorrow morning before daybreak.

"Tell me that you've not murdered anyone else. Promise me that there isn't a pile of bodies somewhere, all dropped by you."

I lower my eyes, concentrating on the food. For the first time since it happened, I wish Mina had kept her mouth shut about Alan. She didn't go to the police when it could have made a difference. She's kept the secret for a decade. Why talk now? And why tell Ivy? Why not a professional, someone who can help her? I know that Ivy is warm enough to make you feel like you can tell her anything but, for the love of all good things, why now?

"There isn't a pile of bodies," I say. I take another bite. I don't bother looking at her.

"Ok then. How many more?"

I hesitate, knowing that I've already said too much. I finish chewing and gulp the food down.

"Two," I say quietly.

From the corner of my eye, I see her clutch her stomach. I finally look up, and see the deep furrow of her forehead. This is the moment my life changes forever. I know it. She really never suspected me of anything like this. It's at once sweet and saddening, life-affirming and soul-crushing. How can an adult be so naïve?

"Anyone I know?"

"There was Beth Meyer. She was Alan's accomplice."

"Beth Meyer? That can't be true. Her death was accidental. She got high and fell out of the window," she says, her confusion evident from the tone of her voice.

"I spiked her weed with something more… lethal; put her in the ground next to her degenerate boyfriend."

She shakes her head, still holding her stomach. She looks at the ceiling before returning her attention to me. "Dad?" Her voice shakes when she asks.

I nod slowly, moving my eyes back to the meal. Five more bites and I'm done.

"You threw him down the stairs, didn't you?"

"What? No! I would never be that sloppy. I poisoned him over some time. One day it kicked in, and not a moment too soon."

She closes her eyes and wraps her arms around herself, rocking back and forth, whimpering.

"Donna," she whispers, "Wh—"

"Stop. Just stop. He hasn't been dead long enough for you to ask why. You remember why. You're not mum; I won't allow you to act like an idiot." My tone is firm, authoritative. Maybe even threatening. Her head snaps up and her eyes fly open. She keeps rocking forward and back. She looks up and closes her eyes again.

"I can't believe this. I can't believe this."

"Yes, you can. You know he had to die; it was the only way we could be free. I wasn't going to let us continue to suffer for his feelings of inadequacy. I had to protect you. I had to save us."

"Do you know how serious this is? Like, in every way? This is evil. You're a murderer!"

"What's going on?" Mum appears, seemingly out of nowhere, in her dressing gown. I don't know how long she's been up or how much she'd heard.

"Who's a murderer?" she asks.

Were it possible for Ivy's face to turn white, it would. Her wide-eyed look clearly broadcasts that things are not as they ought to be.

Mum looks at me. "Donna, is something wrong?"

I don't say anything. I scoop up another spoonful of food and chew quicker this time.

"Mum, please, go back to bed. Everything's fi—"

"What did you do to Ivy, Donna?" she asks, cutting Ivy off.

What did I do to Ivy?

It takes all my willpower not to spew the food out and yell profanities at her. This woman who hated herself and her offspring so much that she was willing to wait until her useless, miserable drunk of a husband beat us to death. If I am evil, it is in part due to her choices.

I finish the food in my mouth and stand up. I reach for the painkillers and pop two pills out of the packet. I toss them in my mouth.

"Donna, did you hear me?" she says.

I chase the pills with some water.

"Donna!"

I swallow the pills and turn to my mother. I can feel my cheeks getting hotter.

"I heard you, mum. 'What did I do to Ivy?'"

"Donna, please, you're exhausted and hurt, you should go to sleep," Ivy says.

"You should be asking what I did *for* Ivy, mum. Actions have consequences, but inaction has consequences, too."

"I don't understand."

"Donna, you need to rest."

"You didn't even ask what happened to my face, mum." I say, pointing at it. "Let me guess, you think I've followed in your footsteps, got a 'man' who likes to beat women up, a coward like your beloved William... or is it that you don't care what happens to your daughters?"

She looks at the bandages on my face for a fleeting moment, says nothing. Ivy puts her hand on mum's shoulder.

"Mum, Donna didn't do anything to me. She's had a long day. Someone tried to hurt her, but she's ok. Thank God, she's ok," Ivy says, starting to whimper.

Mum looks at her, scans her face, turns back to me.

"You said she was a murderer. I heard you."

"I was just..." Ivy loses her words. She doesn't lie, has never been fond of it. She wouldn't even do it to get out of trouble, not even when she knew what William would do to her. That was Before Christ, how much more now?

She bites her lower lip as her face crumples. She turns away from mum and faces the wall, sobbing and wiping her eyes. Mum looks at the back of her head and again at me.

"What did you do, Donna?" she asks.

I stare hard at her and then shake my head.

"You wouldn't understand."

XII

DECEMBER 6TH, 2019

DONNA

No rest for the wicked – that is the truth! It's 4:51 in the morning and I have not slept at all this night. Not one wink. I never expected to tell anyone my secrets. I fully intended to keep them until I died, but now I've done the unexpected and there's no turning back.

Ivy managed to usher mum back to her room before I had a chance to tell her about William. Bless Ivy, the consistent peace maker. I took the opportunity to leave the kitchen; no idea what Ivy made of that. She made no attempt to continue our discussion.

I texted Suzanne, told her to release the information we have on Old Bill. Not all at once – a trickle, not a deluge, like the last time. She responded with a smiley. I get the distinct impression that she likes unearthing and revealing people's secrets. Do what you love and you'll never work a day in your life. The police should get wind of his illegal activities before the day ends. My hope is that they'll take him in and I won't have to worry about any other assassins. It made me feel good to know that the man who twice tried to have me killed is about to have his life upended. Still, sleep eluded me.

If I wasn't thinking about Daryl's attempt on my life, it was Alan's blood I saw. If it wasn't William kicking me repeatedly, it was Mina's torn clothes and the look on her face. And then there was the man choking me – Gary McDonald. Glad to be rid of him. Of all the images that kept me up, Ivy's expression when she realised the extent of my deceit is what bothered me most. It's only a matter of time before she turns me in. She's honest… she cares too much about doing the right thing to let me be, and therein lies her charm.

I'm worn out but I can't sleep. There's no reason for me to keep lying here, hoping for some shut eye. It's too late or early (depending on your perspective) to get any meaningful rest anyway. I get out of bed and stretch. I feel my stitches expand and quickly stop myself. Will I ever know peace? I look around my room.

I'm going to miss this place. It's not long now till I'll have to leave here. I know it. I can feel it in my gut. Even if William Sanders gets what's coming to him, my days of being a lawyer are over. Even if Ivy doesn't turn me in, my days of freedom are over. In short, my life as I know it is over.

I have nothing left to lose. In a fit of resignation, I decide do something different. I haven't prayed since I was a child, so I'm not really sure how to go about it. Ivy always says it's just 'talking to God.' Yeah, because that's a concrete description. *Talking to God.* How do you talk to the one who made everything and knows everything about you? What do you say that won't bore Him?

Hello God, I'm Belladonna, pleased to meet you. I say 'pleased' but I'm being polite. You know how conversations go. They say you know everything about everyone, so I'm not sure why I introduced myself. If you put me in my mother's womb, you surely knew what she'd name me. But anyway, it's Donna here. Since you know all there is to know about everyone, you already know that— you know that I've killed people. I'm a murderer and liar, among other unpleasant things. I'm not sure why you'd want to hear from someone as subversive and criminal as myself, but Ivy says you do… and I've run out of options so here I am.

I don't really know what to say. I don't know if you're real. It's hard to believe you are, given the state of the world. What kind of all-powerful, all-knowing, all-loving being doesn't stop wicked things from happening? How can you be good when you allow so much evil, and then let it go unpunished? If you care about people, why don't you fix the world? How can you be good? Ivy says you're good because you let people choose – you could force everyone to do what you want, but you don't want slaves, you want people to choose you freely. That sounds like a cop-out to me. How is it better to let people choose to do evil than to make them do good? How is that better?

Ugh, she's always whining on about coming to you in humility. Can't roll up to the palace and say, 'Whattup, Queen?!' You have to show her the respect that her office commands. How much more God, the Creator of the universe? Alright then. I'll lay my pride to the side. I don't know why I'm trying this, it's dumb. But… I guess I'm desperate. God, I'm tired of everything. Life, death, people, myself. Sometimes I wish I was dead. Other times, I wish I was never born. But right now, I wish I could sleep, even for an hour. That would be great, if you could do that. I'd appreciate that a lot. Thank you.

I let out a long yawn. Nothing special, I've been yawning all night. I climb back into bed and wrap myself in my duvet. I lie on my back, staring at the ceiling. I yawn again and then I close my eyes, hoping for sleep.

I turn onto my side and look at the clock. It's 7:38am. I blink rapidly. Did I fall asleep? I don't remember nodding off… maybe I didn't. I look at the clock again – 7:39am. I do feel refreshed, almost like I got eight full hours.

Wow, it's a miracle.

XIII

IVY

I wake up at 7 o'clock on the dot. Given the startling nature of Donna's late-night confession, I'm surprised I managed to sleep at all. I've always known that Donna had a strong desire for justice but I could never have imagined that it had mutated into something this dark and destructive. I think I cried myself to sleep.

I'm glad that Donna didn't tell mum what she'd done. We would not have had a moment of rest. She would have wailed and fussed until the cows came home and made it all about her and her loss. I'm not thrilled that Donna is responsible for dad's death, or Alan's or Beth's, but I understand why she did it. I'd be a fool not to. Waiting isn't exactly her strong suit. If she wants something, she'll get it herself. If she needs a rescue, she'll find a way to orchestrate one. It's how she was made. And we certainly needed rescue.

However, I can't get past the fact that it isn't her place to decide who ought to live or die. No one has that right but God, and she's playing with fire if she thinks she can carry on like this. I wish I could see her before I leave today but I don't know if that's wise. I have to be at work early, so I take a quick shower, prepare a salad for her, and leave the house without disturbing anyone.

On my walk to work, I try to get my head around the recent news, try to come to terms with the reality that I've been living under the same roof as a murderer. Correction: a multiple-murderer. I knew she'd killed Alan, but it's another thing to find out the lengths to which she went in order to accomplish that. I don't believe I know who she is. Perhaps I never did.

I want to blame dad for the way Donna has turned out even though it could just as easily have been me. There but for the grace of God, and all that. He was routinely wicked and cruel and there's no doubt that she learned brutish behaviour from him. But no one made her commit murder (several times, for that matter), and as much as I want to absolve her of all guilt, to lay the responsibility for her actions at the feet of our abusive father, I can't. I know better, I know too much. His influence was negative but she made her choice.

I stop briefly at a people crossing, rubbing my gloved hands together while waiting for the man to go green.

I can't believe I've been living with a murderer for ten years and I never once suspected her. How could I be so blind? What signs did I miss? What else is going on right in front of me that I'm oblivious to?

She never talks about work and now she's killed one of her colleagues. Was that premeditated as well? She says it wasn't, but should I really believe her? Should I tell the police what I know, everything she confessed to me? Would that be a betrayal? No, of course it wouldn't. She's committed crimes and she should face the consequences of her actions. But what if the consequences are more than she can bear? What if they're more than *I* can bear? I don't know what to think anymore.

The green man starts flashing. I was so lost in thought that I didn't see when it came on. I cross the street and continue walking.

Should I tell Seth? No, no, that would make him an accessory. Oh no! That's what I am – an accessory.

I stop moving, the weight of the realisation hitting me. I wish I hadn't asked her about Alan. I wish Mina hadn't said anything; I would have been none the wiser. Now I know too much and I have to take action.

As I stand in the frosty air, a feeling of warmth comes over me, like someone covered me in a blanket. I don't know what to do but God does, and He'll help me. He always helps me and this time will be no different. I start moving again, hoping that things work out for the best.

XIV

DONNA

Iknow that mum is volunteering at the church today. I wait until she's gone, leaving my room after 10am. Ivy is out as well. It's just me and my thoughts, like I prefer. I phoned work earlier to let them know I wouldn't be coming in today. Shane answered the phone and I could tell from his tone that he hadn't yet heard about Daryl. I told him that I'd ripped my stitches and had to go to the hospital, and now couldn't come to work.

All of that is true, even if it's the highly abridged version. He told me to take care of myself, which I thought was kind. I hung up and fell asleep again, this time for a couple of hours. I feel great, although I don't know why. It's obvious to me that my life is falling apart but for some reason that doesn't upset me too much.

In the kitchen, I prepare my breakfast. It's nothing special – toast and bacon. I'm not hungry but I need to eat if I'm going to heal properly. I decide to add the salad Ivy has made for me to the mix. I pull it out of the fridge and put the bacon on the grill. While I wait, I switch my phone on.

In a flash, I receive a number of text messages. It takes a while to sort through them, but the important ones are from Suzanne. Her first message, received at

8:20am tells me that 'the floodgates are open.' Her next text, an hour later, declares, 'second batch released.' I'll bet it is. Her final text, which came through at 10:01am says, 'all done.'

The last message makes me smile. Reap the whirlwind, you dog. Old Bill did his best to end me and he failed. He may have slowed me down but he couldn't stop me. It was foolish of him to even try.

I move on to a voicemail which turns out to be from Kat. She sobs about Daryl's untimely death. *'The police won't tell me what happened. They said I should come to the station. I'm scared, Donna. I didn't know who else to call. Where are you? Everyone's freaking out. Please call me when you get this.'* That was over an hour ago. By now, I reckon she knows how Daryl wound up on a slab in the morgue. She probably hates me. It's ok. I'll live.

I put the phone down and remove the bacon from the grill.

I love the smell of bacon in the morning.

I pop it onto the toast, reach for the painkillers and put them where I can see them. I move to take a bite out of my meal when the phone rings. Looking over at it, I see that it's Kat calling. Uh oh, I wasn't expecting that. I take a deep breath. No good can come of this. I put the food down and pick the phone up.

"Hello?"

"I'm outside your flat, I need to see you," she says.

"What?"

"Please, just buzz me in."

The urgency in her voice informs me that she knows the full story. Perhaps I should say she knows what the police know.

"Ok."

I walk to the entrance and push the buzzer, then hang up. There's no time to eat my breakfast before she gets here. I should have left my room earlier.

At least I'm wearing my dressing gown.

I wait by the door until I hear very loud, very frantic knocking. I open it and she hurries in and looks right at my face.

"What did you do, Donna? What did you do?"

Her voice shakes like a leaf in a tornado. She sniffs loudly, staring at me with her mouth open. Yes, she definitely knows what happened.

I shut the door.

"Donna, why… why would you kill him?"

Through her tears, I can just about make out the words.

"He attacked me, Kat. He— he lured me to a remote location and he tried to kill me. I had to save myself."

She wails, clutching her stomach and squatting low. Knowing her, she's likely thinking about all she's lost when in reality she has lost nothing. He was no good for her, and he was not hers to lose. Still, I feel a pang of pity, seeing her so unreasonably distressed.

"Why would he try to hurt you? Daryl would never do something like that. I don't understand."

Of course, she would say that.

"I don't either, Kat," I say, in the softest tone I can muster on an empty stomach. From the kitchen, the food calls to me but I cannot heed said call.

She sobs a bit more. I need her to get a grip and leave. I gently crouch and hold onto her, rocking her back and forth, hoping she'll compose herself faster as a result.

"I know that you cared about him, and I'm sorry this happened. I'm sorry that I had to kill him to stay alive. I'm sorry I've hurt you. I never meant to hurt you or him or Veroni—"

"I don't care about Veronica. Damn her!" Her voice is so loud and her tone, so angry that I leap away from her, taken aback by her reaction.

"What the—"

"All anyone at work is talking about is poor Veronica, poor sweet Veronica. But what about me? What about how hard this is for me? I'm the woman he spent most of his nights with. I'm the one he told his secrets to, his hopes and dreams. I'm the one—"

"You're the one he hid from the world," I say, standing up. I look down at her and continue, "You're the one he would never be seen in public with. You weren't his wife. You weren't even the mother of any of his children. He didn't love you. You were just his side piece, nothing more."

She stands up slowly and stares at me in silence, her eyes glistening with tears.

And then she slaps me across my already bruised face.

Suffice it to say, I didn't see that coming. I hold onto my cheek and look at her in amazement.

Her tear-stained face contorts with what looks like contempt, maybe for me, maybe for herself. "You think I'm beneath you because I was sleeping with a married man, don't you?"

She struck me in my own home. No one has done that since William died. I should break her neck for even thinking about it, let alone doing it.

My cheek feels hot. I rub it gently before lowering my hand. "No, Kat. You know you're beneath me for a whole slew of reasons."

Her eyes widen, leading more tears to trickle out.

"For what it's worth, I never set out to kill Daryl. I only defended myself. Now, get out of my flat and don't ever come back."

Her face crumples as she sobs. She places her hands on her chest. I open the door and she walks out. She turns around, looks like she wants to say something. It doesn't matter. I slam the door shut.

***

Once I got over the shock of being slapped as an adult in the comfort of my own home, I had my breakfast and my painkillers. I still had no appetite, but if I lived by my feelings, most people I know would be dead by now. I have to do what I have to do.

Showered and calmer, I decide to visit Ivy at her work. I'm not sure why. I guess I want to see how she's doing after last night's... *talk*. There's not much else to do since I can't go to work and the police haven't called on me for anything. The car is still in their possession, so I can't even take a drive to the coast. It would take me all day to get there and back. That would have been nice. Well, it's not an option.

I take a slow walk to see Ivy. Today, she's at the nursery entertaining the children of single parents and those who have two working parents that want dirt-cheap (also known as *free*) childcare. Mum is with the over-60s. I may have complaints about the church, but this one at least does useful things in the community. If they aren't helping people, it's not because they're not trying to.

I step into the church building and stand in the lobby area. I walk over to the play room, a short distance from the front door, and peer inside. Ivy is building a block tower with a little girl who I'd say is about two years old. I think I've seen the child around with her parents. Ivy looks adoringly at the child, whose focus and determination are to be commended.

"Another one?" Ivy says, holding on to a toy brick.

The little girl nods and claps enthusiastically.

"Ok, here you go."

The child grabs the brick and eagerly attaches it to the top of the growing tower. It's ugly and unbalanced but I can forgive that since she's a toddler. The girl squeals with delight once she's done, and now it's Ivy's turn to clap with enthusiasm.

I smile and back away from the door. Ivy's busy doing (and enjoying) her job and now I'm here, I don't know why I thought she would have time for me. Had she shown up unexpectedly at the office, there's no way I'd be able – or even willing – to drop everything and see her. What was I thinking?

I shake my head, wondering what came over me. I turn around and start towards the exit. As I approach the door, Pastor Seth spots me. Oh dear. He smiles broadly and walks over to me while I mentally prepare for Small Talk and an attempted hug.

"Donna, Ivy's sister!" he beams.

Well at least he got my name right. Half the people I meet in this church never do, no matter how many times I (re)introduce myself.

"Yeah," I say, smiling and keeping my distance. "How's it going?"

"It's going well. How are you?"

"I'm ok."

"Are you looking for your mum or Ivy? I can get them for you."

"No, that's fine. They're busy. I should let them be. But thank you."

I smile and walk past him. I hear him pick up the pace behind me.

"Donna," he says.

I stop. Turn around. Face him.

"I don't mean to pry, but... Ivy asked for prayers for your health. She told me about the break-in over the weekend and what... happened..."

I nod. "And...?"

"I know we don't know each other, but I wondered if you needed help in any way."

His eyes are clear, though his brows are creased. The state of my face must inspire pity. If I didn't know better, I'd even say he cared. I guess it's his job to at least try.

"The police are handling it."

"As they should," he smiles. "What I meant was – do you need to talk about things? We have a lot of people here are good at listening. Counsellors, therapists... that sort of thing."

"Why talk when you have nothing to say?"

"I understand. If you change your mind, we're here for you," he says.

The sincerity in his voice is unsettling. I'm so used to being around self-involved, self-serving, treacherous people that the thought that there are people in the world that don't live like that is... disconcerting.

I look at him, searching his face for any traces of deceit, looking for any ticks or giveaways. I don't find any at this point.

"Thank you," I finally say.

I turn to leave, then stop as a thought crosses my mind. Facing him again, I say, "What else has she told you?"

"About...?"

I shrug. "Anything, I guess."

"She mentioned that you were in the hospital, and we prayed for you. You're out and on your feet now, so thank God."

"Did she tell you why I was there?"

He nods.

"Did she tell you what happened to the burglar?"

"She did."

I nod.

Is that all she's told him?

"I guess you think I'm going to hell because I killed someone."

"You're not dead yet, so I don't know where you'll end up," he says. It's all very matter-of-fact.

"But what if my heart expired right now? If I dropped dead at your feet, you think I'd wake up in hell because I've killed someone, right?"

Why am I asking about this? I know it doesn't matter.

"No, Donna. You'd end up in hell because you rejected Christ's payment for your sins. You'd have to pay for them yourself. The fact that you killed someone is beside the point."

I shake my head. "How can you say that? That doesn't make any sense."

"Maybe we should chat somewhere quieter," he says.

I look over at the room that Ivy is in. She won't leave there for a while longer, I reckon. I have no pressing matters to attend to, and this is the very opposite of Small Talk. I suppose I have no reason to say no.

"Lead the way."

***

We sit in the counselling room, him on a grey tattered couch and I on a better-quality green one that is placed opposite his. The door is wide open and people walk past in the corridor, chattering as they go by. It's quieter, but it is not quiet. Not by my standards, anyway. He sits, drinking tea from a mug that reads, 'World's Second-Best Dad.' Someone in his family has a sense of humour. I declined to drink anything. I don't plan to be here for long.

"You seem somewhat apprehensive."

"I'm not," I say. "Why would you say that?"

He smiles. "I don't know. It's an impression I get."

"I'm fine, thank you."

He takes a sip of tea.

"You remind me of Ivy when she first started working here," he says.

No one has ever said I remind them of Ivy. Ever.

"How so?"

"She came across as very reserved and… uneasy. It was like she couldn't relax, not really. You give off the same vibe."

I see.

"You said that it didn't matter that I'd killed someone. What did you mean by that?"

"I didn't say it didn't matter, I said regarding where you go after you die, it was beside the point."

"Meaning…?" I say.

"Meaning: you've sinned in ways smaller and less dramatic than ending someone's life. You've sinned maybe in more ways than you can count. And, yes, sinners go to hell, but you're not a sinner because you've sinned – you've sinned because you're a sinner."

I listen intently, trying to properly digest what he's saying.

"You've lied, as all people have. You've not always put God ahead of yourself. No one but Jesus has. It's unlikely that you've always respected your parents. You've killed someone. Right?"

I nod slowly, lowering my gaze. I've killed *people*, but other than that minor quibble we're on the same page.

"You've done those things because humans are corrupt by nature. Jesus said that evil comes from the heart. Your heart is evil because you were born that way. Just as you were born genetically predisposed to certain things, you were born spiritually predisposed to sin. From birth, you've had the desire to be God, to dethrone Him, which at its core is what sin is. And so you do what your nature tells you to – you sin, even if you don't *really* want to sometimes. What you do flows from who you are. And the wages of sin is death – ultimately, eternal death in hell. Think of it as a spiritual prison for all of time's spiritual criminals."

"But I didn't make myself. And I didn't ask to be born. How is any of this my fault?" I ask.

"Yes, no one asked to be born, but here we are. You didn't make yourself black or female; you didn't give yourself brown eyes or dark hair. You inherited those physical traits from your parents, or their parents. And all of us and our ancestors have Adam and Eve to thank for the will to sin – because we're all descended from them, we've all inherited their innate sinfulness. There's nothing we can do about the things we can't control or things we had no say over. We can control what we do about Christ," he says, lifting his mug to his mouth.

I ponder what he's said. For the first time in my life, a religious conversation is actually making some kind of sense. How thrilled would Ivy be to hear that?

"So… I sin because I'm wired for it, and I go to hell because I sin. You know, that actually seems fair."

"It is fair, but it's not ideal."

"Nothing in life is ideal. Nothing," I say. I close my eyes, surprised by how emotionally drained I feel.

"Do you want to go to hell?" he asks. My eyes fly open and my head leans to the side. I look at him, noting his crow's feet.

I didn't think he was that old.

"I ought to. It would make sense for the whole world to go to hell. It would be just," I say, exhaling and leaning into the sofa.

It *would* be right. Humans are the worst thing in the universe.

"I agree that it would be fair, and right, but God loves people too much to give them what they deserve. He is just and He is holy, but He is also love. And since our first nature is corrupt and we can't do anything to change that, He had to help us, hence Jesus."

"Again, meaning…?"

"God came to earth as a human, the man we know as Jesus. He did everything right, by the power of the Holy Spirit – to show that through the Holy Spirit's power, we can live lives that God approves of. We can live holy lives, free from sin's chokehold. Jesus did that. And then He gave Himself up to be killed, so that if we trust in Him, we don't have to go to hell."

Is this fan-fiction?

"Ok, I don't understand that at all."

"It's like this: you sinned, you violated God's sacred law and because God is holy and a just judge, He has to sentence you to hell for the entirety of eternity. But God loves you in a way that you can't even fully comprehend, and He doesn't want you to pay for your sins. Have you ever loved someone so much that you'd do anything to prevent them from suffering? Or you'd go to any length to stop the suffering they're already going through?"

I swallow hard. "Yes."

"Well, God loves you much more than that, and by becoming a man and dying on the cross, He paid the penalty for all your sins – past, present and future. Sin leads to death, both physically and spiritually. You sinned and for that you should die, but Jesus died instead of you. You did the crime and He did the time. Because He died and resurrected, if you accept what He's done for you... if you accept His payment for your sins, you don't have to go to hell for any of the wicked things you've done. You can simply admit your sins to God, tell Him you're sorry for them, leave them behind and start getting to know Him. It's what you would do if you wanted to repair a relationship with someone. As your relationship with Him grows and deepens, it'll be easier to trust Him to walk with you through life, and let His Holy Spirit empower you to obey His laws, which are only good. He loves you so much that He doesn't want to live without you."

I exhale loudly. That was a mouthful. It all sounds strange, a little too good to be true. That means that it most likely is too good to be true. It's like a big cosmic fairy tale, with Jesus cast as the Charming Prince and the human race as the Damsel in Distress. Or maybe Jesus is a superhero, and the humanity is once again the Damsel in Distress.

It sounds like fantasy, yes, but it is starting to make sense to me. Ah, but all this talk of spirit, holy or otherwise, kind of bugs me. I look at him as he silently sips from his mug.

"You really believe all of this?"

He nods, taking the mug away. "I know God and His love and power, first hand. I've seen God do too much to believe anything else."

He comes across as an honest man, and that is not an easy thing to do. As a rule, I assume men are habitual liars, brutal and animalistic, and I've rarely ever been proven wrong. He seems like he might be one of the rare ones. I could be wrong, of course. That too is possible.

I sigh and lean forward. "Thank you for taking time to talk to me."

I stand up.

"Oh, no problem. Do you have any other questions?" he asks. He stands as well, looks eager to keep talking. I've had enough for one day.

I shake my head. "That's all for now. But I know where you are if I think of anything else."

"Wonderful. Will you wait for Ivy or your mum?"

"No, I have... other things to do."

I extend my hand and he shakes it.

"God bless you," he says.

A kind thing to say.

XV

IVY

I had a great morning running around with the children. They are one of the purest joys that life has to offer, like the sunset or moonlight or the sound of the ocean waves on a quiet night. Penelope built a brick tower and christened it Moon Tower, because according to her it's going to moon. It's getting dismantled and going back in the box, but she doesn't need to know that.

Ricky kept me entertained with animal noises and I was very impressed to find that at 2 years old, he knows that both milk and cheese come from cows. As Donna would say, that pleases me.

At no point did I think about my home life. I was happily distracted by the excitement and warmth of these delightful little ones. As they troop out, hugging me on their way, the euphoria starts to dissipate. One by one, I start to think about their futures, wonder whether in two decades' time they too will be murderers, or some other sort of criminal. I try to push the thoughts aside, hugging the little ones tightly, praying their lives don't go off the rails. With a heavy heart, I return to reality.

Lottie, Christina and I put the toys and boxes away. They chat non-stop but I find myself ignoring them. My mind wanders to my new Donna-induced predicament. All this time I thought the thing I had to watch out for was her being rude to mum. It could have been much worse than that. "Inaction has consequences," Donna said last night. I for one am glad those consequences did not involve her poisoning mum to death. Things to be grateful for.

"Ivy!"

I jump and turn around to find Christina and Lottie staring at me.

"What? What's wrong?" I say.

"Are you ok? That's the fourth time she called you," Christina says, her tight eyes full of concern.

"I'm fine, lost in thought, I guess," I say, smiling. "What did you need me for?"

"Nothing pressing," Lottie says, with raised eyebrows. I smile at her, hoping she doesn't ask any more questions.

Seth walks in and spreads his arms wide. "You ladies are amazing!"

"You're too kind, Seth," Christina says.

"I only speak the truth. Anything to report?"

I turn back to the store and shove another box into it.

"No, everything went swimmingly," Lottie says.

Another box goes in and I shut the door.

"Ivy."

I turn around. "Bro Seth."

"Your sister was here earlier. I think she was looking for you."

I freeze upon hearing that.

"Oh, what did she want?" I grab my jumper at the wrist and tug on it.

My words are hurried. I think they notice because they stare at me quizzically.

"She didn't say, but we had a nice chat," he says.

"Oh really?" I ask, curling the hem around my fingers. "What about?"

"Life, death, Jesus, hell – you know, the simple things."

I laugh a little. "Oh ok."

An awkward silence envelopes the room as Lottie, Christina and Seth stare at me. I realise that I've wrapped my jumper's hem so tightly around my wrist that it might leave a mark. I drop my hands and hold them behind my back, smiling sheepishly as my gaze hits the ground.

"Are you sure you're ok?" Lottie asks.

I raise my head and nod. "Absolutely."

They look on, unconvinced.

***

I have to persuade Donna to go to the police. I can't live with this secret – I won't let her do so either. I've made up my mind and there's no turning back. At home, I search the place and find that she isn't here. I left mum at the church. She wanted to come home with me but I convinced her to stay and have coffee with some of the other ladies. Had I known that Donna wouldn't be here, I may have thought better of that. I don't want to be here on my own, not after the break-in.

I hope Donna returns soon. Thankfully, I have no other commitments for the rest of the day. I wonder where she is. I call her and it goes right to answer phone. I hang up without leaving a message. I hope she's not avoiding me. More than that, I hope and pray that she isn't out hurting people. I don't think I can take any more trouble. Well, there's nothing to do now but wait.

I go to my room and change into my indoor clothes – a pink vest, blue hoodie and a pair of black tracksuit bottoms – and sit on my bed eating from a packet of bread. I say eating from, but in truth I have every intention of eating every slice of bread in this packet. I don't need it toasted, that's just being extra. No – soft, fluffy, plain bread does it for me. No one I know seems to understand this.

I'm halfway through the bread when the doorbell rings. I think about who it could be. It's too late for the post and Donna and mum both have keys. I start to panic at the thought of the house being invaded again. Donna has made no attempt to talk about what happened on Friday night. Was she afraid as well? I toss the packet of bread on the bed, but not before wrapping it up. Dry bread is not for me. I step off the bed and pick up a cricket bat that I keep nearby. It's been decorated with glitter and stickers, courtesy of a bunch of the children at church.

I walk to the door, taking each step as stealthily as possible. I know it's unlikely that a burglar would ring the bell before trying to get into the house, but you never know. He might come disguised as a utility worker, or a neighbour's friend. The bell rings again as I approach the door. I peer through the peephole and see a tall, older man that I don't recognise. He's well-dressed, carrying a briefcase. He looks slightly agitated, rocking from side to side like he needs the loo. His coat alone looks like it cost more than all my earthly possessions.

I place the bat by the door, within easy reach, and raise my voice. "Who is it?"

"Miss Palmer, is that you?"

Yes, but no one calls me that.

Either this is someone Donna works with or it's not a social call. Someone from the police, perhaps?

"I said who is it?"

"William Sanders, from Sanders Staunton & Co," he says.

Oh, I see. The man in charge has come to pay Donna a visit. It's less than 24 hours since she killed his son-in-law. I wonder what he wants from her.

"She's not here, sorry."

"To whom am I speaking?" he asks.

I crack the door open and he steps back, putting one hand behind him.

I take in his appearance, leaving the latch on the door. "Do you have any ID?"

He nods. I beckon with my hand. He fumbles around in his coat pocket as I keep my other hand close to the bat. He produces a wallet, takes out his driver's licence and hands it to me. I take a good look at it, and yes, this is in fact the senior partner of Donna's firm. I pass the licence back to him.

"Donna isn't here. I don't know when she'll be back."

"May I wait for her?"

I want to ask why he isn't doing something more productive at this time of day, but that's the sort of thing she would do. That is how I know it would be rude. Besides, she'll probably be back soon anyway. I close the door, unhook the latch and open the door wide.

I smile. "Please, come in."

"Thank you," he says, as he enters the flat.

441

He looks around the entrance hall. I shut the door behind him and pick up the cricket bat.

"Straight through," I say.

He turns to me and lifts his brows when he sees the bat. He tenses up, then smooths his lapels. "Is that for me?"

"There was a break-in over the weekend… just being cautious."

He nods. "Of course, I was sorry to hear that. These are dangerous times."

He turns and walks through to the kitchen.

"Would you like some tea?" I follow a little distance behind him.

"Yes, please."

We get to the kitchen and I point to one of the stools. He takes a seat. I place the bat against the fridge and lift the kettle, filling it with a cup's worth of water.

"Chamomile?"

He nods. "That's fine."

He takes his coat off and drapes it over the adjacent stool, putting his brief-case on top of the coat. He leans forward with his arms folded on the worktop, adjusting his expensive-looking cufflinks. They resemble a pair that dad used to wear. If I remember clearly, they were a gift from his mistress. He probably gave her a black eye in return. As for Mr. Sanders, he's certainly making himself at home without being invited to. I look at him, maybe suspiciously. I can't see my face so I can't be sure.

"Are you Donna's sister?"

The faint lines on his forehead appear more pronounced when he talks.

I nod. "Ivy. Pleased to make your acquaintance."

"And yours, Ivy. That's a pretty name."

I shrug. "I didn't choose it."

"I suppose not. You're here on your own?" He wrings his hands as he asks.

"Clearly not since you're here too," I say, smiling.

I turn the kettle on. He smiles back. I open a cupboard to fetch a tea bag.

"I see that wit is a familial trait," he says, caressing his chin.

I shut the cupboard; put the tea bag in one of our *visitors-only* mugs.

"What brings you to see Donna?"

He sits up straight, looks at the counter. The kettle gets louder in the background. It's a really noisy kettle which Donna is forever threatening to replace. The sound swells until it's in the foreground. He opens his mouth but I smile and put my hand up. He pauses and my hand stays up until the water boils. I pick the kettle up and pour the water into the mug.

"Sorry about that. Milk? Sugar?"

"No, that's fine, thank you."

I present the mug to him.

"Thank you," he says.

"So, you want to talk to Donna about…?"

"The police told me what happened last night. I wanted to check on her, see how she's doing," he says, clenching his jaw.

"The man who attacked her was part of your family."

His mouth moves but he doesn't say anything. He hesitates. Slowly, he starts to nod. "Yes, my son-in-law."

He lowers his eyes until they settle on the mug.

"Do you know why he tried to kill her?"

He shakes his head. "I was hoping that she could tell me more about what happened. Help me understand what was… going through his mind."

He looks up at me, squinting. "It doesn't add up. Daryl was not a violent man."

"I never met him, and Donna doesn't really talk much about work."

"She doesn't?"

I shake my head, folding my arms as I lean against the wall. "No, never. I didn't know she was defending that Casino man until she was on TV."

I sigh, closing my eyes. I open them again and my gaze lands on the fridge, going lower until it rests on the cricket bat.

There's too much I don't know about her.

"We can't always talk about the work we do," he says, before taking a sip from the mug.

443

"Well, she doesn't talk about any of it. I know a few names, fewer faces, but that's all. It's almost like she's a spy."

"I see," he says. "And she has no idea why Daryl would want to hurt her?"

I look at him and shake my head.

"Hmmm," he says. He takes another sip. "My daughter is in a very fragile state."

"I'm sorry to hear that."

He nods. "Thank you. I wish I could comfort her, but…" He looks off into the distance as his eyes go misty.

"But what?"

He blinks, clearing his throat. He looks at me and smiles. "It's nothing. One never expects tragedy to strike, that's all."

"I know what you mean." I bite my lower lip, remembering the feelings of hope and sadness that welled up when dad was declared dead. To this day, my feelings for him are… muddled, but his death could still be classed as an unexpected tragedy. I know now that there was more to it than that. No, I can't let those thoughts in, at least not for the time being.

He gulps down the rest of the tea and stands up.

"Thank you for your hospitality," he says.

Would it be rude of me to let him leave so soon? Will that make her look bad?

"Oh, you don't have to leave. She'll probably be back soon."

He looks at me.

I smile at him widely. "You can have some more tea if you like."

He smiles back. "Thank you, Ivy. That would be nice."

"Ok."

He sits back down.

I fill the kettle with more water and switch it on.

XVI

DONNA

I left the church armed with knowledge but lacking direction. I'm sure I've heard Ivy say some of those things before, but they never really seemed relevant to my life. I walked half an hour to a park in the vicinity. I needed to clear my head. It was a nice stroll. I found a bench near the pond and claimed it, as I like to do.

I've been here for a few hours, turning over this new information in my mind. If it's true, my goose is beyond cooked. If it's true, I'm living on borrowed time. I've had more brushes with death than most normal people, yet I'm still here. That can't be an accident.

I'm staring at the ducks that gather at the edge of the pond, scratching their bellies and sun-bathing or whatever it is they do. They look happy and calm, and that in turn calms me down. I close my eyes and pray silently, *"God, if everything the pastor said is true, help me believe it. I don't want to believe lies."* I open my eyes and feel no different. I'm not sure if I thought I would. Well, I've lost nothing by trying. I lean against the bench. The sun shines brightly but with little heat, struggling to warm my face on this cold day.

I find my phone and switch it on. Though I knew the police might have tried to contact me, I didn't want any distractions while I thought things through. It turns out I didn't miss anything. Ok, that's not strictly true – there is a missed call from Ivy but I doubt it's urgent. I call her back in case she wants me to get something from a shop.

The phone rings three times before she answers.

"Hey Ivy, sorry I missed your call."

"Miss Palmer, Ivy can't come to the phone at the moment."

I freeze when I hear the voice. I recognise it instantly.

"Mr. Sanders…?"

What is happening?

"Your sister is quite charming, Miss Palmer."

I sit up in the bench and my stomach flips.

Why is he in the flat? Why is he taking Ivy's calls? Is she ok?

I do my best to stop my voice from shaking. "What do you want, Bill? Where's my sister?"

"Ivy is making me another cup of tea. She's very good company…"

I leap off the bench so suddenly that the ducks scatter. Very quickly, I start down the winding path that leads to the park's exit.

"If you lay a finger on her—"

"Sorry, the kettle's boiled. I must dash."

He hangs up. I immediately call a taxi company as I get to the park's exit. And then I wait, listening to nothing but the sound of my heart's uncontrollable pounding.

XVII

IVY

We're in the living room now. William, as he insists I call him, is showing me pictures of his daughter. On his phone, he has photos dating back to when she was a foetus in a sonogram. She's his only child, clearly the apple of his eye. I get the impression that any sadness he may feel over his son-in-law's death has less to do with the man and more to do with him empathising with his child. Not once has he mentioned Daryl since he got his second cup of tea.

At his request, I get up to fetch his third brew. When I return to the living room, he's sliding my phone across the coffee table in front of him, away from himself. I look at him, feeling my brows lift and my eyes enlarge.

"Oh, that was your sister," he says, like it's no big deal.

"You answered my phone?"

"Yes, she said to say hello," he says. He reclines on the sofa with one leg crossed over the other. His top foot lightly caresses the bat (a work of art, in his estimation) as it rests against the coffee table. I get the impression that he believes he can do whatever he wants wherever he goes. Maybe I shouldn't have asked him to stay.

"Um, thanks, but I didn't give you permission to touch my phone," I say, holding the mug. I should have taken it with me.

"Oh, I apologise profusely. I thought I was being helpful. Considering how hospitable you've been, it seemed like the least I could do. I didn't mean any harm." He places one hand on his chest and folds over, lowering his eyes.

"That's ok. I— you know what, it's fine. Thank you for being so… thoughtful."

"No, Ivy. Thank you for being so charitable."

For no discernible reason, a chill runs down my spine.

"Well, I'm sorry I've kept you this long. Should you be getting back to your family… or work?"

"No, I'm quite enjoying getting to know you."

If by getting to know me he means talking about his daughter, he's accurate.

"The perks of being the boss," I say, with a nervous laugh.

"Indeed. May I have the drink now?"

I hesitate, clasping the mug in my hands, despite the heat.

He smiles. "Well then, I suppose I should leave you in peace."

As he starts to move, I step forward and place the mug on the coffee table.

"There's no rush, William, really. You can at least finish the tea."

He nods. "I will. Thank you."

I smile at him and he reciprocates. Perhaps it's the crookedness or the reptilian look his eyes possess, but something about his smiling face puts me on edge. I move the cricket bat far away from him, placing it on the table near the corridor.

And then I start praying silently.

XVIII

DONNA

Almost eight minutes and we're here. I practically throw the money at the cab driver when he pulls up outside the building. It might be more than we agreed, but I don't care. He can have it, buy his car some sort of air freshener.

I hold onto my side and race out of the car, into the building, into and out of the lift, to the flat's door. I pause for a moment, catching my breath, stroking my wound. I pull my key out of my bag and put it into the lock. I start to think about all the awful scenarios that may be waiting for me on the other side of the door. Has he hurt Ivy? Will I be able to come back from this? I prayed so hard on the drive over that I feel I must now be a convert.

I turn the key in the lock, open the door.

"Oh, there she is!" I hear Ivy say in a raised voice.

She sounds unharmed. I breathe a sigh of relief even before I see her. I step into the flat and the door shuts behind me. She comes into the hallway, bounding towards me.

"Hey," she says, lowering her voice.

"Are you ok?"

She shrugs and puts her hands up, as though unsure.

I hug her tightly, not wanting to let go. But I have to.

"Are *you* ok?" she asks, looking at me.

I half-nod and half-shake my head at the same time. I walk past her to the kitchen. Bill isn't there.

"Your boss is—"

"I'm in here," his voice calls out from the living room. I brace myself for some form of confrontation and walk across to meet him. He sits on the sofa, spread out as though he paid the mortgage. This man thinks he owns everything.

"Mr. Sanders, what brings you here?" I try to sound cool and in control. No matter what he thinks or how he acts, he's on my territory. I stand in the corridor, waiting for his reply.

"I heard about your unfortunate run-in with Daryl, thought I should see how you're faring," he says. He stands up, towering over everything else in the room.

"That's kind of you." I lean against the table that mum's ugly lamp once rested on. "I suppose I should extend my condolences to you and your family."

"Veronica is devastated, as one would expect."

I bite the inside of my cheek, feeling genuine pity for her and her children.

Ivy comes from behind me, gently touches my shoulder. "Shall I leave you two alone?"

"Oh, please don't," Bill says, "Yours is such pleasant company."

She almost smiles, looks from him to me. Our eyes meet as hers go wide. I know her well enough to register her discomfort.

"There's no need for you to be here, Ivy."

"I disagree." Bill pulls a gun from behind him and points it at us.

Not again.

"What the hell, William?" Ivy says, jumping.

William? In an afternoon, they're on first name basis? Seriously?

"You know what they say – if you want something done right… I can't for the life of me work out how someone as kind as you," he says, pointing the gun at Ivy, "could be related to someone as cruel as her."

He points the gun at me now. Wonderful. My chickens have come to roost in my literal home. At long last.

"The good genes are recessive in me," I say, stepping in front of Ivy.

He smirks.

"Whatever is on your mind, Bill, it's between you and me."

"We're past that now, Miss Palmer. Way past that. You've caused me more pain than I could have imagined."

"Don't be so dramatic. You didn't even like Daryl!"

"True – I hated him, despised him. I should thank you for getting rid of him. Sadly, now that he's dead, I see how much Veronica loved that urchin. She's crushed. Can you believe it? I would comfort her but she's ignoring my calls, because of those recordings."

His voice trembles when he talks about Veronica and his pain. It's strange to see him – or any man of his size – express any emotion other than blind rage.

"What recordings?" Ivy whispers. I squeeze her hand, hoping she says no more.

"Oh Bill, I'm sure she'll change her mind when the hoopla dies down."

"And if she doesn't?" he asks, drily.

I know it's rhetorical. Still, I answer. "Well, Bill, you tried to have me killed – twice. There was no need for that. I— *we* had an understanding, an agreement. I believed you but you broke your word. You did this to yourself."

"What are you—?"

"Ivy, darling, come over here for a second," he says, interrupting her question. He waves the gun at her like he's gesturing to a child. I feel her clutch my hand hard. She squeezes it with such force that I think she might break it.

"Oh God, have mercy," she says in short, sharp breaths.

"She's not going anywhere near you," I say, looking right at him. I step in front of her, shielding her from his view.

"Do you want me to shoot you?"

"You have no power here, Bill. Your career is over; your family hates you;

451

you could shoot me and it will accomplish nothing. You've lost everything – your position, your reputation, your family. I beat you. Get over it," I say.

It's probably unwise to provoke a man who is pointing a gun at me, but I can't help but gloat. I rarely ever get a chance to. If this is my last stand, I might as well do the most. Should he open fire, Ivy will at least have time to get away.

He cocks the gun, looks sternly at me. "I have nothing left to lose."

My chest feels tight.

He continues, "You didn't have to bring my family into this—"

"I didn't bring them into this, Bill. You did. You're the one who betrayed them. That has nothing to do with me."

"Well, I hope you see this the same way. I'm going to kill your sister and then I'm going to kill you."

I look in his eyes and I know that he intends to make good on his threat. Has he thought this through? Does he have an exit strategy? Is a clean-up crew waiting outside to move in once he's done?

There might be an opportunity for one of us to escape, but not both of us. It has to be Ivy. I put myself in this position – she shouldn't have to suffer for my sins. Ah, my sins of which there are so many. I wish she could read my mind, see how sorry I am for all the disappointment and pain I've caused her. I guess she'll never know. I hope she can at least read the room and run at the right moment. I hold her hand for dear life.

"Counter-offer: you kill me and let Ivy go."

"No!" she yells. "Don't listen to her."

Ivy wrenches her hand from mine and walks out in front of me. "She's lost her mind. I don't know what she did to you, but you don't have to kill us. I know that you're hurting and your family is, too, but in time they'll forgive you for whatever it is that you've done wrong. The people who love you always forgive you."

"I often marvel at how the same parents can produce such wildly dissimilar offspring. Your sister is the devil, Ivy, yet you are a saint," he says, shaking his head.

She walks over to him, as I follow close behind her, pawing at her hands which she repeatedly snatches away from me. He takes a couple of steps forward as I reach out for her. My hand is a hair's breadth from her shoulder when he hits her in the face with the gun. She flies into me, and we topple over.

"You're lovely, but I still have to end your life," he says.

I find my footing, lifting her up with me. She holds onto her face, crying. I grab her by the shoulders and shake her. "I'm sorry, Ivy. I'm so sorry that I got you involved in this mess. But it's my mess and I have to clean it up."

I leave her shaking on the spot, still holding her face. I turn to Bill and walk right up to him with my hands in the air. He keeps the gun on me. I hear Ivy sobbing. I can't give that any thought, not now.

I'm right in front of him now, the gun pointed directly at my chest. We're probably a foot apart. There's no *Matrix*-style dodging this.

I shrug. "What now?"

"On your knees," he says.

They always want you on your knees.

I kneel in front of him.

"Please don't do this," Ivy says. She sounds closer than she was a moment ago.

"I'm sorry, darling, but your sister has left me no choice."

"Our Father who art in Heaven…" She audibly recites The Lord's Prayer.

Is now the time? For goodness' sake, run!

He moves the gun so that it's aimed at my head. Not long now.

"Any last words?" he asks, ignoring Ivy's communication with God.

"A few," I say, and then I say nothing.

One beat.

And another.

"Well… what are they?"

Curiosity kills.

"I've met men like you before, William – you're nothing special," I say, lifting my head, fixing my eyes on his. "My whole life, I've been confronted by men who think it's their right to take whatever they want, and do whatever they want, simply because it's what they want. I've known men who have tried to bully, intimidate, force their way into places regardless of whether or not they were qualified to be there or whether or not they were even wanted there. Yes, William, you're nothing special. You're just more of the same. And do you know what all those men have in common?"

"Please tell me, I'm gagging to know."

"They all died by my hand. Every last one of them. Your fate will be no different from theirs, because you are no different from them."

"You say that, but I'm the one holding the gun, and you're the one on your knees," he says, pressing the gun into my forehead. The cold barrel feels hard enough against my skin that it'll likely leave a mark before he dispatches me.

"You say that, but I've recorded every word of this encounter on my phone."

His brow furrows. I reach into my back pocket and wave my phone over my head. He grabs it from me, frantically pushing the buttons. His other hand – the one holding the gun – starts to shake.

As I start to move, I feel the barrel scrape skin off my forehead as it lifts away from me. He stumbles back, and something heavy drops on the ground next to me, missing my arm by mere inches. I look down and see the cricket bat that some children at church vandalized a few months ago. I realise that Ivy must have thrown it right at his head.

Thank you, Ivy.

As he falls, the gun flies out of his hand. Instead of diving for it, I pick the bat up and hit him in the knees. I toss the bat away and out of his reach. I pull the stick out of my hair and hurl myself at him. I mount him, stabbing him three times in quick succession, in the hand with which he held the gun. He screams in pain. Ivy cries out. I turn for a second, see her holding her hands on her head. I'm sorry she has to see this but he came to our house and threatened to kill us, not the other way around. He asked for this.

My breathing is uneven and loud. I should beat him to death with that ugly bat but that would take too much energy. I stand up and find the gun. Old Bill whimpers in an undignified manner. I'd feel sympathy for him if I wasn't offended by his existence. Besides, I made that mistake once and it almost cost me my life.

I point the gun at him as he wiggles around the floor, still whimpering.

"Ivy, I need you to leave. Call the police and don't come back until they get here, ok?"

"Donna, what are you doing?"

"Subduing the enemy." I look at her. "Go, Ivy. Get help."

Our eyes meet. She looks at Bill on the floor. His moans are getting louder and more irritating with each passing second. I want to shoot him if only to shut him up and have some quiet.

"What are you going to do to him, Donna?"

I return my focus to him as he struggles to speak.

"Yes, Miss Palmer," he says, coughing. "What are you going to do to me? Are you going to make my wife a widow? Like you did my daught—?"

"Shut up. Nobody called your name," I say.

"I'll call the police, but I'm not going anywhere until they arrive," Ivy says.

My index finger curls around the gun's trigger, almost as if it was autonomous.

"I'm asking you to leave so you don't have to see something you can never unsee."

"You don't have to kill him, Donna. He didn't do us serious harm," she says, walking slowly to me.

I feel the scratch on my forehead smarting. I touch it, realise that it's bleeding. I look at her face. It's starting to swell up.

"Not for lack of trying, Ivy. Not for lack of trying."

"If you kill him," she steps closer, "there's no turning back. This isn't something you'll be able to walk away from. Not this time. Donna, do you understand that?"

I listen to her, absorbing the words. He tries to retreat towards the sofa, but I shake my head, waving the gun at him. "Don't test me, Bill. You don't want to end up like Gary and Daryl."

"If you kill me—"

"Don't talk, Bill. Just shut up."

He stops moving, grabs his bloody hand with the one I haven't damaged yet.

"If you kill him—"

455

"What? God will hate me? He already does, Ivy."

"No, He doesn't. And He won't. But you will unleash consequences that you probably don't want to have to deal with." She takes another step. She puts her hand on my shoulder and says quietly, "You can take the high road, let the authorities handle him."

Ah yes, the mythical high road that's the supposed solution to every problem. The High Road that leads those who've been victimised to 'forgive' people who then go on to do more rape and murder when they should have been executed, or at least incarcerated, at the first opportunity. The High Road is a hoax, a con designed to free perpetrators to create more victims. I'm not taking that road. Not now, not ever.

"Donna, I know what you're thinking," she says.

"You have no clue what I'm thinking."

I lock eyes with Bill. He narrows his, like he's still got some fight in him. That's a bad sign. He backs up, despite my warning, until he's against the sofa. He lifts his shirt and wraps it around the bleeding hand. Ivy reaches for the gun, but I move away from her.

"If you're not going to kill me, can you at least call an ambulance?" he says, smirking.

"You're thinking that if you let him go," she says, ignoring him, "he'll hurt someone else."

I nod. "If there's only one thing I know, it's that dead people never get to hurt anyone else. If I let him go, he won't stop, Ivy."

I look at her.

She shakes her head. "I know that's a risk. I'm worried about that, too. He has money, he can manipulate the system. But please Donna, don't think about him. For once, think about yourself. All these deaths, all this violence… it's killing you. It's ravaging your soul and if you carry on like this, there's no telling what will happen."

Her voice is cool and unwavering.

"I'll probably wind up in jail," I say in an equally steady tone.

"I'm fairly certain that jail is the least of your worries."

"I think I'll die of boredom before I bleed to death. Are you calling an ambulance or not?"

Bill laughs after he speaks. His goading raises my heart rate. I want to kill him, I really do. Nothing would please me more right now than putting a bullet in his chest. However, I do not want to kill him in Ivy's presence, though this might be the only chance I get.

Is it worth it? In the grand scheme of things, have I actually helped anyone by murdering the people I did? Mina seems worse off than she was before Alan died, though there's a chance that her drug addiction would have manifested regardless of whether or not he lived. Am I really making the world a better place by killing these people? I want to believe I am, but for the first time since Alan's death, I'm not confident about that.

I'm unsure.

I don't do things that I'm unsure of.

I put the gun down, holding it by my side. If there's one thing I'm sure of, it's that I don't want Ivy to watch me kill anyone.

She wins.

From the corner of my eye, I see her exhale and look up, as though she could see God and was thanking Him directly.

"Call the police, Ivy. Let them do their job."

XIX

IVY

The ambulance arrived with the police in tow. Once the officers took our statements, they took Mr. Sanders away, presumably to the hospital. He seemed strangely unperturbed by the afternoon's events. I suppose there are more crazy people in the world than I had realised. I still can't quite believe that a man of his status would stoop to trying to kill someone by himself. Don't they have assassins for that sort of thing? What a weirdo.

Donna and I were both treated and now have new war wounds to silently bond over. It's like being children again, albeit marginally more disturbing. Either way, I'm glad that no blood was spilt today. I don't know that I would have recovered from seeing Donna kill someone, or get killed. I know I wouldn't have recovered from death, and I'm glad that didn't happen either. Praise Jesus for life.

Mum is still out, which is a blessing. It gives Donna and me time to talk things through. She walks the last paramedic out while I stay in the living room, composing my pitch. I organise my thoughts, say a short prayer and walk to the entrance hall in time to hear Donna cursing.

She doesn't do it much, but I hate it when she does.

"Must you curse?"

She apologises without resistance. "Sorry, I didn't… I'm sorry."

I don't say anything. She touches her face, stroking the bruises Daryl gave her last night.

"Does it hurt?" she asks.

"Nah," I say, touching my own cheek. "They doped me up real good."

I smile, but she doesn't.

"You did the right thing, Donna." I know she doesn't agree, but I have to help her see straight.

"We both know that's not true. As long as he's alive, we're not safe here," she says, shaking her head.

She says it like she knows for certain that he – or someone else – will burst in any minute and try to kill us.

"You can't be—"

"I can, Ivy, and I am sure. For all I know, someone is waiting for us outside or they're coming up in the lift to finish what he started. Maybe he'll call them at the hospital, I don't know. All I know is that we have to leave before he tries again."

"No, he won't. He may be desperate, but he's not stupid. If anything happens to us, the police will know he's behind it."

She groans and looks away from me. All this talk of trying again makes me wonder how we ended up here in the first place. He talked about some recordings, said she'd released them. What was that about anyway?

"Why does he want you dead?" I ask. "What did you do to him?"

She sighs. "Does it matter?"

Typical Donna – secretive and evasive.

I nod. "To me it does."

And then she tells me – that she found out about her boss's sexual predilections, both immoral and illegal, and when he tried to fire her, she used her discovery to secure a promotion. She wanted to tell the police about his visits to some massage parlour but she decided to cover her own backside instead. I'd be impressed if I wasn't horrified. This woman has guts, even if she misuses them. As she talks about how she did this for us, it occurs to me that she really believes that.

"This wasn't about keeping your job. It was about power."

"What?" she asks, with narrow eyes. The look on her face tells me that the thought had never crossed her mind.

I shake my head. She's too blind to see herself. "You can't stand the thought of anyone having power over you. You always have to be the strongest one, the one in control. This time was no different."

She raises her voice, just a little. "That isn't true. Do you think we can afford to live in a place like this on your salary? I know you love Jesus, but He isn't exactly the one keeping a roof over your head – I am. We'd have to sell the house and move to God-knows-where! Is that what you want?"

I turn my head to the wall, holding the back of my neck with both hands.

"I understand what you're saying, and I could nit-pick theologically, but whether you like it or not, keeping homelessness at bay is not the only reason you blackmailed your boss. He made you feel weak and small, and you couldn't live with that. And I get it. What we went through growing up – what dad put us through – it wasn't normal and it wasn't right. All the things he did to control us were wrong, and I understand that you never want to feel helpless or weak again. You don't want to be victimised ever again. That's why you blackmailed your boss, and it's why you wanted to kill him. You wanted to show him that you're more powerful than he is. That's why you killed dad, that's why you killed Alan Ellis and Beth Meyer, and the man who broke in here, and your colleague. You wanted to prove that you were stronger than them. You wanted them to know that you had power over their very lives."

She looks at me, dumbstruck. I lower my eyes, till I'm looking at her feet.

"That's not true," she says. "I killed them because I wanted us to be safe. I wanted to— to get rid of people who abuse others for sport. I didn't— I *don't* want to live in a world where people do appalling, irreversible things to one another and then get to walk off into the sunset like nothing's happened, like they haven't damaged lives. I don't want to live in a world where dangerous people are on the loose, free to keep causing destruction."

Her breathing gets louder. Maybe she's lying to herself or maybe she isn't telling herself the whole truth. She swallows hard and I can see that she's trying not to cry. It hurts me to see her so upset. Still, I have to push her in the right direction.

"What you describe is a world where you aren't welcome, Donna. You're dangerous, you've murdered people, and you'll keep doing it for as long as you see fit. Who's going to protect the world from you?"

She doubles over, as if I punched her in the gut. She starts crying and doesn't stop for a little while, sinking until she's sitting on the floor. I feel bad seeing her like this, but I don't try to comfort her. Let her cry it all out.

Even after every beating, she kept her head up. She never cried, no matter what dad did to her. Now, though, it looks like she's exhausted. She's had enough. I think that's for the best. I go to the living room and get a box of tissues, which I place next to her when I come back. I kneel in front of her as she keeps on crying. She wipes her tears and blows her nose.

When she's done, I hold her hands and stare at her. "Donna, you don't have to spend the rest of your life playing God – He's alive and well and He doesn't need you to be judge, jury and executioner. You should let Him do His job."

She nods and speaks quietly. "I can't stop Sanders without killing him. He won't let this go."

She rests her forehead against mine. "The police, Donna… tell the police."

I move away from her and rest my fingers under her chin. I lift her head so we're eye to eye.

"I'll have to tell them about the blackmail."

"I know," I say, nodding. I know and it rips my heart up because I know what that means for her. I know what that means for her future.

"I'll go to jail," she says. She breathes out and rests her head against the door. Her eyes look off into the distance. "Jail has never been in my plans."

"You might or you might not," I say, trying to hold on to the slimmest shred of hope. "You lawyers are always working things out behind the scenes, no?"

Stranger things have happened.

"You want me to tell them everything I did…"

I feel sadness well up in my heart until my eyes get damp. I look away from her, trying not to cry. I can't afford to cry now. We can't both sit here in a puddle of tears – that would be pathetic.

"I would recommend that… for your conscience's sake."

She breathes loudly. "Will you come with me?"

I clasp both her hands in mine. "Of course. I'm with you all the way."

She leans on my shoulder and cries some more. This time, I join her.

XX

DONNA

Ishould just move into the police station or the hospital. It feels like in the last few weeks I've spent more time in one or the other than I have at home. That'll all change soon enough. In due time, my permanent residence will be a prison cell. I'm trying not to think too much about that. If I thoroughly mull it over, I know I'll be inconsolable. I shouldn't give myself an opportunity to lose it. I have to face my fate with dignity.

Detective Miller comes into the interrogation room. He smiles at me, but only looks briefly at my face. I can only assume that, to some degree, he feels that I've let him down. I would have expected him to be beaming with pride, since he was sure that there was something unnatural about my reaction to corpses. His sombre expression takes me by surprise. Maybe gloating isn't something he enjoys. I suppose it takes all sorts.

"Miss Palmer," he says, nodding. He sits opposite me and places a recorder on the table.

"Detective," I say, nodding back. "Will your partner be joining us?"

"In a minute."

He taps a tune on the desk. I don't know if it's a real song or if he's just whiling away time. I look at his fingers as he taps. I lift one hand behind my head and breathe out through my mouth.

"Jeremy Haywood passed away in the last hour," he says, still tapping.

I drop my hand on the desk and look at him. "It had to happen at some point."

"Yeah, I guess."

I fold my hands together, looking at the door.

"I had thought that when we were done investigating his wife's death, you and I could get a drink. I see now that that is unlikely to happen." The tapping slows down.

I look at him as his eyes rise to meet mine. I shrug. "Yeah well, it would be unwise of you to be seen fraternising with a criminal."

"Would you have said yes? I mean, without turning around and cancelling..."

He tilts his head to one side, raising an eyebrow.

I smile wryly. "Your guess is as good as mine."

The door opens and Detective Lawson walks in. She nods in my direction and takes her seat next to Miller, who smooths his hair and adjusts his posture.

"Ready?" he asks her.

"Yes."

He turns the recorder on. Goodbye freedom.

***

I told them everything, from the first kill to my little blackmail scheme. I even told them of my part in the sabotage of Jeremy Haywood's case, though I did not implicate Mina and Suzanne. As I detailed all of my past misdeeds, Lawson looked like she couldn't believe her ears. Miller looked disappointed and shocked, and occasionally impressed.

I gave them all the evidence I had against Old Bill, including the recording of his attempt on our lives earlier in the day. They said they'd look into his involvement with Gary McDonald. Meanwhile, he's under arrest at the hospital for attacking us. The detectives tell me that the massage parlour will be investigated and, should he provide assistance in said investigation, Sanders will likely get less time for trying to kill me and Ivy. For some reason, that doesn't move me one way or the other. At least they were upfront about it.

I will be charged with the murder of Alan Ellis, William Palmer and Beth Meyer. They believed me when I told them that I killed Gary and Daryl in self-defence, which is good. I'm not yet sure that I'll be able to make any deals, since I have nothing to trade. Even if I did, I don't know that I'd be willing.

Miller offered me and Ivy a lift but we turned him down. Well, I turned him down. I wasn't in the mood for his puppy-dogging. Ivy called a cab which we're waiting for in the station's reception area.

As Ivy reclines in the uncomfortable chair, I rest my elbows on my thighs and keep my eyes low, thinking about the past week. In it, my actions – direct and indirect – have left two sets of children fatherless. Perhaps three, if Gary McDonald was a parent. I have a feeling that isn't something to be proud of.

"Donna?"

I raise my eyes. In front of me stands Zach. As I made my confession, I thought about him and wondered what he would think when news of my crimes reached him. Despite his occupation, he tries his best to see the good in people. It's his nature, just as seeing the bad in them is mine. And now he's here. I guess I don't have to wonder any longer.

I'm nervous but despite myself, I smile at him. "Zach… what are you doing here?"

He looks at Ivy, who is now sitting up. "Wow, Ivy, I haven't seen you in ages."

She smiles at him, stands up. "Yeah, it's been a while."

A brief hug, and then she turns to me. "I… need to use the restroom. I'll be back."

She walks away from us, leaving him staring at me. I clasp my hands together, resting them on my thigh. He sits in the spot she vacated, placing his hands on his knees. The subtle scent of musk wafts in my direction.

"What're you doing here?" I ask. I doubt he's here by chance.

"Working." He pauses, and then, "I heard—I heard you confessed to…

murder?"

His voice is quiet. The tone in which he says the last word reveals his shock. His lids look heavy, as he chews his lower lip. I won't bother asking who told him. I nod, then look at the ground.

"I don't know what to say… How do you feel?"

I smile, turning to him again. His eyes are locked on my face. His gaze is soft, one of concern, maybe more.

I shrug. "Unburdened, I guess."

He sighs, and moves to touch my hand. I turn my palm up, until our hands are fused.

"I don't know what you did, but I'm sorry that you felt you had to do it," he says, taking my hand to his mouth and kissing it gently.

He lets it go, then leans back in the chair, staring at the ceiling.

"That means a lot coming from you," I say.

"Yeah, well, you mean a lot to me," he says, glancing at me. A sad smile crosses his face. "But you already know that."

I lean over to him and kiss his cheek. "Thank you."

He faces me as I pull away. He smiles and sits up. "When can we get dinner together?"

He refuses to accept that he dodged a bullet.

I smile at him and shrug. "Maybe next week."

His eyes light up as he nods. "Great. Thank you."

I suppose I have nothing to lose.

***

The cab got Ivy and me home in one piece. When we get inside, Suzanne and Mina are with mum. I don't know why they're here. I didn't ask them to investigate anything. Maybe they have some kind of update on Aisha.

"Hey, what are you doing here?" Ivy asks them. She and Mina hug, while Suzanne salutes us both.

"I— Suzanne has a date and I didn't want to be alone, and… you'd said I was always welcome here…"

466

"And you are, of course," Ivy says.

"I thought I'd drop her off," Suzanne says.

Mum looks from me to Ivy. "Where've you been? I was worried."

If that was true, she would have called. She didn't.

Ivy and I exchange a look. She turns to mum and smiles. She opens her mouth to say something, but pauses and shrugs. She sighs and folds her arms in front of her, and then looks at me. They'll all find out eventually. Now is as good a time as any to tell them what's happening.

"We were at the police station," I say.

"Doing what? Is Haywood dead?" Suzanne asks. "He was still alive a couple of hours ago."

I sigh. "He is, but that's not why—I... I went to turn myself in."

Suzanne cocks her head, narrowing her eyes. "Turn yourself in... to a pumpkin?"

We all look at her and she shrugs, like her suggestion was valid.

"Turn yourself in for what?" Mina asks.

Ivy walks to the sofa and sits down, hands folded on her lap. She looks up at me, waiting for my response.

"Murder."

XXI

MINA

As Donna recounts her victims by name, I feel like the life is slowly ebbing from my body. Alan, Beth, Mr. Palmer. Donna murdered all of them. She plotted their deaths and saw to it that she carried out her plot. She'd made sure no one suspected foul play. I feel like throwing up as she describes in a clear, calm manner how she had concluded that each one of them *needed* to die.

"I thought it was the right thing to do," she says.

She then tells us about her attempt to blackmail her boss, using the information Suzanne and I unearthed, and how that yielded two more bodies and an attack on her and Ivy, mere hours ago.

I lose balance, feeling faint, but Suzanne catches me.

"Steady," she says.

She helps me to the sofa where Ivy shuffles over to make room for me. She manages a smile even under such dire circumstances. As bad as I feel, I appreciate that Donna glossed over her primary reason for wanting Alan dead. She didn't say much beyond stating that he was a bully and rapist. The delicacy with which she handled that bit of information moves me.

"How could you kill your father?" her mother asks. Her face is soaked with tears that tell me that it won't be easy for her to forgive Donna.

"Do you really have to ask?"

To my surprise, the question comes from Ivy. She stares at her mother pointedly. Mama Selene cradles her cheeks as she cries. She does not answer the question.

"You said you decided to kill Alan when you found out he was a rapist. How and when did you find out?" Suzanne asks. As usual, she appears entirely unperturbed by this information. With each revelation Donna has offered, she has seemed unmoved. I think she might be a sociopath.

"Word gets around," Donna says, looking at her feet. I unwittingly let out a sob. Suzanne turns to me, stares at my face as I hasten to look away from her. From the corner of my eye, I see her turn back to Donna.

"I see… Word has a way of doing that."

"What's going to happen to you?" I ask between sobs.

Donna shrugs. "I'll face justice, or something like it."

"For what it's worth, I think you should have taken this to your grave," Suzanne says. "We're all better off because Alan and Beth are no longer here. Never forget that."

Like I said, she's a sociopath.

Mama Selene gets up and leaves the living room. No one tries to stop her. Again, Donna has not made it clear why she felt the need to kill her father, but I'm sure I can work it out. The fact that Ivy doesn't seem too torn up about it tells me her reasons were sound enough. That or Ivy is just tired.

Donna smiles at Suzanne. "Has anyone ever told you that you're crazy?"

"No," Suzanne replies with a straight face.

I sit back in the sofa and hug my knees to my body, crying softly. Suzanne turns to look at me again. "You'll be ok, Mina. Life goes on… and in time, all wounds heal if you let them."

I look at her and she smiles.

"Well, I have a date, so I must go now," she says.

Donna nods. "I'll walk you out."

Suzanne waves at me and Ivy. "See you later."

They go to the door, and Ivy turns to me. "Will you be ok?"

"I don't know… I hope so."

We hear the door shut and Donna comes back to the living room. Our eyes meet. I can't read her. I've always had trouble with that.

"I shouldn't have taken the law into my hands. I should have found someone else to turn him in. I'm sorry… I denied you a real chance at justice. Can you ever forgive me?" she says.

I look at her as her lips tremble and her eyes fill with tears. Part of me thinks that my addiction came about when I realised that Alan's death meant I would never get closure for why he raped me. I don't know if that's true, but sometimes I think it is. But Donna was only doing what she thought was right. She wanted to help me when I was in too much pain to help myself. She did this, at least in part, because she cared about me.

"There is nothing to forgive."

She shakes her head and starts to cry. I get off the sofa and we embrace.

XXII

IVY

When they are done, Donna and I leave Mina in the living room and go to find mum. I knock on her bedroom door. Contrary to my expectations, mum opens it, her face bathed in tears and snot. It's not a pretty sight. She lets us into her room, and the first thing I do is grab some tissue from the box on her nightstand (as if she didn't know it was there). I hand it to her, and she wipes her face.

"What do you want?"

"To see if you're ok," I say.

Donna stands with her back against the door.

"I literally just learned that my daughter killed my husband and made it look like an accident. How can I be ok?"

I look at Donna, and she shrugs. I guess there's nothing to say. Mum looks at me, and then at Donna.

She shakes her head and starts crying again. "How could you have done that? How could you?"

"How could you not?" Donna says. Uncharacteristically, there is no venom in

471

her voice, only coolness. It sounds like a genuine question, like for the first time in her life she wants to understand mum's reasoning.

Mum shakes her head. "I loved him. Despite everything, I loved him. Is that so wrong? Is that so hard to understand?"

"He hurt us, mum. Beat us, threw us down staircases. He broke our bones, kicked us about. He called us awful, degrading names. He treated us like we were lower life forms. And you loved him? After all that, you loved him?"

She gets some more tissue and blows her nose. "I know that he did all those things, I was there. He did them to me too, but... he wasn't like that all the time. He wasn't all bad. He was brilliant and funny and talented, but he was also flawed and complicated. Which one of us hasn't done things we're not proud of? Does that mean we don't deserve love? What makes you think he didn't deserve a chance to do better? I know he would have got better if you hadn't..."

Her hand reaches for her forehead as she whimpers.

"He could have killed us, mum. Multiple times. He would have, eventually," I say.

"What did you want me to do? Go on the run? Spend the rest of my life dragging you two around, hiding from him? Is that the life you wanted?"

"It might have been better than the life we had," Donna says.

"If you really think he was capable of murder, what difference would it have made? He would have found us and killed us. You got to sleep in your own beds every night. Doesn't that count for something?"

"We didn't have to run away – you could have gone to the police," I say.

"And have him thrown in jail?" She shakes her head vigorously. "No, I would never have done that to him."

"How can you say that after all he put us through?" I can't believe her. If she wouldn't involve the police, then she really was prepared to die.

She puts both hands on her head. "I loved him... I still do, with all my heart."

Stockholm syndrome... even after all this time.

I feel a wave of sadness come over me. "The heart is deceitful above all things, and desperately wicked."

"If you'd ever been in love, you would understand," she says.

"Do you truly believe that?" Donna says.

Mum looks at her. Fresh tears spring to her eyes until she's sobbing again.

"Why didn't you kill me as well, like you killed Beth? You think of me as an accomplice, don't you?"

Donna shrugs. "I'm honestly not sure."

"How could you bring yourself to do such wicked things?" Her head is held high, like she's a judge.

"It is my nature."

Donna looks at me and beckons with her head. I walk over to her as she opens the door and leaves. I turn to mum and watch her sit on her bed, still crying. I want to say something, but I don't know what. She looks up at me and I nod slightly at her. I turn around and shut the door.

XXIII

DONNA

I wonder how Rebecca Staunton will react when she learns about this. Did she ever suspect that I had it in me to kill people? I'm sure Kat will be happy to see me imprisoned since I've deprived her of her worthless lover. She can move on to some other married man. Mistress today, mistress tomorrow, mistress forever.

I stop myself from trying to work out what every person I've ever met will think when the news travels. It doesn't matter. What's done is done. I can't change anything now. And though the weight of my actions is bearing down on me more heavily now I'm back home, there's still a part of me that believes that all I've done was for a good cause. Not even mum's ridiculous dramatics can fully convince me otherwise.

I'm sitting on the floor of my room resting my back against the bed, legs outstretched. I haven't done my leg-lifting routine today. I'm already trying to prepare myself for the future when I most likely won't have the luxury. I don't know if that's the best way to go about it, but the sooner I get used to going without, the better. I touch my side, where I was stabbed mere days ago. The bandages are still in place, despite my activity earlier today. They wound seems to be healing nicely. Will I get stabbed in prison? I've managed to get this far in life without being raped. Will that change once I'm 'inside'?

I touch my forehead and pull my legs up, resting my elbows on my knees. I look across at Ivy, who grimaces. She is sitting on the ground, backing the door as she often does.

"What?" she asks. "What's wrong?"

I shake my head and hug my legs tightly.

"All my nightmares are coming true." I laugh a little.

"Why are you laughing?"

"What else can I do?"

She mirrors my seating position and rests her head on her knees. "I'd say something, but you'd just scoff at me."

"Something about God?"

She nods. I shift my position and drop my knees to one side. "I came looking for you at church today, found your pastor instead."

"He said you two talked." I nod. "Was it— how was it?"

I breathe out through my mouth and rest my arm on the bed behind me. I use it to support my head. "It was… thought-provoking. I don't know… the things he said were rational, coherent."

She crosses her legs and leans forward slightly. She looks away from me, chewing the inside of her cheek, and then looks back at me. "I'm surprised to hear you say that."

"Yeah, I thought you would be. He told me that I'm a murderer because I was born that way," I say, smiling softly.

"He said that?"

"Not in so many words, but that was the crux of the matter… born with an evil, corrupt heart or will, like you always say. I deserve hell as much as dad and Alan… and all the others. It's hard to accept that that's true…"

I look up at the ceiling, massaging my scalp with my fingertips, as though that could relieve the tension I feel in my heart.

"But do you accept that it's true?"

I look at her. Her big eyes get bigger, almost like she's alarmed. I nod. "I do, yes."

She stands up and walks over to me. I take my hand off the bed and fold both hands together, placing them on my knees. She sits next to me, a little distance away.

"So what does that mean? What are you going to do about it?"

Her voice is quiet and soothing.

"I don't want to go to prison. Even though I know I've earned it, I don't want to go there... and I get the feeling that hell will be much worse."

"Oh, it will," she says, nodding her head very fast. "You don't want to know first-hand."

"I need help. I don't know if I can make it through another day in my... current state. I need Jesus. Only His blood can wash all this blood off my hands, take my sins away," I say, my voice getting quieter. "I can't think of anything or anyone else that can help me."

I bite my lower lip and start to cry.

"Hey, it's ok Donna. It's ok." She pulls me in for a hug and rests my head against her chest. "If you want Jesus, tell Him that. All you have to do is ask."

I sob and sniff and think about it.

Is this really what I want? Do I actually believe that this is the right thing to do, the right way to live?

The more I think about it, the more I realise that I do believe everything that Pastor Seth said. I believe that I need Jesus, and I would need Him even if I wasn't a murderer, or staring at a long prison sentence. And... if it turns out that I'm wrong I can always change my mind. I have nothing to lose.

Yet, I am afraid.

"What if it's too late for me? What if He says no?"

"As long as you're alive, it's not too late, and He would never say no. He said that He wouldn't turn anyone who comes to Him away. He's better than that," she says in a wobbly voice.

"Will you pray with me?"

"Absolutely."

Finally, her voice cracks.

XXIV

ONE YEAR LATER

IVY

I t's scary how quickly time passes. It drags and flies at once. I'm sitting in waiting area of the prison. It's almost Christmas again and I've brought Donna some gifts. Well, it's not much really, only a devotional book for next year. She's been devouring these things lately and it's a pleasant surprise.

In April she was sentenced to 8 years for each murder she confessed to, but because of the mitigating circumstances (her friend Zach recommended an excellent lawyer), she will serve them concurrently. Weirdly, she seemed disappointed to find that she wouldn't necessarily die in prison. She won't be able to practice law when she's out and I guess that upset her. What upsets me is knowing that she's not guaranteed to survive prison.

She also got a lighter sentence because the evidence she provided about the massage parlour helped the authorities in their investigation of a human trafficking ring. In June, Mr. Sanders (who did not cooperate with the authorities) was sentenced to 10 years for attempted murder, being an accessory to human trafficking, and a few other crimes. I didn't memorise the charges. It goes without saying that he was disbarred. After two months inside, he was killed by an inmate.

The firm is now called Staunton Mensah & Co. The only constant thing in life is change.

I see Donna walking to the seat, and I smile. She has a bandage over her eyebrow. It hurts me to see that. I guess I shouldn't be surprised. This is not the safest place to live, if television shows are to be believed. That said, it may be no more dangerous than the house we grew up in.

"Hey," I say, once she picks up the phone.

She smiles. "Hey."

I touch my eye. "You got into a fight?"

She shrugs. "How are you doing? How's life?"

It's funny – she never asked me such questions when we lived together.

"Yeah, I'm fine I guess."

She nods. "How is everyone?"

She no longer asks for mum by name, possibly because mum has made no effort to see her since she started her prison sentence. She also skipped every court date Donna had and basically avoided her from the night of her confession.

"Mum is… well, you know." She nods. "Mina is doing alright, you'll be happy to hear."

Her eyes light up and she flashes a big smile. "That's great."

"Yeah, she was going to come with me but Suzanne called her at the last minute for a job. I should have started with, 'Mina sends her love, wishes she could be here.'"

"That's fine. I don't expect anyone to come here. It's… so drab," she says, rolling her eyes comically.

"She says her counselling sessions are going well. Graham's also clean now. You should see them together – they seem so… content," I say, locking eyes with her.

"I'm glad. Really, I am," she says, looking down.

"Suzanne said that Aisha wants an internship with her. She's hasn't said yes, but she hasn't said no."

She smiles again. "Amazing! I'm glad Aisha's doing well."

I smile, lifting my shoulders to my ears.

She sighs, scratching her head. "How're things with Micah?"

I pout. "Uh… yeah, it's going ok. He's… he's nice. He treats me well. I think you'll like him."

She makes eye contact. "Good. Because if he hurts you—"

"I'll break up with him! You don't have to make any threats," I say. She smiles and laughs.

I nod and smile as well, until the smile fades of its own accord. I swallow hard. "Are you really ok?"

She blinks slowly, doesn't answer.

"If you weren't, would you tell me?"

"You don't have to worry about me, Ivy. I'm fine. And you don't have to come here every month, you know? It… it's a waste of time. You're better off doing something else."

"I *like* coming here. It's a change of scenery. And you're here, so it's fine." I speak firmly but gently.

She sits back in the chair and massages the back of her neck with her free hand. "I had a weird dream last night."

"Oh, what about?"

She looks up. "That day at the beach. With the sandcastle, and the seashells… it was a nice day."

Our eyes meet. I feel mine moisten but I will the tears away. I smile at her and move my head around like a dog wagging its tail. "Yeah, it was."

"I took your advice, asked the church folks who visit to hook me up with a counsellor. My sessions start next week."

My mouth opens slightly. "Wow. That's—I wasn't expecting you to do that."

"Nor was I, yet here we are."

I smile and put my hand on the glass. She mirrors my actions. We look at each other, physically separated but forever connected. She smiles back.

I have a feeling that everything will be alright.

EPILOGUE

S
ilence.

As always, it offers comfort.

It's my second day in solitary and I feel good. I never quite understood what it is about solitary confinement that people find so off-putting. It's quiet, serene even. There are no threats other than your own imagination, or perhaps your conscience. But when your conscience is clean, washed by the blood of God Himself, how can it give you trouble?

They put me here because some of the other inmates were bothering me. I haven't quite mastered this whole 'turn the other cheek' thing. I retaliated with force… quite a lot of it, in truth. I want to blame my fellow inmate Bland Barbara (as I think of her) for the injuries she sustained, say it was her fault for attacking me but I could have diffused the situation without violence.

Yes, in a misguided attempt to cow me, she did try to stab me first but I know I could have talked her off the ledge with some anecdote about changing what you sow in order to reap better things. I *could* have. Instead, I got the knife away from her and stabbed her in the arm, so here I am. I am a work in progress.

I lie in the same spot I've been in for what I estimate to be 45 minutes. I slept through the night, a new trend since turning to Christ. I look up at the ceiling, see nothing but darkness. Even then, the weight that I unknowingly dragged around for years and years is gone. I'm inclined to say that despite my living arrangements, I feel free.

A tune comes to mind and I let it fill my head until there's nothing to do but sing.

I saw the light, I saw the light

No more darkness, no more night

Now I'm so happy, no sorrow in sight

Praise the Lord, I saw the light.

As the sun starts to rise, light creeps into the room.

A new day has dawned.

ACKNOWLEDGEMENTS

To my family and friends –

your love, support and encouragement are priceless.

To Korede and Myriam especially –

I appreciate your time, energy and feedback.

Your critiques, opinions, questions and suggestions

are worth their weight in gold.

ABOUT THE AUTHOR

J.H. Harrison lives in Surrey, England.

This is the author's first novel.

A short story collection is due in late 2020.

To get in touch, email jacob.h.harrison@outlook.com.

Printed in Great Britain
by Amazon